PIMLICO

187

# PRIMA DONNA

Rupert Christiansen studied at the universities of
Cambridge and Columbia. He is the author of
*Romantic Affinities* and *Tales of the New Babylon*,
and has had long associations with the *Spectator*,
the *Observer* and *Harpers and Queen*. He lives in
London, and is currently working on a book about
nineteenth-century travellers to England.

# PRIMA DONNA

## A History

---

## RUPERT CHRISTIANSEN

### Second edition, fully revised and updated, with a new final chapter

PIMLICO

PIMLICO
An imprint of Random House
20 Vauxhall Bridge Road, London SW1V 2SA

Random House Australia (Pty) Ltd
20 Alfred Street, Milsons Point, Sydney
New South Wales 2061, Australia

Random House New Zealand Ltd
18 Poland Road, Glenfield
Auckland 10, New Zealand

Random House South Africa (Pty) Ltd
PO Box 337, Bergvlei 2012, South Africa

Random House UK Ltd Reg. No. 954009

First edition published by The Bodley Head Ltd 1984
Pimlico edition (fully revised and updated) 1995

1 3 5 7 9 10 8 6 4 2

Papers used by Random House UK Limited are natural,
recyclable products made from wood grown in sustainable
forests. The manufacturing processes conform to the
environmental regulations of the country of origin

Typeset by Deltatype Ltd, Ellesmere Port, Cheshire
Printed and bound in Great Britain by
Mackays of Chatham plc, Chatham, Kent

ISBN 0-7126-7466-7

# CONTENTS

# LIST OF PLATES

They were born, they learned to sing, they sang, they made money and bought diamonds, they got Royalties to write in their autograph albums, and they died.

Ernest Newman on the lives of prima donnas, from a review on Albani's autobiography

Love of money, luck, snobbishness, coolness, powers of observation, egotism, sexual attributes, individuality, need for father figures, attitude to men, independent spirit, obstinacy, honesty, romanticism, love of singing, dominating personality, unforgiving nature, growing sense of isolation, desire to be remembered after death, generosity to other singers, humility, sense of humour . . .

From an entry in the index of Garry O'Connor's biography, *The Pursuit of Perfection: A Life of Maggie Teyte*

Self-censorship, hypocritical modesty, insecurity, girlishness, self-deception, hostility towards one's fellow-strivers, emotional and sexual dependency upon men, timidity, poverty and ignorance . . .

'Traits of the oppressed personality': from Germaine Greer's history of women painters, *The Obstacle Race*

# Introduction

This book is a history of women's part in one of the most magnificent and extravagant phenomena of western culture—opera. Specifically, it focuses on the prima donnas, the singers who for 300 years have been at opera's epicentre, both worshipped and reviled.

The *Oxford English Dictionary* gives 'the first or principal female singer in an opera' as its major definition of 'prima donna', and records examples of the usage in English from the end of the eighteenth century. Although it is commonly assumed that the term arose in Italian around 1650, in fact '*virtuosa*' was the ordinary way of referring to a principal female singer until about 1800; '*cantatrice*' (meaning simply 'female singer') was also internationally used. Such words were neutrally descriptive, and in the earlier phases of opera a prima donna was the *cantatrice* who sang the greatest number of arias in the course of any particular work.

Not until the middle of the nineteenth century and the highly publicized and promoted careers of Grisi and Patti did 'prima donna' come to bear an innuendo. In 1862, for example, Henry Mayhew, in his survey *London Labour*, identifies the prima donna as a sort of courtesan, idling her way through wealth and fame; and by the twentieth century, particularly in English, the term had stuck as a label of abuse on a level with virago, shrew, or bitch. To be a prima donna was not so much to be a great interpreter of operatic music as to be an outrageous *grande dame*, 'exacting, torrential, and exasperating', and often lazy, greedy, stupid, conceited, and 'impossible' as well. It has proved a powerful stereotype. A woman who wants her own way is a prima donna. A woman who makes a complaint is a prima donna. A woman who changes her mind is a prima donna.

The truth about the prima donnas is more complex, and rather than treating them as either gorgons or freaks, I have tried to put their lives and their art into historical context. The picture then emerges rather differently. Many of the women in these pages

I

worked their way up from unprivileged backgrounds, fought tooth and nail to get a hearing in a male-dominated world of ruthless intrigue, braved enormous risks, and accepted the necessary sacrifices. The rewards—fortune, independence, public acclaim, the chance for self-expression beyond the roles of wife and mother— were incomparably high, but so were the odds against success, let alone happiness. Opera has always been a highly-strung profession, running on dynamic and creative clashes of will and temperament. Given such a gamble in such circumstances, a woman had to be alert and aggressive in order to survive. 'Acting the prima donna' may have been the only way to avoid exploitation, and a prima donna's 'greed' was often only the hard-headed refusal to work for less than her market value. Her infuriating 'whims' were often based on rational instincts of self-protection: not only were there artistic standards to maintain, but the singing voice is a sensitive physical instrument which requires careful handling and husbanding. A woman who refuses compromises is a prima donna. A woman dedicated to her talent is a prima donna.

It would be possible to make a feminist defence of the prima donna. She proved that women of no inherited rank or moral virtue could stand up in public—something Jane Austen or Emily Dickinson never had to do—and make their lives for themselves.[*] However, feminist writers have shown little interest in prima donnas, despite massive and justified attention paid to their sister painters, writers, and scientists.[†] Why should this be? Not, I think, because all lastingly successful operas to date have been written by men and largely present women in passive or dependent situations; but perhaps because prima donnas are, almost by definition, *successful*. They have not been the victims of oppression and intimidation, they have grabbed at the glittering rewards of their success; they often fought against the very women they should have helped. (When asked to comment on Grover Cleveland's dictum

---

[*] Why women in music have had so much more success as performers than as composers is another fascinating question.

[†] The work of the fashionable intellectuals like Catherine Clément and Susan McClary (see the Bibliography p. 314 for details) fancifully attempts to 'deconstruct' opera from a feminist perspective and interpret it in terms of 'gender politics'. The results, in my view, are unilluminating: the reader would be far better directed towards the solid and sensitive research of John Rosselli's *Singers of Italian Opera* (Cambridge, 1992).

that 'a woman's place is in the home', the American prima donna Emma Eames replied that it might be appropriate for 80 per cent of women, but that was no reason to stifle the other 20 per cent.) And if prima donnas have been mocked, they have also been adulated. Like the sirens of the *Odyssey*, their voices were sexually alluring and morally dangerous. In the nineteenth century a prima donna also became a *diva*, a goddess, receiving the homage of flowers, diamonds, applause, flattery, and removing themselves beyond the ordinary condition of womankind.

Alongside this idealizing of the *diva* came the journalistic emphasis on charisma, genius, and mystique, and a failure to appreciate the technique, intelligence, musicianship, and plain hard work which make a first-rate singer. Nor was there much attention given to the prima donna's creative role in the development of opera—*Norma* and *Anna Bolena*, for instance, are as much an expression of Pasta's genius as they are of Bellini's and Donizetti's; the capabilities of Schröder-Devrient, Stolz, and Jeritza were vitally inspiring at various times to Wager, Verdi, and Richard Strauss; while in our own day, Berio gave Cathy Berberian music which trusted a great deal to her own improvisation, rather as the eighteenth-century *virtuosa* would completely transform a written melody with fantastic embellishments. In other words, we turned working women into mannequins.

The aim of this book is to restore some reality to our image of the prima donna and to create a sense of actual individuals—all with their own struggles and frustrations, virtues and vices—beyond the myths and anecdotes of *diva* adoration, now somewhat tiresomely appropriated by the Camp camp. I am afraid that limitations of space—and the reader's patience—have inevitably meant that many fine singers are not even mentioned, and others find less than their fair share of space: I am aware that the bias is Anglo-Saxon, that the French and Russians are under-represented and that no sort of justice has been done to the *verismo* school of sopranos which flourished in the early years of this century. My apologies to them all, but it seemed more important to provide a broad cross-section, including some not strictly eligible castrati and mezzo-sopranos (in some periods a prima donna was invariably a soprano), than to cram in names and facts just for the sake of being encyclopedic. For similar reasons, I have excluded singers whose careers have been almost exclusively in *lieder*, concert, or operetta. I have also avoided

3

technical terms and analysis, while assuming a reader acquainted with the basics of musical vocabulary. Anyone wanting more detailed comment on specific recorded performances than I have provided can do no better than turn to J. B. Steane's *The Grand Tradition* (1973), a book I have found truly inspiring.

This second edition of *Prima Donna* takes into account scholarship and journalism published since I first researched the field in 1982–3, as well as a constellation of young stars and rising talents which I review in an entirely new last chapter. But this book remains a preliminary study of an under-explored field; I hope one day someone combining the skills of historian, musicologist and sociologist will dig it deeper.

London, 1995

I

# *From* Opera Seria *to Mozart*

'The Dutchis of Molbery had got the Etallian to sing, and he sent an excuse, but the Dutchis of Shrosberry made him com, brought him in her coach, but Mrs Taufs huft and would not sing because he had first put it ofe; though she was thear yet she would not, but went away . . . I wish the house would al joyne to humble her and not receav her again.'

In this semi-literate letter written in 1708 by one Lady Wentworth to her daughter is perhaps the earliest recorded instance of 'prima donna' behaviour—'Mrs Taufs huft'. Caprice, bad temper, greed, hauteur—Mrs Taufs, or Tofts, as she is ordinarily known, embodied the popular and enduring image of the female opera singer, and her career certainly contains many elements and situations which will occur repeatedly in the course of this book. Already we see an ignorant public gleefully creating a *monstre sacré*, oblivious to the difficulty of singing. Lady Wentworth, for instance, never considers the possibility that Mrs Tofts was rightly affronted at the 'Etallian's' unprofessional failure to appear at the right time: what most concerns her is that Mrs Toft's impudent presumption broke the codes of social deference. The prima donna is already a noisy threat to female decorum ('let your women keep silence in the churches' enjoined St Paul in Corinthians) and Mrs Tofts realized that she could afford to withhold her labour. It made her unpopular among the aristocrats who patronized her. When Mrs Tofts went mad, people of fashion giggled: it was her deserved come-uppance.

Katharine Tofts's origins are obscure: she was probably born about 1685, and emerged in London musical life at the beginning of the eighteenth century, when the vogue for Italian opera was just beginning there. Lady Wentworth's 'Etallian' was the famous castrato Nicolino, making his English début. On the occasion at which they were present—a gathering of aristocrats for a private

5

recital in the rehearsal room of the Queen's Theatre—he and Mrs Tofts were to sing from a new opera, *Pirro e Demetrio*, probably a *pasticcio*, a piece cobbled together from various sources and typical of its time. Nicolino would have sung in Italian, Mrs Tofts in English, a common and much-ridiculed practice. Italian finally won the day, perhaps as much because of the chic attached to a foreign language as because of its wonderfully singable vowel sounds.

Mrs Tofts first came to fame singing songs in concert at the Drury Lane Theatre. Of her voice and its qualities we know next to nothing. She was a soprano, probably with a degree of agility unusual for her time and place, although soon to become a necessity. The infamous hack dramatist Colley Cibber wrote that 'The beauty of her fine proportion'd figure and exquisitely sweet, silvery tone of voice with the peculiarly rapid swiftness of her throat, were perfections not to be imitated by art or nature'—which is about as far as the contemporary vocabulary of music criticism can take us. In December 1703 she cancelled an appearance 'by reason of a great cold', an announcement which then, as now, probably met with incredulity. Then in early 1704 another singer made a highly successful first appearance at Drury Lane. This was Margherita de l'Épine, an Italian resident in England, longer established than Mrs Tofts and considered a very fine artist. During her second appearance on Mrs Tofts's territory a violent outbreak of hissing and orange-throwing occurred and an arrest was made, the culprit being embarrassingly identified. The following letter was published shortly afterwards, originally addressed to the manager of Drury Lane:

> Sir, I was very much surpriz'd when I was informed that Ann Barwick, who was lately my servant, had committed a rudeness when Mrs L'Épine the Italian gentlewoman sung. I hope no one can think that it was in the least with my privity, as I assure you it was not. I abhor such practises and I hope you will cause her to be prosecut'd, that she may be punish'd as she deserves. I am, sir, your humble servant Katharine Tofts.

We may doubt the sincerity of this repudiation, but it is known that the two ladies continued to sing at the same performances, even if never in duet.

Madame L'Épine was extremely plain, and was publicly known as the 'Tawny Tuscan'; Mrs Tofts was a beauty, and had the added advantage of being British. Fashion, chauvinism, and political faction played their parts in the subsequent partisanship.

> Music has learn'd the discords of the state
> And concerts jar with Whig and Tory hate.
> Here Somerset and Devonshire attend
> The British Tofts and every note commend . . .
> There fam'd Lepine does equal skill employ
> While listening peers crowd to the ecstatic joy:
> Bedford to hear her song his dice forsakes
> And Nottingham is raptured when she shakes* . . .

So wrote the poet Hughes; while the newspapers carried further epigrammatic and poetic compliments to the ladies, one of which has been attributed to Pope:

> So bright is thy beauty, so charming thy song
> As had drawn both the beasts and their Orpheus along,
> But such is thy avarice, and such is thy pride
> That the beasts must have starved, and the poet have died.

What gave Mrs Tofts real glamour, however, was her association with Italian opera. In 1705 she appeared in *Arsinoe, Queen of Cyprus*, a piece by Thomas Clayton which, like the majority of early operas, has long since vanished. It has its significance as the first English attempt to emulate the Italian style, and it had a certain popular success, but critical feeling was hostile, one authority finding 'nothing in it but a few sketches of antiquated Italian airs, so mangled and sophisticated that instead of *Arsinoe*, it ought to be called the Hospital of the Decrepit Old Italian Operas'. Before *Arsinoe*, the English operatic tradition had (with notable exceptions such as Purcell's *Dido and Aeneas*) been rooted in the legitimate theatre. Plays and court entertainments were commonly performed with interpolated songs and musical interludes, but the Italian conception of opera which began in the late sixteenth century as an attempt to recreate what was thought to be the practice of Greek tragedy and which soon became, roughly speaking, a series of elaborate songs linked by accompanied recitative, had not caught on till then.

* i.e., a shake or trill.

7

In Italy the female singer had long been familiar as the object of honours and flowery compliments. In Renaissance courts, the singing of songs and madrigals was considered an estimable occupation for ladies, and the d'Este palace in Mantua was particularly celebrated for its 'golden-throated nightingales', including the Duchess Isabella herself. The earliest female opera singer we know of is Vittoria Archilei (1550–c.1618), who sang and danced in many of the first operas performed in Florence, where she was attached to the court of the Medicis. We know somewhat more about another Mantua-trained *virtuosa*, Leonora Baroni (1611–70). She did not sing in opera, but in the courts, where her recitals would be accompanied on the *lira* by her mother Adriana, who had also been a singer. She was said to be 'highly accomplished . . . graceful, frank and full of intelligence' and her renown spread abroad: in 1644, at the behest of Cardinal Mazarin, she sang in Paris. The young John Milton heard her in 1638–9 during his Italian tour, and was impressed enough to write three conventional Latin sonnets in tribute to her:

> *Nam tua praesentem vox sonat ipsa Deum . . .*
> *Quod si cuncta quidem Deus est, per cunctaque fusus,*
> *In te una loquitur . . .*

(For the sound of your voice makes it clear that God is
    present . . .
If God is all things and omnipresent, nevertheless
    he speaks in you alone)

It was in Venice that opera became a commercial entertainment, and the first public opera house opened there in 1637; but we know virtually nothing about any of the singers from this period, and it is only in London with Mrs Tofts that the historian first finds a prima donna adulated, exploited, fought over, fighting back, publicly excoriated, and probably libelled. Hers is not a happy story with which to begin, but Pope's view that she was simply motivated by 'avarice and pride' is not a fair one (although it has to be said that her fee for a performance in 1705 was £16 13s. 4d., over four times as much as that of Mrs Bracegirdle, the leading actress of the day). Eventually Mrs Tofts pleaded for redress with the Lord Chamberlain, the court official who licensed the theatres, claiming that the manager 'tooke all the Opportunitys he could to be Revenged on her: which was in calling on her to sing oftener than she was able to performe', thus causing her to lose her voice and require expensive medical attention. She also demanded money for costumes and stage ornament, as well as two bottles of wine to refresh 'the Gentlemen that practice with her'. She won her case, and went on in 1706 to the great triumph of her career in the title-role of Bononcini's *Camilla*, an Italian opera that was played repeatedly over the next few years and which remained popular throughout the century. A scene in which Mrs Tofts as Camilla shoots and kills a wild boar passed into contemporary theatrical legend—the *Spectator* even published a letter, purporting to come from the shade of the unfortunate animal: 'Camilla's charms were such that beholding her erect mien, hearing her charming voice and astonished with her graceful motion, I could not keep up to my assumed fierceness, but died like a man.'

Soon Mrs Tofts was again petitioning the Lord Chamberlain for better terms, on the basis of 'this climate being much worse than any other for voices, and in short the misery . . . if seiz'd with a cold'. She also threatened not to sing again until she received reimbursement for the eighty guineas she had spent on gowns for *Camilla*. Again she got her way, but in 1708 she left Drury Lane and signed up with the new Queen's Theatre in the Haymarket, where she and Madame L'Épine each received a fee of £400 for the season. She supplemented her already large income by giving private recitals like the one Lady Wentworth attended. The theatrical gossip Chetwood records how in 1709 she went to the Duke of Somerset's 'where there were about thirty gentlemen, and every kiss was one guinea; some took three, others four . . . but none less than one'. In the twentieth century, plenty of prima donnas have been prepared to sing in night clubs or musical comedy, but of her kind only the wretched Mrs Tofts seems to have sunk as low as this. Two months later she made her last British appearance in an opera called *Love's Triumph*. The *Tatler* shortly issued a report that Mrs Tofts

. . . has had the ill-luck to break before her voice, and to disappear at a time when her beauty was in the height of its bloom. This lady entered so thoroughly into the great characters she acted, that when she had finished her part, she could not think of retrenching her equipage, but would appear in her own lodgings with the same magnificence that she did upon the stage. This greatness of soul had reduced that unhappy princess to an involuntary retirement, where she now passes her time among the woods and forests, thinking on the crowns and sceptres she has lost, and often humming over in her solitude

> I was born of royal race
> Yet must wander in disgrace.*

But for fear of being overheard, and her quality known, she usually sings it in Italian.

We know nothing else about this nervous breakdown, and we can only conjecture at the pressures which might have caused it or the reality of her mental state. The music historian Dr Charles Burney (1726–1814), writing towards the end of the eighteenth century, considered the story exaggerated. It is certainly true that Mrs Tofts reappears in Venice in 1712, singing 'in all the great Assemblies that were held at the Electoral Prince of Saxony's', apparently with great success. The *Spectator* devised a 'letter from Camilla', which shows, if nothing else, that people had not quickly forgotten her.

> I live here distinguished, as one whom Nature has been liberal to in a graceful person, an exalted mien, and heavenly voice. These particularities in this strange country are arguments for respect and generosity to her who is possessed of them. The Italians see a thousand beauties I am sensible I have no pretence to, and abundantly make up to me the injustice I received in my own country, of disallowing me what I really had. The humour of hissing, which you have among you, I do not know anything of, and their applauses are uttered in sighs . . . P.S. I am ten times better dressed than ever I was in England.

Does this hint at the possibility that Mrs Tofts retired from the London stage, not because she was mad, but because she had suffered from some stormy audience behaviour and could not recover her nerve? In Venice she never sang in opera again—strange if *folie de grandeur* was her complaint—only in concerts. In 1716 she married—her original 'Mrs' was probably meaningless, and Tofts

* A well-known air from *Camilla*.

her maiden name—one Joseph Smith, a faintly shady consul in Venice, who was busy acquiring, perhaps with his wife's earnings, Canalettos which came to form the basis of the royal collection now in Windsor Castle. She again fades from sight, residing in the Palazzo Balbi, where she was said to live in great state until her death in 1756. An unreliable source, Sir John Hawkins, later repeated the *Tatler* story—in her Venetian seclusion Mrs Tofts suffered a relapse: 'Sequestered from the world [she] had a large garden to range in, in which she would frequently walk, singing, and giving way to that innocent frenzy which had seized her in the earlier part of her life.' Even more fanciful was the news that, having turned Roman Catholic, she sang for the Pope, who had subsequently paid her scandalous attentions. The blend of fantasy, deliberate falsification, vindictiveness, and detached amusement which make up this tale will be another recurrent factor in the following pages.

What were early prima donnas such as Mrs Tofts singing? It was a difficult period for the operatic form, and no amount of special pleading can make even its best works fully alive today, for we have lost the idea of theatre they were composed around—an idea indifferent to naturalism in speech, deportment, gesture, and plot, but centrally concerned with putting forward a strong moral case for one of the approved virtues—constancy, clemency, honour—which made men and women noble. Even Handel's operas, written 1705–41, only survive today through their wonderful tunes and the fancy notions which producers hang on to their flimsy plots. We don't *believe* in Handel's emotional world as we can believe in Monteverdi's, perhaps because the latter's use of *arioso* (a continuous melodic speech) is so much more dramatically direct than Handel's long solo arias, with their relentless *da capos*, so many of them apparently interchangeable and without any evident function in terms of the action or the character's psychology. But that's not how composers of the early eighteenth century thought. They worked on premisses alien to us—on the one hand, the action on stage showed aristocratic or mythological personages, allotted a definite prominence in the plot and a certain number of arias appropriate to their status in a system of hierarchies which operated from the king's court right down to the seating arrangements within the opera house; on the other hand, performances were conducted in a state of near-uproar, with noisy audiences, under-rehearsed stagings, and the singers allowed a since unheard-of degree of liberty to interpret or embellish the music as they wished. What in the mere printed score now appears to be an intolerable monotony of formula was subverted in performance by a spirit of licence and improvisation. The chief vehicle for this freedom was the *da capo* aria—in which the initial melodic idea would be repeated with runs, trills, and all the other ornaments associated now with the term 'coloratura'. Of course, many used the opportunity just to show off their high notes or breath control, but the greatest singers were always recognized for their ability to make their inventions dramatically memorable and relevant, an intensification of the aria's basic emotion—anger, jealousy, relief, joy, grief—which the 'original' composer had set out in skeleton form. Some singers changed their ideas from performance to performance, others were more consistent. And it was only the better musicians who devised their own decorations. The run-of-the-mill prima donna hired a hack. The Italian composer Marcello satirized the practice: 'The singer . . . will at the first possible moment take all her arias . . . to her Maestro . . . so that he may write in the passages, the variations, the beautiful ornaments etc.—and Maestro Crica, without knowing the first thing about the intentions of the composer [will write in] everything he can think of.' This improvisatory principle has recently been revived, but in a manner perhaps rather genteel and academic—we probably get a better idea of its exhilarating effect from 'scat' singing in jazz.

Perhaps the Baroque opera house is better compared to a night club than to the modern darkened and silent temples of art. In the eighteenth century, audiences would come and go throughout the performance, in and out of auditoriums kept fully lit, talking, eating, drinking, conducting amorous intrigue, and generally treating the entertainment with what in some ways was a healthy lack of respect. In such an atmosphere the singers had to work hard to shock the audience into attention. Sometimes they would themselves behave with a corresponding disdain of audience and drama. 'All the while the *ritornello* [orchestral introduction] of his air is being played the singer should walk about the stage, take snuff, complain to his friends [seated in stage boxes] that he is in bad voice, has a cold, etc.' wrote Marcello in his ironic account of the common practices of the time.

The decorum of opera in this period was a strange mixture of high formality, low informality, and something like hysteria. Admission was expensive: in London it was over four times what it was for the playhouse, and the opera house in the Haymarket (variously called the Queen's, King's, and Her Majesty's), built by a committee of noblemen and ultimately policed by the Lord Chamberlain, charged a box subscriber of 1721 twenty guineas to hear fifty performances. Many of these subscribers would attend every night—one must bear in mind the dearth of alternative public diversions—but their engraved ivory or silver ticket was transferable. The pit was filled with young gallants who liked to cruise up and down the aisle known as 'Fop's Alley'; the gallery was usually known as the 'Footmen's Gallery' and was largely populated by that class, waiting for their masters. The amount of seating was variable, the general principle being to cram in as many as would pay. Another oddity was the habit of allowing standing room on the stage: this was frequently condemned as a nuisance but seems to have lasted throughout the eighteenth century.

The success of Italian opera in London was initially sporadic, and profitable only when a fashionable foreign singer could pack the place out. A major setback was the immense success of Gay's *The Beggar's Opera* (1728), a play in English set in the pits of London low life, the music of which is made up from folk-ballads and street ditties and which can be seen as a straight satirical inversion of the pretensions and conventions of Italian opera, to the point where they were no longer viable. For instance, the duets between Polly Peachum and Lucy Lockit, rivals for the hands of the highwayman Macheath, commemorate a performance of Bononcini's *Astianatte*, given in the presence of the Princess Caroline, at which the respective partisans of the two prima donnas, Faustina and Cuzzoni, caused a near-riot with their cheering and booing. The story soon developed that Faustina and Cuzzoni themselves had gone for each other in the ensuing fracas, and it was this apocryphal fight that Gay immortalized:

> Why how now Madam Flirt,
> If you thus must chatter
> And are for flinging dirt,
> Let's try who best can spatter!

Faustina and Cuzzoni were the first in a great line of rival prima donnas which includes Grisi and Viardot, Lehmann and Jeritza,

Tebaldi and Callas. Their feuds have always been very popular with the public, and the press has relished feeding the real conflicts by inventing inflammatory remarks and slanders. The tale of Faustina and Cuzzoni is one in which all the virtue, and the reward, was seen to be on one side.

Francesca Cuzzoni was born in Parma in 1698, and began her career in the Italian opera houses, as well as being court singer to the Duchess Violante of Tuscany. She was, wrote Walpole, 'short and squat, with a doughy cross face, but fine expression; was not a good actress; dressed ill; and was silly and fantastical'. Others found her 'of turbulent and obstinate temper', governed by 'ingratitude and insolence'. On her arrival in London in 1723, her singing in Handel's opera *Ottone* created a sensation. In rehearsal she proved fractious, and according to Burney, 'treated the composer with but scanty respect; making alterations in the passages he had written, and affecting inability to sing them in their original form'. This is interesting as it shows Handel protective of his compositions and unhappy with the prima donna's assumed prerogative to alter and ornament at her discretion, even though he was prepared to insert new arias designed to show off her technique. Composers of lesser eminence would not have been able to pull such weight, and Handel only got his way, it was said, by seizing Cuzzoni round the waist and threatening to throw her out of the window unless she sang what he had written.

Cuzzoni was the rage—her salary was £2,000 for the season, handsomely supplemented with private and provincial appearances. Black market tickets for her benefit performance (a gala at which all takings accrued to the star honoured) went for as much as fifty guineas. Her extravagance was said to measure up to these vast sums. In Handel's *Rodelinda* she appeared in a 'brown silk gown, trimmed with silver', which was much imitated by ladies of fashion, among them the Countess of Pembroke, leader of her band of aristocratic admirers. Cuzzoni's only rival in London, where she lived for five years until 1728, was the castrato Senesino: until, that is, the arrival of her fellow-countrywoman Faustina Bordoni in 1726.

Faustina, as she was always known, was a darling of the gods. Born in Venice in 1700 of patrician family, she was beautiful, charming, a fine actress, and a great singer. She had a brilliant career, made an excellent marriage and lived to enjoy a vivacious old age. Cuzzoni was always either on her trail or one step ahead of her: but their

quarrel cannot have been caused by competition for the same parts—
Cuzzoni was a soprano, Faustina a mezzo. They had first sung
together in Venice, but the trouble came to a head in London, where
the audiences were fiercest. It was during an opera by Handel called
*Alessandro*, according to Burney, that 'they began to kindle the
flames of discord among the frequenters of the opera and patrons of
the art, which increased to a more violent degree of enmity than even
the theological and political parties of high church and low, or Whig
and Tory, which then raged in this country'. Lord Hervey wrote:

> No Cuzzonist will go to a tavern with a Faustinian. And the ladies
> of one party have scratched those of the other out of their lists of
> visits. I was t'other night upon the water, and heard nothing till
> three o'clock in the morning but invocations of one and
> execrations upon the other.

Horace Walpole tells how the Prime Minister's wife Lady
Walpole bravely invited them both to sing at one of her *soirées*:

> . . . an assemblage of the first people in the kingdom were present
> . . . Finding it impossible to prevail on the one to sing while the
> other was present, she took Faustina to a remote part of the house
> under the pretext of showing her some curious china, during
> which time the company obtained a song from Cuzzoni, who
> supposed that her rival had quitted the field. A similar device was
> practised in order to get Cuzzoni out of the room while Faustina
> performed.

At subsequent grand dinner parties, they were seen to behave
'politely . . . and relieved their hostess by mutual concessions'. The
situation was eventually resolved by a sordid financial expedient.
The opera house managers realized that one or other of them had to
go, and Cuzzoni was indisputably the greater headache. She had
sworn never to accept a smaller salary than Faustina, and they had till
then been equally paid. Faustina was now offered an extra guinea,
and Cuzzoni left London in pique: perhaps exhausted by the
continual tension, Faustina almost immediately fell ill and the opera
season came to a premature halt. The year was 1728, and *The
Beggar's Opera* was considered more novel and exciting than the

Italian opera—the theatre of the Royal Academy of Music, to which Handel was contracted, collapsed shortly afterwards.

Cuzzoni's subsequent progress is an unhappy one: she priced herself out of the Viennese opera market by demanding a salary of 24,000 florins, but toured Naples, Venice—where Faustina was also passing through—Florence, and Genoa. Handel, working for another opera house, refused to have her back to London, but she eventually returned in 1734 for a further three seasons, when she sang at the opera house in Lincoln's Inn Fields, established in opposition to Handel. It was a time of general disenchantment with the Italian opera, and Cuzzoni made less impression than before. She returned to the Continent, singing in the major cities, but things now went very wrong. In 1741 a report reached London that she had poisoned her husband, a harpsichord-maker, and was to be beheaded. However, she reappeared in 1745 as a court singer in Stuttgart, where she settled until 1748, and where her contract held the proviso that if she lost her voice it would be made void. Perhaps in absconding to Bologna, leaving massive debts behind her, she was anticipating the worst. Certainly her voice seems to have collapsed thenceforth. When she made a final trip to London in 1750–1, she gave a benefit concert which was regarded 'less as a musical entertainment than as an act of charity'. Dr Burney was there, and recorded an evening that must have been even more pathetic than comparable efforts by Pasta and Callas: 'Her voice [was] reduced to a mere thread; indeed her throat was so nearly ossified by age, that all the soft and mellifluous qualities, which had before rendered it so enchanting, were nearly annihilated.' A couple of months later she was arrested for debts of £30. The Prince of Wales bailed her out, and in 1751 she had one final benefit appearance which she advertised to the public as 'the last I shall ever trouble them with, and is made solely to pay my creditors'. Burney wrote that 'there was but little company', and she left England 'more miserable than when she came'. In Holland, she was again thrown into prison for debt, working her release by giving concerts on parole. Her last years were spent in Bologna, living in extreme poverty as a button-maker and dying in 1770.

Happily, Cuzzoni is also commemorated as a great singer. Handel may have hated her, but she excelled in his music—during a performance of his *Admeto* there was a cry from the gallery, 'Damn her! She's got a nest of nightingales in her belly!' Burney translated a more considered Italian critic thus:

> . . . so grateful and touching was the natural tone of her voice, that she rendered pathetic whatever she sang, in which she had leisure to unfold its whole volume. The art of conducting, sustaining, increasing, and diminishing her tones by minute degrees, acquired for her among professors the title of complete mistress of her art. In a *cantabile* air, though the notes she added were few, she never lost a favourable opportunity of enriching the *cantilena* with all the refinements and embellishments of the time. Her shake was perfect; she had a creative fancy, and the power of occasionally accelerating and retarding the measure in the most artificial and able manner by what the Italians call *tempo rubato* . . .

Given her rival's nemesis and the wonderfully complementary qualities of their two voices, there is something brutally unfair about Faustina's smooth passage through life. After London, she made successful appearances in the major Italian opera houses and in 1730 married the prominent operatic composer Johann Hasse. For more than thirty years the couple lived at the Saxon court in Dresden, where Hasse was *Kapellmeister* and for which he wrote numerous pieces in the classic *opera seria* form. Their two daughters trained there to be singers, while Faustina continued a fêted international career, promoting her husband's operas. After the upheavals of the Seven Years' War, the couple went to Vienna and finally Venice, where Faustina died at the age of eighty-one. Burney visited her in Vienna, and found her 'a short, brown, sensible and lively old woman . . . with good remains, for seventy-two, of that beauty for which she was so much celebrated in her youth, but none of her voice'. That voice had been a penetrating mezzo-soprano, with a wide range: whereas Cuzzoni had excelled in the slow and pathetic, Faustina was a virtuoso. Burney again:

> She in a manner invented a new kind of singing, by running divisions [fast florid passages] with a neatness and velocity which astonished all who heard her. She had the art of sustaining a note longer, in the opinion of the public, than any other singer, by taking her breath imperceptibly . . . her professional perfections were enhanced by a beautiful face, a symmetric figure, though of

small stature, and a countenance and gesture on the stage which indicated an entire intelligence and possession of the several parts she had to represent.

We should not forget that Mrs Tofts, Faustina and Cuzzoni were still pioneers for their sex. At the end of the seventeenth century Pope Clement XII had fulminated that 'for a woman to keep her virtue in a stage career is like making her jump into the Tiber expecting her not to get wet'; and as John Rosselli puts it, between the nunnery and a circumscribed career on contract to a court, the only territory open to women was 'an ambiguous zone' where they might appear on stage only 'at the cost of being deemed a courtesan'. By the early eighteenth century, this suspicion had scarcely lessened: if a prima donna wasn't a courtesan, then her status remained between stairs (in 1708 the Countess of Sunderland agreed to invite an Italian soprano and her husband to her house to sing 'provided that they would not be above dining with the servants or by themselves'). This problem was to persist for women in opera even longer than the other great obstacle they faced throughout the eighteenth century—the castrato.

'It had all the Warblings and Turns of a Nightingale, with only this difference, that it was much finer and did not a man know the contrary, he would believe it impossible such a Tone could proceed from the throat of anything that was human.' This description, written by an anonymous Englishman in 1718, is typically awe-struck at *castrato* singing, a phenomenon which at its best combined unearthly beauty of tone, the flexibility of a coloratura soprano, unnatural breath control, and enormous volume. We may assume it had a womanly sound, yet it also had some quality which put it beyond definite sexual identity. More suggestive is a contemporary Frenchman, Charles de Brosses: 'The timbre is as clear as a choirboy's, and much stronger . . . their voices almost always have something dry and piercing in them . . . but they are also brilliant, light, full of sparkle, very strong and extensive.'

The sound of the castrato just survived into the era of recording. One Alessandro Moreschi, who conducted and sang in the Sistine Chapel choir, made some records of sentimental religious music in 1902–3, but they are apparently little more than tantalizing— Moreschi was middle-aged when they were made, and had a mediocre technique. J. B. Steane, in his authoritative review of recorded vocal music, *The Grand Tradition*, found their impact 'sadly comical'. But in the eighteenth century the great castrati were the wonder of the civilized world, and a history of the prima donna has to pay tribute to them, because in terms of salary, status, glamour, the castrati were the true prima donnas of their age and, for the only time until Caruso and Chaliapin, made male singers a greater box-office draw than female. 'As the male singer was at once more respectable and more thoroughly artistic than the singing actress,' wrote Vernon Lee, a nineteenth-century commentator on eighteenth-century Italy, 'it was he who had all the social advantages of the art for himself . . . when he sang people remained silent and breathless, and occasionally went into hysterics; when he ceased the applause was perfectly frantic; everyone possessed his printed portrait . . . the ladies wore miniatures of him, sometimes four at a time; and the wits of the coffee-houses and lecture rooms wrote sonnets in his honour.'

Eunuchs had long been common and convenient in Eastern courts, but the practice of castrating boys to create this extraordinary vocal situation dates possibly from the end of the Roman Empire and was certainly known in Byzantium. In the sixteenth century, presumably via Moorish influence Spanish 'falsettists'—who were either what we today know as counter-tenors, or true castrati—became popular in the choirs of the Catholic church, where women were not allowed to sing. By the end of the sixteenth century Pope Clement VIII had sanctified the use of castrati in the Sistine Chapel choir, and the rise of Venetian opera soon gave them an even more spectacular arena.

The exploitation of castration was confined to Italy. The operation itself was strictly illegal, and those who perpetrated it faced death, their accomplices (parents included) excommunication. However, various blind eyes belonging to various interested parties were turned, and while many indulged in nominal moral outrage, many more were happy to accept the sad 'accident' that had befallen the child, and to profit from its happy side-effect. It has been estimated that by the mid-eighteenth century as many as 4,000 pre-pubescent boys a year, mostly from poor or peasant backgrounds, were thus assaulted, the parents sometimes receiving a sum from a singing teacher, who in turn would take a percentage in his protégé's career. Of all these, a mere handful would mature to make a decent living as singers. The operation itself was easily performed. One technique was to drug the victim with opium and cut the vas deferens leading from the testicles to the urethra. The testicles, deprived of 'the vein that conveyed their Proper Aliment and Support . . . grow lank and flabby, till at last they actually dry up and come to nothing'.

The consequent hormonal imbalance had many strange physical effects: an enormous amount of hair on the head but none on the body, a tendency to grow extremely tall and in later life obese and very wizened among them. Castrati's speech remained pipingly boyish, while their gait was often so loping and awkward that in compensation they cultivated a variety of affectedly elegant postures on stage. Most significant was the fact that the vocal cords did not thicken, and that the chest developed to the point where the rib cage came to look almost busty. Their lung capacity was enormous, allowing them to exhale for a minute or more.

Many castrati spent their lives as church singers, but it was in opera that they became big business. Those of the second rank would often take up long-term contracts at one of the smaller German courts, where the Italian opera was the centre of artistic and social activity—Hasse and Faustina's appointment in Dresden is a remarkable instance of this sort of patronage. The most famous names had international careers and commanded enormous sums of money. They would travel with their 'suitcase arias' or *aria di baule*, a form of signature tune which they would insert into whatever opera they were appearing in, regardless of dramatic context. Their vanity sometimes went further—Luigi Marchesi, wrote Scudo, liked to

> . . . play the part of someone who could wear a gilded helmet crowned with red or white feathers. He wanted to make his entry descending a hill, from the top of which he could cry, '*Dove son io?*' ('Where am I?'). Then he demanded that a trumpet gave forth a blast, after which he could declaim '*Odi la squillo della tromba guerriera*' ('I hear the blast of the war-like trumpet'). Having sung this, he advanced to the front of the stage and invariably sang the same rondo . . . in which he lamented his cruel lot.*

Some of the castrati's impact on eighteenth-century society came

---

* Lucrezia Agujari, a famous eighteenth-century soprano, was even more specific in her demands, requiring an aria which contained the word '*ombra*', shadow, intoned on specific notes in her beautiful lowest register.

from their sexual ambiguity, both on and off stage. Some were homosexual. Obviously they were peculiarly attractive to married women looking for liaisons which could not result in pregnancy. Voyeuristic curiosity provided a further *frisson*: sniggering innuendo must have been another occupational hazard. Forbidden to marry though still able to perfom sexually, they took advantage of a licence sometimes granted to anomalies. In opera they were called upon to play women's roles, and some habitually wore women's clothes. This gender-bending became even more contorted when, to avoid the papal ban, women in Rome took to the stage masquerading as castrati dressed as women. Balzac was to write a short story, 'Sarassine', on these lines, and Casanova's memoirs report some embarrassing encounters. Sitting in a café, he noticed an attractive man:

> At the appearance of his hips I took him for a girl in disguise, and I said so to the Abbé Gama; but the latter told me that it was Beppino della Mamana, a famous castrato. The abbé called him over, and told him, laughing, that I had taken him for a girl. The impudent creature, looking fixedly at me, told me that if I liked he would prove that I was right, or that I was wrong.

The first internationally famous castrato was Baldassare Ferri (1610–80), about whom relatively little is known, but who is reported to have visited London around 1670; then came Nicolino, one-time partner of Mrs Tofts and the first to establish himself in London. Nicolino was more appreciated for his acting than his singing, although his success, especially in Handel's music, did much to further the initially shaky cause of Italian opera. Even the thoroughly cynical *Tatler* praised him for 'the grace and propriety of his action and gesture, [which] does honour to the human figure . . . There is scarce a beautiful posture in an old statue which he does not plant himself in.' Nicolino was succeeded by Senesino, whose relations with Handel were stormy, but who sang alongside Faustina and Cuzzoni in some of his operas. In 1734, another young Italian castrato made his London début. Senesino sang opposite him as a furious tyrant, but was so overcome by the beauty of the newcomer's singing that he completely forgot his character, rushed over to the young man and embraced him. Senesino was prickly, but he had the good sense that night to acknowledge one of the noblest names in the history of singing—Farinelli (or Farinello; his real name was

Carlo Broschi). Senesino was not the only fellow professional to be overcome. The aspiring Gizziello fainted with despondency on first hearing Farinelli, convinced that he could never sing again after encountering someone he considered so superior to himself.

Farinelli was born in Apulia in 1705, possibly of a patrician family that had fallen into disgrace.* He was taught by both his brother Riccardo, later the composer of some of his 'suitcase arias', and in Naples by Nicolo Porpora, himself a pupil of the elder Scarlatti and indisputably the greatest singing teacher of the eighteenth century. It was in opera in Rome that Farinelli first became famous, and a story told of him at the time (later transcribed by Burney) demonstrates something of his breathtaking—or non-breathtaking—technique. Farinelli boasted a bravura aria with trumpet obbligato. Singer and instrument engaged in competition:

> . . . after severally swelling a note, in which each manifested the power of his lungs, and tried to rival the other in brilliancy and force, they had both a swell and shake together, by thirds, which was continued so long, while the audience eagerly waited the event, that both seemed to be exhausted; and, in fact, the trumpeter, wholly spent, gave it up . . . when Farinelli, with a smile on his countenance . . . broke out all at once in the same breath, with fresh vigour, and not only swelled and shook the note, but ran the most rapid and difficult divisions . . .

Farinelli's early days were spent mostly between Naples and Rome, often appearing in vehicles specially tailored for him by Porpora. In 1726 Frederick the Great's flute-teacher, Quantz, described the voice as 'a penetrating, full, rich, bright and well-modulated soprano . . . His intonation was pure, his trill beautiful, his breath-control extraordinary, and his throat very agile . . . But the fire of youth, his great talent, the general applause and his ready throat brought it about that at times he proceeded in too spendthrift a fashion.' Passing on to Vienna at the end of the decade, the Emperor Charles VI confronted him with Quantz's reservation. 'If you wish to reach the heart,' he said, 'you must take a more plain and simple

---

* The recent eponymous French film based on Farinelli's life is not to be taken seriously, although its electronic mixing of a counter-tenor and soprano voice is an interesting attempt to recreate the castrato timbre.

road.' Farinelli took the royal judgement very seriously, and purged his singing of excesses. By 1734, when he arrived in London for what became two and a half years' residence, he was probably at his peak.

Farinelli was pure singer and although tall and handsome, clearly made no attempt to act. Like Flagstad or Melba, his genius lay in the perfect production of a glorious sound, built on a rock-solid musical foundation. Burney wrote of his London performances that 'without the assistance of significant gestures or graceful attitudes, [he] enchanted and astonished his hearers by the force, extent, and mellifluous tones of the mere organ . . . though during the time of his singing he was as motionless as a statue, his voice was so active, that no intervals were too close, too wide, or too rapid for his execution.' A tiny doubt creeps in that he might have been a little dull after a while.

London fell: the opera orchestra were so thunderstruck when they heard him that they could not play; a noble lady in the audience cried out after an aria, 'One God, one Farinelli!'; Hogarth represents him in 'The Rake's Progress', surrounded by hangers-on; the Prince of Wales sent him 'a fine wrought gold snuff-box, richly set with diamonds and rubies, in which was enclosed a pair of brilliant diamond knee-buckles, as also a purse of one hundred guineas'. In all, he probably made about £5,000 a year while in London. Handel, in the rival opera house, was virtually ruined, but even Farinelli could not long stem the rot that had set into Italian opera in London. The public were at bottom tired of it, and by 1737 the sensation of 1734 was said to be singing to £35 worth of takings.

Nevertheless, he left England fully intending to return: London must have been a charming haven from the suffocating provinciality and intrigue which infested the opera in Central Europe and Italy. But his life now took its strangest twist. Philip V of Spain was neurotically withdrawn, and his court in decline. Philip had already abdicated once in favour of his son, but the boy had died, forcing his father to reassume the throne. Washing, shaving, and changing his clothes were as much anathema to him as attending to matters of state. Nothing engaged his interest, and his scheming Italian wife Elisabeth Farnese was terrified that he would die, leaving her to dowagerhood, and her unpleasant stepson Charles to the throne. Farinelli was the last hope, or at least an outside chance, and Elisabeth lured him to Madrid in the hope that he could work a miracle—which he did. The British ambassador sent this dispatch to London:

> Philip was struck by the first air sung by Farinelli, and at the conclusion of the second sent for him [he was singing from a room next to the King's bedchamber], loaded him with praises and promised to grant whatever he should demand. The musician, who had been tutored by the queen, entreated him to rise from his bed, suffer himself to be shaven and dressed and attend council. Philip complied, and from that moment his disorder took a more favourable turn.

Farinelli was to stay in the Spanish court for over twenty years. He immediately became the victim of his own success. His salary was enormous, but his duties insufferably monotonous. Philip lived another nine years, kept from catatonia by the beauty of Farinelli's singing. It was said that the King was only interested in hearing the four same arias, and that Farinelli had to sing them all every night between 12 and 5 a.m., interspersing them with soothing and elegant conversation. If this is true, he would no doubt have taken advantage of singer's licence and varied the ornamentation—Philip may have found this part of the fascination. After the King's death he stayed on under Ferdinand V as an *éminence grise*, gathering power and influence like a beneficent musical Rasputin. No one had a bad word for him: he was above political and amorous intrigue. Vernon Lee speaks of him as 'modest and self-respecting in the most corrupting position, unselfish and forgiving amidst baseness: something which makes him appear like almost an idyllic hero among the artificial worthless people around him'. The truth may be that he was just intelligently diplomatic, and knew when not to open his mouth. He was now in effect retired, and so took over not only the direction of royal church music and opera—which he conducted with exemplary firmness and to a very high standard—but also concerned himself with the canalization of the River Tagus, with the interbreeding of Spanish and Hungarian horses, and in the cause of the Prime Minister Ensenada, who had quarrelled with the Queen. Paintings of the period depict him with all the regal trappings, surrounded by cherubim and trumpets, garlanded with laurel.

But then everyone was ready to make a myth out of Farinelli. First came the myths about his singing; then came the stories of his magnanimity and largesse, such as this pretty tale. A tailor who had made Farinelli a superb suit of clothes for a court gala refused payment from him, but asked instead to hear him sing. Farinelli, accompanying himself at the harpsichord, willingly obliged and 'exerted himself in every species of excellence'. When he had finished, the tailor thanked him and made to leave.

'No,' says Farinelli, 'I am a little proud; and it is perhaps from that circumstance that I have acquired some small degree of superiority over other singers. I have given way to your weakness, it is but fair, that, in your turn, you should indulge me in mine.' And taking out his purse, he insisted on his receiving a sum amounting to nearly double the worth of the suit of clothes.

If we refuse to believe in such unmitigated virtue, Farinelli's personality remains somewhat mysterious. His surviving letters to his lifelong friend, the librettist Metastasio, are gushing, formal, and unexceptionable, but hardly vivid.

In 1759, Farinelli finally left Spain—against his will, but forced out by the conflict of loyalties provoked by the Seven Years' War. He retired to Bologna, living in a villa he had been planning for years, with a fortune, a handsome pension, and a fine collection of keyboard instruments. He became melancholy: Casanova claimed to have visited and found him 'bored and boring . . . One day while I was speaking to him of Spain, he burst into tears: his heart was still set on the high position he had lost.' Other visitors included Gluck, Mozart, Burney, and the Emperor Joseph II. He died in 1782, a year before his most considerable contemporary, the mezzo-soprano castrato Caffarelli. As is so often the case with these operatic 'rivalries'—as indeed with Faustina and Cuzzoni—one party is made out to be all virtue and the other all vice, while the two voices in question are so different as to be properly incomparable. In fact, these two seem to have got on well enough, and Farinelli engaged Caffarelli to sing in his opera house in Madrid.

The latter was born in 1710, and trained like Farinelli with Porpora (who loathed him, but thought him a singer superior to Farinelli). Caffarelli's career was centred in Naples, and his only visit to London in 1738, in the wake of Farinelli's departure and the doldrums of operatic activity, was a failure, although Handel there composed for him the famous so-called *Largo*, 'Ombra mai fù'.

Considered reports of his voice are few: it is his temperament that has been passed down to posterity. He fought a duel, one of many, with a double-bass bow; spent a night in a cistern having been surprised *in flagrante* by a jealous husband; was given three days leave to France after a duel over the relative merits of French and Italian music; and was briefly imprisoned in 1741 for 'disturbing other performers, acting in a manner bordering on lasciviousness with one of the female singers, conversing with the spectators in the boxes from the stage, ironically echoing whichever member of the company was singing an aria, and finally refusing to sing in the *ripieno* [ensemble]'. He is even known to have sulked in the lavatory. In latter years his singing became erratic, but at his peak, he must have been very exciting— what descriptions of his voice there are suggest that it was unusually dark in timbre. Metastasio wrote to Farinelli that in Rome 'numerous critics' had found his voice 'out of tune, strident, and uncontrollable: so that he can make no effect without forcing it, when it becomes harsh and unpleasant'. This reminds one of the later Callas, and that perhaps gives a hint of his personality. For all his success he was persistently querulous. Unlike that friend to the great, Farinelli, he seems to have had a rooted distaste for nobility and royalty—when Louis XV sent him a gold snuff-box, Caffarelli disdained it; on being informed that similar gifts had been gratefully received by ambassadors, he retorted, 'Let the Ambassadors sing!' He was however absurdly high-handed himself. The pompous inscription above his palazzo in the Calabrian dukedom he bought himself—*Amphion Thebas, Ego Domum* ('Amphion built Thebes, I built this house')—gave rise to the neatly deflating rejoinder, *Ille cum, tu sine* ('He with, you without'). Yet in retirement, away from the aggravation and pressures of a performer's life, he became much nicer, giving large amounts of money to charity and taking to religion. Burney met him in 1770 and found him 'very polite', entering into 'conversation with great ease and cheerfulness'.

With Gaetano Guadagni (*c.*1725–92) we come to a singer whose singing did not fit the standard style and accomplishment. He is instead a singer representative of the general reaction against contemporary *opera seria* that set in about 1740, and to which Gluck's was the most lasting contribution. Guadagni's training and earliest years are obscure, but his first prominent engagement was not in a church choir or in *opera seria*, but in the eighteenth-century equivalent of musical comedy. *Opera buffa* developed out of the great traditions of Italian *commedia dell' arte*, and its light, usually premarital, intrigues perpetrated by a variety of stock characters. In Italy, the *buffa* was originally played in the intervals between the acts of the *seria*; later it became an afterpiece. Musically, *buffa* was predominantly swift and bright with, like Gilbert and Sullivan operas, patter songs and much attention paid to musical setting which allowed the words to come through clearly. The bass voice played an important part, being used for old codgers, crotchety fathers, and the forces of authority, while ensembles were much more common, extended arias much rarer, than in *seria*. The triumph of this form is Mozart's *Le Nozze di Figaro*, and its principles can still be felt through Verdi's *Falstaff*.

Guadagni sang juvenile lead, and came to London with an Italian company in 1748. He was considered to have no technique, and the management of his contralto voice was 'wild and careless'. But he was good-looking, 'his countenance replete with beauty, intelligence, and dignity', and a strong actor. He attracted the attention of both the elderly Handel, who gave him the mezzo part in *Messiah*, and the actor-manager David Garrick, who 'took great pleasure in forming him'. All this encouraged Guadagni to become a 'serious' singer, and he began to study with Gizziello (the castrato who had fainted on hearing Farinelli), emerging with a stronger sound in a wider compass. In 1762, in Vienna, he created the role of Orfeo in Gluck's opera and thereby won his place in history.

Gluck's 'reform' operas were part of the general culture move away from Baroque excess towards more restrained Neo-classicism. At first influenced by the independent and insular French opera, which had never surrendered to the supremacy of the aria and never accepted the castrato, and then by the theory of the Italian musicologist Algarotti, Gluck sought to purify Italian opera. Like so many operatic reforms—be they the early Florentines' or Wagner's—this one was an attempt to bring opera closer to drama. Ornament and elaboration gave way to simplicity, singer's licence to composer's law, and the music became the servant of the text, faithfully reflecting and intensifying human feelings. Gluck did not quite fulfil his own best ideals, and there are still elements of older styles in his operas, but he managed to break a mould. So did Guadagni. He was the singer Gluck needed, possessing, wrote Angus Heriot in *The Castrati in Opera*, 'the grandeur and nobility that Gluck demanded, [while] his powers of execution were not great enough to tempt him to introduce unsuitable *fioriture* [decorations] or cadenzas, and thus mar the Neo-classic severity of the conception'. His personal demeanour was correspondingly uncompromising. In the name of dramatic propriety, he refused to break from his character and take bows after an aria, or to encore anything. Audiences were often angry at being so ignored, but Guadagni believed in 'the dignity of the singer's calling'. Burney wrote that, 'He had strong resentments and high notions of his own importance, which revolted many of his warmest friends and augmented the malice of his enemies.' And yet when he returned to London in 1769, he sang Orfeo in a version which included extra music by J. C. Bach and others, as well as interpolating an aria composed by himself. This fact should warn us against the mistake of overestimating the completeness of Gluck's 'revolution'—if he had broken the mould, there was still life in the shattered pieces. *Orfeo* was popular, but audiences continued to flock to bravura singing rather than to severe conceptions. Guadagni never had the drawing-power of Farinelli, and his voice, though 'perfectly delicate, polished, and refined', was always too thin and weak. Burney remarked that his most notable technical accomplishment was his 'artful manner of diminishing the tones of his voice like the dying notes of an Aeolian harp'. He continued to travel round Europe until 1776, finally retiring to Padua, where he last sang Orfeo behind the scenes in a domestic marionette performance of his own devising.

In retrospect, Guadagni seems like the first of what are now called 'singing-actors'—a dubious label, which too often implies third-rate singing and second-rate acting. Guadagni may not have been guilty of that, but he could not match the sheer vocal splendour of the next of the great castrati, one who was considered to uphold all the technical standards of the previous generation.

Gasparo Pacchierotti was born in 1740 and may have trained at San Marco in Venice, where he certainly began his professional life. The unusual longevity of his voice may well have been due to the fact that he did not start singing publicly in his teens. In 1770 he passed into opera, taking up an appointment in Palermo.

From Sicily he moved steadily northwards through the opera houses of Rome, Florence, Milan (where he sang in the inaugural performance at La Scala), Padua, and Genoa. His repertory included Gluck's *Orfeo* and other 'reform' operas, but he was unusual in his taste for music of the old school, especially the arias of Handel. His great friend Bertoni also wrote operas adapted to his gifts and accompanied him to London.

In London Pacchierotti was to find his finest eulogist, Richard, Earl Mount Edgcumbe, whose musical reminiscences are among the most valuable of their kind. Mount Edgcumbe is categorical in his insistence that Pacchierotti was 'the most perfect singer it ever fell my lot to hear'. He continued:

Pacchierotti's voice was an extensive soprano, full and sweet in the highest degree; his powers of execution were great, but he had far too good taste and too good sense to make a display of them where it would have been misapplied, confining it to one bravura song (*aria di agilità*) in each opera, conscious that the chief delight of singing, and his own supreme excellence, lay in touching expression, and exquisite pathos ... As an actor, with many disadvantages of person, for he was tall and awkward in his figure, and his features were plain, he was nevertheless forcible and impressive: for he felt warmly, had excellent judgment, and was an enthusiast in his profession ... As a concert singer, and particularly in private society, he shone almost more than on the stage; for he sung with greater spirit in a small circle of friends, and was more gratified with their applause, than in a public concert room, or crowded theatre.

If history had played fair, what a singer of Schubert's *lieder* he would have been! Mount Edgcumbe also details his amazing powers of sight-reading, his talent for improvisation, and the expressive power of his recitative—an aspect of singing neglected by the early virtuosi, but which became more vigorous and subtle after Gluck. Burney also records that his voice ranged over more than three octaves from the tenor pitch up to a soprano top C.

Burney never heard Farinelli or Caffarelli, but he was a close friend of Pacchierotti, and his daughter, Fanny, the novelist-precursor of Jane Austen, made a pet of him. She also paid him the supreme novelist's compliment—putting him into one of her books, *in propria persona*. In *Cecilia* the heroine attends an opera rehearsal as part of her initiation into polite society: the opera was *Artaxerxes*, the theatre the King's, Haymarket, and Pacchierotti was the singer. In her fascinating journal, Fanny Burney also recorded the progress of this 'very grave and very sweet man' through his triumphant seasons in London between 1778 and 1780.

First we gather that Pacchierotti was no Guadagni: being on stage and in character was no excuse to omit social courtesy: 'Pacchierotti found me out and gave me several smiles during the performance: indeed, he could never look either to the right or the left without a necessity of making some sort of acknowledgement in return to the perpetual bows made him from almost every box in the house . . .' Later we see him the subject of female adoration at a *soirée* of Lady Mary Duncan, who became notorious for sending him a scandalously large sum of money. Although lanky and awkward, he had numerous female admirers, who, one suspects, exploited his good nature and innocence: 'Oh how the Miss Bulls do idolise him! They profess thinking him quite angelic, and declared that they should even look upon it as a favour to be beat by him! I laughed violently at this extravagance . . .' In a conversation with a friend of the Burneys, he is shown in an even more vulnerable light.

'This is a climate' said Pac, 'never in the same case for half an hour at a time; it shall be fair, and wet, and dry, and humid forty times in a morning at the least. I am tired to be so played with, sir, by your climate.'
'We have one thing, however, Mr Pacchierotti', he answered, 'which I hope you allow makes some amends, and that is our verdure; in Italy you cannot boast that.'
'But it seem to me, sir, to be of no utility so much ever-green; is rather too much for my humble opinion.'
'And then your insects, Mr Pacchierotti; those alone are a most dreadful drawback upon the comfort of your fine climate . . .'
'I must own,' said Pacchierotti, 'Italy is rather disagreeable for the insects: but is not better, sir, than an atmosphere so bad as they cannot live in it?'
'Why, as I can't defend our atmosphere, I must shift my ground and talk to you of our fires, which draw together society.'
'Oh, indeed, good sir, your societies are not very invigorating! Twenty people of your gentlemen and ladies to sit about a fire, and not to pronounce one word is very dull.'

Fanny's comment on this is interesting: Pacchierotti became very animated during this exchange, since most of the people he met in

London 'affect a superiority to conversing with him, though he has more intelligence, ay, and cultivation too, than half of them'—which suggests that, for all its 'lionizing', the higher echelon of society still regarded its singers as beyond its pale.

Pacchierotti returned regularly to London, but spent most of his remaining active years in Venice. On his last visit to London, he coincided with Haydn, who persuaded him to perform his solo cantata 'Arianna a Naxos', the composer playing the pianoforte part. 'It is needless to say,' wrote Mount Edgcumbe, 'that the performance was perfect.' Pacchierotti finally retired to Padua, living in a villa furnished in the English style and surrounded by an English garden. He studied English and Italian literature and worked on a treatise on the art of singing which, by the time it was published in edited form in 1836, had become an anachronism, a commemoration of a lost art. The French invasion of Italy upset him deeply, but he came out of retirement to sing before Napoleon in 1796, and made a final appearance in 1814, at the age of seventy-four, singing in a Requiem for Bertoni. In 1817 Stendhal visited him and was very moved, finding him 'still sublime when he sings a recitative . . . I learnt more about music in six conversations with this great artist than from any book.'

After Pacchierotti, the art of the castrato went into irreversible decline. As so often, this was due to a complex of causes rather than a single one. The new spirit of liberalism and republicanism condemned castration as an aberration of pampered tyrants and their decadent courts, while the full-blooded tastes of Romanticism preferred voices that were 'natural', rather than fabricated by surgery. Changes in musical composition and the inevitable withering of *opera seria* left the castrato redundant. The last of the operatic line, Velluti, who will appear in the next chapter, had to compete with a new vogue for the tenor voice, as well as a magnificent generation of female singers, capable of assuming the roles, male and female, that the castrati had previously monopolized. But the dream of the castrato voice, its power and beauty, lingered on: it is known that Wagner wanted a castrato to sing the wizard Klingsor in *Parsifal*, and approached the Sistine Chapel, where the type survived the strenuous efforts of the Napoleonic government to eradicate the operation. He was forced to abandon the idea, though the association of the castrato with preternatural power became a familiar Romantic notion.

The Elizabethan falsetto counter-tenor voice, popular since the 1950s and useful in productions of Baroque opera, probably bears little relation to the castrato timbre, none to its flexibility and volume. So, in an age obsessed with recovering authentic performance practice, if we are ever to retrieve a fundamental aspect of eighteenth-century opera, there is no alternative to accepting the unspeakable view expressed in 1966 in a notorious letter to an American music magazine:

> I have many friends, some of them quite prominent in musical circles, who agree with me that if there is to be a serious and widespread revival of Baroque and *bel canto* opera, there must necessarily be a return of the *castrati* to sing the roles they alone can handle with dramatic and vocal legitimacy . . . I definitely do not advocate force, but if a young singer should possess a fine voice which he wishes to preserve, I can sympathize with no reason for discouraging him . . .

Few women singers reached a dominating position during the great era of the castrati. Their sweet clear tone was simply no competition for the unearthly magic and variety of castrato timbres. One of the few to create a stir was Caterina Gabrielli (1730–96), as much because of her unquenchable self-will as because of her talent. She was the daughter of a cardinal's cook and through the patronage of her father's employer, and despite the Church's disapproval of women singers, she became yet another pupil of Porpora's. Her voice was a light, brilliant soprano, and she was a compelling actress. In 1770 in Palermo, when Pacchierotti was singing opposite her, Gabrielli 'exerted herself in so astonishing a manner, that, before it was half done, poor Pacchierotti burst out a-crying and ran in behind the scenes, lamenting that he dared to appear on the same stage with so wonderful a singer.'

Burney found her 'the most intelligent and best bred virtuosa with whom I have ever conversed'. Her love life was complicated and uninhibited—'she was supposed to have achieved more conquests than any woman breathing', whispered one contemporary—but what made her scandalous was her constant refusal or failure to sing when contracted to do so. She once alleged that the reasons for this were physical and genuine, and it is as well to respect this. Opera singing requires a delicate physiological equilibrium, and many people are not aware, for instance, that women find it difficult to sing in pitch while menstruating, owing to the relaxation of abdominal tension it involves. Audiences tend, equally naturally, to feel slighted when an advertised favourite cancels at short notice, especially as some strongly constituted singers never miss a performance. But Gabrielli, according to Sutherland Edwards, was in a class of her own.

> Some years ago [the viceroy of Sicily] gave a great dinner to the principal nobility of Palermo, and sent an invitation to Gabrielli to be of the party. Every other person arrived at the hour of invitation. The viceroy ordered dinner to be put back, and sent to let her know that the company awaited her. The messenger found her reading in bed. She said she was sorry to have made the company wait, and begged he would make her apology, but that really she had entirely forgotten her engagement. The viceroy would have forgiven this piece of insolence, but when the company came to the opera, Gabrielli repeated her part with the utmost negligence and indifference, and sang all her airs in what they call *sotto voce*, that is, so low that they can scarcely be heard. The viceroy was offended; but as he is a good-tempered man, he was loth to make use of authority; but at last, by a perseverance in this insolent stubbornness, she obliged him to threaten her with punishment in case she any longer refused to sing. On this she grew more obstinate than ever, declaring that force and authority should never succeed with her; that he might make her cry, but never could make her sing. The viceroy then sent her to prison, where she remained twelve days; during which time she gave magnificent entertainments every day, paid the debts of all the poor prisoners, and distributed large sums in charity . . .

Reading between the lines this sounds as though Gabrielli ('reading in bed') might have been ill; what one notices is the appalling condition of a singer beholden to a patron with law on his side. (Gabrielli was later incarcerated again for screaming at the pestiferous Infante of Parma, '*Gobbo maledetto*,' 'Accursed hunchback.') Outside Italy, she sang for Catherine the Great in St Petersburg and with Farinelli's company in Madrid. In London, she made little effort and frequently replaced herself with her sister Francesca, a vastly inferior singer who was her constant companion.

33

Of the next generation of prima donnas, three of the most famous excited an extraordinary amount of abuse, in a generally tempestuous but *louche* period.

Brigitta Banti was the roughest of them. She was born in 1756 and began, like Piaf, as a street singer in Paris, never losing the air of a *femme du trottoir* and finding it quite unnecessary to make any concessions to gentility. No one could teach her anything—one of those who tried and failed was Piozzi, whose marriage to Mrs Thrale so mortified Dr Johnson—and many said that she could not even read music, learning everything by sharpness of ear and instinct. Mozart's librettist Lorenzo da Ponte loathed her, calling her a 'musical Messalina'. He worked with her in London in 1794 and his memories of the experience were not pleasant. 'She could make any theatre at which she was engaged tremble at the sound of her name . . . she brought to opera, where her voice alone had introduced her, all the habits, manners and customs of an impudent Corsican. Free in her speech, still more in her actions, given to debauchery, licentiousness and drinking . . .' Yet there must have been more to her personality than this. In the noble role of Gluck's Alceste her acting was judged 'sublime'; and if the discriminating Mount Edgcumbe had found Pacchierotti the most perfect singer he had ever heard, Banti was the 'most delightful', 'her voice, sweet and beautiful throughout, had not a fault in any part of its unusually extensive compass. Its lower notes, which reached below ordinary sopranos, were rich and mellow; the middle, full and powerful; and the very high, totally devoid of shrillness.'

Slightly older than Banti was Mara, born Gertrud Schmeling in 1749, and the first German prima donna. Her biography was written in her own lifetime, and we have an unusual amount of verifiable facts about her career and experiences. Mara's childhood was cruel. She suffered both a tyrannical violinist father and rickets, from which she never fully recovered. As an infant, she once snapped one of her father's violin strings, and as punishment was made to learn the instrument: later she ascribed her perfect intonation to her violin training. Soon she was good enough to be trapped in that heavily exploitable form of child labour, the infant prodigy. At the age of six she was playing publicly in Vienna, but in 1759 in London the pathetic little bubble burst, leaving father and daughter stranded and penniless. They set out to tour the more gullible provinces, little Gertrud by now having shown signs of vocal ability. Somehow they

34

reached the quiet cathedral town of Wells, where the father played the flute to his daughter's soprano and guitar. Fortunately they were heard by a local musical dilettante, who was impressed by the girl's voice and arranged for a concert in more glamorous nearby Bath, from which they earned enough to get back to Germany.

One of Mara's first engagements was in Leipzig, where Goethe heard her. In 1771 she bravely made her way to the court of Frederick the Great in Berlin, with a letter of recommendation from the Electress of Saxony. Bravely, because Frederick was notoriously averse to the idea of German singers, and patronized only Italians. The one-time friend of Voltaire and enlightened despot had become a crabbed old man, running his court opera like a department of state. He conducted the orchestra himself on occasion, and had been known to lash at the players with his baton. The King received the girl coldly. Her nerves must have been steely, because her initial reaction was to walk round the room examining the paintings. Then, her spirit inflamed by his silent sarcasm, she gave a flawless display, and won both his admiration and a contract.

At first all went well enough. She took lessons from Porporino, Frederick's court castrato, and foreign visitors, including Burney, were impressed with her. But her very success became the problem, since Frederick became possessive of his prima donna to the point of keeping her under close surveillance lest she escaped to the fleshpots of the international scene. She was aware of her own value too, and within a year of arriving in Berlin had attempted to enlist Frederick's support in an unattractive quarrel with her father.

She then fell in love with Giovanni-Battista Mara, a court cellist, who resembled her father in being lazy and drunk. Frederick opposed the match, and even locked her up in Spandau fortress when she tried to elope, but they were eventually married on the condition that they remained in Berlin. The King now had a third party to play with in the battle of wills, and whenever there was trouble Herr Mara was sent off to play in the band of a front-line regiment.

Mara now tried to get herself dismissed, and refused to sing music commanded by the King. During a state visit by the Grand Duke Paul of Russia she announced that she was ill and took to her bed. Frederick needed her for the entertainment, and sent eight dragoons who carried her off on the mattress. She at first sang without enthusiasm and almost inaudibly, until natural vanity reasserted

35

itself. The Maras became a byword for impertinence and *lèse majesté*, and when they eventually did escape from Berlin—in 1780, on the pretext of taking a spa cure for an attack of pleurisy—Frederick released her without vindictiveness and perhaps with relief. The story is a sad instance of the perils of patronage, in which security of tenure hardly compensated for the restrictions on personal liberty.

Over the next four years Mara sang in Vienna, Munich—where Mozart was appalled by the couple's arrogance and unimpressed by what he found over-artful singing—and Paris. In 1784 she arrived in London, where she was to settle for the next eighteen years. Her husband became impossible (she divorced him and he drank himself to death in Holland) but her career prospered. She sang opera with Pacchierotti, and 'I know that my Redeemer liveth' in the grand Handel commemoration concert of 1784 in Westminster Abbey. Mount Edgcumbe has this to say of her:

> Mara's talents as a singer (for she was no actress, and had a bad person for the stage) were of the very first order. Her voice, clear, sweet, distinct, was sufficiently powerful, though rather thin, and its agility and flexibility rendered her a most excellent bravura singer, in which style she was unrivalled; but she succeeded equally well in some of Handel's most solemn and pathetic songs, though there appeared to be a want of that feeling in herself, which, nevertheless, she could communicate to her hearers.

By 1790 her voice was beginning to lose its strength, and she made the mistake of singing the part of Polly Peachum in *The Beggar's Opera*, to which she was hardly suited. In 1802, 'in the maturity of her charms, which had never been great', she left London with a young flute-player and made a farewell tour of Europe, settling first in Moscow, where she lost everything in the 1812 conflagration, and then in Tallin, where she taught. Then, continued Mount Edgcumbe:

> When she was almost forgotten, she re-appeared as suddenly and in as singular a manner as she had vanished. A very few years ago, 1819, an advertisement from Messrs. Knyvett announced for their concerts a most celebrated singer whom they were not yet at liberty to name. This mysterious secret was soon after explained by another announcement, that *Madame Mara's* benefit concert

would take place at the King's theatre on an evening specified, no one being at all aware of her return to England, or even of her existence. She must have then been at least seventy; but it was said that her voice had miraculously returned, and was again as fine as ever. But when she displayed these wonderfully revived powers, they proved, as might be expected, lamentably deficient, and the tones she produced were compared to those of a *penny trumpet*.

She returned to Russia, wrote her memoirs, and lived to the age of eighty-four. Goethe sent her two poems on her eighty-second birthday, paying tribute to her singing in 1767, sixty-four years earlier.

One of the most significant facts about the third of these women, Mrs Billington (1768–1818), was that, for all the operatic activity in London, she remained until the 1920s the only English-born prima donna to achieve real European fame. Her life appears miserable, and one biographer claimed that she suffered throughout from a neurotic depressive condition; but then many claims were made for her, including those of the gutter press. In 1792, a book was published which showed Mrs Billington 'immersed in the horrible depths of human depravity', deflowered by her father, and saddled with both an impotent husband and venereal disease. On the other hand, Reynolds painted her as Saint Cecilia, and she received the tributes of doggerel:

> With beauty's soft blandishments arm'd to delight
> Resistless and charming, she bursts on the sight;
> From her eyes issue rays of voluptuous mirth,
> And she catches applause, ere the judgment has birth.*

Born Elizabeth Weichsell, she was the illegitimate daughter of a German wind player and a mother who had studied with J. C. Bach and sang in Vauxhall Pleasure Gardens. The young Elizabeth was also taught by Bach, but started off, like Mara, as another tiresomely talented infant instrumentalist. At the age of twelve, two sets of her pianoforte sonatas were published.

She married her second teacher, James Billington, and made her first stage appearance in Dublin. In 1786 came success at Covent

* Pasquin's *Children of Thespis* (1792).

Garden, which she consolidated with further intensive study in Paris. Interestingly, Mrs Billington continued to take voice lessons throughout her career, and she seems to have been exceptionally conscientious. Her repertory was never distinguished, but it was the pretty pastoral music of Arne, Shield, and Arnold that the public wanted.

Haydn, then resident in London, became a tremendous admirer of hers, and in his biography of the composer, Stendhal reports a meeting between the composer, Mrs Billington, and Reynolds, at which Haydn commented on Reynolds's portrait: 'You have painted her listening to the angels: you should have painted the angels listening to *her* divine voice.' Mount Edgcumbe judged that voice, 'though sweet and flexible', to be 'not of that full nature which formed the charm of Banti's, but was rather a *voce di testa*, and in its very high tones resembled a flute . . . she possessed not the feeling to give touching expression, even when she sung with the utmost delicacy and consummate skill.' George III privately criticized her for excessive ornamentation of 'pathetick songs', when taste was moving towards something simpler. She also constantly used her brother as orchestral leader when she was singing, doubtless to ensure sympathetic *tempi*.

After the publication of the scurrilous attack on her morals, Mrs Billington left England in 1794. She answered the accusations and sued the publishers, but the scandal stuck. Making her way to Naples, where 'her only desire was to live in seclusion', in a climate recommended as beneficial to her mental condition, she was persuaded by the English ambassador, Sir William Hamilton, to sing before the royal family. Some say that she became Hamilton's lover, others that she was the intimate of the notorious Emma Hamilton, Sir William's wife and a fine amateur singer herself. Whatever the truth, she made a strong impression in her début at the Teatro San Carlo in an opera written for her. Almost immediately her husband died of an apoplectic fit after a large dinner with the Bishop of Winchester; there was also an eruption of Mount Vesuvius. A female Protestant heretic was vulnerable to blame in such circumstances, and many thought she had poisoned her husband, with whom she was known to be unhappy.

Mrs Billington proceeded to tour the major Italian opera houses, and in Milan was received by the Empress Josephine. She remarried there, a young Frenchman called Félissent, and bought an estate near

38

Venice. When Félissent maltreated her, she returned to England in 1801. He followed and harassed her for money, but was arrested and deported as an alien. London found her even better than remembered, and she took contracts at both Drury Lane and Covent Garden simultaneously. In her first season back home she must have earned in the region of £15,000. She sang at the farewell performances of both Mara and Banti in 1802, and remained supreme until her retirement in 1811, when her voice was still at its peak but her spirit broken. She had become comically fat, and her first child had died in infancy. A second, probably illegitimate, had been placed in a Brussels convent. Félissent reappeared in 1817 and took her back to Venice. Her unstable life ended, possibly at the hands of her husband, less than a year later. *The Times* commented in its obituary: 'Into whatever human errors she might have fallen, she possessed an excellent heart and a truly benevolent disposition . . . it is impossible to describe the anxiety with which her numerous friends implored her not to leave the country with her husband who, after having lived separate from her abroad for 16 years, came to England, and declared he could no longer live without her.'

Towards the end of the eighteenth century opera seemed ready to collapse into utter banality, at least in England. Standards were generally as low as public taste, and there was still an obsession with *pasticcio*—the stitching-up of popular tunes, in the absence of copyright, from various sources, irrespective of musical or dramatic integrity. As we have seen, even Gluck's operas received this treatment, and *Orfeo* is still performed with a florid interpolated aria by Bertoni at the end of Act I. Banti, Mara, and Mrs Billington were prima donnas with nothing of much worth to sing outside oratorio. The great operatic music of the time hardly reached them; which is to say, Mozart hardly reached them.

Mozart's operas are accessible to us today in ways that those of other eighteenth-century composers cannot be. In them we find that ambiguity and anxiety, a sense of tragedy in comedy, and the complexity of human feeling and motive, that we find in neither the austerities of Gluck nor the cheerful energies of *opera buffa*. Yet Mozart inherited these traditions and genres, developing and working with the possibilities they offered. His early operas are distinguished only by the youthful genius in the music: theatrically, they look pretty much like anyone else's product.

But with the mature Italian operas, *Don Giovanni*, *Figaro*, *Così fan tutte*, he takes the surface subject-matter of farce and *opera buffa*—courtship, seduction, the cynical old against the cunning young, the servant outwitting his master—and gives it a depth and pace that it had never previously had. *Figaro* is the first opera to be developed intelligently from a good modern play (Beaumarchais' *Les Noces de Figaro*); while the old story of Don Juan is used not to point a finger at the fate of libertines so much as to create an atmosphere of dangerous confusion in which the villain might also be a hero and the victims take their share of the satire. In *Così* another familiar farcical situation is turned inside out by the emotion Mozart invests in it. With *Die Zauberflöte* he manages an even more staggering transformation. The pantomime entertainment and spectacle which distinguished the German *singspiel* is taken as a basis for an exploration of some of mankind's most solemn questioning of moral conduct and religious truth.

None of these works offer the prima donna easy options. Ensemble and recitative, unrewarding in terms of applause, require as much effort and artistry as the arias. They offer no easily achieved effectiveness: rather, they mercilessly expose the fraudulent. Mozart had the incomparable gift of making the smallest nuance in the vocal line sing with meaning, and the ability to articulate that detail is perhaps the ultimate test of a Mozart singer.

Mozart's music is both uniquely gratifying and cruelly testing to sing. It lies very well for the voice, and does not strain the vocal equipment—in fact, singers very often say that it 'refreshes' the voice. But it poses complex technical challenges too. Elettra in *Idomeneo* and Donna Anna in *Don Giovanni* both require a heroic dramatic compass that can effortlessly scale itself down to produce a liquid legato. Donna Anna's first aria, 'Or sai chi l'onore', for example, needs a Brünnhilde's aggressive force, and stamina and accuracy in negotiating wide intervals; while the second, 'Non mi dir' starts in icily smooth calm before launching into the sort of supple coloratura that most 'dramatics' cannot muster. Then there are the infamous arias of the Queen of the Night in *Die Zauberflöte*, and Constanze's bravura 'Martern aller Arten'. However, the Mozart that is most deeply loved by both singers and listeners is found in the more lyrical roles—the Countess, Susanna, Donna Elvira, Zerlina, Pamina, Ilia in *Idomeneo*—where the challenge is in sustaining and interpreting a melodic line rather than in virtuosity.

Today we associate such parts with singers such as Schwarzkopf, Te Kanawa, Margaret Price, and Lucia Popp, all great exponents of the purified Mozart which has developed since the Second World War. Precise in intonation, clean in execution, stricter in tempo than previously, but allowing a limited amount of decoration, usually at the discretion of the conductor rather than the singer, the enlightened modern Mozart style has cut out the slurring and swooping which pre-war Mozart singers employed to make the music sound more 'romantic' and emotional. But style in Mozart is never enough. Mozart's operatic music uniquely conveys *personality*: Susanna is wonderfully differentiated from the Countess or Cherubino—or Zerlina or Despina—and the singer has to understand that psychology, to convey it in her phrasing and tone. If she cannot communicate a particular human being, she is not singing Mozart well. Nothing human is shut out of his imaginative world, and in the Italian operas in particular his music bespeaks a variety of female desires, strengths, and failings: the pathos of Fiordiligi's yielding to Ferrando—'Fa di me qual che ti par', 'Do what you like with me'; the Countess's weary forgiveness and Pamina's assertion of 'Die wahrheit', 'the truth': to realize such things, the prima donna must understand something more than style.

Mozart's feelings about singers and their capabilities were predictably mixed: the demands his music made were considerable, and he had many struggles with the inadequate and recalcitrant. Yet inasmuch as he wrote carefully for individual voices and was prepared to insert extra music as required, he was a composer of his time—to survive, he had to be. His ideal was a castrato of the *vieux école*, Manzuoli, who taught him singing when he was a boy in London, and he found no one in adulthood to measure up to him. By the time Mozart's mature operas were being written in the 1780s, a good castrato was hard to find. The role of Idamante in *Idomeneo*, the most beautiful and moving of all *opera seria*, was taken by one Vincenzo dal Prato, who infuriated the composer: 'I have to teach him the whole part as if he were a child,' he wrote to his father: he had 'no intonation, no method, no feeling'. With prima donnas he had better luck. He was in love with two of them. The English singer Nancy Storace was the first Susanna in *Le Nozze di Figaro*, and for her Mozart composed a lovely aria for concert singing, 'Ch'io mi scordi di te?'; Aloysia Weber, elder and initially preferred sister of

Mozart's wife Constanze, also had such arias written for her in a florid style.

The outstanding contemporary Mozart singer was indisputably Catarina Cavalieri (1760–1801). In *Die Entführung aus dem Serail*, Mozart sacrificed dramatic credibility, and composed a long, heroic and fiendishly difficult aria, 'Martern aller Arten', to show off what he called her 'flexible throat'. With a long instrumental introduction, it is a producer's nightmare, and often the prima donna's too. Cavalieri also sang in the first performance of *Der Schauspieldirektor*, a one-act squib which satirizes the folly of two rival prima donnas, each trying to outbid the other vocally and financially. Mozart clearly enjoyed poking fun at these ladies and the music they sang: *Così fan tutte* contains an aria, 'Come scoglio', which, with its perfervid sentiments of constancy, its leaps and runs, is a superb parody of *opera seria* at its silliest. For Cavalieri Mozart inserted an aria— Donna Elvira's 'Mi tradì'—into *Don Giovanni*, and in a revival she also sang the Countess in *Le Nozze di Figaro*, a role requiring the utmost control and smoothness of line. Even though she was the mistress of his rival Salieri, Mozart remained on very cordial terms with her until his miserable end. A few weeks before his death he took her and Salieri to see *Die Zauberflöte*: in a letter to Constanze, Mozart reported their verdict that 'they had never seen such a delightful show'.

Only *Figaro* and *Don Giovanni* survived Mozart's death as popular works (although *Die Zauberflöte* appeared sometimes as *Il Flauto Magico*), and it was not until the middle of this century that his other masterpieces won the central place in the repertory that they now hold. The first Mozart opera to be heard in London was *La Clemenza di Tito*, in which Mrs Billington sang in 1806. A work of great virtues and some originality, it was also a throw-back to the ethics and structure of conventional *opera seria*. London considered it 'modern' at first, because of the unfamiliar sophistication of its harmony and orchestration. Within twenty years, however, it would look and sound hopelessly old-fashioned. For out of the unprecedented turmoil of the revolutionary and Napoleonic period a new culture was growing, in which opera found new fresh roots and shapes. The great age of the prima donna was about to begin.

# Romantic Opera

John Keats once admitted that 'there is a tendency to class women in my books with roses and sweetmeats—they never see themselves dominant'. One of the fascinations of early Romantic opera lies in the fact that at one level it deals in the standard 'roses and sweetmeats' female fantasy-role—woman as passive victim and virginal innocent; as intercessor, the bearer of pity and mercy; woman waiting and praying—while at another, it gives women that vocal domination which Keats found lacking in his poetry. In many of these operas women become genuinely heroic, put centre-stage and made agents of their own destinies: Beethoven's Leonore or Bellini's Norma and Cherubini's Medea, modelled on classical tragedy, are notable examples of this. Opera thus provides the most potent image of woman in any Romantic art form. Neither the novel nor painting gave women such an open field of action, such a number of revolutionary possibilities. Nowhere else was a woman put so firmly at the structural centre. The great prima donnas of the period both seized and forged these possibilities, asserting their individualities and taking control.

The political and intellectual upheavals of the time had had their inevitable radical effect on public taste. The *ancien régime*, with its fixed moral and class codes, had been unsettled, not just in France but throughout Europe. From the turn of the century, war, or the prospect of it, became a norm. The fixed form of *opera seria* became as anachronistic as the absolutist monarchies under which it had flourished, and a new music developed for a new social dispensation.

But revolutions are never immediate or clean, and the new era began with the triumph of two magnificent dinosaurs, Angelica Catalani and Giovanni-Battista Velluti. Mount Edgcumbe spoke of Catalani as 'the last great singer heard in this country whose name is likely to be recollected in musical annals'. He also thought that there was something a little silly about her.

Her throat seems endued (as has been remarked by medical men) with a power of expansion and muscular motion by no means usual, and when she throws out all her voice to the utmost, it has a volume and strength that are quite surprising, while its agility in divisions, running up and down the scale in semi-tones, and its compass in jumping over two octaves at once, are equally astonishing. It were to be wished she was less lavish in the display of these wonderful powers, and sought more to please than to surprise; but her taste is vicious, her excessive love of ornament spoiling every simple air, and her greatest delight (indeed her chief merit) being in songs of a bold and spirited character . . . in which she can indulge in *ad libitum* passages with a luxuriance and redundancy no other singer ever possessed, or if possessing ever practised, and which she carries to a fantastical excess.

This extraordinary coloratura soprano was born in Sinagaglia in 1780 and had little musical education. In early days she sang with Mrs Billington and the castrato Marchesi in Italy, where she was always regarded with a degree of scepticism, and then spent about six years in Lisbon. In France she became a favourite of Napoleon, but even the blockade of the Channel could not stop her from reaching London, where she made her début in 1806 in Portogallo's *Semiramide*. The *Morning Post* was beside itself in search of superlatives. Her first performance was good enough: 'There never was perhaps a singer of any age or country, who possessed such powers of voice and execution, as this Lady . . . we must notice her bravura at the end of the first act, which exceeds all possibility of description'; but her second far exceeded 'any description that is within the scope of language to justly characterize'; while 'on Saturday she exceeded her former efforts beyond all description'.

Her head turned by such praise, Catalani's repertory became progressively more ridiculous. When she did sing Mozart (she was London's first Susanna in *Figaro*), the result was considered admirable, but nothing could wean her away from bravura show-pieces specially composed for her by contemporary hacks. 'It was no matter how unmeaning or preposterous these displays were: it was quite enough if they were astonishing.' Two of the ultimate idiocies were an arrangement of Figaro's aria 'Non più andrai', in which she would drown 'by the force and volume of her organ, the whole

brazen instruments of the orchestra', and, much to Mount Edgcumbe's distaste, a vocalized version of some variations for violin.

Catalani was a woman of immense amiability, unspoilt by her
success and extremely generous. She was also very beautiful. Mount
Edgcumbe found 'the outline of her features ... decidedly tragic
(almost Siddonian), yet she can relax them into the most charming
smile, and assume the character not merely of gaiety, but even of
*niaiserie*, and of arch simplicity.' Like so many of the more rapacious
prima donnas, she left the negotiation and collection of her fees to her
husband—a miserable French army officer called Paul Valbrèque.
She, meanwhile, charmed one and all. 'No woman,' wrote Michael
Kelly in his *Reminiscences*,

> ... was ever more charitable or kind-hearted, and as for the
> quality of her mind, I never knew a more perfect child of nature.
> At Bangor she heard the Welsh harp for the first time. The old
> blind harper of the house was in the kitchen; thither she went, and
> seemed delighted with the wild and plaintive music which he
> played. But when he struck up a Welsh jig, she started up before
> all the servants in the kitchen, and danced as if she were wild. I
> thought she never would have ceased.

She was in London regularly until 1814 and became a feature of
fashionable life. It has been estimated that she amassed £50,000
while in England, but things were not always easy. Once she went on
strike when the management's payments to her fell in arrears: this
provoked a riot in the theatre—chandeliers and musical instruments
were smashed and a week's closure ensued. The size of her fee was
also a major cause of the 'Old Price' riots at Covent Garden in 1809.
But beyond the charge of avarice, no breath of scandal was ever
attached to her: 'She pursued her course with undeviating propriety,' wrote one commentator approvingly. Valbrèque eventually
tried to buy the King's Theatre as a permanent base for his wife, but
after he failed, the couple left for Paris, and London may have felt
some relief when in 1815, amid the drama of Napoleon's return from
Elba, the French state handed them the Théâtre-Italien, along with a
generous subsidy.

Four years of fiasco ensued, as Catalani gave way to tendencies
already noted in London. Not only could she not endure any sort of
rivalry, but she deliberately surrounded herself with ninth-rate

singers in supporting roles and sacked half the orchestra and chorus in draconian economy measures. 'My wife and four or five puppets—that's all you need,' replied Valbrèque, when asked on what principle he ran his opera house. In performance nothing much mattered except the display pieces, and the repertory was consequently abysmal, with rehearsal and production cut to a minimum. The monotony soon overpowered the French, and Catalani seems to have sensed that her time on stage was up. She began a grand series of concert tours. Stendhal reported her visit to Milan:

> Signora Catalani is come to town with the promise of four recitals. The tickets are to cost ten francs each, and the whole of Milan holds up its hands in horror. (The price of a seat at *la scala*, on a regular subscription, is precisely six and thirty centimes) . . . Everyone who heard her concurs in the verdict: for pure vocal quality, Signora Catalani has no rival within living memory . . . What marvels then, were it our fortune to witness, had nature but seen fit to bestow upon her the gift of a *soul*! But, alas! in the event, she sang every single aria on the programme *in exactly the same style* . . . It is fully eighteen years now since Signora Catalani first came to Milan and sang 'Ho perduto il figlio amato' and she has not made an iota of progress.

In Naples, she charged seven times the usual amount and billed herself unequivocally as '*prima cantatrice del mondo*'. In 1824 she returned to London and to opera, appearing in a comic piece to which her considerable (when she bothered) acting talent was well suited. Her voice was deemed to have retained all its glory, and in four months of London performances she made over £10,000. As a portent of the times, Pasta and Rossini were also in London and the composer and Catalani sang a duet together at a music festival in Cambridge.

Catalani sang on regardless until she retired in 1828, and Valbrèque continued to get her the best possible terms. A Catalani contract of 1826 (not, incidentally, accepted by the management) contained the following clause:

> Madame Catalani shall choose and direct the operas in which she is to sing; she shall likewise have the choice of performers in them;

she will have no orders to receive from anyone; she will find all her own dresses.

Further down the page, we gather that Madame Catalani would also expect to receive half the total takings. Valbrèque also insisted that a large number of free tickets, presumably for a claque, should be made available to him. In such a light, it would be possible to regard Catalani's entire career as a monument to exploitation and artistic malpractice. Yet she commands respect: however intransigent and narrow-minded, she was aware of her strengths, and she did not disappoint her audiences. (The composer Spohr records a touching sign of weakness in her otherwise near-flawless vocal equipment, a characteristic which immediately makes her a more sympathetic performer: she suffered terribly from nerves and was observed before a concert to 'tremble from head to foot . . . hardly able to breathe'.)

Her retirement was marked by the endowment of a school for aspiring prima donnas. There were no fees, but a stipulation was made that every pupil had to adopt 'Catalani' into their surname. The venture was not a success, and all her money seems to have vanished, as money does. In her latter days, Catalani sat in Paris in genteel poverty, knitting obsessively. A correspondent of the *Musical Times* interviewed her: 'I hate music,' she exclaimed. 'Fifty years of humble invocation to the Virgin not for a blessing on my dearly beloved children, not for the health and happiness of myself, but for a benediction on my crotchets and quavers.'

Catalani was one of those singers whose greatness was thrust upon them by virtue of a unique physical organ: she did not need to make concessions to the art of music. Our second dinosaur, the castrato Giovanni-Battista Velluti (1781–1861), tried harder, to no avail. He arrived in London at the same time as the notorious 'Living Skeleton' Claude Seurat, and society went from staring at one physical freak to listening to another. Velluti was an epigone, and capitalized on his novelty value—London had not heard a castrato for a quarter of a century when he appeared there in 1825. The sniggering was widespread, and he was the subject of 'scurrilous abuse', some of it probably justified. Extremely handsome, he was notorious for his dalliance with ladies of quality. 'Childishness,' wrote Stendhal, who admired his art, 'is the predominant facet of his character, and a footman can lead him around like a bear on a string.'

47

Even more than Catalani, he suffered from his own obsolescence. For one thing, his voice was not particularly strong. Mount Edgcumbe, admittedly hearing him only late in his career, was disappointed: 'His general style is the *grazioso*, with infinite delicacy and a great deal of expression, but never rising to the grand, simple and dignified cantabile of the old school, still less to the least approach towards the *bravura* . . . there is a great want of variety in his performance, as well as a total deficiency of force and spirit.' He had to compete with a new fashion for tenor heroes and with the Rossini *travesti* parts for women. His response was largely defensive, and the operas written for him were largely old-fashioned, pallid, and replete with ornaments and antique vocal effects. When in 1813 Rossini (who as a child had himself narrowly evaded the knife which was Velluti's fate) wrote a part for him in *Aureliano in Palmira*, there was an argument—Velluti had an enormous success with his principal aria, but Rossini was furious at the way his original simple melody had been decorated and embellished out of all recognition. On that occasion young composer had to yield to established singer, but Rossini was soon in a position from which he could enforce his insistence that what he wrote was meant to be sung without the singer's creative collaboration. Stendhal understood the momentous significance of this transference of power when he wrote that 'The revolution inaugurated by Rossini killed the gift of originality in the singer.' Perhaps 'killed' is too strong a word, and 'restricted' more accurate: throughout the nineteenth century prima donnas continued to decorate at their pleasure, though never to the extent that Catalani did.

In 1824 Meyerbeer wrote the last role ever composed for a castrato, Armando in *Il Crociato in Egitto*. It was, as Mount Edgcumbe puts it, 'quite of the new school', and Velluti took it to London. Among the other singers at his début was the seventeen-year-old Mlle Garcia, soon to be famous as Malibran. *The Times* maintained that a male soprano, or representative of the 'epicene gender', as he was delicately referred to, was a nasty foreign thing, and 'will never suit the unsophisticated palate of that people who for years fought the battles of Europe and came from the contest victorious'. Velluti himself was 'distinguished by a melancholy placidity', his face speaking of 'a heart that knows no joys. It is a painted sepulchre.' Mount Edgcumbe was more dispassionate: 'At the moment when he was expected to appear, the most profound silence reigned in one of the most crowded audiences I ever saw, broken on his advancing by loud applauses of encouragement. The first note he uttered gave a shock of surprise, almost of disgust, to inexperienced ears, but his performance was listened to with attention and great applause throughout, with but few *audible* expressions of disapprobation speedily suppressed.' His success, founded in curiosity, never consolidated itself, and he continued to be something of a joke. One evening, having sung the words 'il nostro casto amor', 'our chaste love', a gallery wit shouted, 'What else could it be?', which caused waves of mirth.

In 1826 he took over the musical direction of the King's Theatre, where he was noted for his attention to historical accuracy in costume. At forty-five, he was ready to bow out gracefully, but his professional end was ignominious. The ladies of the chorus successfully sued him for non-payment of a promised bonus, and he left the country in disgust. His long retirement was spent farming in the Brenta, where he used his fortune to try out novel agricultural methods. He and the also-retired Rossini mellowed into friends and giggled at the *avant-garde* peculiarities of Berlioz.

Far more suited to Rossini's mature style was a Spanish soprano, Isabella Colbran. (There have been many great Spanish Rossini singers, perhaps because the characteristic Spanish sense for subtleties of rhythm relieves his music of its frequent four-square predictability.) Rossini worked at a staggering pace, and liked the short-cut of his chosen formulas, frequently sweeping up material from his last unsuccessful serious opera and dumping it surreptitiously into his next comic one. At the same time, he was a true liberator, learning from the example of Mozart in matching the flexibility and swiftness of *opera buffa* to dramatic subjects, as well as increasing the amount of effect gained from the orchestra and from vocal ensemble, particularly in his famous finales. Rossini's music is very noisy—Mount Edgcumbe objected to it for that very reason. It uses a lot of brass and percussion, a lot of martial rhythms, a lot of *crescendo*, *accelerando*, and *sforzando*. It retains a lot of the verve and melodiousness of *opera buffa*, but it has a cruder energy as well, whipping its audiences into little fits of excitement. In sum, Rossini established a new set of operatic clichés and brought to an end the long-drawn-out death pangs of *opera seria*, even while using the time-honoured classical plots in works such as *Maometto Secondo* or *Semiramide*. His success was remarkable for a mere composer, and

49

Stendhal begins his gloriously ramshackle biography with a tribute to his eminence. 'Napoleon is dead; but a new conqueror has already shown himself to the world; and from Moscow to Naples, from London to Vienna, from Paris to Calcutta, his name is constantly on every tongue. The fame of this hero knows no bounds save those of civilization itself; and he is not yet thirty-two!'

Rossini first encountered Colbran as a boy of fifteen in Bologna. She was seven years older than he, and already well known. Her startling theatrical presence is described by Stendhal:

It was a beauty in the most queenly tradition: noble features, which, on the stage, radiated majesty; an eye like that of a Circassian maiden, darting fire; and to crown it all, a true and deep instinct for tragedy. Off-stage, she possessed about as much dignity as the average milliner's assistant; but the moment she stepped on to the boards, her brow encircled with a royal diadem, she inspired involuntary respect, even among those who, a minute or two earlier, had been chatting intimately with her in the foyer of the theatre.

Queenly, noble, fire, majesty, 'true and deep instinct for tragedy'—these became the familiar attributes of the new race of prima donna, and Colbran was the first of the breed.

In 1815 Rossini went to the recently rebuilt Teatro San Carlo in Naples and signed a long-term contract with its impresario, Domenico Barbaia. This man became the greatest power in early nineteenth-century opera, managing at various times opera houses in Milan and Vienna as well. He began life as a waiter and was said to be the first to crown a cup of coffee or chocolate with whipped cream. He made a fortune out of gambling concessions in opera house foyers and elsewhere. More significantly, he had real artistic instinct, and knew that to commission good composers was as important to opera as engaging good singers. Colbran also had a contract with Barbaia, or probably two, since she appears to have been his mistress as well as his prima donna. She was also favoured by the King of Naples, which made her extremely unpopular with the Republican element of the audience.

Rossini's reputation, then as now, was largely based on his comic operas, but Colbran was no comedian, and she weaned Rossini away from *buffo* librettos to matter more fiery and majestic. Their professional partnership began with *Elisabetta, Regina d'Inghilterra*, a bizarre distortion of the Queen's involvement with the Earl of Leicester, an early instance of the new 'historical' opera, which caught on in the wake of the vogue for the novels of Scott. Stendhal's impassioned description of Colbran as Elisabetta gives a good idea of her arrestingly economical style. She

> . . . used no gestures, did nothing melodramatic, never descended to what are vulgarly called *tragedy-queen poses*. The immensity of her royal authority, the vastness of events which a single word from her lips could call into being, all this lived in the Spanish beauty of her eyes, which at times could be so terrible . . . it was the unmistakable absence of the least shadow of doubt concerning the devoted obedience which would greet the most insignificant and capricious of her commands, which characterized the acting of this great artist; all this wealth of exquisitely-observed detail could be read into the statuesque calm of her every gesture. And when, rarely, she did move, it was as though the breaking of the stillness were forced upon her from within . . .

Between 1815 and 1823, Rossini wrote nine further parts for Colbran. But from 1816 onwards there was, according to Stendhal, a major problem: 'Signorina Colbran revealed a marked tendency to sing either above or below the required pitch, and her singing became what (in inferior mortals) would certainly have been termed execrable; but God forbid that one should have suggested anything of the kind in Naples . . . This, to my mind, represents one of the most flattering victories achieved by rank despotism . . .'

This tendency to poor intonation was a common one among Romantic prima donnas, probably the consequence of both the fervour of their histrionics and the fashion for forcing the voice to create a violent or arresting effect. In any case, Stendhal and the Neapolitans reacted strongly:

> If we found that she was firmly resolved to sing out of key, we likewise took a firm resolve and chatted away ostentatiously among ourselves until it was all over, or else escaped into a coffee-house and ate ices. After a few months of these and similar excursions, the audience began to grow bored with the whole thing, gave up the pretence of deluding itself that poor Signorina

Colbran was all she had been in her younger days, and waited expectantly for the management to get rid of her. Nothing happened . . . In 1820, one thing alone would have made the Neapolitans happy: not the gift of a Spanish constitution, but the elimination of Signorina Colbran.

Rossini and Colbran married in 1822, having lived together for some years. It was not a happy idea, even though it was a partnership built on great mutual respect. Some said that he had married her for her money—not a fortune by Catalani's standards, but still a lot more than a composer could hope to earn. They left Naples, and Rossini's version of *Semiramide*, with Colbran as the eponymous heroine, the last part he composed for her, was premièred in Venice in 1823. Passing on to London in 1824, Rossini was fêted by royalty and high society, the fame of his operas preceding him. Colbran made little impact, however—Mount Edgcumbe found her 'entirely *passée* . . . her powers are so diminished that she is unable to produce any effect on the stage'. Her career swiftly distintegrated, and when in 1830 Rossini finally opted to settle in Paris, she stayed behind in Bologna, demoralized and listless. Her extravagance became neurotic, and she developed—perhaps an inheritance from her days with Barbaia—a taste for gambling. To cover her losses she started giving singing lessons. Rossini's father, deputed to oversee and hand out her monthly allowance, fulminated to his son, 'a spendthrift who looks only for ways to show spite, and that because one doesn't want to kowtow to her grandeurs and insanities'. Colbran herself was clearly desperate. She wrote to a friend, 'When fortune is remote from you, everything conspires against you. I must tell you that my health is always bad, that my affairs go from bad to worse, and in order to distract myself I have turned to gambling, with such disaster that I cannot take a card that doesn't become a victim.' Rossini meanwhile had found a new and less demanding companion, the *demi-mondaine* Olympe Pélissier, and in 1837 he was legally separated from his wife. She died in 1845, the composer at her bedside.

The utter collapse of Colbran's career in London was not only due to whatever vocal deficiencies she may have had. The problem in 1824, as for Catalani and Velluti, was the triumph of Giuditta Pasta, greatest of all Italian prima donnas, who, said the critic Henry Chorley writing in 1861, 'has printed deeper impressions on the memories of those that heard her than any other female singer'. Not that Chorley ever heard Pasta in her vocal prime—he came to her art late, when she had begun to sing consistently out of tune. For the Pasta of the 1820s we have Stendhal, a friend as well as her most articulate admirer.* He had originally toyed with the idea of falling in love with this woman of genius, but soon contented himself with regular visits to her *salon* in Paris's rue Richelieu. He used to stay so late that the porter, who had to get up to let him out of the building, began to hate him. Eventually, he moved into an apartment above Pasta's, whiling away the small hours in her company, playing faro and talking to visiting Milanese: in this building, Stendhal wrote his *Life of Rossini*, which contains the encomium to Pasta.

The liaison was innocent, and Pasta's married life remained perfectly respectable. In fact, one wonders whether Stendhal was ever allowed to get very close to his goddess—for such a perceptive analyst of women, his picture of her personality is oddly one-dimensional: 'She was in my view without vices or faults, a simple, consistent, just, natural person.' On the qualities of her singing, however, he is vividly suggestive.

> Madame Pasta's voice has a considerable range. She can achieve perfect resonance on a note as low as bottom A and can rise as high as C# or D . . . the true designation of her voice is *mezzo-soprano*, and any composer who writes for her should use the *mezzo-soprano* range for the thematic material of his music . . . one of the most uncommon features of Madame Pasta's voice [is that it] is *not all moulded from the same metallo*, as they would say in Italy [i.e. possesses more than one timbre]; and this fundamental variety of tone produced by a single voice affords one of the richest veins of musical expression which the artistry of a great *cantatrice* is able to exploit . . . Without such a palette of breath-taking colour deep within her own being, and without such an extraordinary and compelling natural gift, Madame Pasta could never have achieved the over-mastering force of natural expression which we have learnt to associate with her—a miracle of emotional revelation, which is always true to nature . . . always alive with that unmistakable, burning energy, that extraordinary dynamism which can electrify an entire theatre.

* Did he name the heroine of *La Chartreuse de Parme* after her daughter Clelia?

One important fact emerges here—Pasta was not a true soprano, but some sort of mezzo: did she, in her long and rigorous apprenticeship, force her voice up to the C#s and Ds against its natural inclination, and was it that forcing which caused her particular failures of intonation? Against this shortcoming are ranged the splendours of her art, its superb line and *portamento*; the austerity and meaningfulness of her ornamentation; the voice's facility at changing from 'head' to 'chest' voice; and her subtle rhythmic instinct. What made her style 'modern' was the ability, as Stendhal implies, to 'colour' her voice, to give the same note different emotional overtones. Her singing lacked the purity of Mrs Billington's or Mara's, but it was infinitely more interesting. For Chorley, Pasta's greatest 'grace' was her 'depth and reality of expression . . . Her recitative, from the moment she entered, was riveting by its truth . . . the impression made on me was that of my being always subdued and surprised for the first time. Though I knew what was coming, when the passion broke out, or when the phrase was sung, it seemed as if they were something new, electrical, immediate.' She was indisputably a great tragic actress, and, like Callas, the power of her performances lay in their complete commitment to the highest ideal of opera—the expression of human emotion through music. Her acting was as linked to singing as a Shakespearean actress is to her speaking voice. She presented a severe and noble intensity that women have rarely been allowed in art outside classical drama, and which found its fulfilment in Bellini's *Norma*.

Giuditta Negri was born near Milan in 1797. She started singing in Milan and in 1816, sponsored by the composer Paër, joined Catalani's company at the Théâtre-Italien in Paris. It was not an auspicious beginning and, according to Chorley:

> . . . her voice was originally limited, husky, and weak, without charm, without flexibility, a mediocre mezzo-soprano. Though her countenance *spoke*, the features were cast in that coarse mould which is common in Italy. Her arms were fine, but her figure was short and clumsy. She walked heavily, almost unequally. No candidate for musical sovereignty ever presented herself with what must have seemed a more slender and imperfect list of credentials.

Her will was superior to her endowment, however, and she

continued to slave at her technique. After an unremarkable season in London, she retired to Italy with her husband, the lawyer Giuseppe Pasta, and had a baby. She then sang in secondary Italian opera houses. (A fascinating letter from this period survives, written to Pasta by the composer Nicolini, who was writing an opera for the Roman winter carnival season, in which Pasta was to appear. Like a dressmaker asking for measurements, he asks her for 'the music of two arias which suit your voice well so that I can get a fair idea of your method and skill'.) She returned to Paris and the Théâtre-Italien in 1821, a transformed artist. At first her chief vehicles were the operas of Rossini; Desdemona in *Otello*, Colbran's role of Elisabetta, and the title-role of *Tancredi*, in which she sang the famous 'Di tanti palpiti', at the time virtually Rossini's signature tune. Her *salon* became famous too, and a large number of letters survive written to her by male admirers. Some were prostrate with infatuation, of course, but many are simply and strikingly friendly. Pasta's relationships with men appear truly adult, and make one suppose that her *salon* was a place of real frankness, intelligence, and mutual respect, with the singer as a comrade rather than a goddess.

In the timely year of 1824, Pasta braved London again. Disappointed by Colbran and Velluti, bored by Catalani, the city which had been electrified by Edmund Kean was ready for a new theatrical grandeur. Pasta repeated her Desdemona, as well as Semiramide and Romeo in an operatic version of Shakespeare's play by Zingarelli. Her success was such that the management of the King's Theatre offered her a contract worth £14,000 for the season, but went bankrupt before they could fulfil the sum. Back in Paris, she significantly took over the part written for Velluti in *Il Crociato in Egitto*: her repertory also included a Mary, Queen of Scots, Otello himself, and the Medea of Mayr's not-quite-forgotten *Medea in Corinto*, which gave her great histrionic, if not musical scope.

Her relations with composers were notably cordial. Rossini frequently conducted her and one can only lament that he never wrote anything substantial for her. That privilege was reserved for Donizetti and Bellini, whom she inspired to some of their finest music, in collaboration with the efficient librettist Felice Romani. Donizetti's *Anna Bolena* gave Pasta a great historical character, suitably romanticized, and a superb final *scena* which, as William Ashbrook has written, 'vividly presents the stages of Anna's retreat from unendurable reality, through longing for release, to triumph, once her reason is restored, as she finds the spiritual strength not to curse but to forgive those who have brought her to her death'. Donizetti wrote much of this opera at Pasta's villa on Lake Como, with the voice on hand, as it were, for reference. Bellini's talents were both gentler and deeper than those of Donizetti, whose historical melodramas are well turned but hardly moving. Bellini died young, and his harmony and orchestration are thin and unsophisticated compared to those of his major rivals. He is most admired for his long-spun melodies, which had their effect on Chopin's Nocturnes, and were valued by Wagner, but there is more to his operas than beautiful tunes. The music for Pasta in the bucolic *La Sonnambula*, the story of a village maiden who sleepwalks her way into trouble that impairs her good reputation, may now seem pretty and anodyne, but *Norma*, which followed it in the same year of 1831, has a power that no other opera of this school possesses. The title-role is at the very acme of the soprano's repertory, considered more challenging than Brünnhilde or Isolde and rarely sung even competently. Its range and grandeur is an impressive indication of Pasta's stature.

Norma is a Druid high priestess who has borne two children to a Roman proconsul, Pollione, only to discover that he now loves her friend and junior priestess Adalgisa. After struggling against feelings of vengeance, she is persuaded by Adalgisa not to kill her children. Norma then exposes her own personal treachery against her oppressed people before the assembled Druids and commits herself to the pyre: Pollione, moved by her sacrifice, dies with her. Underlying this is a not very subtly modified version of the Medea story, which also exploited Italian nationalistic feeling in the Druidic animosity against the occupying Roman forces. No self-respecting tenor has ever volunteered to sing the part of Pollione, and Adalgisa fades from the drama unsatisfactorily. But the depiction of Norma herself is nobly conceived. Her opening scene involves the test of 'Casta Diva', with its spacious dreamy line and exquisite chromatic cascades, followed by a *cabaletta* which is not brilliant and angry but a sweet musing on the joys of love—and much the more difficult for that. This aria requires from its singer impeccable control of pitch and rhythm at a very early stage in the evening; later she has to steer her way through two long-breathed lyrical duets with Adalgisa; a ferocious and florid part in a long trio-finale; and stretches of declamatory *arioso* and recitative. Nothing in Norma's music is emotionally neutral: there is a scene of frenzy and remorse as Norma comes close to killing her children, and hard-edged irony in her confrontation with Pollione. In the last act finale Bellini demands one final marshalling of resources in Norma's moving plea, 'Deh! non volerli vittime', which flowers into a vast climax.

Simply to pass muster, then, a Norma needs power, stamina, flexibility, beauty and variety of tone, as well as theatrical presence and intelligence. Even Pasta doubted whether she could measure up. She complained to Bellini that 'Casta Diva' was not suited to her abilities, but he made her promise to work on it for a week. A few hours before the première, she sent the composer a bouquet of cloth flowers, a parchment lampshade decorated with motifs of warriors and maidens, and a note: 'Allow me to offer you something that was some solace to me for the immense fear that persecuted me when I found myself little suited to performing your sublime harmonies, this lamp by night and these flowers by day witnessed my studies of *Norma* and the desire I cherish to be ever more worthy of your esteem.' After an initial fiasco at La Scala, the opera became very popular and was repeated there thirty-nine times in the first season. But its demands exhausted Pasta's vocal resources, and by the time she sang the part in London, in 1833, one reviewer claimed that 'It would not be exaggerated to say that not a single phrase of the entire opera was sung in the correct pitch . . . it required her power as an actress to save her from disaster.'

The English singer Adelaide Kemble, who studied the part of Norma with Pasta, has some interesting observations on Pasta's difficulties with pitch:

Even at her best, she had always sung false upon three notes in the middle of her voice—the C of the third space, with the D and E which follow, were invariably considerably too flat. One day that she was teaching me to sing 'Casta Diva', the great air of the 'Norma', when I came to the words 'spargi in terra', which falls upon these particular notes, she suddenly stopped me. 'Crescete, mia cara' ['Rise higher, my dear'], said she. I began again, and was again stopped at the same place. Anxious to ascertain the fact, about which I had my doubts, I repeated the passage for the third time, very gently touching the piano at the concluding note, and finding myself in perfect unison with it . . . [She] then herself sang the notes a full quarter of a tone too flat . . . a very curious proof that her falseness of intonation was an imperfection of the ear, and not of the voice, for these three notes of the scale—a most remarkable peculiarity which I have never since met with in any one. . . . Over her bedroom door hung innumerable birds in cages. 'J'aime à les entendre le matin' she said; adding, with a comical shade of bitterness, 'Ces petits coquins, ils chantent toujours si juste' ['I like to hear them singing in the morning . . . the little rascals, they always sing in tune'].

In 1833 Bellini unsuccessfully asked for Pasta's daughter's hand in marriage, and also honoured her with the title-role in *Beatrice di Tenda*, her last creation. By now, although she maintained all her command and exceptional musicianship, she simply could not be relied upon to sing in tune. Her unsparing commitment was her downfall. Reluctant to retire, perhaps partly because she had lost most of her money in the Guymuller bank crash, she gave some more performances in London in 1837 and made a trip to St Petersburg in 1840, by which time her voice was in a miserable state. Adelaide Kemble heard her during the last but one of her engagements in England: 'I remember while I was sitting in my stall worshipping this great goddess and thanking Heaven for a new revelation of happiness, hearing a well-known old dandy [ancestor, no doubt, of the modern opera queen] who was just before me exclaim, while he applauded her with a sort of good-natured condescension, "Oh, poor dear old thing! How stumpy she is! How old she has grown, to be sure! She oughtn't to have come back again!" ' Then, ten years later, when she was fifty-two, she was seduced back to London to sing some scenes from *Anna Bolena*. Chorley's account of this tragic occasion is magnificent. In the audience were the great French actress Rachel (who was overtly sarcastic about the proceedings) and Pauline Viardot, Malibran's sister, a great singer herself, then at her peak. 'Nothing more inadvised could be dreamed of,' began Chorley: the voice's 'state of utter ruin on the night in question passes description . . . [yet] Dismal as was the spectacle, broken, hoarse, and destroyed as was the voice, the great style of the singer spoke.' She attempted the final *scena*:

By that time, tired, unprepared, in ruin as she was, she had rallied a little. When, on Anna Bolena's hearing the coronation music for her rival, the heroine searches for her own crown on her brow, Madame Pasta wildly turned in the direction of the festive sounds, the old irresistible charm broke out; nay, even in the final song, with its roulades, and its scales of shakes ascending by a semitone, the consummate vocalist and tragedian, able to combine form with meaning—the moment of the situation with such personal and musical display as form an integral part of operatic art—was indicated: at least to the apprehension of a younger artist, 'You are right' was Madame Viardot's quick and heartfelt response (her eyes full of tears) to a friend beside her; 'You are right! It is like the *Cenacolo* of da Vinci at Milan—a wreck of a picture, but the picture is the greatest picture in the world!'

Prosper Mérimée visited Pasta in retirement on Lake Como, and found 'Git', as she was familiarly known, happily growing cabbages. She loved gardening and the country life. In her heyday there had been Pasta fêtes on the lake, with fireworks and famous 'Pasta arias' played throughout the night by a band on a boat, but the life of this incomparable prima donna ended quietly. George Sand saw her once in Venice: 'In her old hat and coat, Pasta could have been mistaken for a box attendant. Yet she made a sign to the gondolier to indicate the direction she wanted to take, and in that gesture the great Queen, if not the *diva*, reappeared.' J. E. Cox, an English music critic, was sailing across Lake Como in 1861, and caught sight of her chasing some turkeys with a switch; Sutherland Edwards quotes from the account of some other English visitors:

We did not see her at her best, for having just risen from her siesta, in which we had disturbed her, she was only half awake. We found her very friendly and evidently gratified by our visit. Her mouth and teeth are still lovely, the great eyes full of fire, her black hair in a dishevelled state, and her dress an extremely original medley of oddities. She never ceased talking of old times, and told us that she had given up living in the villa because both her mother and her husband had died there. She afterwards wrote something for our albums, and gave us some beautiful flowers.

Devoted to her family, warm-hearted and sensible, Pasta nevertheless rarely emerges to history as a vivid human being, nor do portraits suggest any startling individuality. Perhaps, like so many great actors and actresses, her magnetism was reserved for the stage. None of which could be said of Maria Malibran. If, as one French critic put it, Pasta embodied the spirit of Sophocles and Racine, Malibran embodied Shakespeare and Victor Hugo. To Chorley, she was just 'thoroughly, fearlessly original'.

It has become a cliché of operatic journalese to compare Callas with Malibran, but Callas was surely closer to Pasta, imperious and grand, a tragedienne of instinctive nobility and reserve. Malibran was wild, impetuous, and uninhibited. She loved to improvise on stage, to the point of both embarrassing her colleagues and of making a fool of herself. In the middle of love scenes, she tickled her tenors or pinched their behinds; she introduced absurd dances at inappropriate moments, once falling flat on her face; she even sang the part of an old hag in Cimarosa's *Il Matrimonio Segreto*, just for the joy of dressing up. She was deadly competitive—'The idea that the fame of any living artiste could approach hers, was enough to eat her heart away,' wrote one of her observers—and performed in a spirit, not of dedication to art, but of doing one better or that much more than anyone else. Compared with Pasta, a lot of her effects were simply startling and even cheap: in his journal, Delacroix remarked on the way in which she ripped her handkerchief and gloves to pieces in a fraught moment of Donizetti's *Maria Stuarda*:

> She thus achieved moments full of energy and seemingly full of truth, but it also happened that she would seem exaggerated and faulty in her timing . . . I do not recall ever having seen her *noble*. When she came nearest to the sublime, it was only to such a conception of it as a bourgeoise might possess; in a word, she was completely lacking in the sense of the ideal.

Her singing, however, was of the same school as Pasta's. Both had instruments made great by will, rather than by nature, and both lacked Catalani's natural vocal endowment. Chorley describes Malibran's voice clinically:

> It was not naturally a voice of first-rate quality. It was a mezzo-soprano, extended upwards and downwards by that hardy and tremendous exercise the introduction of which has been ascribed to the appearance of her father . . . the girl was early put into possession of an instrument two octaves and a half, if not more, in compass, weakest in the tones betwixt F and F—a weakness

audaciously and incomparably disguised by the forms of execution, modification, and ornament which she selected. Her topmost
and deepest notes were perpetually used in connected contrast . . .

Ernest Legouvé is more evocative:

Malibran's voice was like gold, but like gold it had to be dug from
the bowels of the earth; it had to be separated from the ore; it had
to be forged and beaten, and made pliable like the metal under the
hammer . . . One day in Rome when she was to play Rosina, I
heard her study the shakes of her *cavatina*. Every now and then
she stopped short to scold her own voice saying 'Obey me! I'll
make you obey me!' The struggle therefore was a necessity.

The necessity of struggle began pathetically early: Malibran's
childhood must have been agony. To the end of her short life, she
retained a weird naïvete. She always loved playing with dolls, but
farmed out her own child. She stayed up all night, rode bareback all
morning, sang all afternoon and evening, before collapsing into a
trance of sheer exhaustion. Her frenzied intensity battled with a frail
constitution, but she had been taught to ignore all such limitations.
Her father was Manuel Garcia, founder of the greatest of operatic
families, and himself an important figure in the history of singing.
The son of Spanish gypsies, Garcia became the first of the newly
liberated batch of tenors, given, in the operas of Rossini, a
prominence they had not known before. He created the part of
Almaviva in *Il Barbiere di Siviglia* and was Otello to Pasta's
Desdemona. His singing was florid, loud, excitable, and immensely
popular in Naples, London, and Paris. Maria was born in 1808, and
could read music before her alphabet. She made her stage début at
the age of five in an opera by Paër: the first of many Malibran stories
has it that when the prima donna of the evening suffered a memory
lapse, the child immediately filled in her part. Apocryphal or not, the
little girl was tyrannically drilled by her father, who did not stop at
brute force. Paër was once walking past the Garcia apartment with a
friend. Screams were heard, and the friend exclaimed, 'Someone is
being murdered!' Paër walked on calmly and replied, 'It's just Garcia
beating trills into his daughter.' This unremitting trauma, inflicted
on her by a father she loved deeply, formed her voice and her
personality. If Garcia takes the credit for schooling a rough and

uneven instrument, he must also take responsibility for her manic self-destructiveness and desperate need to be loved. 'If I were near you, you would have neither face nor body, because I would eat all of you. Love me, love me as I love you, and if you have the chance, *for the Love of God*! write to me even though it be two lines,' she wrote to Pasta, whom she worshipped.

Maria's childhood was itinerant. She made her first proper public appearances in London in 1825, singing opposite her father in *Il Barbiere di Siviglia* and with Velluti in *Il Crociato in Egitto*. Garcia, nearing the end of his vocal life, then had the idea of taking his family and the Italian opera to New York, where both were entirely unknown. The American impresario was one Dominick Lynch, who had been inspired by hearing Pasta. He and Maria tried to persuade Pasta to lead the troupe, but a tendency to sea-sickness, and a reluctance to leave her family for a long period made her refuse. The whole enterprise smacked of that well-known American phenom-enon, the quick buck, but it gave Maria solid stage experience and some easily won adulation from a gullible audience, ready to approve of it all as another genteel European import. One of her admirers in New York was a middle-aged French-born merchant, Eugène Malibran. When she announced that she wanted to marry him, Garcia only gave his permission on condition that Malibran promised a large sum of money in compensation for removing his bankable daughter from his company. Garcia and family left New York for Mexico. Free from the stifling presence of her father, Maria married and retired from the operatic stage. Problems began soon afterwards. Malibran lost all his money and proved to be something of a charlatan. Maria resumed her career in a loyal effort to save him from embarrassment and grossed large sums in New York and Philadelphia. By the end of 1827, the marriage had obviously deteriorated, and the most respectable way of separating was for Maria to return to Europe and for Malibran himself to follow when business improved. She does not seem to have undertaken to send him money, although she may have agreed that anything she earned might be deducted from the money he still owed to her father. In Paris, Maria began by singing at fashionable *soirées*, where even Colbran 'who in her whole life never gave a compliment to anyone, approached, arms open, before a numerous group to embrace me, to pay me a thousand compliments'. After the departure from the Théâtre-Italien of the reigning prima donna, Henriette Sontag,

Maria was ready to take her place. She triumphed in two of Pasta's Rossini roles, Semiramide and Desdemona, and then wrote to her husband to say that he need not bother to leave New York—she was happy where she was and as she was, living a respectable chaperoned life and presiding over a cheerful-sounding *salon*, full of pranks and party games. In 1829 she attacked London again, where, according to Chorley, she was initially found 'unequal, bizarre, and fatiguing'. Her Zerlina, for instance, in *Don Giovanni* was not the usual demure Petit Trianon shepherdess, but 'a coarse, vulgar country lass, agog for enjoyment', who at the ball 'jumped and jigged about, out of time and out of place'. Authenticity in costume was important to her. She sang the sleepwalking scene in *La Sonnambula* not in a muslin négligé, but a peasant's coarse gown, woollen stockings, and night cap; for Donizetti's *Maria Stuarda*, she sketched from Tudor tombs in Westminster Abbey.

There can be no doubt that Maria Malibran irritated a section of public taste. She was not, as has sometimes been implied, a harbinger of naturalism, but a vehement over-actress, who would throw into her interpretations extraneous detail and an excess of emotion. A Parisian friend of Pasta's, Albert Stapfer, wrote to her that Malibran 'hadn't the strength of mind to resist the death-dealing acclaim of the Parisian public. Day by day, she becomes more mannered and exaggerated.' She was often inspired, but she was occasionally ridiculous and even, as Delacroix thought, 'unbearable'. Yet it was this 'over the top' quality which must have made her so exciting. Like Judy Garland, she seems to have communicated a sense of danger, a sense of someone pushing her own resources beyond all reasonable limits and who was prepared to risk failure in the attempt. How long her magnificent voice and hard-earned technique could have stood up to the anarchic schedule of her life is an unanswered question; but, as Gautier put it, 'she had the genius to die very young'.

Malibran's off-stage personality was completely at one with this, and for all her fervent kindness and generosity, one imagines that she was hardly a relaxing companion or someone for the close sympathies of intimate friendship. She was lucky to find, in 1829, Charles de Bériot, a famous Belgian violinist, darkly handsome, shy and diffident, who provided her with steady moral support as well as being an object in whom she could satisfy her thwarted desire for love. Unlike most prima donnas, she was faintly prim about sex, and she longed to be publicly acknowledged as Bériot's wife—which is how she privately presented herself. For the next five years the drama of trying to get rid of Eugène Malibran (who had returned to Paris and who, under the Napoleonic Code, was entitled to all his wife's property) brought further tension into her life. It was not until 1836, with the patronage of General Lafayette and a change in the hitherto inflexible law, that she won an annulment and could remarry.

Until 1832 Malibran sang chiefly in London and Paris, alternating between frenzy and collapse. Apart from her theatrical engagements, she also sang in concert and at private parties, and if she did drink heavily, as was rumoured, it was hardly surprising. She became notorious for cancelling performances at the last minute, but also sang in the most painful circumstances—a broken arm, pregnancy, lips scalded by sal volatile—nothing could stop her when she chose. In 1832, on a whim, she left for Italy and sang in Rome (where she was heartbroken to receive news of her father's death), Bologna, and Naples, accompanied throughout by Bériot, who adapted his own engagements to hers. Back in London in May 1833, she sang in English one of her very finest roles, Amina in *La Sonnambula*, a performance which quite besotted Bellini. The manager of Drury Lane, Alfred Bunn, was forced into paying her £2,000 for fifteen performances and comments in his memoirs on her 'inordinate love of money . . . it would be sheer humbug to say she had not that passion'. But avarice went with truly massive donations to friends and to charities, gifts that were often anonymous. Somehow she managed to give her time too, and one of the silliest and most charming Malibran stories concerns a visit to a hospital for orphans. Malibran, swathed in inconspicuous black, toured the wards. A dying child needed a bath and was making violent resistance. Malibran: 'If I sing to you, will you get into the bath?' Malibran sings a *bolero*, so exquisitely that the nuns' eyes fill with tears. The child continues to screech, but Malibran has a further inspiration, takes all her clothes off, gets into the bath herself, and is soon followed by the child, stunned no doubt into acquiescence.

Alfred Bunn was another who was stunned into acquiescence, as he dredged up ever larger sums of money to keep Malibran at Drury Lane. Their relationship was a lively one, and one of the letters he reproduces in his memoirs gives an idea of Malibran's entrancing childishness and manic mental energy: it concerns an operetta she was trying to learn.

> St James's Street, Mardi
> Again and again, alwais me, and eternally me, my dear Mister Bunn. I have been tormenting poor Chelard out of his wits. I want to have my part to practise it, know it, and be able to play it in 10 days the latest. I am sure if you give proper orders for the copy of the parts, *we* shall be all ready, at least I will be ready in 8 days . . . but—rehearsals, parts, orders, rehearsals, no rehearsals without parts, no parts without orders, and no orders without my eternal hints, and my never ending letters, since it appears you will not do me the high honour of comming at my house for a quarter of an hour to have a little settling chit-chat. However it may be, I wait your pleasure, noble cousin, and humbly beg for an answer when it may suit your Majesty. Nonsense apart, pray say YES or no . . .
> To A Bunn !!!!!!
> Esquair!!!!!!

Back in Naples, Malibran repeated *Sonnambula* and, again measuring herself against Pasta, sang *Norma* for the first time: unfortunately no coherent description of her in this latter role survives. It is easy to imagine her charm as the sleep-walking maiden, but less easy to conceive how she coped with the simplicity and restraint necessary to a Norma. With a signal lack of tact, she chose the part for her début in La Scala in 1834. The Milanese identified the part with Pasta, and one of a lunatic fringe of 'Pastists' threatened her life. Pasta herself was in the audience, and was greeted with ferociously partisan applause. Even the fearless Maria Malibran was overcome with nerves, and the 'Casta Diva' *scena* was disastrous, although she redeemed herself later in the evening. After the second performance, there was what the Italians call a *furore*, and the police were called in to evacuate the theatre. A huge crowd escorted the prima donna back to the Visconti *palazzo*, where an orchestra and chorus waited to present a cantata in her honour. The next major addition to her repertory was Leonore in *Fidelio*, a role associated with her Teutonic counterpart, Wilhelmine Schröder-Devrient, and in which Malibran indulged her leanings towards melodrama, flourishing two pistols at the climax of the dungeon scene, where everybody else flourished one. Back in Milan she sang the eponymous heroine of Donizetti's *Maria Stuarda*, which was not a success, despite the high possibilities of Mary's situation. She was 'voiceless' at the première, and the censors considered the subject-matter sufficiently inflammatory to demand debilitating cuts. The opera seemed quite dead after its first five performances, but was successfully resuscitated in the 1960s as a vehicle for Sutherland, Caballé, Sills, Janet Baker, *et al.*

Malibran never created a major repertory role, and it is sad to realize how much of a unique talent was spent on second- or third-rate music. Her last new assumption is a case in point. *The Maid of Artois*, a bastardized version of the Manon Lescaut story, was written for Drury Lane by Balfe, the only nineteenth-century English opera composer of European standing. It contains pretty melodies and an action-packed plot, both designed to show off the prima donna, but it hardly extended or challenged Malibran as *Norma* did Pasta—except that she needed a pint of porter, variously conveyed to her while on stage, in order to get through a last scene which required a top E and a trill on a high C!

In the middle of 1836 Malibran, now legally married to Bériot, was pregnant, not for the first time—her one surviving child, brought up by Malibran's mother, became a pianist and died in 1914. She nevertheless accepted an invitation to an aristocratic hunting party in Surrey, and, with customary bravado, insisted on riding the roughest mount in the stable. In a truly hideous accident, she was flung head first to the ground after her foot had slipped through the stirrup. A superficial recovery was followed by bursts of manic depression, blinding headaches, and an intensification of activity in all spheres. Bériot had discouraged her from the expedition in the first place and she never dared tell him the true origin of her malaise. Her last months were spent in Belgium, her nominal home, France, and England. She finally collapsed in Manchester after a concert in which she had insisted on singing an encore, and died in the Mosley Arms Hotel a few days later. She was twenty-eight.

A Romantic for any age, Malibran had been admired by Verdi, Liszt, Rossini, Chopin, Mendelssohn, Hans Christian Andersen, and George Sand. Fifty thousand people lined the streets of Manchester to watch her funeral cortège; Alfred Bunn recited his own commemorative ode from the stage of Drury Lane:

Enchantress of the nations! She who breathed

The sweetest notes that ever music wreathed . . .

and Alfred de Musset wrote some finer, if untranslatable lines:

> *C'est ton âme, Ninette, et ta grandeur naive*
> *C'est cette voix du coeur qui seule au coeur arrive*
> *Que nul autre, après toi, ne nous rendra jamais . . .*

It is difficult not to feel a touch of scepticism after this brief and magnificent explosion—can she really have been that good? But like Nijinsky, Rachel, or Paganini, the myth of the phenomenon of Malibran is more important than a balanced, comparative, and historical assessment of her achievement as an opera singer. 'If life is not a crime, it is at least an expiation,' she mysteriously told Ernest Legouvé, and perhaps the lingering emotion on pondering personalities such as Malibran's is a sense of pity for the harsh and inexorable hand that they were dealt, with no choice but to exhaust their lives through their genius, denied the joys of being ordinary.

The Garcia dynasty, however, lasted into the twentieth century. Garcia's son, also called Manuel, died in 1906 at the age of 101. After some unsuccessful appearances in opera, he became one of the greatest of all singing teachers, his pupils including Jenny Lind and Mathilde Marchesi, who herself taught Melba. His first wife and their son were also successful opera singers. The Garcia method, as laid out in *Traité complet de l'art du chant* (1847) is still respected today, and is notable for its scientific approach to the physiology of voice production. Garcia also invented the laryngoscope, a mirror apparatus which allows the throat to be observed in action.

His sister Pauline, thirteen years younger than Maria and born in 1821, was one of the most remarkable women of the nineteenth century, a prima donna of intelligence rather than instinct, and someone who, like George Eliot or George Sand, her closest female friend, triumphed over the irregularities of her personal position to become a social figurehead and an embodiment of the highest potential of the female. As George Sand told her, 'You are the priestess of the ideal in music and your mission is to spread it, to make it understood, and to reveal to the recalcitrant and ignorant the True and the Beautiful.' That she was to some extent able to fulfil this injunction was not due to extraordinary vocal resources, and her career in opera lacked the *éclat* of Malibran's. Instead she built her fame on the Victorian belief in the religion of art, and a repertory far more sophisticated and interesting than her sister's had been.

Pauline Viardot-Garcia was born in Mexico, whither, in 1826, her father had taken the family on an operatic tour after their fateful visit to New York. When civil war broke out, the Garcias tried to escape the country, but they were waylaid by brigands who robbed Garcia of the entire takings of the tour. They made their way back to Paris and the patronage of the now wealthy Maria. By the age of seven, Pauline could play the piano well enough to accompany her father's pupils, and herself eventually became a pupil of the young Liszt, with whom she was briefly infatuated—perhaps the only occasion in her life when she almost careered out of emotional control. She also took singing lessons from her mother after Garcia's death, but rarely came into close contact with her peripatetic sister, who was none the less intensely interested in her burgeoning talent. After Maria's death, her considerable gift as a pianist fell into the background as she was inevitably pushed forward as Malibran's younger sister and heir. The roles she initially took reflect this—Desdemona, Rosina, Amina, Norma, even the old hag in *Il Matrimonio Segreto*: all Malibran vehicles—and they were not well suited to her. Chorley tells the familiar story:

> It was to be felt that nature had given her a rebel to subdue, not a vassal to command in her voice. From the first she chose to possess certain upper notes which must needs be fabricated, and which never could be produced without the appearance of effort. By this despotic exercise of will it is possible that her real voice—a limited mezzo-soprano—may have been weakened.

She would probably have had a steadier reputation if she had not taken on such parts. But as it was, Gounod, who later fell in love with her, found her at thirty 'already nearing her end, and singing out of tune all the time'. Later, she realized that she had made a mistake, and told one of her pupils, 'Don't do as I did. I wanted to sing everything, and I spoilt my voice.'

Yet her early years were successful enough. Some found her not quite as forthright as they wished, and she was once, interestingly, criticized as following 'psychological inspirations derived from novels of the day'. One of her admirers was the elderly Duke of Wellington, who commented on her London début, 'The impulse is in her to be great, and great she will be, whoever lives to see it.' He was magnificently right.

Rossini was the first composer to treat the possibilities of the dramatic coloratura mezzo, and wrote for two magnificent exemplars of the type—the hideous Benedetta Pisaroni* and, later, Marietta Alboni† (Marilyn Horne is their phenomenal modern counterpart). Pauline Viardot extended this repertoire into the style of French Grand Opera, and her art was an inspirational factor in the creation of such mezzo roles as Dalila in Saint-Saëns's *Samson et Dalila*, Cassandra and Dido in Berlioz's *Les Troyens*, and perhaps even Carmen.

More directly, Viardot worked with Meyerbeer, the most successful opera composer of the period. He and his librettist Eugène Scribe wrote unashamedly for the rich bourgeois audience of the rampantly commercial and cynical society we know from Balzac's novels of Parisian life. This audience wanted something showy and effective, something Romantic—but only in a reassuring way. It wanted value for money and immediate gratification, not an art for connoisseurs. The Italian audiences always had a genuine interest in music and singing: in Paris they wanted a superior floor show, a good evening out, exciting without being disturbing. Auber's *La Muette de Portici* (1828) and Rossini's *Guillaume Tell* (1829) established the conventions which Meyerbeer's operas so adroitly exploited. The plots are historical, usually based on themes of the Middle Ages or the wars of religion, and the action is vivid and heroic. Variety was important, hence the frequency of ballets, tableaux, processions of clergy or royalty, crowd scenes, and scenic *coups de théâtre*: the

---

* 'Distorted, deformed, dwarfish Pisaroni' lamented Lady Granville, a contemporary ambassador's wife. 'She has an immense head, a remarkably ugly face. When she smiles or sings her mouth is drawn up to one ear, with a look of a person convulsed in pain. She has two legs that stand out like sugar-tongs, one shorter than the other. Her stomach sticks out on one side of her body, and she has a hump on the other.' Despite these disadvantages (the result partially of smallpox), Pisaroni was both a superb singer and a convincing actress. Pacchierotti was one of her teachers; Rossini wrote three major roles for her.
† Whose obesity caused Rossini to dub her 'the elephant which swallowed a nightingale'.

Triumph Scene in Verdi's *Aida* is a late and famous example of this; Meyerbeer himself came up with a midnight orgy of ghostly nuns in *Robert le Diable*, the Massacre of St Bartholomew in *Les Huguenots*, and a shipwreck in *L'Africaine*. Extended arias play a smaller part than ensembles; gimmicky instrumental effect and harmonic effect replace sustained or developed melody; a degree of sheer noise, bright orchestration, and five long acts (it is almost impossible to perform a complete Meyerbeer grand opera in under five hours) made up the slick and glittering package. The sensational success of the lurid *Robert le Diable* in 1831 established Meyerbeer's supremacy after the premature retirement of Rossini, and although the Théâtre-Italien continued to fill seats with the older Italian pieces, Meyerbeer at the Opéra itself in rue Le Peletier made everything else look and sound a little *passé*.

What did such vulgarity offer to a sensibility as refined as Pauline Viardot's? Chiefly, vocal lines far less taxing than Italian opera and the histrionic possibilities of sophisticated melodrama, with its wide range of extreme emotions emerging in striking situations. Viardot seized on this new repertoire, playing leading roles in *Robert le Diable* and *Les Huguenots* as well as Rachel, who dies in a boiling cauldron, in Halévy's *La Juive*. In 1849, at Meyerbeer's particular request, she gave the first performance of Fidès (who meets her end in the conflagration of the palace of Münster) in his *Le Prophète*. Playing this simple burgher woman, filled with maternal love yet forced to renounce her son and, at one point, forced to beg for alms, Viardot was found deeply affecting. It was in such parts that she had her most undisputed success at the major operatic centres. In Italian opera she was overshadowed by Grisi, and during the early 1840s, when she was in her vocal prime, she performed mostly in Berlin, Dresden, and St Petersburg, where she was idolized. But perhaps her finest role was Orphée in the French version, edited by Berlioz, of Gluck's *Orfeo ed Euridice*. The melancholy and simple dignity of the piece was balm to the truly musical public of Paris, by then sated by a long diet of Meyerbeerian excess, and in Viardot it found a noble interpreter. Between 1859 and 1861 she sang the part over 150 times. Dickens went to one performance and found himself in her dressing-room afterwards, his face 'disfigured with crying'. Chorley here found her technical shortcomings an asset:

The peculiar quality of Madame Viardot's voice—its unevenness, its occasional harshness and feebleness, consistent with tones of the gentlest sweetness—was turned by her to account with rare felicity, as giving the variety of light and shade to every word of soliloquy, to every appeal of dialogue. A more perfect and honeyed voice might have recalled the woman too often to fit with the idea of the youth. Her musical handling of so peculiar an instrument will take place in the highest annals of art.

It was as Orphée that she made her last operatic appearance, in Weimar in 1870. Berlioz describes her interpretation in some detail: by modern standards of Neo-classical style, it sounds rather frenzied. She sang 'J'ai perdu mon Eurydice' at first in a slow tempo, 'then after the adagio "Mortel Silence! Vaine esperance!" in *sotto voce* (*pianissimo*, with a trembling voice, choked with a flood of tears); she finally took up the theme in a more animated tempo, withdrawing from the body of Eurydice, beside which she had been kneeling, and rushing away with mad despair towards the other side of the stage, the very picture of frenzy in her outcries and sobs.'

Pauline Viardot's latter years are full of musical novelty. She was the first London Azucena in Verdi's *Il Trovatore* (a part modelled on Meyerbeer's Fidès) and sang his Lady Macbeth in Dublin—cruel stuff for even a voice of steel, so she transposed almost all the music down, a frequent practice of the time. Then there was a revival of Gluck's *Alceste*, Gounod's first opera *Sapho* (the title-role written for her), a concert première of extracts from Berlioz's masterpiece *Les Troyens* in which she sang Cassandra, and a private recital with an audience of two, one of them Berlioz, of the newly composed Love Duet from *Tristan und Isolde*, Wagner taking the part of Tristan: an outstandingly unsuccessful occasion. Finally, in 1870, she gave the first performance of Brahms's Alto Rhapsody.

Parallel to all this activity was a personal life of some complexity. Throughout she was sustained by a necessary streak of blinkered selfishness. For all her fascination, she does not seem to have had any of her sister's desperate warmth, and in the name of her mission to art she was capable of using people without giving them much back. She personally knew almost every name of music, literary, and artistic distinction of the mid-nineteenth century. Romantic love seems never to have overcome her: Alfred de Musset found his passion for her unrequited, and the lovesick Gounod was only flirted with; Berlioz had one of his brief obsessions for her, but was ultimately disappointed at her coldness. She played the game skilfully. On the advice of George Sand, worn down by her unsatisfactory affair with Chopin, she had married in 1840 Louis Viardot, then impresario of the Théâtre-Italien. He was middle-aged, level-headed, and reliable, a man of principle and patience, who provided the calm and stable conditions in which her art could best flourish. The marriage survived even the extraordinary intrusion of Ivan Turgenev, the most persistent of Pauline Viardot's admirers. He first fell in love with her in St Petersburg, and through his mediation she introduced Russian music to the West: later in her career she made a speciality of Russian songs, and Tchaikovsky wrote 'None but the lonely heart' for her. Another happy side-effect of the relationship is the play *A Month in the Country*, to some extent inspired by the situation with Gounod, of whom Turgenev was wildly and unjustifiably jealous: Pauline can be seen as Natalya, Viardot as Islayev, Turgenev as Rakitin, and Gounod as the callow young tutor Beliaev.

Turgenev followed her back to France and remained in love with her for the rest of his life. He and Louis Viardot became great friends, and their last years were spent *à trois*: the two men died within a few months of each other. Although Turgenev and Pauline frequently lived under the same roof, it is perfectly possible that they never had any sort of physical relationship. It would be equally plausible to assume that one of her children was his, and she brought up his illegitimate daughter in her own household. Pauline destroyed most of her significant letters to him, and Turgenev's surviving corre-spondence is ambiguous. One moment he addresses her respectfully as his 'dearest beloved, best friend'; the next he is more extravagant: 'My God, I could lay my whole life, like a carpet, under your dear feet, which I kiss a thousand times.' Shortly before he died in 1883 he cried out that she surpassed Lady Macbeth in her wickedness. Henry James, who visited the Viardot *salon*, wrote that 'she has made him her property'; Flaubert branded him as 'a man in leading-strings'.

Pauline Viardot worked on. From 1863 onwards, she cut back on her operatic appearances, singing only in concerts or small provincial opera houses and basing herself for some years in Baden-Baden. She taught, played the piano or organ, composed operettas (some to librettos by Turgenev) and songs to Russian texts. Most important she continued to patronize younger composers, including Brahms, Saint-Saëns (who characterized her voice as 'not velvet nor crystal

. . . but bitter-sweet oranges'), Massenet, and Fauré. She died in 1910, in the Paris of Proust and the Ballets Russes.

If Pauline Viardot was one of the major exceptions, then Giulia Grisi (1811–69) fulfilled the popular archetype and proved the rule. She was imperious, exacting, and devious: if she liked you as she did the English impresario Mapleson, she could be 'most obliging: full of good nature'. Others found her 'irritable and ambitious'. The young Queen Victoria adored her, but was upset when her singing teacher Lablache, Grisi's colleague, expressed reservations: 'I do not think he quite *likes* her,' the Queen admitted to her journal. Lablache also pointed out the bad habit she had of swallowing before starting a *roulade*, 'a habit she has contracted from fear of failing'. This was a small flaw, however, in a strong and true dramatic soprano voice which had no need of the elaborate faking cultivated by Pasta and Malibran. And if Grisi lacked their interpretative genius and musicality, she had a compensating stamina and reliability.

Chorley witnessed all her major assumptions and described her voice as 'rich, sweet, equal throughout its compass of two octaves . . . without a break, or a note which had to be managed [viz. produced by means of some acquired trick], capable of any required violence, of any advisable delicacy.' He also noted its 'essential fitness for the theatre' and its sheer reliability—'the number of apologies, post-ponements etc. etc., to which she has given occasion is small without precedent in the history of the Italian prima donna.' On stage, she gave rein to 'those bursts of spontaneous emotion and energy which are more popular than the sublimer and finer qualities of a Pasta.'

Ultimately, she lacked individuality and originality: 'I have never tired of Madame Grisi during five-and-twenty years: but I have never been, in her case, under one of those spells of intense enjoyment and sensation which makes an epoch in life, and which leave a print on memory never to be cancelled by any later attraction, never to be forgotten so long as life and power to receive shall endure.'

Giulia Grisi came from another remarkable musical family. Her father was a Napoleonic general who lived to over a hundred, but her aunt Josephina Grassini was a noted contralto of Mrs Billington's time, Pasta's teacher, and rumoured to be, at various times, the mistress of Napoleon, Wellington, and Castlereagh; her elder sister Giuditta had a brief but considerable career as a mezzo; while her younger cousin Carlotta, who also began as a singer, became one of the greatest ballerinas of the nineteenth century, the lifelong love of Théophile Gautier, and creator of the role of Giselle in 1841. Giulia's early vocal development was rapid and unproblematic—hers was clearly a naturally strong and facile instrument. She made her début in Bologna at seventeen and at the age of nineteen was put under contract to La Scala. The young Giulia sang with Pasta in *Anna Bolena* and as Adalgisa in the first performance of *Norma*— '*Benissima! bene, trè bien—pas mal, la piccola,*' the great prima donna exclaimed in rehearsal.

When her reputation increased, Grisi broke her terms with La Scala on the grounds that she had been a minor when the agreement had been made. She never sang in Italy again, but shrewdly—Grisi was almost invariably shrewd—concentrated her efforts on Paris and especially London, where she missed only one season between 1834 and 1861.

Grisi had a regular and imposing beauty which contributed considerably to the effect of her grander portrayals, further enhanced by the bearing of her tenor partner Mario. Gautier was reminded of '*un tableau de Titian ou Giorgione*'. In the 1830s she was a figure of some notoriety, and bore an illegitimate child to Lord Castlereagh's son. Her marriage to an indolent French nobleman was brief and unsuccessful. She was unable to divorce him, indeed she had to pay him an annual allowance of £2,000, a fact which infuriated her. '*Porco infame*', 'infamous pig', she later exclaimed in a letter to her lawyer: 'Let the devil take him, I'll not give him another penny.' Her subsequent personal union with Mario was one of the most glamorous matches of the time. They made a devoted couple, despite Grisi's outbursts of irrational jealousy over the possibility that some member or other of the female opera public might be paying Mario untoward attention.

The most bizarre of his fans was one Miss Giles from Gloucester-shire, a lady of private means who had already made a name for herself by following the actor Charles Kean around. She was very ugly and fantastically dressed. Grisi detested her, decided that she was casting the evil eye, and referred to her as 'the Skull'. 'There she sits,' wrote a newspaper columnist, 'alone in her spacious box, dressed in the costliest of lace and brocades, perfectly indifferent to everything but Mario . . . lorgnettes are levelled towards the place where she sits from all parts of the house . . . but she heeds nobody, and when not looking over the fringe of her splendid fan . . . at the object of her burning passion, she sits like a sphinx.' She went to the incredible length of stowing away on the ship that took Grisi and Mario to America in 1854, and was discovered by Mario under a tarpaulin over which he had tripped, a story one imagines Grisi found highly implausible. In Paris she mortally embarrassed Mario during a performance of *Faust* by showering him with rose petals from her box, thus causing hysterical mirth among the rest of the audience. A few days after this, a lamp in her hotel room fell over and she was burnt to death: Mario paid his respects to the corpse.

Grisi and Mario's domestic life was otherwise dull and blameless, passing between the fabulous Villa Salviati above Florence, in which they were visited by heroes of the Risorgimento, a French *château*, and a series of West London mansions. Their commitments included their three daughters, Grisi's fanatical homoeopathy ('Her medicine chest,' reports Mapleson, 'held, besides orgeat and other syrups, brandy, whisky, hollands, port-wine, and bottled stout'), little society, charitable donations, and regular habits—all very good for the preservation of the voice, and all run on staunchly Anglophile lines. Mario himself was the son of a general and lineal descendant of the Borgias. Born a Cavaliere di Candia, he only became a singer to escape financial embarrassment, but was so ashamed of tainting his family name with the stain of the stage that professionally he used only one of his many Christian names. Like Grisi, he had a naturally strong voice and suffered only from never having to try very hard. He was the most successful tenor of the period, despite his nonchalant manner and chain-smoking of cigars. In her petty and vicious campaign against Pauline Viardot, he served as Grisi's key weapon.

In the Italian dramatic repertory—a Norma so convincing that tenors singing opposite her took her fury personally, Semiramide, Anna Bolena, Donizetti's Lucrezia Borgia—Grisi was unrivalled. If she lacked what Chorley called 'the originating faculty', she had sterling vocal equipment which rarely let her down and a fine stage presence. Her reputation and popularity were immense: she even had the great Mario as well. But she could still not tolerate Pauline Viardot and her success in the new operas of Meyerbeer. She herself failed in the modern repertory, and made something of a fool of herself in *Le Prophète*—but then Viardot could not have sung Lucrezia Borgia. Matters reached a head in the first season of the Royal Italian Opera at Covent Garden. Pauline Viardot had been kept out of London by Grisi between 1839 and 1848, for she had never liked the idea of Malibran's brilliant sister. But Viardot returned in the latter year to sing Amina in *La Sonnambula*—a poor choice, both because it was not a role which gave her much scope, and because it had been one of Grisi's favourites in her younger days. Mario was due to sing opposite her, but he was suddenly and inexplicably withdrawn, leaving Viardot with an inexperienced and unrehearsed tenor. The same tactic was repeated on the evening of Viardot's benefit performance. *Les Huguenots* was scheduled but it was announced on the morning that Mario was too ill to sing. Grisi, with double-edged graciousness, offered to appear that night in *Norma*, should the management agree to the substitution. What she meant, of course, was that she would be prepared to steal Viardot's evening by taking the title-role, leaving Viardot to the secondary position as Adalgisa. Viardot outpointed her: thanking Grisi for her kindness, she announced that, if all else failed, she would be happy to sing Norma herself to Grisi's Adalgisa, but that she had found a tenor who could stand in for Mario. *Les Huguenots* was normally sung in Italian, and the tenor only knew the part in French, so Viardot re-learnt her every line by curtain up. The excitement was intense, and the performance was a complete triumph for the tenor and for Viardot. And yet Grisi tried again in 1850, pulling Mario out of the London première of *La Juive* at the ninth hour. Viardot was ready with another substitute tenor, the performance was again a triumph. Grisi, sitting prominently in a box, was furious.

This is not the only story of Grisi's machinations. From the mid 1830s to 1840s she was the ring-leader of a tight little cabal of singers who united themselves to extort the maximum amount of money out of managements and exert a self-perpetuating stranglehold. This quartet, also known as the *vieille garde*, consisted of Grisi, Mario, the baritone Tamburini, and the great *buffo* bass Lablache: the tenor Rubini and the coloratura soprano Fanny Persiani were also involved. The central quartet were most famous for Donizetti's *Don Pasquale*, of which they gave the first performance in 1843; Bellini's *I Puritani* was their other major vehicle. The manager Benjamin Lumley bitterly describes how they announced 'their determination to resist every effort of the director to vary the composition of the phalanx, by declaring that not one of them would engage singly—in other words that M. Laporte, then manager of Her Majesty's Theatre, must agree to take them collectively or not at all. The *prima donna*, who was looked upon as the "head and front" of the coalition, had confessed as much to the manager, although she declared that she had reserved herself the right of acting separately when she chose.' In 1840 Laporte refused to engage Tamburini. He was a brave man—the defection of four such stars could have been as disastrous to his receipts as their collective presence was to seat prices. A modern equivalent might be a hypothetical team of Freni, Domingo, Nucci, and Raimondi: no one could complain about mediocre standards, but the situation was clearly undesirable. At the end of one Tamburini-less performance, a riot took place, vividly reported by Dick Doyle in his Journal of 1840:

> There was a party of noblemen in the omnibus box who, with Prince G[eorge] of Cambridge (so says the paper) were the ring-leaders. The orchestra attempted to play the overture to the ballet but was quite smothered in the deafening cries for Tamburini and Laporte ... Mr Laporte at length made his appearance amid a most desperate volley of screams which the majority of the house cried down every time he tried to speak. Others called out 'No Tamburini, no intimidation'. The manager in the mean time was carrying on a conversation with the occupants of the omnibus box, but did not seem to come to a satisfactory conclusion. He retired, the drop curtain rose, and the dancers appeared but just as the orchestra struck the first note, one of the most terrible outcries that were ever given vent to ran through the house. The manager was again forced to appear and attempted to make a speech, but his voice was drowned amid the cries of 'Engage Tamburini!' 'Yes or no. No conditions.' This game was kept up till one o'clock when Mr Laporte, having promised that he would engage Tamburini, the whole pit and the boxes that conveniently could do it, rushed simultaneously onto the stage to the great bodily fear of any of the corps de ballet who happened to be there, and waved their hats in token of their triumph.

When Lumley himself became manager he took a harder line, but Grisi and Mario did not toe it, and eventually defected to Covent Garden.

Grisi did get her come-uppance, in the grand style. She made an over-long business of giving up, and came to grief. Her 'farewells' began in 1849: by 1860 *The Times* music critic asked drily 'Does the word *last* bear an esoteric idiom in operatic parlance other than that ordinarily accepted?' In 1861 she sang in *Don Giovanni* with the young Adelina Patti, and in *Norma*, *Les Huguenots*, and *Lucrezia Borgia*. J. E. Cox was present at her farewell concert in the same year and reported her humiliation:

> On retiring from the orchestra, after a peculiarly cold reception— as unkind as it was inconsiderate, seeing what the career of this remarkable woman had been—there was not a single person at the foot of the orchestra to receive her or to accompany her to her retiring-room! I could imagine what her feelings must have been . . . I could not resist the impulse of preceding her, without obtruding myself upon her notice, and opening the door of the retiring-room for her . . . Her look as I did this and she passed out of sight is amongst the most painful of my Recollections, for it uttered more than words could speak, how sweet that small drop of consolation had been to her at such a moment.

But as if this was not enough, she returned five years later and gave one final performance of *Lucrezia Borgia*, which descended to farce:

> At the end of the first act . . . Mdme Grisi, accustomed to the stage of the Royal Italian Opera, remained too far in front . . . and when the curtain came down the Lucrezia of the evening found herself kneeling on the ground . . . and cut off by the curtain from the stage behind. This placed the unfortunate singer in a ludicrous and, indeed, painful position; for she had a stiffness in one of her knees, and was unable on this occasion to rise without the help of the stage attendants.

After recourse to homoeopathy, she finished with only the added indignity of failing to reach a high A. She was played out, and died of cholera in Berlin three years later, on her way to join Mario in St Petersburg.

# The Victorian Nightingales

Before we look at a strain of prima donna peculiarly adapted to the official Victorian sensibility, it will be as well to give a rough picture of the nature of the business we are dealing with in an age which saw a revolution in communications, spanning the introduction of the railway and the gramophone. The focus is on London, not only because it is the best-documented operatic centre of the nineteenth century, but also because it is the most interesting, inasmuch as it never knew the public or court subsidy that existed in Europe. Private capital and public demand were the twin pillars between which the prima donna balanced herself, and there were plenty of moments, then as now, when the entire structure looked ready to collapse.

The second King's Theatre (called Her Majesty's after 1837), built after a fire had destroyed the first in 1789, was the centre of opera in London. Drury Lane and Covent Garden both held occasional seasons, and Drury Lane was particularly noted for its English opera, but the King's was the regular opera and ballet house. It was a little larger than the present Covent Garden and rather smaller than La Scala, probably holding about 2,500 people. Its early years were beset by endless legal wranglings over leases and sub-leases, constant changes of management, and eventual closure. Only with the arrival of a publisher/bookseller, John Ebers, in 1821 was any sort of order restored, and in his seven-year stint as tenant-manager even he lost £44,000 and was declared bankrupt. Ebers concentrated on improving the standard of ensemble and production, sticking out against the more outrageous of Catalani's financial demands—Pasta, who at £2,365 for about twenty performances, did not come cheap, was nevertheless better value.

After Ebers came a French Actor, Pierre Laporte, another man of artistic acumen and financial incompetence, who was at one point imprisoned for debt. His release was engineered by a young Jewish solicitor, Benjamin Lumley, who then became Laporte's right-hand man and successor. Lumley was tough over money and contracts, and by 1845 had re-established the theatre's liquidity, lifting it out of litigation for the first time since the 1780s. Unfortunately, he lacked much musical initiative, playing safe in terms of repertory and giving more attention to the ballet. In 1847 a permanent company, the Royal Italian Opera, was established at Covent Garden, taking Lumley's musical director and the *vieille garde* (with the exception of Lablache), with whom Lumley's relations had progressively deteriorated. The defection was a blow, a relief, and a challenge to Lumley: he found his trump card in Jenny Lind (of which more later). Lumley was offered the management of La Scala, which he refused, although he did make a brief and disastrous incursion on Paris. In 1852, he boldly tried to turn Her Majesty's into a joint-stock company, thus relieving himself of some of the financial burden, but his plans were thwarted by legal complications. A lean season followed the scandalous default of a German prima donna, Johanna Wagner. Musical standards had fallen irreparably. In 1853 the theatre was left empty and it only reopened in 1856 after Covent Garden, under the management of Frederick Gye, had burnt down after a masked ball. Lumley had handed over the lease to Lord Ward for safe-keeping, and Ward assigned Lumley a sub-lease in 1856 to allow a reopening under his management. Despite the new popularity of Verdi, the pretty Marietta Piccolomini and the magnificent Therese Tietjens, Lumley could not raise the arrears of rent, and Ward foreclosed on him: the theatre again went dark in 1858.

Then followed the remarkable E. T. Smith, a restaurant owner and lessee of Drury Lane, later a tin merchant, who, it was said, could not tell the difference between 'La Troviata' and 'Il Traviatore': he, in his turn delegated to Colonel James Mapleson, a violinist, unsuccessful tenor, and, most intriguingly, London's first full-time concert agent, who sought out and signed up singers for both Lumley and Gye. Mapleson took over Her Majesty's in 1862 and through this and other ventures dominated the English and American operatic scene for the next twenty-five years. His long-serving musical director Luigi Arditi described his success thus:

I have known prime donne enter his office infuriatedly, vowing that they would not depart from his presence without a 'little cheque' or hard cash, and these same irate ladies would sally forth, after waiting his leisure for some considerable time, with their angry looks transformed to absolute serenity . . . there never lived the man whose suave, gentle art in calming the irrepressible creditor was more conspicuous or effective.

So much for the prima donnas' *éminences grises*, who wrote their memoirs and articulated their grievances: we know much less about their ultimate paymasters, the public. There were no market research surveys in Victorian England, and we can only guess at the constitution of the audience. An early turning-point was the increase in 1807 of the subscription price of boxes from 180 to 300 guineas. This put them out of reach of even many of the nobility and meant that boxes were increasingly rented out for single performances only, thus causing a distinct lowering of the general tone. It is interesting to note, in Lumley's memoirs, that the Duke of Wellington sat in the pit in an orchestra stall, not in a box. 'Fop's Alley', as the aisle through the pit was known, remained a prominent feature of the auditorium, even in Lumley's day: 'All that was aristocratic, distinguished, fashionable, or (still more) would-be fashionable, met, swarmed, greeted, babbled in an ever-seething, ever-varying crowd.' But fashion alone could not keep the opera solvent. There was not enough cultured aristocracy to fill Her Majesty's two-hundred-odd boxes at up to fourteen guineas each, especially after Covent Garden had opened: rich tradesmen had to be made welcome too. Tickets were put on sale not only through the box office, but through booksellers who, acting as agents, seem to have bought block bookings at a concessionary price: in 1852, Lumley sold £10,000 worth of seats to a Mr Mitchell. It is safe to say, then, that the mid-nineteenth-century opera audience showed a far wider distribution, socially and geographically, than the narrow metropolitan one of the pre-railway era. Trains and tourism were two salient factors in this—London was a centre of both, particularly after the Great Exhibition of 1851—and Lumley rather snobbishly deplored the alteration:

The Opera House—once the resort and the 'rendezvous' of the *élite* of rank and fashion, where applause received its direction from a body of cultivated, discriminating 'cognoscenti', and the treasury of which was furnished beforehand by ample subscriptions in reliance upon the provision to be made by the manager—

now mainly depends for support upon miscellaneous and fluctuating audiences; audiences composed in great part of persons who, in hurried moments of visits to the metropolis, attend the opera as a kind of quasi-duty, in order to keep pace with the musical chit-chat of the day.

This period also sees the start of labour problems in the opera house: both chorus and orchestra were roused by the spirit of trade unionism. Just before the 1867 conflagration of Her Majesty's the all-male orchestra went on strike against the employment of a female harpist, and in 1861 Mapleson had sacked the entire chorus after they struck over what he called an 'exorbitant claim'. He re-employed more docile Italian immigrants, a practice which continued in London until the First World War. The disparity in salary between the prima donna and everyone else in the establishment must have been thoroughly inflammatory. Pasta's 1827 fee of £2,365 for a summer season is nearly £1,000 higher than anyone else's, while some soloists earned as little as £75 or £100. This was not necessarily extortionate. A prima donna sang at her market value, relative to her drawing-power. Managers were only too thankful to secure her services and fill the house.

The Victorian prima donna is a frailer creature than her early Romantic counterpart. Compared with the heroic characters of Medea, Norma, Semiramide, or Anna Bolena, the Victorians turned to a more anodyne femininity and to a vocal style which in some ways was a throwback to that of Mrs Billington—pure silvery tone without *vibrato*, firm in intonation but limited in colour and emotional range, with a pellucid top register and an easy coloratura, but nothing in the chest to give out the splendid rage of a Pasta. The parts the 'nightingales' preferred—Zerlina in *Don Giovanni*, Lucia di Lammermoor, Amina in *La Sonnambula*, later Gounod's Juliette and Marguerite in his *Faust*—were those of innocent victims, sweet-tempered, yielding, and duped. They are the virgin maidens of old men's sexual fantasy; in parts such as Marie in Donizetti's *La Fille du Régiment*, Rosina in *Il Barbiere di Siviglia*, or Zerlina, a hint of the little minx gave further spice. In general, they answered the Victorian male culture's obsession with women as ministering angel. The dichotomy between the dramatic singer—a Pasta, Grisi, or Tietjens—and the nightingale is made clear in George Eliot's great novel *Daniel Deronda*, with its two contrasting singers. Mirah Lapidoth is all sweetness and light, with a voice 'not strong enough for opera', while the Alcharisi is a woman of 'desire, will, and choice', who acted as powerfully as she sang.

The development of the maiden or nightingale prima donna was probably much encouraged by the popularity of the Romantic ballet in the 1830s and 1840s. Dancers like Marie Taglioni or Grisi's sister Carlotta danced in *La Sylphide* or *Giselle* with the utmost ethereality swathed in white gauze and illuminated by the new glow of gas lighting. Soft, malleable, the object of desire and mystery, they gave the illusion of weightlessness as their male partners scooped them off the ground into exquisite lifts, their pointe shoes and willowy arms allowing them the same sort of flexibility of manoeuvre as a coloratura technique gave the soprano.

Fanny Persiani (1812–67) may serve as a point of introduction. In 1835, while at the Teatro San Carlo in Naples, Donizetti wrote his most famous 'tragic' opera, *Lucia di Lammermoor*, for her. Lucia is orphaned, fey, and given to feverish imaginings—a far cry from the grand sexual passions of a Norma or Medea. She is easy prey to the manipulations of her ambitious brother, who forces her into a profitable but loveless marriage. Her plighted lover Edgardo interrupts the wedding ceremony and, unaware of the scheming, denounces Lucia, who goes mad, kills her husband and then dies herself after the most popular of all 'mad scenes', in which the voice echoes a flute obbligato and which contains poignant reminiscences of the earlier love duet and other arias. It is a long virtuoso showpiece which can be successfully negotiated by a light voice. Persiani's timbre was white and silvery and *pace* the weight and colour later brought to the role by Callas, Donizetti clearly intended Lucia to sound girlish, both in her opening *scena* and in the famous sextet with its piping top notes. The role became one of the nightingales' calling-cards: it contains opportunities for all the vocal tricks, requires little acting ability beyond conveying the plight of a virgin abused, and the situation, rather brutally adapted from a Scott novel, has plenty of atmosphere. Persiani sang Lucia throughout Europe and became identified with it. She was plain and sickly, but a fine musician much appreciated by connoisseurs and admitted by Grisi into the all-powerful *vieille garde*. (It was her husband, a composer, who put up much of the initial capital with which the lease of Covent Garden was secretly bought in 1846.)

If Persiani lacked charm and grace, her contemporary Henriette Sontag held those qualities in abundance. Sontag's career was a strange one. She was born in 1806, in the proverbial theatrical trunk, her father a *buffo* bass and her mother a provincial actress, neither of them at all respectable. Henriette appeared a few hours after her mother had been on stage in Koblenz, and was christened Gertrud Walpurgis, a name she wisely forgot. After her alcoholic father's death, her mother moved to Prague, where little Henriette played numerous juvenile roles. She entered the Conservatory there, and in 1821 made her adult début to considerable acclaim. From the beginning everything about her was pretty—big blue eyes, pouting little mouth, a demure smile, mild temperament, and a voice sweet, pure, and accurate, backed up by what was probably the soundest technique of her era, Catalani always excluded. The great Neapolitan impresario Barbaia immediately engaged her for his opera house in Vienna, where she sang Mozart and Rossini, and where she was given the title-role in the first performance of Weber's bizarrely plotted opera *Euryanthe*. Amazingly, she also sang in the first performances of Beethoven's Ninth Symphony and *Missa Solemnis*, much to the composer's pleasure—amazingly, because Sontag's was never a very powerful voice and Beethoven is a notoriously awkward vocal composer, who never made the usual concessions to natural limitations of breath or range. It is a considerable tribute to Sontag's underlying strength as a singer that at the age of eighteen she could tackle such music without ruining that sweetness, purity, and accuracy.

In 1825 she was engaged for the season in Berlin and became the darling of the town. One German writer observed:

> One might put the prize of a hundred ducats on the invention of an adjective that has not been used for Sontag, and none would win the prize. She has been called 'the indescribable, the heavenly, the incomparable, the divine, the universally admired, the matchless, the adorable, the adored, the delicate pearl, the dear Henriette, sweetest of maidens, darling little girl, the heroine of song, divine child, the champion of melody, the pride of Germany, the pearl of opera . . .'

Outside the German-speaking world she had, like Mara, to surmount the initial hurdle of prejudice against Teutons singing

Latin music. Her successs in Paris from 1826 onwards was nevertheless enormous, despite the rival presences of Pasta and, later, Malibran. But there were plenty who found her irritating. Pasta's friend Stapfer wrote to her that 'Even with her fine development, pretty figure, charming foot, etc. . . . she [Sontag] somehow finds a way of making herself utterly disagreeable . . . with her simpering and mannerisms . . . no expression—even musical—no verve, no soul, no intelligence.' Doubtless Sontag was not a singer of great emotional range, nor a very impassioned actress, but she embodied the 'nightingale' type to perfection. There was no aggression in her voice, just a fragile artless charm. Put at its bluntest, old men could and did slaver over her, as they slavered over a sexless yet totally 'feminine' ballerina like Taglioni. 'On she carols,' rhapsodized Berlioz, 'higher and higher, like the lark at heaven's gate, so soft, so clear, so wonderfully distinct that, like the silver bell from the altar, it is heard through the pealing organ.' The *Harmonicon* more intelligently noted her trick in florid passages of sacrificing volume so as to keep accuracy: 'She executes *arpeggio* passages with the neatness of a good finger on the pianoforte, and her *staccato* notes are not less finished; they are like drops of sound, each a whole in itself and completely detached; but when playing thus wonderfully on her vocal organ, she abates its power, all such passages being given *a mezza voce*.'

When Malibran came back to Paris from New York, it was Sontag she had to meet and match. She was thunderstruck at the German's accomplishment and, being Malibran, felt that she had to do better. The press was anxious to uncover a deadly rivalry between the two, but, as so often, it is difficult to find any solid evidence for it. They sang together in *Semiramide, Don Giovanni*, and *Tancredi* in both Paris and London, making elaborately deferential gestures to each other when bouquets were thrown. The rivalry, if anywhere, was off-stage. Charles de Bériot, Malibran's second husband, had previously proposed marriage to Sontag and been devastated at her refusal. More insidiously, Sontag's demeanour made her acceptable in high society whereas Malibran's vehemence often left her *de trop*, much to her chagrin. In London Sontag was courted by the Duke of Devonshire and a caricature of 1829 associated her with Golbourn, the current Chancellor of the Exchequer; in Paris, Sir Walter Scott presented her with a souvenir album filled with literally hundreds of signatures from members of the *beau monde*. 'The Sunday papers,' wrote Chorley, 'told of Dukes dying for her, of Marquises only waiting to offer her their coronets at her feet. Royalty itself was said to mingle in the dance.'

Then from Paris appeared a strange report: Mademoiselle Sontag, having slipped on a cherry stone in her boudoir, had twisted her knee, and would not be appearing in public, either socially or professionally, for a certain period. This kind of story could only mean the embarrassment of pregnancy and Sontag's reputation in polite society plummeted. Malibran was full of righteous indignation, and a touch of glee. 'She has dropped in public favour like a fallen soufflé,' she wrote, 'I am very angry about this, but very angry, for she was very nice.' Sontag lost her baby and returned to the stage looking wan and pale. The question of paternity was endlessly discussed in every *salon*. In 1830 the story came out. Sontag had been 'secretly married' since 1827 to Count Rossi, a young diplomat from the Sardinian court in Turin. She was now to leave the stage and marry Rossi in public—in other words, she had never been married at all. The King of Sardinia had refused to sanction the marriage and three years of negotiation had been necessary to secure his permission, Sontag's retirement being a primary condition. According to Chorley, the King of Prussia helped 'and made his wedding present by bestowing on her a patent of nobility. The daughter of the people was extinct. She had her escutcheon and quarterings and a "von" to her maiden name—as was only befitting one who was henceforth to figure in court circles.'

Over the next twenty-odd years, she made various private or charity appearances in concerts in the cities to which she and her husband were assigned—The Hague, Frankfurt, St Petersburg, and Berlin. She took to the study of composition, and brought out a cantata, *Il Naufragio Fortunato*, for herself and chorus. In St Petersburg she once sang at the court opera for Tsar Nicholas I, but the rebuke from Turin was swift and absolute. In Berlin, she sang duets with the royal princes and princesses of Prussia. Other noble amateur after-dinner singers were eclipsed, and her natural vanity must have been mildly gratified. But Chorley suspected that she was unhappy, bored by the 'regulation nothings' of diplomatic functions and keen to talk about her days as a trouper. The theatre had been her whole life and seven children were not compensation enough. At least she kept her voice alive, and fate was to take its turn . . .

The next of the nightingales came from an unexpected source—

Sweden. She was Jenny Lind, a figure perfectly attuned to the middle-class morality of the age, despite a career and a fame which must rank among the most sensational of the nineteenth century. Above all, she was respectable. She brought pure Protestantism to a profession tainted with Catholicism and made her private conduct part of her public appeal. Nowadays it is difficult not to feel impatience or even suspicion at her thoroughly Victorian integrity. We look for, and find, a degree of hypocrisy in her massively publicized charities, her ecclesiastical connections, her white gowns, and unadorned person. A modern writer, Henry Pleasants, thinks that 'The insignificant, snub-nosed, plain, simply dressed, hesitant, unassuming, poor-little-me, pining for the northern homeland, pure of heart and noble of thought, was the greatest of her roles.' But her contemporaries found her angelic in the purity of her sentiments, and she never failed to say the proper thing. Thus in the middle of her American tour, managed by the ruthless showman Barnum, from which she spun $176,675, the Swedish Nightingale wrote to a friend, 'Few people realise what an inwardly beautiful and quiet life I lead, how infinitely little the world and its vanities have intoxicated my mind! Herring and potatoes, a clean wooden stool and ditto wooden spoon to eat porridge with, would make me happy as a child and set me dancing with joy.'

Jenny Lind's childhood had its share of wooden spoons but little joy. She was born illegitimate in Stockholm in 1820, and never managed to form a stable relationship with her mother, who continued to plague her through her years of fame. Variously farmed out to relations and foster parents, the little girl's natural exuberance and desire for maternal love were never answered. However, at the age of nine, the maid of a ballerina at Stockholm's Royal Opera heard her singing at an open window, and via her mistress arranged for an audition at the Royal Opera School. Despite her mother's distaste for the stage, she was immediately admitted, and from the age of ten sang, danced, and acted in a number of juvenile roles. At seventeen, she sang Agathe in Weber's *Der Freischütz*, soon followed by Lucia, Donna Anna, and Norma, imbuing them all with the soft wan tenderness and pathos which from the first made her acting style so distinctive. The young Wagner was to speak of her 'curious pensive individuality'. She identified herself with her roles in what we would now think of as 'Method' style: 'It seems to me when I act that I feel fully all the emotions of the character I represent. I fancy myself—

indeed believe myself—to be in her situation, and I never think of the audience.' Not surprisingly, by the time she was twenty-one her voice was showing signs of being over-taxed: she had already given over four hundred performances in Stockholm. Further tension was caused by the husband of the family with whom she was then lodging. Lind loved both the composer Adolf Lindblad and his wife. She sang his songs and thought of herself as their daughter. But when Lindblad declared his passion for her and hinted at the possibility of a *ménage à trois*, she received a considerable moral shock. The only solution was to leave Stockholm.

In 1841 she made for Paris, to take lessons from Malibran and Viardot's brother, Manuel Garcia. 'Mademoiselle, you have no more voice,' he told her, in what she later described to Mendelssohn as the worst moment of her life. He advised her, literally, to keep her mouth shut for three months. When she came back, he set to work with science, correcting her breathing technique and building up her control of dynamics. He found her hard-working and intelligent, but doubted her ultimate success. By the standards of the day she had none of the bearing of a prima donna, Paris was anathema to her, and she was desperately lonely. She heard Grisi and Persiani, and saw Rachel act: 'The difference between Mlle. Rachel and me,' she wrote back to Sweden,

> is that she can be splendid when angry—but tender she cannot be. I am desperately ugly, and nasty too, when I am angry, but am better at being tender, I believe. Of course I do not compare myself with Rachel. Heaven preserve us. She is infinitely greater than poor me!

With Garcia's help, she not only recovered but developed her instrument. The return to Stockholm was triumphant, and over the next few years her reputation grew steadily throughout Northern Europe. In Copenhagen Hans Christian Andersen, in some sense, fell in love with her, but she would call him only 'dear brother'. He sent her copies of 'The Ugly Duckling', 'The Emperor's Night-ingale', and 'The Snow Queen', which severally dramatized the position. In Berlin Meyerbeer treated her like 'the tenderest father' and Henriette Sontag was deeply impressed ('modesty forbids me to repeat what she is said to have said'). It was Mendelssohn who came close to breaking her moral self-possession and her modern biographer Joan Bulman is convinced that with him 'she found a companionship deeper and more satisfying than anything she was ever to know for the rest of her life'. He was happily married, however, and his manifest influence on her remained musical. He did not live to write the opera he promised her, but she was the inspiration for the soprano part in his oratorio *Elijah*, which became the corner-stone of her repertory in later life and which exploited the peculiarly beautiful tone of her high F#s.

She had become famous, but she had still not ventured beyond the secondary opera circuit. The thought of the London–Paris nexus daunted her, and by 1845, with her customary mixture of diffidence and arrogance, she was talking about giving up the stage, with its freight of draughts, fatigue, and nerves. Then began the Bunn Affair. Alfred Bunn, manager of Drury Lane Theatre, offered her a not very generous contract for twenty performances in London. Urged on by Meyerbeer and the British ambassador's wife, she signed in the interval of a performance, later claiming that she had been *distrait* and hampered by her lack of English. She then panicked and tried to negotiate an annulment. Thanking Mr Bunn for his compliment to her 'trifling talent', she announced that she would not meet London standards: 'I possess neither the personal advantages, the assurance, nor the charlatanism of other *prime donne*.' Moreover—and perhaps this was the real crunch—she could not sing in English as was the custom at Drury Lane. Bunn understandably refused to release her. Some months later, desperate for someone to fill the gap left by the *vieille garde*'s defection to Covent Garden, Lumley entered the fray. After consulting Mendelssohn, she signed a very generous contract worth £4,800 for the season, plus expenses but minus the right to sing in concert anywhere else. Lumley also undertook to settle with Bunn. An equivalent contract with Berlin had been worth about a quarter of this. Then, in a fit of terror and without warning Lumley, she wrote to Bunn and offered him £2,000 if he would release her. Again, he refused. Enormous amounts of publicity were accruing, and London burned not just to hear Lind, but to know whether she was coming at all, and, if so, where she would sing. Chorley had already wearied of her. He was irritated at the 'herald-trumpets' which 'spoke of charities done, in a tone as if charity was the exception not the rule among musical artists'. The long anticipation 'had racked our opera world into a state of fever, and elevated it into a firm faith, moreover, that that which had cost so much trouble to secure must be, indeed, something unspeakably precious'. She delayed her arrival in London to the point at which Lumley had to go to Vienna to collect her—someone had told her that she risked imprisonment should Bunn decide to strike. When she did finally appear in April 1847, she was appalled at the size of the theatre and refused to give Lumley a date for her début. Lumley was beside himself, but the press coverage continued to fuel the romance of the timid Swedish songbird. *Punch* published the lament of Mr Bunn:

> Thy talents I would fain requite
> Though Lumley gives thee more,
> They say thy salary is, per night,
> One six six thirteen four.
> The Haymarket may hear thy strain
> But discord to thy mind
> Whispers will come from Drury Lane
> Of faithless Jenny Lind.

Finally, she sang, in Meyerbeer's *Robert le Diable*.

Orchestra stalls went for five or six guineas, boxes for twenty. The Queen and Prince Albert led an audience that included the Duke of Wellington, Prince Louis Napoleon, Mendelssohn, and Lablache, as well as the crush of nobility and fashion. Lind was not making her début in a familiar opera, like *La Sonnambula* or *Il Barbiere di Siviglia*. She had chosen the 'modern' music of Meyerbeer, which would be less immediately telling of her technique. But after a superb trill at the end of her first solo, Lablache let forth a stentorian '*brava*', and the rest of the audience followed suit. By the end of the evening the enthusiasm was maniacal, and the Queen herself threw down a bouquet. Chorley sceptically noted that he had 'never seen anyone so composed as Mlle. Lind as on that night . . . the absence and the semblance of emotion, at once, in the midst of such overcoming excitement, were strange.' In the ensuing months she sang in *La Sonnambula*, *La Fille du Régiment*, and the unsuccessful première of Verdi's *I Masnadieri*, her popularity spreading far beyond the ordinary opera audience. Her private virtue was as much praised as her singing. Horses, dogs, dolls, a tulip, a pub, and a whistling kettle took her name in vain. She rode along Rotten Row with the Duke of Wellington and was repeatedly received at court. Bunn meanwhile had instigated legal proceedings against her.

Did her singing justify the fuss? Thackeray found her 'atrociously stupid. I was thinking of something else the whole time she was jugulating away', and he could not wait to get out 'and have a cigar'; J. E. Cox, in his *Musical Recollections*, says little more than that he was 'extremely disappointed'; the columnist 'Fast Man' in *Punch* moaned: 'We have had enough of Jenny Lind. She don't suit us . . . We admire an actress who comes out, and is jolly. Jenny Lind does the gentle, and the interesting, and the angelic. So do young people in a consumption. We call that sort of thing spoony.' Chorley is again perhaps the best guide. He paid tribute to what Garcia had nurtured—her extraordinary breath control, glorious top register with its peculiarly beautiful *pianissimo*, and general technical mastery. She was, however, limited in dramatic range to the lyrical and pathetic, and even in the thickening atmosphere of adulation her Norma was considered pallid in a London with living memories of Pasta, and Grisi still in command at Covert Garden. She was inhibited by Italian, which she never pronounced with 'finished clearness'. Chorley also felt that the other side of her creditable 'resolution to offer the very best of her best to her public' was a certain 'over-calculation' in her performances, an excess of earnestness. Yet what finally gave Lind her appeal as a singer was a unique colour in the voice, an unmistakable and recognizable sound, which, like that of Supervia or Lotte Lehmann, immediately evoked a particular personality. Chopin described it as 'a kind of Northern Lights'; others babbled of woodland freshness.*

After the London season had ended, she went on an extensive tour of the provinces by railway.

Trains not only brought in audiences from outlying parts. They also sent out singers in relative comfort and vastly increased the possibilities of touring schedules. In a comparatively small country like England with relatively good roads the railway made less difference—Catalani had made extensive tours of the English provinces, reaching deep into the West Country. But in Europe and, later, America the effect was revolutionary. (The most eccentric of

* On the subject of the comparison of voices to natural phenomena, Lumley records a friend of his who found that voices he disliked variously conjured up 'snails, stale beer, sour milk, curry powder, rhubarb, mud splashes, and tea leaves from which the water has been strained'.

nineteenth-century prima donnas, Ilma di Murska, had her own special view of it. According to Mapleson, she

> never thought it worth while, when she was travelling from some distant place on the continent, to announce that she had started . . . Her geographical knowledge, too, was often at fault, and some of the routes—'short cuts' she called them—by which she reached London from Vienna, were of the most extraordinary kind. She had taken a dislike to the railway station at Cologne, where she declared that a German officer had once spoken to her without being introduced; and on one occasion, partly to avoid the station of which she preserved so painful a recollection, partly in order to get to London by a new and expeditious route, she travelled from Vienna to St Petersburg, and from St Petersburg took a boat to Hull, where she arrived just in time to join my opera company at the representations that I was then giving in Edinburgh. We had not heard of her for weeks, and she came into the dressing-room to find Madame Van Zandt already attired for the part Mdlle di Murska was to have played, that of Lucia. She argued, with some truth, that she was in time for the performance.)

The climax of Lind's railway tour was a visit to Norwich where she was invited to stay with Bishop and Mrs Stanley. Cathedral bells pealed to welcome her, and the church establishment was outraged at the liaison of the cloth and the stage, however impeccable the latter in this case was. The spirit of Trollope hovers deliciously over the incident. But for Lind it was a turning-point, consolidating her desire to quit the impure world of the theatre for something with more uplift. She had liked London and the English from the first, but at the Stanleys', in Joan Bulman's words, 'she had come face to face with Victorian ecclesiastical England, and it touched something very deep in her . . . Never had her religious yearnings found such encouragement. With the Stanleys she could discuss her inmost thoughts and feelings.'

Other factors combined to determine her. Late in 1847 her mentor Mendelssohn died, and a few months later Bunn's suit against Lind was decided in favour of Bunn, with the award of £2,500 damages. Considerable and humiliating doubt was cast on Lind's purity of motive, and Bunn later published a book containing the papers of the case. She was also encouraged by Queen Victoria, who expressed approval of her moral delicacy.*

Lind returned to Lumley and Her Majesty's after operatic farewell visits to Stockholm and Berlin. She added Lucia and Elvira in *I Puritani* (very much Grisi's property) to her London repertory and repeated last season's favourites, following it up with another concert tour and another visit to the Stanleys in Norwich, where the proceeds of two of her concerts went towards the establishment of the still extant Jenny Lind Hospital. She dithered over making a straightforward public announcement of retirement from opera, partly because she was anxious not to let Lumley down, but finally made her last appearance, in *Robert le Diable*, in May 1849. She was close to breakdown after over-work and two broken engagements, one to a dull Swede and one to an even duller Englishman whose strict piety even she found hard to take.

At this point she was contemplating complete retirement, when she was approached by an agent of Phineas T. Barnum, the American impresario who until then had specialized in freak shows and was most famous for the exhibition of a midget known as General Tom Thumb. For all his chicanery, Barnum was a genuinely imaginative showman who rightly realized that he could sell Lind as a curiosity, putting a Swedish Nightingale on a par with Tom Thumb and the Feejee Mermaid. He knew nothing about music and had never heard her sing, but what signified was his command over American credulity and the railroad. The money he offered her was a fortune in itself, enough for a lifetime of that favourite Victorian combination, capital and charity. An advance of $187,500 was deposited in a London bank and Lind consented. She would sing only in concert, retaining complete control over her repertory and associates.

Barnum was the first impresario to exploit the potential of advance newspaper publicity and he personally propagated a number of

* The Queen loved 'the dear opera' and attended regularly until Prince Albert's death, recording her views in her diary and in letters. She was devoted to Mario and Grisi, but as she wrote to the King of the Belgians, 'Poor Grisi is quite going off, and after the pure angelic voice and extremely quiet, perfect acting of J. Lind, she seems quite *passée*. Poor thing! She is *quite* furious about it, and was excessively impertinent to J. Lind.' Grisi, we know, was at this time engaged in a vendetta against Pauline Viardot, yet it is difficult not to side with her here.

stories to herald her arrival, including that she 'changed all men's ideas of music as Bacon's system revolutionised philosophy'; that her primly dressed hair disguised the fact that she had no ears; that she had secretly married the Duke of Devonshire. When she actually arrived in New York, huge crowds gathered at the harbour: cheers, serenades, bouquets, flags, and speeches were all carefully stage-managed. The campaign worked triumphantly, and in the ensuing fever for tickets Barnum decided to auction seats for the first concert—bidding reached up to $225. Then there was the merchandising spin-off, as commemorated in a doggerel song of the time:

> Yes, all is Jenny Lind now,
> In ev'ry shop she's found;
> Jenny Lind you get there retail
> By the yard, quart, pint, or pound.
> We've Jenny Lind shirt collars,
> And round my neck—Oh fie!
> I've fastened lovely Jenny Lind,
> A charming op'ra tie.

Under Barnum's efficient management Lind went on to sing a total of ninety-five concerts throughout the eastern and southern states. Barnum grossed a total of over half a million dollars *after* he had paid Lind's fees and was a happy man, but for her the strain and irritation were ceaseless.

Conditions were often uncomfortable: in Madison, Indiana, she was even required to sing in an abattoir. As a sympathetic journalist recorded, she had to receive a constant flow of visitors every day, starting with

> . . . the lady beggars, who, in some instances, have 'put the screws on her' . . . To such unexamined and unexpected applications, Miss Lind has usually offered twenty or thirty dollars, as the shortest way to be left to herself. In almost every instance, she has had this sum returned to her, with some reproachful and disparaging remark, such as 'We did not expect this pittance from you!' 'Excuse us, we came for a donation, not for alms' . . . With one or two such visitors, on the morning we speak of, were mingled applicants for musical employment; passionate female admirers who had come to express their raptures to her; a dozen

ladies with albums; one or two with things they had worked for her, for which, by unmistakable tokens, they expected diamond rings in return; one who had come indignantly to know why a note containing a poem had not been answered; and constant messages meantime from those who had professional and authorized errands requiring answers . . . This sort of 'audience' lasted at Miss Lind's rooms all day. To use her own expression, she was 'torn to pieces'—and it was by those whom nothing would keep out. A police force would have protected her, but, while she habitually declined the calls and attentions of fashionable society, she was in constant dread of driving more humble claimants from her door.

It is scarcely surprising that reports of the Swedish Nightingale's brusque wilfulness and peremptory bad temper filtered out.

After she and Barnum had amicably terminated their arrangements, Lind resumed a less exhausting schedule, but the novelty was wearing off. Without Barnum's tough tactics, her image became tarnished and receipts plummeted. The situation was exacerbated by the man she married in Boston, Otto Goldschmidt, a short and serious German Jew, nine years younger than Lind, who had been a pupil of Mendelssohn's. He had no glamour or publicity value whatsoever, except as 'a model of virtue, industry and domesticity' (thus did his wife describe him to a friend), and the way in which his second-rate pianism was blatantly pushed forward at every Lind concert infuriated audiences. For his part Goldschmidt simply did what he was told, serving his wife with a dog-like devotion which gratified her innate sense of spiritual superiority. He also gave her life the steady anchorage it had lacked, and when in 1852, after eighteen months in America, Lind sailed back for Europe, she was finally in the domestic position to make the withdrawals she had long professed to want.

London had missed her, and it was hard for the opera-house managers to know what to do after she had left.

Then something extraordinary happened: Lumley's desperate stroke of genius. He had suffered a disastrous Lind-less season, and something radical had to be done. As soon as Lind's departure was confirmed, he sent to Berlin as his agent the pianist Thalberg with the idea of approaching the Countess Rossi, Henriette Sontag. Many thought her dead, but reports had steadily come through of her

95

private appearances and the miraculously good state of her voice, kept in trim but not over-taxed. Thalberg wrote back that 'The prospect of returning to the stage seemed to affect the Countess greatly: she even shed tears at the thought of it.' And in 1848 anything was possible. It was the year of revolutions, and with a new regime in Turin, Rossi was in danger of being dismissed from his ambassadorship, leaving his wife free to do what she pleased. The political situation see-sawed, Countess Rossi hesitated, Lumley waited. Finally, Rossi was stripped of office and his wife became Sontag again, returning to London on a contract worth £6,000 over six months. She was now in her mid-forties and had not been a professional singer for nearly twenty years. Such a return is surely unparalleled in operatic history, and Lumley was taking a risk. The press was incredulous and a report even circulated to the effect that the public was in fact going to hear Sontag's daughter. But all went extremely well. She appeared as Donizetti's Linda di Chamounix: 'the cheering was universal, genuine, unusually prolonged'. Remarkably, she went on to master the 'new' (to her) repertory of Bellini and Donizetti, rather than merely repeating her earlier impersonations. The romance of the situation was not the only reason for her success. If anything, she seemed to have developed her artistry. Conditions had changed during her absence, particularly in regard to the expansion of the orchestra; she had been a contemporary of Catalani's and was now one of Viardot's. But Chorley thought her superior to Lind in *La Fille du Régiment* and she was as happy in *La Sonnambula*. She went on to sing in Paris and Brussels, and kept Lumley's London receipts buoyant for two further seasons. He also organized for her a gruelling provincial concert tour of which the high point was a visit to Stonehenge, at that time assumed to be Druidical, where Sontag was inspired to sing 'Casta Diva' from *Norma*; and the low point, her near-death from exposure when the train had to be abandoned in a snowstorm between Glasgow and Aberdeen.

In 1852 Sontag collapsed completely from exhaustion and spent the summer recuperating at a German spa. She announced a second retirement from music in Europe, but the Rossis still needed money, and again following in the wake of Jenny Lind's success, they decided to brave America. The schedule was as hectic as the material rewards were great, and she was singing in opera, not just concerts— the first great soprano to do so since Malibran's youth. At least once she was *la fille du régiment* in the afternoon and Lucrezia Borgia in the evening. In 1854 she died of cholera in Mexico City.

The search for nightingales continued. There were plenty of silly gimmicks, like the Black Malibran, a Cuban lady who sang to a small guitar and caused passing enthusiasm. Marietta Piccolomini, popular in the mid-1850s, made Verdi's *La Traviata* famous. She may be compared to the film-star prima donnas of the 1930s like Grace Moore—wonderful ankles, smile, teeth, hair, publicity agent, etc., but fatally lacking in one needful quality. 'As for singing,' wrote J. E. Cox, Piccolomini 'had not an idea of what the meaning of that accomplishment really was . . . If it had not been an insult to common sense, whenever she came in contact with a difficulty, the manner of her shaking her little head, making a dash at it, and then scrambling helter-skelter through it, would have been amusing . . . On one occasion she was known indeed to have said "They call me little impostor, and they give me bouquets, applauses, moneys: why not be a little impostor?" ' Lind was not to be won back to opera. She eventually settled with her husband in England, singing in concert and oratorio, usually for charity, rearing three children, teaching at the Royal College of Music, and becoming ever more severe.

Her charities became as burdensome to her as her voice. Here, from the end of her life, is a letter complaining of an importunity. The Lind tetchiness is very evident.

Dear Miss Pearson,
I must take for granted that you are one of the daughters of [illegible] although you give no address or date on your letter. I am very much occupied—I always work for others—and I have been so particularly busy before our first performance of Bach last Wednesday that I could not answer the threescore letters addressed to me from all sorts of people. I return the letter you sent me. Numbers of applications from perfect strangers to me arrive every week—and of course I take no notice of them . . . I have already more duties in that line than I am capable of, yet I will gladly send you a post office order for two pounds if you think that this family is still in need . . . but in sending this—I only do it for your sake, as I have been obliged to lay down the rule not to send money to people who are perfect strangers to me. I am too overwhelmed with similar cases . . .

Lind died in 1887 at her last home in the Malvern Hills. More than any other prima donna, she helped raise the moral and social status of performers. The purity of her singing was interpreted as evidence of the purity of her soul, and her Victorian audiences were happy to be applauding the two simultaneously. But, as the above letter shows, the fervour in her charity left no room for the spontaneous and easy-going generosity which characterizes theatre people at their best.

The undisputed prima donna of the second half of the Victorian age had something of that quality. Adelina Patti was as expensive as Catalani and her intractability made her the despair of managers, but she was fundamentally amiable. Her egotism was the natural response to a lifetime in the hothouse of public adulation. Getting what she wanted was all that she was ever to know. The critic Hanslick described her as a 'child of nature, half-timid and half wild, what the French call *sauvage*, good-humoured and violent, inclined to sudden quickly passing fits of temper'. Even into her forties her appearance remained touchingly girlish, her face dominated by dark, eager, and inquisitive eyes.

Like Sontag, she was born to the theatre. Her Italian mother gave birth to her in 1843, just after singing Norma in Madrid, and family lore insisted that Adelina's first scream was a perfectly pitched high F. Her father was an impresario, who took his wife and children to New York in 1846, settling in the Bowery. He was fruitlessly engaged in establishing an Italian opera company in America, along the lines of the Garcia effort. In 1848 he was joined by the enigmatic Maurice Strakosch, an ex-pupil of Pasta's turned impresario. He married Patti's sister, but it was clearly the 'passionate and vindictive' Adelina who engaged his fullest attentions. From a very young age, she adored performing and made it the stuff of her playtime fantasy, often impersonating the audience, as she later recalled, 'applauding and flinging myself nosegays, which I manufactured by no means clumsily out of large newspapers crumpled up together'. The young Henry James heard her as a child prodigy, dressed in plaid with long white drawers, and a red hussar jacket, 'mounted on an armchair, its back supporting her, wheeled to the front of the stage and warbling like a tiny thrush'. Strakosch exerted a Svengali-like influence over her earliest professional years, touring her round the States and promoting her with the calculation of a Barnum, but wisely forcing her into temporary retirement at twelve so that the voice could develop without strain. In 1861 she came to London under his management and tutelage. She had been singing in opera in New York and New Orleans for about two years, but it was in Europe that her reputation had to be made.

Patti and Strakosch arrived at the office of Mapleson, who was sufficiently excited by her rendition of 'Home, sweet home' to engage her on the spot. He rushed off to organize a company and a theatre to put her in, but returned to Patti and Strakosch's hotel to find them in possession of a £50 personal loan from Gye at Covent Garden, 'which intelligence reduced my height by at least two inches'. They had signed up with the Royal Italian Opera. Patti began a twenty-five-year reign at Covent Garden; Mapleson was left with a company, a theatre, and an announced season, but with Patti as his opposition. It was the beginning of a long battle.

Patti made her London début in *La Sonnambula*, and continued through the gamut of Rossini, Bellini (though never *Norma*), Donizetti, and Verdi up to *Traviata*. It could be said that she and her imitators 'held back' public taste in the era of *Tristan* and *Otello*, but this is not altogether fair. The nightingales did take up new roles in the second half of the nineteenth century on the less exalted plains of French opera. Lyrical and sentimental romances like Gounod's *Faust* and *Roméo et Juliette* or Thomas's *Hamlet* or *Mignon* suited them admirably, the lyrical soprano parts written with due consideration to their style and type of voice. Patti loved Wagner's music, and late in her career sang a little of it in concert, but she lacked the necessary heroic temperament as much as the technique. Some worthless showpieces written for her died the death, and her only two real gambles in new music were Carmen and Aida. Her Carmen proved a total miscalculation, but her Aida was successful. She was coached in this enormously challenging role by Verdi himself, who admired her unreservedly, despite her cavalier cuts and transpositions. She could be a good actress, especially in comedy, but no one could claim that she advanced the cause of music drama. She disliked the strain of rehearsals, and even in the early days Strakosch would often attend them on her behalf: later she sent her maid along to find out something about the new sets or what the tenor looked like. In the 1880s she wrote her exemption from these tiresome functions into her contracts, along with a demand that the size of her name on the billings should be at least a third higher than anyone else's.

But she was no fool, nor was she irresponsibly idle. Patti's overriding principle was vocal health, and her life was dedicated to it. She never drank tea, coffee, red wine, or spirits, nor ate bread, sweets, or cold food. She avoided all unpleasantness like the plague. Her daily routines when she was performing, wrote a French journalist, were rigorous: 'chocolate in the morning, at eleven o'clock lunch of eggs and white meat, a few hours' siesta, and a walk towards four o'clock; on her return, some vocal exercises, and then, after some consommé, departure for the concert or theatre . . . Nothing could make this singer deviate from this regularity to which she attributed the preservation of her organ.' Of her technique, she knew nothing, beyond that she had to avoid stress. At the slightest hint of a cold, she cancelled. 'I sing comfortably,' she once said.

Patti's emotional life may have been under less control than her voice. Her first marriage was to Louis Napoleon's equerry, the Marquis de Caux. He was something of a handsome bounder and the match was not approved, but Patti would have her way. According to her companion Louisa Lauw she pined in the Marquis's absence and would sit up all night in her room, playing 'fantastic strains on the guitar'. After she had married him they became part of the Prince of Wales' smart set, but they 'soon found that there was scarcely a question upon which they were of one mind', and he annoyed her intensely by slouching in her dressing-room after a performance and sighing 'Well, that's another show in the bag' in a bored sort of a way. Patti began to flirt with a married French tenor, Ernest Nicolini. The Marquis was inflamed with jealousy, to the point at which he and Patti came to blows. Much to the delight of the newspapers Patti then eloped with Nicolini—'Patti's running away with a common tenor, after being for so many years a titled and respected lady, held up as a model to all young ladies, was almost beyond conception,' exclaimed a prim *New York Times*—but like her godmother Grisi she at first found it impossible to obtain a divorce, and for some years she and Nicolini openly lived together, her celebrity allowing her to ride the social embarrassment. Nicolini was a boor and a third-rate singer ('Which is your favourite opera?' a journalist once asked him. 'The one I sing in least,' snapped Nicolini), but he was very good at keeping unpleasantness at a distance, so Patti went on singing while the rest of the world ran around keeping her comfortable.

As with Jenny Lind, one wants to know whether somewhere, sometime, a mental constitution like Patti's experienced blind panic, terrifying *ennui*, desperate loneliness, or anything deeper than stage nerves or a fit of pique. Perhaps Patti was as inwardly calm as she appeared; perhaps, suggested her contemporary Clara Louise Kellogg, it was the secret behind her singing: 'A great deal is heard about the wonderful preservation of Patti's voice. It *was* wonderfully preserved. How could it have been otherwise, considering the care she has always taken of herself? Such a life . . . she has allowed herself few emotions. Every singer knows that emotions are what exhaust and injure the voice.' Hanslick went further and noted Patti's complete lack of moral or intellectual imagination. He once gave her Dickens's *Great Expectations* to read, but she threw it back at him after a few chapters: 'That an old woman wouldn't give up her old bridal dress and old wedding cake can't be true and isn't possible,' she complained of Miss Havisham. 'I am no longer a child to whom one can give such things to read.'

In the twenty years following her London début she sang all over Europe, winning over even those like Hanslick who despised her 'empty and ineffectual' repertory. The elderly Rossini was infuriated by her ornaments for one of his arias, but charmed enough to write her some new ones. In 1868 she and the great contralto Alboni sang the *Stabat Mater* at his funeral. In St Petersburg the Tsar allowed her to call him 'Papa': one of her visits is commemorated by Tolstoy in *Anna Karenina*. In 1881 she returned to New York, and in 1882 Mapleson finally caught the bird for some transcontinental tours. Six years later he published his memoirs. Brought to a peak of exasperation by the failure of his American fortune-making schemes, he revenged himself in print on Patti, whose decision not to renew her contract lost him a chance of lasting success. The stories he tells are irresistibly funny, classic prima donna anecdotes, but they do not necessarily give accurate accounts of real events. Instead, he gave the public a parody of prima donna behaviour that it has still not forgotten: 'Madame Adelina Patti,' wrote Mapleson, 'is beyond doubt the most successful singer who ever lived. Vocalists as gifted, as accomplished as she might be named, but no one ever approached her in the art of obtaining from a manager the greatest possible sum he could by any possibility contrive to pay.' What he failed to add at this point is that without Patti he would have had no audience at all.

Mapleson's company toured in a special train, in which Patti had her own sumptuously appointed carriage. One of her constant companions was a parrot called Ben Butler, which according to Mapleson shrieked 'Cash! Cash!' every time he crossed the portal.

The fee she demanded was £1,000 a performance and she had to have it by 2 p.m. on the day of the performance. On occasion Mapleson had to stand at the box office, waiting for the last monies to come in, but, fortunately, the Americans were universally mad to hear her. 'Amongst the numberless inquiries at the box office several were made as to how long Mdme. Patti remained on the stage in each of the different operas; and the newspapers busied themselves as to the number of notes she sang in each particular work; larger demands for seats being made on those evenings when she sang more notes.' In *Lucia*, for instance, it was calculated that Patti was paid 42½ cents for every note she sang.

Apart from cash and the delicate state of Patti's health there was, records Mapleson, another serious problem on one of the tours, in the form of a coloratura soprano in the company, the Hungarian Etelka Gerster, who was later treated by Freud's mentor Charcot for hysteria. After a humiliating incident at a bungled curtain call, Patti conceived an unquenchable loathing for poor Gerster.

> If anything went wrong, from a false note in the orchestra to an earthquake, it was always, according to the divine Adelina, caused by Gerster and her 'evil eye'. 'Gerster' was her first exclamation when she found the earth shaking beneath her at San Francisco . . . Whenever Gerster's name was mentioned, whenever her presence was in any way suggested, Mdme. Patti made with her fingers the horn which is supposed to counteract or avert the effect of the evil eye; and once, when the two rivals were staying at the same hotel, Mdme. Patti, passing in the dark the room occupied by Mdme. Gerster, extended her first and fourth fingers in the direction of the supposed sorceress, when she found herself nearly tapping the forehead of Mdme. Gerster's husband, Dr Gardini, who, at that moment, was putting his boots out before going to bed . . .

Gerster had her revenge when Patti was kissed in public by the overcome Governor of Missouri. A journalist asked Gerster for comment on this scandalous incident: she replied simply, 'There is nothing wrong in a man kissing a woman old enough to be his mother.' Despite all this, Patti gratified her American audiences to the hilt, receiving the most fulsome tributes graciously, and dropping small bombs on her rivals in newspaper interviews:

Christine Nilsson's day 'has passed', she announced (Nilsson's invitation to the Vanderbilts' famous ball in 1883 infuriated her), Gerster 'cannot act'. Her life remained basically simple—she sang, smiled and took the money. No other prima donna radiated so little effort.

A spirit of the crassest commercialism and snobbery runs through Patti's American tours and their fabricated razzmatazz, repeated *ad nauseam* in every visited city. Theatrical conditions and acoustics were usually totally unsuitable for opera, and the level of perform-ance can have been nowhere near as high as the level of publicity. It was a phenomenon worthy of Mark Twain's witheringly sceptical eye. What mattered to the audiences was not opera, or even entertainment, but the cachet of witnessing yet another European cultural import. In San Francisco, one of America's great opera cities, the rage to hear Patti caused a latter-day Gold Rush.

On the day of the performance it took the whole of the police force to protect the theatre from the overwhelming crowds pressing for tickets, although it had been announced that no more were to be had. Long before daylight the would-be purchasers of Patti tickets had collected and formed into line, reaching the length of some three or four streets; and from this time until the close of the engagement, some four weeks afterwards, that line was never broken at any period of the day or night. A brisk trade was done in the hiring of camp stools, for which the modest sum of 4s. was charged. A similar amount was levied for a cup of coffee or a slice of bread and butter . . . Ticket speculators were now offering seats at from £4 to £10 each, places in the fifth row of the dress circle fetching as much as £4, being 400 per cent above the box-office price . . .

To describe the appearance of the house at the performance would be impossible. The toilettes of the ladies were charming. Many were in white, and nearly all were sparkling with diamonds. In the top gallery people were literally on the heads of one another, and on sending up to ascertain the cause, as the numbers were still increasing, the inspector ascertained that boards had been placed from the top of an adjoining house on to the roof of the Opera-house, from which the slates had been taken off; and numbers were dropping one by one through the ceiling on to the heads of those who were seated in the gallery. (Mapleson)

As a result of all this speculation, Patti built up as grand a fortune as any Victorian industrialist, and she spent it as they did, becoming the *châtelaine* of a large and ugly Victorian country house called Craig-y-nos, in a superb position some miles north of Swansea. Over £100,000 was spent on improvements, although it is interesting to note that only three bathrooms served thirty-four bedrooms! There were electric lights in the reception rooms and an elaborate system of electric burglar-alarms designed to protect the Patti treasury and her wardrobe of over 300 gowns. Forty servants were permanently employed. Among the installations were a billiard room, a conservatory, a winter garden, a tennis court, an ice plant, a chapel, and a huge orchestrion organ ('It was with the aid of her splendid orchestrion,' cooed Hermann Klein, 'that Mme Patti first began to comprehend the intricacies of Wagner's more advanced works'); but most spectacular of all was the construction of a private theatre seating a hundred which by means of a hydraulically lifted floor doubled up as a ballroom. The drop curtain depicted Patti as Semiramide in a chariot driven by four white horses. She gave some small-scale operatic performances there, but her greatest joy, oddly enough, was to take part in plays mimed to musical accompaniments—a fashionable genre at the end of the nineteenth century—and she even appeared in such an adaptation of Sardou's play *La Tosca*, made popular by Sarah Bernhardt and later used by Puccini.

After marrying Nicolini and buying Craig-y-nos, Patti's career became even less energetic and even more profitable. In 1885 she abandoned Covent Garden for concerts, and in 1887 made her operatic farewell to New York. She then visited Montevideo and Buenos Aires, where her fee reached new heights, and sang in various other less exposed operatic centres. Her last significant effort on opera's behalf was her Parisian appearance in a new version of Gounod's *Roméo et Juliette*, conducted by the composer. Patti sang opposite the great tenor Jean de Reszke, and together they made the piece a popular favourite. But as she approached fifty she began to husband her resources and carefully contract the scale of her operations. One sharp amateur critic was Jeannette Marshall, the pert daughter of a Savile Row surgeon, who vividly described her Albert Hall concert of 1889

Now for Patti, who after all, was *the* person we came to hear. First she looks *fully* her age (50?), [46!] and has dyed her hair auburn which goes particularly badly with a faded complexion very much powdered, and thick black eyebrows. The lower part of her face must always have been plain, & is now quite ugly & she grimaces and smirks so that I could see scarcely any resemblance to her portraits, which give her a far more refined & intellectual look than she has. She is getting stout, & her neck is red, and therefore she has wisely eschewed a low dress. Her costume was a triumph of art . . . I will say it was 'chic'. Her manner is that of a coquettish ingenue of 17, which sits very ungracefully on her to *my* way of thinking. Her voice is still very powerful, but harsh when forced, & with a peculiar metallic ring, which *I* don't like. Her execution is phenomenal & of course all her songs are chosen to show this off. 'Ombra leggiera' (encore, ''Twas within a mile'), 'La fille du Paria' (encore, last part) & 'Robin Adair' (encore, 'Home sweet home' & 'Gin a body') [Comin' through the Rye]. I liked the last best as 'Robin' was given with real feeling, & I must own that my favourite aversion 'Home, sweet home' was more than bearable. Delibes' Paria was very difficult, owing to the extraordinary intervals, and was perfectly sung, but I frankly speaking think it *ugly* and rubbishing. ''Twas within a mile', and 'Gin a body' were very *knowingly* sung, as one would expect, & the Dinorah song ['Ombra leggiera'] was taken swimmingly, but I think the occasional yelling notes, like rockets, were quite painful. Altogether I was interested, to a certain extent not disappointed, and somewhat astonished, and yet she does not touch me in the least. She is all artificial & artifice, & gives one the impression of not being truly & earnestly musical, as the great German singers are— She thinks much more of herself than of her art.

But the shrewdest commentator on this part of Patti's progress was George Bernard Shaw, then a music critic writing as Corno di Bassetto, and an ardent Wagnerian dedicated to the idea of opera as intellectually challenging music drama, but also a lover of fine Italian singing. Thus his feelings about Patti were genuinely mixed. He deplored her stage manners and the endless courting of, and responding to, applause—'Patti will get up and bow to you in the very agony of stage death if you only drop your stick accidentally.' Yet his admiration for her singing could be almost unbounded, especially when she left off coloratura showpieces and put her heart into a simple ballad.

I never fully appreciated Patti until one night I heard her sing, not *Una voce* or anything of that sort, but God save the Queen. The wonderful even soundness of the middle of her voice, its beauty and delicacy of surface, and her exquisite touch and diction, all qualify her to be great in expressive melody, and to occupy a position in the republic of art high above the pretty flummery of newspaper puffs, flowers, recalls, *encores*, and so forth which makes it so difficult for people who take art seriously to do justice to the talent and the artistic pains with which she condescends to bid for such recognition.

Her dabbling in Wagner brought a similar tribute: she attacked the 'Prayer' from *Tannhaüser* 'with the single aim of making it sound as beautiful as possible; and this being precisely what Wagner's own musical aim was, she goes straight to the right phrasing, the right vocal touch, and the right turn of every musical figure, thus making her German rivals not only appear in comparison clumsy as singers, but actually obtuse as to Wagner's meaning.' Shaw regarded Patti's career as a waste of a great voice and musicianship on a bad old system in which 'it was still possible for a *prima donna* to bounce on the stage and throw her voice at the heads of the audience with an insolent insistence on her position as a public favourite, and hardly the ghost of a reference to the character she is supposed to impersonate'.

But the system had plenty of life in it—it still does—as was witnessed by the excitement generated by Patti's return to Covent Garden in 1895 for six 'farewell' performances in three of her most famous roles, *La Traviata*, Zerlina in *Don Giovanni*, and Rosina in *Il Barbiere di Siviglia*. The timing was perfect. She was in magnificent voice and had been away from opera in London long enough to cast enormous glamour over the proceedings. At Flora's party in *La Traviata*, Patti emblazoned her bosom with over £200,000 worth of diamonds, and two costumed detectives lurked round on stage to protect them. After this, Patti's operatic career was virtually over. She planned to sing Elsa in *Lohengrin*, but perhaps wisely, perhaps sadly, never did.

Craig-y-nos had become famous for its lavish hospitality and Patti wanted to spend as much time there as possible, receiving homage from foreign nobility, ambassadors, musicians, and journalists. Here she took up cigarettes and kept her public image polished via her patronage of various charities. Meanwhile her sublime self-centredness scarcely quivered, as this charming letter of 1896 to her favourite niece Marie, ingenuously reveals:

. . . I am so frightfully busy, that it is almost impossible for me to do my letter-writing just now, but I will not allow another day to pass without sending you these few lines, to tell you how much I appreciate your kind thoughts of me—I can well imagine how terribly anxious you must feel about your sons and your property in Cuba, with all this dreadful fighting going on there—I hope most sincerely that the disturbances will soon end, and your anxiety be over . . . My season here in the South [Nice] has been a series of colossal triumphs—I only wish I had more time to tell you all about my success in 'Traviata', 'Lucia', the 'Barber', 'Don Giovanni', and 'Mirka' [mimed play] which we gave for the Czarewitch, and of the autographed portrait he gave me of himself . . . two concerts I had arranged to give in London at the Albert Hall proved such an enormous success that I was obliged to return and give an extra one, and even then it was found impossible to seat all the people who struggled for admission . . . I am going to give my Charity concert at Cardiff, which I think will be an exceptionally grand affair, as it will be the first time I have sung there for charity—my concert was to have been given in Swansea, but owing to the impertinent interference of some of the Swansea Committee, who upset all the arrangements I declined to sing there, and am giving the concert in Cardiff instead, but I have arranged that part of the proceeds of the concert shall go to the Swansea hospital and the poor of the district as I do not want them to suffer for the stupidity of the Swansea Committee . . .

After Nicolini's death, Patti's health declined somewhat, and Craig-y-nos closed its doors as her third husband Baron Cederström, a celebrated masseur, owner of a military gymnasium, and barely twenty-eight when she married him, disapproved of any over-excitement. Farewell and charity concerts saw her into the first years of the twentieth century. Her last operatic appearance was in 1907 at Jean de Reszke's private theatre in Nice, but as late as 1914, when she was seventy-one, she sang for the Red Cross at the Royal Albert Hall. She also visited Bayreuth, where she adored both *Tristan*—'all *too* lovely and poetic for anything'—and *Parsifal*.

The great fact of these last years is, however, her recordings, made when she was sixty-two. The story of the gramophone's technical evolution has been so authoritatively told by Roland Gelatt in his book *The Fabulous Phonograph* that it seems pointless to give even a resumé here, although its importance to the prima donna cannot be over-estimated. Yet how tantalizing and how misleading these shreds of aural evidence are! How many 'great singers' sound almost comically inadequate on early records, leaden, expressionless, off-pitch, or terribly rushed. Often this is due to transcriptions made at fractionally the wrong speed or to the limitations imposed by the four-minute 78 rpm disc, but some voices—Nordica's and Frem-stad's, for instance—were just too big for the equipment recording them, others were simply inhibited by the cramping circumstances of the studio. Nor should it be thought that the early gramophone brought opera into every lowly thatched cottage. Records were enormously expensive—Patti's pink label records cost one guinea for about seven minutes of music. At such prices, the industry grew slowly, but its potential was never in doubt, and the capture of Patti's voice was one of its greatest coups.

Like several others, Patti was slow to be won over to the idea of recording, and her initial reluctance may have been further fuelled by the poor critical reception of her 1903 farewell American concert tour. When after long negotiations she finally agreed in 1905 to receive the Gramophone Company at Craig-y-nos, she was still apprehensive. The crew waited for days, as Patti prowled about the machine with a small girl's curiosity. Then, after dinner one evening, the accompanist Landon Ronald (from whom the following account comes) was playing from *Tristan* on the piano: Patti began to sing along softly, 'just to see if she was in voice'. The next morning she agreed to record, and first sang Mozart's 'Voi che sapete'.

When she had finished her first record she begged to be allowed to hear it at once. This meant that the record would be unable to be used afterwards, but her wish was immediately granted. I shall never forget the scene. She had never heard her own voice, and when the little trumpet gave forth the beautiful tones, she went into ecstacies! She threw kisses into the trumpet and kept on saying, 'Ah! mon Dieu! maintenant je comprends pourquoi je suis Patti! Oh oui! Quelle voix! Quelle artiste! Je comprends tout!' . . . Her enthusiasm was so naive and genuine, that the fact that she was praising her own voice seemed to us all to be right and proper. She soon settled down and got to work in real earnest, and the records, now known all the world over, were duly made.

They are indeed lovely records, even if one cannot be as sublimely uncritical about them as Patti was herself. The faults are manifest. The voice has clearly frayed with age. In the parlour songs and ballads she can sound arch, as in the bracing jollity of 'Comin' through the Rye' or in the exaggerated dolefulness of 'The Last Rose of Summer'; in the art songs and arias she is often over-taxed and plain over-ambitious—she scampers through 'Batti, Batti' from *Don Giovanni* and loses the pianist towards the end in her attempt to sing it at the fast tempo common in her day; elsewhere her intonation can suddenly turn sour, while her *portamento*, scooping, and over-emphatic attack on climactic notes are not to modern taste. But what wonderful, almost reckless exuberance, what pleasure in singing, what riches of detail and phrasing! Not for a minute is her singing dull or pompous. In the comfortable middle of her range, she combines clean diction with beautiful tone, and she can colour her sound to bring out the implications of a word or change of mood. In an aria from *La Sonnambula* or Thomas's 'Connais-tu le pays?', she sounds warm and dreamy, the tone veiled and withdrawn; in Lotti's 'Pur dicesti', she is graceful and witty, giving out a trill which sounds natural and spontaneous, rather than a mere special effect; while in concert songs like 'Il bacio', 'La Serenata', and the Spanish 'La Calasera', she is boldly extrovert—the Baron was reputedly shocked at her Hispanic whooping in the latter—singing with youthful rhythmic crispness. 'Hearing, one can believe,' says J. B. Steane—but the story of Patti could never have suggested a singer of such abandon and involvement, of such imagination and originality.

Patti's sovereignty was undisputed. No other singer of her era had the same longevity or drawing-power, the same glamour or salary: perhaps no other singer was as good as she was either. But if Patti was queen there were plenty of royal princesses. We have already encountered the Eastern European coloratura sopranos Etelka Gerster and Ilma di Murska, and there are other sopranos whose biographies would all merit exploration, among them Pauline Lucca, famous for her Meyerbeer and romantically linked with the Kaiser; the second Swedish Nightingale, Christine Nilsson, a woman of disconcerting beauty and 'undisciplined genius' according to Shaw, popular in London and New York, where she sang in the opening performance at the Metropolitan Opera House; and the French Canadian Emma Albani, who was the regular alternative attraction to Patti at Covent Garden and who also excelled in the early Wagner repertory.

The prima donna became a grander creature towards the end of the century, more womanly in person and more statuesque in manner, although silvery pure 'choirboy' tone remained in fashion. Some of these singers could act quite powerfully when they chose, yet any attempt at presenting ordinarily credible or consistent human behaviour on stage was generally eschewed, as the prima donna regularly broke out of character to acknowledge applause and any other sort of tribute. There was little respect for accurate musical texts. Cuts and wanton transpositions were common. The prima donna could sing much as she chose, and conductors and colleagues had to follow suit. Touring, the voracious new American market, and, later, recording doubled her money. Her social position consolidated itself, simply because she was unassailable: no one could gainsay her. Talent, money, and popularity made up for birth. In short, the prima donna had reached the height of her power—no longer just a free woman, she became a positive tyrant. No singer took firmer advantage of this situation than Dame Nellie Melba.

Melba was anything but fey or vague, and she could not be bothered with the finesse of Patti's velvet gloves. She was brusque, business-like, organizing, sometimes downright rude. 'I am Melba,' she would announce categorically to anyone who threated to cross her will in any way. She was totally uninhibited. After a royal command concert at Windsor Castle at which a number of distinguished musicians performed, she turned to the Lord Chamberlain and complained in a loud voice, 'What a dreadful concert this would have been if I hadn't come.' To those who pleased her, she could be regally patronizing—issuing Melba warrants to favoured tradespeople and distributing Melba tiepins, graded in splendour, to those who had served her well. She adopted a series of young musicians who were generously treated while they remained absolutely loyal. She could equally be absolutely dismissive of the claims of others who came into her domain. The accompanist Gerald Moore remembered her as 'the terrible Melba'. On concert tours in her latter days, he recalled, she put great store by flattering lighting, but only got round to testing the effects 'while her assisting artists were performing: during the first group of violoncello solos . . . lights were raised and lowered, spots, foots, flashed on and off until the diva was satisfied with the result. That cellist and audience were disturbed was of small moment . . . Dame Nellie was not personally inconvenienced.'

On stage, she moved pieces of scenery and discarded props which offended her. 'What's this bloody thing?' she would exclaim, and fling the unhappy object into the wings. The writer Beverley Nichols, who 'ghosted' her prim and mealy-mouthed autobiography, *Melodies and Memories*, was once dragooned into helping her change round the furniture in a hotel foyer. When challenged by the hotel management as to what on earth she was doing, she gave her customary reply of 'I am Melba,' then graciously added, 'But don't worry, I'm not going to charge you for it.'

But the primary fact about Melba is, of course, her nationality, which to an unusual extent identified and explained her. She was one of the first Australians to give her country any sort of glamour or appeal—as she was fond of saying, 'I put Australia on the map'—but her own attitude to the place was always ambivalent. She was both worshipped and reviled when she returned there, and she was characteristically frank about what she considered its shortcomings. 'Hopeless' is how she privately described her compatriots. Melba the prima donna had been made in the teeth of Australian values and opportunities.

Her beginnings were not romantically outback, but solidly middle class. She was born Helen Mitchell in 1861, and was brought up in a respectable suburb of the respectable city of Melbourne, whence 'Melba' was later derived and which she aptly described as full of 'parsons, pubs and prostitutes'. Her father, a Scots Presbyterian, was a prosperous building contractor to whom she remained devoted, despite his initial scepticism of her ambitions, and she inherited from him a tough and canny business sense which later helped her to turn her enormous earnings into a solid fortune. As a child she hummed and whistled incessantly, a practice which she later considered to have provided her basic vocal training. At her Girls' College she also took singing lessons from an Italian, Pietro Cecchi. The teenage Melba therefore had the natural musical equipment and a good Italian teacher: what she lacked was a social climate which could nurture her art. The amount of opera, or indeed of any sort of orchestral music, in nineteenth-century Australia was small, and

Ilma di Murska was the only prima donna of note to visit the continent in Melba's youth. Nor was the idea of professional, independent, middle-class women generally acceptable, and at first Nellie Mitchell looked like meeting an ordinary destiny. At the age of twenty she followed her father north to Queensland, where she married Charlie Armstrong, a handsome black-sheep adventurer from England. This, however, proved a mistake from the start. Her father did not approve of Armstrong and gave the couple no money. Armstrong himself had not bargained for a woman with a will, let alone an incipient prima donna. In despair, Nellie wrote to Cecchi:

> I do not mind telling you that times are very bad here, and we are as poor as it is possible for anyone to be. We have both come to the conclusion that it is no use letting my voice go to waste up here, for the pianos are all so bad it is impossible to sing in tune to them . . . I am anxious to leave Queensland as soon as possible. *I must make some money.* Could not you form a small company and let us go touring through the colonies, for of course I should like to study for the opera . . .

This, according to Melba's biographer John Hetherington, is the first evidence of her ambition to be anything more than a polite after-dinner singer. In fact, she had quarrelled violently with Armstrong and had decided to return to Melbourne with her baby. Supported by Cecchi's belief in her potential, she worked like a fury and was soon earning her living by singing in concerts throughout the state of Victoria. Her father neither helped nor hindered her; her husband stayed up in Queensland farming. Then in 1886 her father was sent to London as a delegate for a Colonial Exhibition: Nellie with her baby went too, armed with a sheaf of introductory letters. Sir Arthur Sullivan told her to come back in a year and he would consider her for the D'Oyly Carte chorus. Others were even less encouraging. Her last resort was Mathilde Marchesi, a pupil of Manuel Garcia's, who herself taught in Paris and numbered Gerster and di Murska among her protégées. Marchesi was fortunately overwhelmed and took the girl on immediately. It was only on this trip to Paris that she entered an opera house for the first time.

In later life Melba liked to make out that Marchesi had done everything for her singing, and she appears to have been one of the very few women Melba really loved. The truth is a little more complicated. Nature had given her a fabulous sound and Cecchi, over six years, had drilled her with basic technique. Marchesi came in at the last stage, and could be said to have exploited Melba (as she now became) for her own glory, presenting her to the operatic world as her own creation. Another contemporary pupil of Marchesi's, the American soprano Emma Eames, put it thus: 'This brilliant new soprano had little to learn and in truth was well along the road to vocal sophistication before Madame ever saw her, and lacked only taste and imagination and musical intuition.' These last three qualities would be a lot for any teacher to provide, but many would say that they were precisely what Melba's singing *always* lacked.

Yet Marchesi was obviously an inspiring teacher, as well as one who could arrange useful introductions: through her, for instance, Melba met Gounod, Thomas, Massenet, and Delibes, in all of whose operas she would perform. The trademarks of the Marchesi style were purity of intonation, evenness of scale, clean, forward diction, and a free upper voice. It is the true style of *bel canto* (a term now misapplied to the Pasta era, or confused with coloratura) in which tone and line take precedence over expressivity, and it is appeciated in the now-familiar metaphors—Marchesi herself described Melba's voice as more like that of 'a bird than of a human creature' and 'as clear as a silver bell'.

Marchesi introduced her successfully into Parisian *salons*; and Maurice Strakosch, Patti's mentor, offered her a contract but shortly afterwards dropped dead. She made her real début in 1887 at the Théâtre de la Monnaie in Brussels when she was twenty-six. It is worth noting that compared with Sontag, Lind, and Patti, this was relatively late: nowadays it would be considered a little early. Her success as Gilda in *Rigoletto* was instant, and only marred by the unpleasant reappearance of her husband, whom she now determined to discard. In 1888 she sang Lucia at Covent Garden, but things did not go well, and she returned first to Brussels and then to Paris. She was soon lured back to London, however, partly through the offices of one Lady de Grey, a powerful figure of the time who exerted influence over the opera house and who liked Melba as both woman and singer. She was properly launched in a prestigious production of Gounod's *Roméo et Juliette* with Jean de Reszke, a singer she adored and respected; without any acting ability or any great beauty, she won the power she craved through the indisputable physical superiority of her voice.

Melba's triumph as a singer went hand in hand with her speedy social climb. By the 1890s the London *haut monde* was sufficiently relaxed to admit representatives of the arts as something more than entertainers, and Melba saw no reason to be daunted. She revelled in money, chic, and titles, candidly announcing, 'I'm a damned snob.' Lady de Grey was her guide, and in her memoirs Melba tediously relates the splendours of her drawing-room:

> The Duchess of Leinster, robed in white satin with marvellous sapphires round her neck, holding her head like a queen. Lady Dudley, with her lovely turquoises, so numerous that they seemed to cover her from her head to her knees; and Lady Warwick, then at the height of her beauty, the old Duchess of Devonshire, making somewhat pointed comments on those around her, the brilliant Duchess of Sutherland . . .

Nor was it only the ladies she admired. In 1800 she fell in love with the twenty-two-year-old Duke of Orléans, Bourbon Pretender to the French throne, then exiled in England. Melba was thirty, a commoner, still married, and a Protestant. There was little hope of anything permanent emerging from such circumstances, but their affair was intense and glamorous while it lasted, and he accompanied her to Vienna, St Petersburg, Paris and Brussels. Highly discreet but also much talked about, it probably won Melba a certain *cachet* among those spangled duchesses, even if the Queen stopped inviting her to sing at Command Performances. Real ruinous scandal threatened, however, when Armstrong served a divorce writ, a hearing of which would have brought the liaison firmly into the public eye. The writ was later mysteriously withdrawn, but the Duke found it all too hot, went off on a long safari, then came back and married an archduchess. Melba was left alone and never found anyone else to whom she could commit herself although her sexual voraciousness has remained the stuff of opera house gossip ever since. Armstrong, from whom she was finally divorced in 1900, even took their son away to America. But if at bottom she was a lonely woman, there was little else that her life lacked. She was an Edwardian rather than a Victorian by temperament, and described the King's reign as 'an immense week-end party in which everybody was intent on getting the most out of life'. Her own London house in Great Cumberland Place was furnished in the manner of Versailles:

she was pleasure-loving and self-centred, spending lavishly on comfort and show, and scoffing at conventional morality.

Yet the professional Melba was tight-fisted and sharp-eyed. In John Hetherington's words, 'She remembered how hard the climb had been, and she had no intention of letting all that effort go for nothing. She never committed the deadly sin of being complacent.' 'If I'd been a housemaid, I'd have been the best in Australia – I couldn't help it,' she said once. 'It's got to be perfection.' She knew that her real power lay not in having desserts named after her (Pêche Melba, as devised by Escoffier), but in her voice; just as her real palace was no *ersatz* Versailles, but Covent Garden. No one there crossed Melba, and her disapproval, expressed with a trooper's command of expletives, was said to have stifled the careers of Selma Kurz, Emma Eames (both Marchesi pupils), and Geraldine Farrar, though it is hard to find concrete evidence of this. If she did operate to get rid of rivals, she must have employed subtle rather than overt means. What did matter to her were her unique privileges. She had her own dressing-room to which she kept the key—'MELBA. SILENCE! SILENCE!' was inscribed across the door; and her own fee—Caruso had to be content with £399 per performance as only Melba was permitted to earn £400. Her real power base was the loyalty of her audience, particularly its fashionable end, and from 1890 onwards 'Melba Nights' at Covent Garden were one of the major events of the fashionable calendar, on a par with the races or charity balls. Shaw was a jaundiced observer of the earlier of such occasions, noting tartly how Melba 'received flowers in those large baskets which English ladies and gentlemen invariably carry with them in the theatre, and which they present to singers in moments of uncontrollable admiration'. Appropriately enough, the last Melba Night before the outbreak of the First World War was attended by two kings, four queens, and a dowager empress.

These were the conventional trappings of prima donna-hood, but Melba was not a conventional singer, and her operatic repertory was substantially more contemporary than her nightingale predecessors. She sang no Mozart, no Bellini; Rossini and Meyerbeer only a little; Lucia was her sole major Donizetti role. The Italian nexus was fast giving way to the modern French one. It could be said that Gounod, Thomas, Delibes, and Massenet gave the world updated Donizetti, with efficient plots softened with plenty of pathos, waltzing melodies in place of coloratura, lushly orchestrated sentimentality in place of rough-edged energy. Melba studied with all these composers and made their music a corner-stone of her repertory. The only two roles she created, in now forgotten pieces, were also by Frenchmen, Saint-Saëns and Bemberg. She even sang some of the new *mélodies* of Debussy and Reynaldo Hahn. In later Italian opera, she briefly assumed Aida and Nedda in Leoncavallo's *I Pagliacci*, but her two most famous parts here were Desdemona in Verdi's *Otello* and Mimi in Puccini's *La Bohème*—both of which, again, she studied with the composers, and which she sang until the very end of her career. There was also Wagner to reckon with. Melba genuinely loved Wagner's music and because she must have foreseen a time when Wagner would be as essential to a soprano as Rossini had been seventy years previously, she decided to dive in to its deepest waters: the irritating example of Lilli Lehmann, who could apparently sing anything, must also have goaded her on. In 1896 at the Met she sang Brünnhilde in *Siegfried*. The part consists of one very long scene with a crucifyingly taxing climax, and it was quite beyond Melba's vocal capacities. Despite the support of her beloved Jean de Reszke as Siegfried, she had a bad cold and scarcely got through the forty-minute ordeal. After that one evening she suffered a severe vocal collapse, developed a nodule on her vocal cords, and was advised not to sing for some months. The baritone David Bispham witnessed the fiasco and noted how ludicrously old-fashioned her stage deportment became in such an opera: 'apparently forgetful of the Wagnerian tradition to remain well within the scene', she kept Jean de Reszke, 'in the heavy fur coat of Siegfried . . . busy patrolling the forward part of the stage to keep the white-clad Melba from rushing into the footlights, over which she had so many times sung to delighted audiences'. She was probably also trying to prevent her voice being drowned by the Wagnerian orchestra.

Melba should not have worried: what she could do in the French and Italian line was enough to keep her in power. Covent Garden was her 'artistic home', but she was also supreme in New York (which she hated: 'so vulgar'), and even won over the thoroughly chauvinist audience of La Scala, Milan, when she sang Lucia there in 1893. Her returns to her native Australia began in 1902 with a concert tour; in 1909 she set up house in a village near Melbourne, where she christened herself 'the Countess of Coombe', only half-jokingly; in 1911 and 1924 she became chief mover and attraction of an Australian touring opera company. She herself made enormous sums of money there, netting £2,350 from one concert alone in 1902, but equally ploughed a considerable amount back into Australian music, closely involving herself in two Melbourne music conservatories. As she got older, she spent more time in Coombe, playing jazz on the gramophone and entertaining herself with a series of mostly homosexual courtiers.* 'Poor little me,' she would sigh. A baseless newspaper report of her alcoholism was the first of many trials by which she was dogged, but the last Melba story has remained the most notorious. In 1928 a biography of the contralto Clara Butt appeared in which Melba was quoted as advising Butt on her forthcoming Australian tour: 'All I can say is—sing 'em muck! It's all they can understand.' Melba furiously denied the remark and insisted that the publishers delete the page in question. But Australia could not forget the insult, and 'sing 'em muck' passed into the common currency. Melba was right to be indignant inasmuch as she had always tried in a small way to educate public taste, but she had often spoken more politely to the press of her disappointment at the Australian failures of musical appreciation, and 'sing 'em muck' does have an authentic ring to it. Melba could not resist one final dig: 'It would be quite unnecessary to advise Clara Butt to sing muck, since that's all she sings anyway.'

During the First World War Melba raised over £100,000 for the wounded, and was created a Dame of the British Empire for her efforts. But post-war society was not as diamond-studded as she would have liked. She returned to Covent Garden after its five-year closure to find her dressing-room repainted without her permission and men in 'shabby tweed coats' sitting in orchestra stalls once occupied by those in full evening dress. Although now fat, sour-faced, and well past her peak, she continued to sing in opera. In 1926, at the age of sixty-five, she made her Covent Garden farewell, singing scenes from her Desdemona, Juliette, and teenage tubercular Mimi. There is a fascinating recording of the evening in which we can hear not only Melba's still intermittently impressive singing, but also her farewell speech. 'A long farewell to all my greatness!' She thanks audience, orchestra, management, stagehands, stage-doorman, but it is the thought of the opera house itself that most seizes her—'I love it more than any place in the world,' she

---

* According to Blanche Marchesi, she introduced the taxi-cab to the continent. She was a keen driver herself.

announces in a warm speaking voice, boldly charged with emotion, even though she had not sung there much since 1913. By the end of the speech she sounds close to breaking down, and her last words are mercifully drowned in applause. It is hard not to be moved at the thought of what such a moment must have meant, even to someone as hard-boiled as Nellie Melba. She continued to visit Covent Garden as Queen Dowager. Many stories are told of her in this new role, the most innocuous of them being that of her delight at a performance of *La Bohème*, when the audience began shouting for the tenor Martinelli. Melba, now slightly deaf, turned to her companion. 'Listen,' she said. 'They're still calling for their Auntie Nellie!' The dimunition of her fame was something she could not tolerate. One of her courtiers, Tommy Cochran, describes her fury in Harrod's when an assistant refused to accept her cheque for some china figurines. 'I am Melba!' she thundered. 'You know the name, don't you?' 'No, Ma'am, I'm afraid I don't,' replied the poor shopgirl, as Melba summoned the managers. But her time was up. Although she had her fortune, a mass of friends and enemies, and an unassailable reputation, singing was the great thing in her life, and once she had given up public appearances, her iron constitution gave way to erysipelas, a consequence of infection contracted after a bungled face-lift, and she died in 1931.

There is a lot of controversy about Melba's singing that her recordings, spanning over twenty years, cannot resolve. What is beyond doubt is that it had an extraordinary natural radiance of tone, magnificently projected. This quality is suggested in two of the most quoted descriptions of its character. The American critic W. J. Henderson emphasized that 'It had splendor. The tones glowed with a starlike brilliance. They flamed with a white flame.' From the box-like acoustics of the early recording studio, one gets the whiteness and the brilliance, but not the splendour or the flame. Mary Garden, the great Scottish-American prima donna, carries it further. Speaking of the last floated high C with which Mimi closes Act I of *La Bohème*, Garden found Melba's

> . . . the strangest and weirdest thing I have experienced in my life. The note came floating over the auditorium of Covent Garden; it left Melba's throat, it left Melba's body, it left everything, and came over like a star and passed us in our box, and went out into the infinite. I have never heard anything like it in my life, not from

any other singer, ever. It just rolled over the hall of Covent Garden. My God, how beautiful it was . . . Since then I always wait for that note . . . they reach and reach for it, and then they scream it, and it's underneath and it's false, and it rolls down the stairs . . . That note of Melba's was just like a ball of light. It wasn't attached to anything at all—it was out of everything.

Melba recorded the scene with Caruso and the note in question is indeed very beautiful in a lunar sort of way. From records, one can also appreciate the precise articulation of both word and note, and the evenness of tone. There are no weak moments, nothing smudged or breathy. Everything is truly and cleanly sung, without tremulousness or *vibrato*, and with near-impeccable accuracy of pitch.

But here one's reservations begin: that precise articulation often becomes reminiscent of a music box's mechanical rigidity. In 'Ah, fors' è lui' from *La Traviata* Melba's phrasing is absolutely square and literal, the emotional dynamics—halting, then yearning, then ardent—reduced to mere *crescendo* and *diminuendo*, learnt rather than felt. Her singing always has tremendous determination and aggression. It knows what to do, where to go, and why it's going. Other shades of feeling are hard to find—her 'Lo! hear the gentle lark' never merits the adjective; her 'Caro nome' has no wistfulness; Juliette's waltz-song sounds as if it is meant for puppets to dance to; and compared with Patti's infinite coquettish charm, her 'La Serenata' has no lilt or allure. 'I do not think anything in the world could have hindered me from becoming a singer,' claimed Melba, and this wilfulness* cuts through her singing, which in that sense is highly expressive of her personality—even her Mimi can sound hectoring.

And yet the Melba sound has a drug-like effect. Listen to it for half an hour, and even though no impression of depth or sensitivity is left, the tone will ring on in the head, obsessively insistent. It would be pointless to deny Melba greatness. Hers was a magic voice, as magic as that of Trilby in George du Maurier's famous novel of that name, published in 1894, in the first years of Melba's fame. Trilby is a simple Irish lass who cannot even sing in tune until mesmerized by

* 'I hate those boys,' she whispered when she heard the choir at Chartres Cathedral. 'They are doing what it took me years and years to accomplish, and I don't know if they aren't doing it better.'

the charismatic Svengali. Then she becomes the paragon of nightingales:

> Every single phrase is a string of perfect gems, of purest ray serene, strung together on a loose golden thread . . . waves of sweet and tender laughter, the very heart and essence of innocent, high-spirited girlhood, alive to all that is simple and joyous and elementary in nature . . . all the sights and scents and sounds that are the birthright of happy children . . . All this, the memory and the feel of it, are in Trilby's voice as she warbles that long, smooth, lilting, dancing laugh, that shower of linked sweetness, that wondrous song without words . . . a clear, purling crystal stream that gurgles and foams and bubbles along over sunlit stones; a wonder, a world's delight. And there is not a sign of effort, or difficulty overcome.

# 4

# *The Wagnerians*

No revolutionary is ever quite consistent with himself, or lives up to the implications of his ideals, and Richard Wagner (1813–83) is no exception. His attempt to overthrow the Meyerbeerian conception of grand opera, 'forced down people's throats by the spirit of speculation, and lazily swallowed by the social *ennui* of the dwellers in our large cities', was sincere, even if fuelled by personal animosities. He was a high Romantic, standing for pure Art in an age of commercialism and exploitation; he was made, and to some extent made himself, an outcast from the bourgeois norms of success that Rossini or Meyerbeer had happily embraced. Wagner had his vision, and because he knew himself to be a genius, he saw it as the duty of others to sacrifice themselves to it. No singer at the first Bayreuth Festival was to receive any payment beyond living expenses: 'A lot of use to me a singer would be who came to me only for the sake of a silly salary. Such a person would never satisfy my artistic demands.' Equally, no one would be charged to attend a performance. Equally, rich people had a duty to finance the operation, and, equally, Wagner, as a genius, exempted himself from the ordinary exigencies of debt repayment.

Yet when one looks coolly at Wagner's operas, there is less purity of purpose. In his voluminous prose polemics he proposes the idea of the *Gesamtkunstwerk*, a union of music, drama, and the visual arts: opera should be a communal celebration, like Greek tragedy, deeply expressive of the people's dilemmas and spiritual values. But, as Shaw originally pointed out, he was more than ready to exploit the despised trappings and conventions of French and Italian opera to gain his effects. Theatrically speaking, the gathering of the Gibichung and the destruction of Valhalla in *Götterdämmerung* is pure Scribe-and-Meyerbeer, as is the Venusberg orgy in *Tannhäuser* or the procession of the Knights of the Grail in *Parsifal*. With his purified non-denominational Christianity, his attempts to exalt the erotic and his fascination with the idea of self-sacrifice, Wagner was much more of the Victorian than he would have liked.

So how much of a revolutionary was he? This question is not easily answered. We cannot examine closely here his harmonic practices and their impact on twentieth-century music, nor the development of those ever more complex webs of orchestral themes, built up throughout the later operas and individually known as *leitmotivs*, which act on the listener something like an authorial commentary in a novel—judging, reminding, pointing ironies and parallels, sometimes dominating the action, sometimes burrowing deep into the subconscious. Wagner 'elevated the dramatic dialogue itself as the main substance of the musical production'—in other words, he returned to Gluck and to opera's roots in Monteverdi by seeking to eliminate all formal musical divisions, such as that between recitative and aria, and to create a continuous flow of speech, heightened in beauty and meaning by being set to music. He deplored the repetitions, paddings, and clichés of expression in Italian libretti. In his operas the drama was not a mere peg on which to hang a succession of musical numbers, nor was the orchestra just accompanist and colorist—it too was given, through the *leitmotivs*, what Wagner called 'a faculty of speech'. Thus the Wagnerian singer had to master two things above all: the art of intelligent musical declamation, of 'talking to music'; and how to ride a sometimes ruthless and unprecedented volume of orchestral sound which at times could contradict, rather than support, the vocal line. Wagner was not interested in catering to singers: rather, it was singers who should cater to him and his art. And so they did, as voices of new types and powers were trained.

What early Wagner audiences most missed was definite melodic contour, regularly phrased and repeated often enough to become what is popularly known as a tune. One of his most formidable critics was Eduard Hanslick, whom Wagner resented violently enough to satirize in the figure of Beckmesser in *Die Meistersinger von Nürnberg*. Hanslick tried very hard to appreciate Wagner and the 'music of the future'. He was happy to pay tribute to his energy, originality, and masterly instrumentation: there were passages he acknowledged as lovely or exciting. But he also found most of it insufferably tedious: 'the intentional dissolution of every fixed form into a shapeless sensually intoxicating resonance; the replacement of independent articulate melody by vague melodization . . . those extended scenes in which one takes in little more than a continuous fluctuation of featureless, fluid tonal matter. Melody, self-sufficient melody from which alone the intrinsic musical body can be constructed, is lacking . . .' It was precisely the last point that Wagner would have taken up, much as he loved melody in Mozart, Bellini and Weber. He mourned contemporary German music's unmelodiousness—'Song, song, and again I say song, you Germans!' he exhorted in an early essay on the virtues of Bellini—but his idea of what constituted melody was wider ranging than Hanslick's. Melody was not necessarily 'self-sufficient': indeed, in opera it had suffered from being irrelevant, and Wagner was aiming at melody constantly bent towards fulfilling the drama, rather than towards vocal display, pretty tunes, or any other sort of immediate audience gratification. George Eliot, a cultivated amateur musician, saw a little further than Hanslick. She was in Weimar in 1854, where she heard Wagner's three early major works, on which she reported in her journal:

I had not the patience to sit out more than two acts of *Lohengrin* . . . The declamation appeared to be monotonous, and situations in themselves trivial or disagreeable were dwelt on fatiguingly . . . With the *Fliegende Hollander* I was delighted—the poem and the music were alike charming. The *Tannhäuser* too created in me a great desire to hear it again. Many of the situations and much of the music struck me as remarkably fine. And I appreciated these operas all the better retrospectively, when we saw *Der Freischütz*, which I had never before heard and seen on stage. The effect of the delicious music with which one is so familiar was completely spoiled by the lack of recitative and the terrible *lapsus* from melody to ordinary speech.

In an essay written shortly afterwards she admits that Wagner 'has pointed out the direction in which the lyric drama must develop itself', and concedes that 'It is just possible that melody, as we conceive it, is only a transitory phase of music.' Love his music, however, she could not: 'You long for the sound even of a street organ to rush in and break the monotony.' Such a response remains common a century and a half later: most people still find most of Wagner hard work, with as many obvious 'highlights' as any Italian opera, despite his determination to 'through-compose' and achieve a constant musical and dramatic flow. Yet most people would also agree with George Eliot—after Wagner, nothing could be quite the same again.

Wagner's first crucial operatic experience was hearing Wilhelmine Schröder-Devrient sing the title-role of *Fidelio*. He was an impressionable boy of sixteen, in the first flush of a passion for Beethoven, but he was never to forget

> . . . the almost satanic ardour which the intensely human art of this incomparable actress poured into [my] veins. After the performance I rushed to a friend's house and wrote a short note to the singer, in which I briefly told her that from that moment my life had acquired its true significance, and that if in days to come she should ever hear my name praised in the world of Art, she must remember that she had in that evening made me what I then swore it was my destiny to become. This note I left at her hotel, and then ran out into the night as if I were mad . . .

This extraordinary woman was born nine years before Wagner in 1804, the daughter of a baritone and one of the finest tragic actresses of her time, Sophie Schröder, sometimes labelled the German Mrs Siddons. She passed on to her daughter an acting style of heightened naturalism, teaching her the gesture, diction, and ability to project intense emotion characteristic of the new Romantic school. At fourteen, Wilhelmine was already playing Shakespeare and Schiller in Vienna. Her vocal training, on the other hand, was relatively casual. Good teachers were hard to find in Germany: many were Italian, and there was a lot more money to be made in London or Paris than in the backwaters of Germany. Schröder-Devrient had no Garcia to drill her into accuracy and agility or the steady emission of tone, and she was always to rely too much on the rasping and emphatic exaggeration that has dogged bad Wagner singing ever since.

German opera was not yet the popular international commodity that Italian opera was, and Schröder-Devrient was never happy with the latter's vocal requirements. Her *Norma*, *La Sonnambula*, *Anna Bolena*, *Otello*, etc. did not match up to the contemporary competition from Pasta and Malibran, and the blatant inadequacies of her singing restricted her career abroad. But apart from her theatrical genius she did have one other great advantage, in the form of the

German role with which she was always identified and in which she so thrilled Wagner—Leonore in Beethoven's *Fidelio*, which she first sang in Vienna in 1822 at the age of seventeen and which she did much to make popular. Beethoven himself rehearsed her and was sufficiently moved to promise to write her another opera, which he sadly never did. In London Chorley was dismayed at her singing of Leonore—'Her tones were delivered without any care, save to give them due force. Her execution was bad and heavy. There was an air of strain and spasm . . .'—but he paid tribute to her portrayal of the woman who risks all to save her unjustly imprisoned husband: 'There was a life's love in the intense and trembling eagerness with which she passed in review the prisoners when they were allowed to come forth into the air—for *he* might be among them! There was something subduing in the look of speechless affection with which she at last undid the chains of the beloved one, saved by her love—the mere remembrance of which makes the heart throb and the eyes fill.' One of her most famous moments as Leonore was at the phrase 'Noch einen schritt und du bist todt' ('One more step and you are dead'), when she flourishes the pistol at the prison governor Pizarro. The last word 'todt' ('dead') would be barked out with a convulsive laugh, rather than sung at its proper pitch. But this *parlando* became one of her worst mannerisms and an easy way out, as Chorley noted, of any vocal difficulty: 'She cared not whether she broke the flow of the composition by some cry, hardly on any note, or in any scale—by even speaking some word for which she would not trouble herself to study the right musical emphasis or inflexion—provided only she succeeded in continuing to arrest attention.' Berlioz felt even more strongly about it:

She would have considered herself to have failed if she did not monopolize the attention of the house, rightly or wrongly and by whatever piece of stage business, in every scene she appears in. Her whole manner suggests that she sees herself as . . . the only character with whom the audience need concern itself. 'What? Listening to that fellow? Admiring the composer? Interested in that chorus? How can you be so misguided? Look over here, this is what you should be attending to . . .' Her singing, as I have said, is often wanting in accuracy and intonation and taste. The cadenzas and the numerous alterations which she now inserts into her roles are in poor style and clumsily managed. But her spoken interjections are in a class apart. Madame Devrient never sings the words, 'Dieu! o mon dieu! non! est-il vrai? est-il possible?' etc. She speaks the whole passage, or rather shouts it at the top of her voice.

Wagner was outraged on reading this, but not because he thought she was a great 'pure' singer: 'She had no voice at all,' he candidly admitted, 'but she knew how to use her breath so beautifully and let a true womanly soul stream forth in such wondrous sounds, that we never thought of another voice or singing.' He saw that 'her tendency to exaggeration was at times almost painful'. But he compared her with the run of prima donnas, or 'female castrati', as he scathingly called them, and extolled her powers of expression and 'womanliness' against their mindless *bel canto*.

In 1835 Wagner, now launched on his musical career, had conducted his goddess when she visited the small town of Magdeburg. Among the operas in which she appeared under Wagner's direction was Bellini's version of *Romeo and Juliet*, *I Capuleti e i Montecchi*, in which she sang Romeo: many years later Wagner told his wife Cosima that the memory of her ardour in that role had inspired him to the second act of *Tristan*. She, for her part, recognized Wagner's talent, if not his genius, recalled his adolescent letter of 1829, and was flattered by his attentions, becoming his patron and friend. Wagner was deeply affected by her interest in him: when on his first visit to London, he dropped a snuff-box she had given him into the River Thames, he nearly drowned trying to retrieve it. The power of this fixation continued long after her death: Cosima's diaries of her life with Wagner in the 1870s record the number of dreams in which she figured, and their house in Bayreuth, Wahnfried, had a *sgraffito* above the portal depicting Schröder-Devrient as Tragedy. Yet he was never in love with her. She had become blowzy and plump by the time he knew her, and altogether lacked the delicate mystique that he found so attractive in women: he was particularly appalled by her theatrical coarseness of language.

The opera house with which she was most closely associated, for more than a quarter of a century, was that of Dresden, and it was here that Wagner and she came together again in 1842. *Rienzi*, Wagner's third opera, was to be given its première and Schröder-Devrient agreed to sing the *travesti* part of Adriano. *Rienzi* is written squarely in Meyerbeerian format and was originally intended for production at the Paris Opéra. It is a five-act historical drama set in fourteenth-century Rome, with a strong theme of 'people against the nobles', a large role for the chorus, and some spectacular stage effects, culminating with Adriano's suicidal ride into the burning Capitol. Schröder-Devrient had great difficulty with it all. She was well past her peak, and found the idiom of the music difficult. At one point, after failing to master some unexpected modulation of key, she flung the score at Wagner's feet and stormed out. Wagner showed unusual (for him) forbearance and tact. The opera was fortunately an immediate and stunning success of an unproblematic kind that Wagner never again experienced. His next work, *Der Fliegende Holländer* (1843), shows the influence of the other great German opera of the early Romantic period, Weber's *Der Freischütz* (1821), in which Agathe was another of Schröder-Devrient's most famous parts. Weber was himself a considerable operatic reformer, many of whose ideas Wagner inherited and developed. *Freischütz* is based in folk-lore, full of imaginative orchestration, with some gorgeous melody and the *frisson* of the supernatural. *Fliegende Holländer* follows it in these respects, and with its movement towards a continuous musical flow, as well as the embryonic use of the musical *motiv*, it also contains features of Wagner's mature style. At the middle of the opera stands Senta, the Norwegian village girl obsessed by the legend of the ghostly Dutchman doomed to wander the sea until a woman's love redeems him. She would be prepared to make any sacrifice to save him, and when he does appear, kills herself to prove it. This nexus of ideas—woman-love-death-salvation—is one of Wagner's persistent themes, both in his art and in his life, and we shall return to it.

Schröder-Devrient was the first Senta. Rehearsal was a terrible time. Wagner privately referred to her as a sow and a bitch, for she was in a permanent state of near-hysteria. Her love-life was notoriously complicated and unhappy, involving three marriages, four children, and a succession of infatuations with thoroughly unsuitable younger men. Her first husband divorced her for adultery and won custody of their children; her second embezzled her money. After her death an anonymous pornographic book appeared entitled *A Singer's Memoirs*, which she was widely thought to have written. Stylishly composed, with a certain amount of insight into sexual psychology and featuring lesbian orgies and an English milord named Sir Ethelred, it is a good example of elegant erotica. There is, however, very little indication of her career as a singer in it, and if it does derive from papers or journals she left, the elaboration must be considerable. What is interesting about it is the simple fact that Schröder-Devrient should be associated with uninhibited expressions of libido.

In the rehearsals for *Fliegende Holländer*, this association manifested itself to Wagner's ultimate benefit. The cause of her mental unrest was the abandoning of a long-standing liaison for a passionate and ill-advised one. Racked with guilt and uncertainty, she ate nothing and looked deathly. Confiding in an egoist like Wagner cannot have been very reassuring, and he regarded her carryings-on with a mixture of amusement, sorrow, and contempt. She in turn mocked him as an innocent in matters of illicit passion—'Oh, what do you know about it, tied to your wife's apron strings?' she complained, little knowing that she was talking to the future composer of *Tristan und Isolde* and one of the most scandalous adulterers in Europe. Finally, the only cure was work. She flung herself into the role 'as a matter of life and death', and her high pitch of emotion, thoroughly suited to Senta, was exacerbated on the first night by the presence of her new lover in the audience. The opera was not a success, but Schröder-Devrient evidently gave a staggering performance and saved the evening from disaster.

In 1845 Wagner produced *Tannhäuser* at Dresden. This romantic opera set in medieval Germany carried his style a stage further. Although it contains some definite arias, there are also passages of freer musical dialogue and monologue that were highly original. Such sustained and complex music made impossible demands on singers and orchestras of the time. Schröder-Devrient sang Venus, the goddess of sensual love who tries to keep Tannhäuser from his nobler spiritual life. She did not understand her music at all and was by now absurdly fat for the role. In rehearsal she warned Wagner that the public would not appreciate his innovations, especially in such an inadequate production, and she was right. A further problem was her jealousy of Wagner's adopted niece, the nineteen-year-old Johanna, who sang the hero's other love, Elisabeth. Still in a highly nervous state over her love affair, she was convinced that Wagner had deliberately set Johanna up in the same opera with the intention of humiliating her. In revenge she decided to call in a loan she had generously made Wagner for the publication of his operas and which he could not conceivably repay. When she instituted legal proceedings, Wagner had to take a further loan from somebody else, and was thus flung deeper into a spiral of debt from which he was never to extricate himself. It marked the end of their relationship—Wagner saw her only once more, when she made an inflammatory public speech during the 1848 revolution for which she was nearly imprisoned. She retired from opera in 1847 and devoted herself to *lieder* singing: Schumann dedicated the great chin-up song 'Ich grolle nicht' (from *Dichterliebe*) to her, and one can imagine how heroically she must have interpreted its stern and hectoring phrases. In 1850 she married a Livonian baron and made an attempt to domesticate herself. 'She would wear a big apron and an immense bunch of keys hanging at her waist, insist on dusting the drawing-room, and even sweeping the floor, especially when visitors were coming; she would go to the kitchen and stir the scrambled eggs.' This particular performance did not last long: nor did her efforts to teach. 'The poverty of heart and spirit was too great,' she wrote to Clara Schumann in 1850, 'the soil too barren, to nourish the strong roots torn from my own heart.' She died in 1860. Wagner bore her no grudge for the considerable trouble she had caused him. In his autobiography, he talks of the 'turbulence and force' of her 'inner daemon, combined with such genuine femininity, lovableness and kindness of heart'. Few of the others who crossed him met with such indulgence.

Wagner had also taken up the revolutionary cause in 1848, and was obliged to leave Germany when the Dresden uprising collapsed. He moved to Paris, then to Zürich, and the première of his next opera, *Lohengrin*, was given in his absence, at Weimar, in 1850 under the direction of Liszt. Over the next fifteen-odd years Wagner lived in exile, his life taken up with his prose writings, conducting, the gestation of the enormous *Ring* project, and with growing estrangement from his wife Minna, a woman sadly ill-equipped to cope with his egotism and ambition. In 1857 they were living together in a cottage on the Swiss estate of a wealthy silk merchant, Otto Wesendonk. Here he began work on *Tristan und Isolde*, fuelled by an ultimately disastrous affair with his host's cultivated wife Mathilde. He set some of her poems to music—one of the rare occasions on which he used anyone else's texts. These secret hymns to an unfulfillable passion, known as the *Wesendonk Lieder*, are unrelievedly yearning and plangent, and contain some of Wagner's kindest and most purely lyrical writing for the female voice.

*Tristan* takes up many of their musical themes and expands on their ideas about love—renunciation, the conflict of night and day, the desire for oblivion. It is easy enough to see these as the future clichés of a thousand novels, films, or fantasies, and the opera's originality as erotic philosophy has been overrated—no one ought to claim that *Tristan* tells us as much about adult sexual relationships as *Phèdre*, *Antony and Cleopatra*, or *Anna Karenina*. Its power lies not in its 'message'—the aspiration towards a perfect love which can only be reached through death—but in the hypnotic sensuality of the music, with its notorious lack of harmonic definition; the vast single impetus of each of the three acts; and its relentless concentration on absolute emotional states—'One thing alone left living,' wrote Wagner, 'longing, longing unquenchable, a yearning, a hunger, a languishing forever renewing itself.'

The part of Isolde requires a soprano capable of projecting two radically opposed personalities, and few of the great Isoldes have ever held the perfect balance. Elsa in *Lohengrin* or Elisabeth in *Tannhäuser* can be sung by lyric sopranos with a pure line and white tone: but Isolde requires much more. Act I presents Isolde the sorceress, self-deceived and even slightly crazed, suffocating with suppressed rage at her humiliation, sarcastic in her dialogue with Tristan, impatient with her servant Brangäne. Fury has to ring out scaldingly from her first utterance, and even the softer passages must have something insinuatingly sinister to them. Any hesitation or insecurity ruins the dramatic illusion of her obsessiveness. But from the drinking of the potion onwards a rapturous warmth has to flood through the voice, melting the ice, cracking the steel, releasing a pulsating desire which culminates in a graphically orgasmic climax. In her relatively brief appearance in the third act, Isolde is transfigured, tender with the dying Tristan, then rising to the *Liebestod* in 'calm of mind, all passion spent'. This, at least, is the Isolde of one's aural dreams: no singer could be humanly expected to encompass such a range—but then, Wagner's later operas were not written with a tremendously realistic sense of ordinary mortals' musical capabilities.

*Tristan* had its first performance in 1865 in Munich, under the new-found patronage of Ludwig II of Bavaria. Wagner's fortunes had sunk even lower after the Wesendonk episode and the disastrous performance of *Tannhäuser* at the Paris Opéra in 1861, for which the composer had refused to make alterations necessary to please an audience with definite notions of what it wanted for its entertainment. Ludwig's lavish financial support and hero-worship were what he needed to survive; he had also won the fanatically complete devotion of Cosima von Bülow, Liszt's daughter and a married woman, who later became his second wife. Over the next few years Wagner lived happily at Triebschen on Lake Lucerne, where he completed *Die Meistersinger von Nürnberg*, which was triumphantly produced in Munich in 1868, and continued work on the *Ring*.

Wagner's impatience with the restrictions and unimaginative management of existing opera houses had long been simmering. Ludwig had promised him a theatre in Munich, but the scheme was blocked by the King's opponents and Wagner had to organize his own solution to the problems of staging his operas. In 1872 the north Bavarian town of Bayreuth gave him a site on the top of a hill, and work began on what would incidentally become the largest free-standing timber-framed building in the world. More importantly, it was to be free of commercial considerations and run by neither impresarios nor prima donnas. Money was raised by public subscription and a massive subvention from Ludwig. Worlds away from Patti's Covent Garden, Wagner stated his principle:

It would be well to keep in mind the fact that this undertaking has nothing to do with a money-making theatrical enterprise, the performances will be attended only by invited guests and the patrons of the undertaking: no one will be allowed to pay for admission. On the other hand, I have already provided for a sufficient number of seats to be placed at the disposal of the citizens of Bayreuth—these to be distributed free of charge.

Needless to say, it did not work out quite like this, but by 1876 Wagner was in complete artistic control of the most advanced theatre of its time.

The admirable features of the auditorium are well known—the sunken orchestra pit, the superb acoustics, the simplicity of decoration and the spartan seating arrangements, ranged as in an amphitheatre, without the usual tiers of boxes. There was a huge stage, elaborate machinery, and remarkably sophisticated lighting equipment. The lowering of the house lights during performance was not quite as unprecedented as is usually made out—Wagner took the idea from the Vitinghoff Theatre in Riga, also deeply raked and wooden, where he had been a conductor in 1837–9. But despite all this advanced technology and noble thinking there must have been something faintly comical about the first festival in 1876, even if only, as poor Nietzsche found, the reality was so very far from the ideal. Over the years great curiosity about the project had been aroused throughout Europe and the town was quite unable to accommodate the influx of visitors. The pilgrims, who included Grieg, Liszt, Bruckner, and Saint-Saëns, spent much of their time trying to find something to eat—'throughout the whole duration of the Festival,' wrote another, Tchaikovsky, 'food forms the chief interest of the public; the artistic representations take a secondary place. Cutlets, baked potatoes, omelettes—all are discussed much more eagerly than Wagner's music.' An air of bathos hung over the proceedings, and even today there is still something pompous in the conception of Bayreuth—as dishonest in its way as the sensational-ism of the Paris Opéra, but much more significant as a national monument: as one critic Josef Stolzing-Czerny put it, 'as the Moslem sinks trembling to his knees at the sight of Mecca, so we Germans are moved when we behold the summit and culmination of German cultural achievement.' Bayreuth is as much a temple as it is an opera house.

None of this aura of incense, however, can detract from the greatness of *Der Ring des Nibelungen*, which was first presented in its entirety at the first festival. Although the *Ring* takes its ambience and some of its plot and characters from Norse mythology, its ethics and structure are based in Greek tragedy: specifically, in the dynastic working-out of justice after an initial wrong, which Aeschylus had explored in *The Oresteia*. It is a work which bites deep into the spirit of its age, but also raises some of the basic questions about moral and social life which pose themselves, in some form or another, to every epoch and culture. For the prima donna it offers first and last the supreme and exhausting challenge of Brünnhilde as a test of endurance and also a test of intelligence. She begins in *Die Walküre* as her father's obedient daughter, blindly fulfilling the militarist notions of Valhalla, until Siegmund shows her the real loneliness of the hero, and the tragic but necessary consequences of defiance. She sides with the outcast rebels against her father's weary assertion of the old law, and is duly punished, her godhead taken away. Reborn as an isolated mortal, she falls in love with Siegfried, a wild boy of the woods, who knows no fear and is completely open to experience—

qualities which might save the world. The ring he gives her is a pledge of love, and not the poisoned crux of a desperate power struggle: she refuses to give it up, even to save her father. When she believes herself betrayed by Siegfried, she becomes mad for vengeance, in music similar in idiom to that given to the Isolde of Act I. Then, when every treason is uncovered and the boy she loves is dead, she reaches her own plateau of ecstatic acceptance, gladly sacrificing herself to whatever comes after the curse on the ring has been lifted. As vocalist, a Brünnhilde has to meet the whooping of 'Ho-jo-to-ho', hard to pitch accurately; the solemn unearthly stillness of the *Todesverkündigung* scene with Siegmund; the long modulations of emotion of the last scene of *Siegfried* (which prostrated Melba), building towards its final reckless laughter. In *Götterdämmerung* there is no shirking the sheer volume required in the opening duet or the ferocious second act, and the opera ends with what *The Guinness Book of Records* claims as the longest aria in the repertoire—the 'Immolation' scene—which must seem like a marshalling of all that has gone before, a meditative and exalted final statement. Successful Brünnhildes, like successful Normas, can be counted on the fingers of perhaps two hands. It is not so much a matter of hitting the high notes—indeed Birgit Nilsson has pointed out how much of the role lies in the lower-middle of the soprano range—as of passing the test of stamina to the point at which one can find some energy to inflect and shade the text. A Brünnhilde cannot get through on sheer brutal accuracy of attack.

By the end of the first Bayreuth Festival, Wagner's debts had rocketed still further, and he seriously considered emigrating to America to escape his creditors, the sickness of Germany, and the Jewish influences which he so feared and hated. But his music was slowly making its way out of the *avant garde* into the standard repertory. In 1875 the first Wagner opera had been presented at Covent Garden—*Lohengrin*, in an Italian translation by Marchesi's husband. A company from Leipzig toured the *Ring* round Europe. Bayreuth closed for lack of funds, but Wagner decided to stay in the domestic calm of his mansion Wahnfried ('Peace from delusion') and worked on his last opera *Parsifal*, which he completed in Palermo and which reopened Bayreuth in 1882, a year before his death in Venice.

Wagner's relations with prima donnas were generally tetchy. After Schröder-Devrient, there was none he held in any great awe.

He had an edgy time with Pauline Viardot, with whom he had sung the *Tristan* duet in front of an unimpressed Berlioz, and finally he quarrelled with her over the Jewish question. He wanted Therese Tietjens for Isolde, but could not get her, and the part went to Malvina, wife of the first Tristan, Ludwig Schnorr, who died shortly after the first performance moaning, 'Farewell, Siegfried! Console my Richard!' Malvina Schnorr later became an agent in the revelation to King Ludwig of the adulterous relations between Wagner and Cosima, with difficult consequences for all. A soprano from Vienna, Amalie Materna, sang the first Bayreuth Brünnhilde and Kundry in *Parsifal*. She suffered from what became a familiar Wagnerian problem: although a fine and strong singer, her appearance was homely. Wagner's 'favourite child' was a young lyric-coloratura soprano from the Court Opera at Berlin.

Lilli Lehmann (1848–1929) came from a family of professional singers, and her mother was an old friend of Wagner's. In the first Bayreuth *Ring* she was cast as a Rhinemaiden, a Valkyrie, and the carolling Woodbird of *Siegfried*—all parts lying at the lightest and brightest end of the vocal spectrum. Her account of the rehearsal period (the only one to survive from any of the singers) is unfortunately stronger on adulation and rapture than precise detail:

> These days were, in their way, unique and never to be repeated—Wagner in his full creative power, the splendidly liberating ambience and those particular artistic and stimulating perform-ances that are gone forever. There was the sound of the orchestra, made up only of the greatest players; and the music itself which lifted us up to the great genius—all combined to produce a state of inspired exaltation. It was a powerful and strange magic spell that remains in my memory and, all pettiness gone, still works on my emotions . . .

She does, however, describe how Wagner wept with joy when he first heard the Rhinemaidens sing their trio; how vividly he assumed various characters in rehearsal (flinging himself into the role of Sieglinde with such passionate abandon that the stolid Siegmund blushed at his embrace); how he told her of his plans to perform other composers' great operas at Bayreuth; how he 'sat on the stage, his legs crossed and the score on his lap'. After the festival was over he wrote to her expressing his gratitude—she was also one of the artists who had not insisted on a fee:

> Oh Lilli, Lilli! You were the most beautiful of all—and you are right, dear child—it will never come again. That was the magic of it all—my Rhinemaidens! Fidi [Wagner's son Siegfried] sings their songs all the time . . . And now you are really engaged—my congratulations!

The engagement proved, in fact, a minor disaster for Wagner. Lehmann was maltreated by her fiancé, later Bayreuth's technical director, and broke off the liaison. In 1882 Wagner summoned her back to Bayreuth to lead the Flower Maidens in *Parsifal*. She accepted, and took over the responsibility of rehearsing the ensemble. Wagner was again enraptured by the result, but at the eleventh hour she withdrew, feeling that she could not stomach the proximity of her ex-fiancé. Since 1870 she had been restricted to Berlin by an imperial contract which only allowed outside performances with a special dispensation from the Kaiser. Now her international career had just begun, with appearances in Vienna and London. She probably benefited from the enforced stability of her early years, for despite her enormous repertory (170 roles in 119 operas), she was no infant marvel. Her gifts were a tenacious will and a patient musical intelligence. In utter contrast to Schröder-Devrient, she sang after the best classical models. Preparing Isolde she sought, in her own words, 'a beautiful legato in the fine Italian style; for after all there is only one perfect art of song', rehearsing 'every phrase hundreds of times . . . gradually increasing my physical and vocal endurance'. She was in the process of making an extraordinary passage, from being a singer of the 'nightingale' mould and timbre to one who could master Wagner's sternest demands. Her achievement turned out even more extraordinary than that, for somehow she managed to keep her voice slim and firm enough to continue singing coloratura parts. She managed this less through physical stamina as through her deep understanding of the technicalities of singing, and her book on the subject, *Meine Gesangskunst* (translated as *How to Sing*) shows a thorough grasp of the physiology of voice production. Few prima donnas have had such a strong intellectual awareness of their art.

Lehmann's first Isolde was sung in 1884 in London, a city which did not meet with her approval. She roundly deplored the carryings-on of Mapleson's management, the prima donna Christine Nilsson, and the fogs which even in spring 'smothered every pleasure'—they must indeed have been a deadly hazard to singers' delicate throats, and their prevalence in winter must have been one consideration in generally starting the opera season in May. Contemporary verdicts on her interpretation are oddly mixed: Wolf objected to her making a virago of Isolde, while Hanslick urged her to be cautious—'Her far from heroic voice is no match for the merciless surf of the Wagnerian orchestra.' Caution was not, however, in Lilli Lehmann's nature. In the words of Henry Pleasants, she 'revelled in the accomplishment of the impossible; she accepted challenges with the self-destructive zest of a Malibran, with the advantage that hers was a more resilient constitution'. Her next bold move was in the direction of New York and the newly opened German-oriented Metropolitan Opera House. To get there for a decent period she had to break her Berlin contract, incurring the Kaiser's wrath, an enormous fine, and an order banishing her from all German opera houses which lasted until 1891. It was well worth the trouble, for she got exactly what she wanted at the Met, becoming its first regular dramatic soprano. She sang Brünnhilde there for the first time, as well as her other major roles of Isolde, Leonore, Aida, Donna Anna, Norma, Carmen, and Violetta—the latter in Italian as well as German when the Met modified its language policy.

Lehmann loved the Americans, finding their high moral tone and earnestness sympathetic. She was a fanatic vegetarian and anti-vivisectionist, and nothing pleased her more in New York than the fact that the whipping of horses was forbidden. Society ladies who appeared before her with feathers or plumes in their hats were treated to a stern lecture. She also became known for the austerity, bordering on stinginess, of her personal life. The chambermaids in her New York hotel were shocked to discover that Madame Lehmann not only washed her own stockings and handkerchiefs, she even hung them up to dry in the bathroom. She refused to tip the liftboys and preferred to stand on the streetcar rather than hire a cab and waste a dime on comfort.

In 1891 she began teaching, and two of her pupils, Geraldine Farrar and Olive Fremstad, became the outstanding American prima donnas of the pre-war years. Lessons were conducted in conditions of Prussian discipline: the over-emoting Farrar had her hands tied behind her back—'Now express your feelings with your voice!'

commanded Lehmann. One day Lehmann threw a book at Fremstad, who then stormed out in tears, vowing never to return. On the stairs she met Lehmann's soon discarded husband Paul Kalisch, a second-rate tenor she had peremptorily married in the vain hope of drilling him into a great Siegfried and Tristan. 'What are *you* worried about?' he said to Fremstad on hearing her story, 'She does that to me the whole time.'

In 1896, Lehmann met her real match when she returned to Bayreuth and came up against Wagner's widow Cosima, who now governed the place like a beleaguered high priestess defending the purity of the cult. In 1886 Cosima had invited Lehmann to sing in the first Bayreuth *Tristan*, but Lehmann had furiously declined when she learnt that the role she was being offered was not Isolde, but Brangäne. Cosima's zeal, as so often in such situations, had led to a hardening and narrowing quite alien to Wagner's pioneering theatrical sense. She did not lack her own production ideas, but in the event of any argument, she referred back to the authority of her dead husband, often seeking confirmation from her son Siegfried, who had been aged six at the time of the first festival. Absolute and exclusive rights were kept over *Parsifal*, performances of which became the centre of the Bayreuth mystique. The opera could be seen nowhere else, and owing to its elements of Christian ritual, applause was forbidden. This was an unjustifiable tradition, since Wagner had actually encouraged the first audience to applaud at the end of the opera and was even said to have let out a loud 'bravo' at the end of the Flower-maidens' scene in the second act. More lastingly serious in its effects was the growth of a Bayreuth-sanctioned conception of Wagner singing. It flourished under the tutelage of the chorus-master Julius Kniese and consisted of bringing Wagner's vocal line as close as possible to speech, at the expense of rhythm and tone, rather than allowing it a natural musical flow. Wagner, on the contrary, had always insisted on his music's melodiousness and appreciated the legato that Italian singers brought to it. But Kniese's coaching led to rasping, barking, forcing: Shaw found the 1894 *Parsifal* 'an abomination . . . German singers at Bayreuth do not know how to sing: they shout; and you can see them make a vigorous stoop and lift with their shoulders, like coal-heavers, when they have a difficult note to tackle, a *pianissimo* on any note above the stave being impossible to them.'

Lehmann came back to Bayreuth as the most famous Brünnhilde

in a world obsessed with Wagner. After his death, the controversy faded and his status was undisputed. For the *fin de siècle* generation, he was the great image of the Artist—titanic, uncompromising, visionary. It was not only the initiated writers, artists, and composers who worshipped him, but the mass of music lovers. Bayreuth had become a major tourist destination ('miserable public' wrote Romain Rolland of the 1896 festival, 'phonies, Jews, snobs, hypocrites, Yankees, slow-witted English and repulsive Germans, stinking as high as the Alps'). Ordinary public taste had adjusted to Wagner's originality to the point at which Shaw in 1889 could tease:

> Oh Bayreuth, Bayreuth, valley of humiliation for the smart ones of the world! To think that this Wagner, once the very safest man in Europe to ridicule, should turn out the prime success of the century. To be reduced to a piteous plea that you always admitted that there were some lovely bits in *Lohengrin*! . . . Yes, the cranks were right after all. And now—now . . . it is not merely a question of whether he or Offenbach is the more melodious, but of whether he is to be accepted as the Luther of a new Reformation, the Plato of a new philosophy, the Messiah who is really to redeem the fall and lead us back to the garden of Eden . . .

Queen Victoria herself commanded a performance of *Lohengrin* at Windsor Castle and wrote in her diary, 'I was simply enchanted. It is the most glorious composition, so poetic, so dramatic, and one might also say, religious in feeling and full of sadness, pathos and tenderness.' Would-be fashionable young ladies like Jeannette Marshall (whose sneer at Patti is quoted on p. 105) played piano arrangements of the Ride of the Valkyries and the Good Friday Music from *Parsifal*. Cosima's stagings even made it all eminently respectable, and Shaw found Rhinemaidens swimming about in muslin tea-gowns, giving 'a strong impression that they had forgotten their gloves and hats'. The romance of opera was German and Wagnerian: Italian opera now seemed meretricious, slightly vulgar, even laughable. Without the continuing patronage of the prima donna it would have been even more scorned.

Lehmann was deeply offended by Cosima's slighting attitude to her present eminence as well as her authority as a member of the original 1876 cast. There was a tight-lipped quarrel between the two women over a red wig, which neither won. Lehmann's pique is evident in her account of the events, from which one gets the distinct impression that she would very much have liked Cosima's job herself.

> I suffered to see how the form of the *Ring*, which we had all so lovingly absorbed and taken away with us, together with our thoughts of its creator, was now being dislocated in the very place that was its home . . . All roads may lead to Rome but to the Bayreuth of today there is but one—the road of slavish subjection. There is no true conception of how valuable individual artistry can be . . . Cosima was not only very clever and well-informed. She had also assumed the authority of judgment peculiar to the aristocracy, so that what she announced was accepted as infallible.

Ironically, Shaw was reluctant to judge Lehmann's Bayreuth Brünnhilde the exemplar of 'individual artistry': 'She acts intelligently, sings effectively and in tune, and is attractive enough, attaining in all these respects a degree of excellence that makes it impossible to call her commonplace; but for all that she is conventional, and takes the fullest advantage of the fact that plenty of ideas suggested by Wagner will attach themselves to her if she only stands her ground impressively.'

Shaw's final comment on this Brünnhilde was that she would doubtless make a very good Marguerite in Gounod's *Faust*, a role she did indeed sing. This is telling. One suspects that Lehmann, for all the praise given to her versatility, was not a true Wagnerian soprano—or rather she became one by training and will-power, not by the exploitation of a physical resource as was the case with Flagstad or Birgit Nilsson. Her fame as a Wagnerian was due to the fact that there were very few singers at the time capable of understanding how to sing his music at all. When her recordings were made in 1907, when she was almost sixty, she bequeathed only one Wagner extract—a bumpily phrased 'Du bist der lenz' which most lyric sopranos can match up to—and the outstanding items come from the more familiar repertory of Mozart, Bellini, Verdi, and even Meyerbeer. Oddly enough, the singer she most suggests is Melba—a Melba with more piercing attack and intelligent colouring. But there is the same limpid tone and smoothness of production, apart from the odd jerk between head and chest register, attributable to age, the same brilliance without weight, and the same no-nonsense briskness. Anything nostalgic, wistful, or seductive finds her lacking: Marchesi's daughter, herself a well-known singer, thought her ice-hard on stage. Her 'Casta Diva', for instance, is extraordinarily accurate and secure, but it fails to suggest a veiled high priestess: she cannot slide down those chromatic runs in a trance or suggest a woman with a secret passion. What is truly magnificent is her scaling of the harsher reaches of Mozart's music. The coloratura is amazing—far neater and truer than Patti's efforts at the same era of life. Her 'Martern aller Arten' in J. B. Steane's words 'meets every technical demand, and has power and majesty beyond comparison'; Donna Anna's long narrative and aria beginning 'Don Ottavio, son morta' is truly arresting and grand in conception—here is a woman well able to bludgeon her fiancé into submission and fight back against her seducer. The fact that she had suffered from asthma as a child makes her technique all the more astonishing.

Mozart played a large part in the long twilight of Lehmann's career. She found the opportunity to satisfy her autocratic tendency in Salzburg's early Mozart festivals, where she managed to sing, produce, assemble casts, and dictate artistic policy. Nothing daunted her: she disapproved strongly of Mahler's 1906 *Don Giovanni* and brought forth her own competing version for Salzburg, which she rehearsed in her Berlin home. Mahler found the result absurdly amateurish. In 1910 she left Salzburg and opera, but continued to sing publicly until her seventy-second year. She paid eloquent and justifiable tribute to her own sterling achievement in her auto-biography:

I have gone my own road proudly, the way of the will, of knowledge, and of capacity, in accord with my aspirations and abilities. Thanks to my education, my talents and industry, I have been able to pursue it with increasing authority. I quickly grasped what availed in art, and gladly learned of everything, with the firm resolution to attain the greatest possible perfection in the realm of art.

By the beginning of the twentieth century, a number of definite types and career patterns had emerged from the Wagnerian soprano. There was the great might-have-been, Hedwig Reicher-Kinder-mann, who died at twenty-nine; the latter-day Schröder-Devrient,

Katharina Klafsky, persistently out of tune but 'elemental, tremendous in everything'; the steely-voiced Rosa Sucher, favoured by Cosima at Bayreuth; and above all these, the Croatian Milka Ternina. Her performances of Isolde with Jean de Reszke as her Tristan in London and New York were written into legend, and her Brünnhilde, Tosca, and Fidelio were equally celebrated; but she was cut short in her prime by a muscular disease which had the embarrassing side-effect of making one side of her face twitch in a manner which made her appear permanently lascivious. The next generation had been trained with the possibility of Wagner from the start, but their records do not reveal a Golden Age beneath the hissing. J. B. Steane's verdict is of 'a higher proportion of plodding ungainliness then than now, more choppy phrasing, less attention to detail and less understanding of the need for light and shade . . . careless over the precise length of notes and occasionally getting intervals wrong'. In time, the baneful absolutism of Cosima at Bayreuth lost much of its influence. The festival closed at the beginning of the First World War, when the copyright on *Parsifal* expired, and it only reopened in 1924 under Siegfried Wagner, whose policy was cautiously liberal. Bayreuth became a symbol of Wagnerism rather than the opera house which set standards and arbitrated style.

In the inter-war years Wagner performance came to maturity with an incomparable generation of singers and conductors, whose nobility is evident in the surviving records of Frida Leider (1888–1975), the most celebrated Isolde and Brünnhilde of her time. What the New York critic W. J. Henderson said of Lehmann's Brünnhilde is also good for what we hear on record of Leider's: 'She was possessed of that rare combination of traits and equipment which made it possible for her to delineate the divinity in womanhood and womanhood in divinity, the mingling of the unapproachable goddess and the melting, pitying human being.' There is no sense of strain at any part of the range of Leider's voice, and she sounds as rich and full in the vital lower reaches as in her glowing top notes. She hadn't the sharp brilliance or agility of Lehmann, but the voice's 'natural' tone was weighted with more colour and feeling. Even more remarkable is its liquidity—the ability to move through long phrases with the values of good Italianate *legato* kept prominent throughout. Second-rate Wagnerians always make the listener aware of the edges and corners in the music, points at which the singer snatches a bit of breath or fudges one note to get to another on schedule. Leider never loses her poise or sonority: her fault, if anything, is the opposite. The recording situation gave her, she admitted, a sort of inverted stage-fright, and she found it much easier to sing when moving about a stage in costume than when standing still in an empty hall at eleven in the morning. She reports one occasion when the first half of the *Fidelio* aria was recorded in one hall, from which she had to move to finish in another hall, with completely different acoustics and atmospheric conditions. There are times, such as her 1928 recording of Brünnhilde's Immolation, when verbal point and urgency are absent, and a disengaged smoothness of line takes over. Yet this slight dullness never affected her in the theatre: 'Leider was quite incapable of a routine performance,' wrote Vincent Sheean. 'She was good or bad, she was often great, but she was never mediocre.'

In her quaint and unrevealing memoirs, she describes her modest Berlin upbringing and a brief early career as a bank clerk. Her aspirations were initially charged by the acclaim showered on visiting prima donnas like Emmy Destinn or Geraldine Farrar, but Lilli Lehmann's autobiography soon put her on the straight and narrow path of artistic idealism. Her teachers included Alban Berg's sister, and she made her provincial début at the relatively late age of twenty-six. Unlike Materna, Lehmann, or Flagstad, she did not skip about for a while in operetta: Venus in *Tannhäuser* was her first role, and she never ventured far out of the dramatic soprano repertory. Apart from her Wagnerian roles, she was also admired as Donna Anna, Leonore, Strauss's Marschallin, and Amelia in *Un Ballo in Maschera*; in her early years she even sang a few Normas. By 1923 she was prima donna at the Berlin Staatsoper, and in 1924 she first went to London, where she sang in the golden Bruno Walter seasons with Lotte Lehmann, Maria Olczewska, Lauritz Melchior, and Friedrich Schorr: her popularity at Covent Garden proved immense and lasting. In 1927 she sang Brünnhilde in Italian at La Scala, which she significantly considered 'extremely beneficial to my technique. In using the open Italian vowels, my throat expanded without effort, my breath moved more freely. I succeeded in carrying this over into my German performances . . .' In 1928 she sang for the first of four years in Chicago, until the company there fell victim to the

Depression. Leider's success had been uninterrupted but exhausting, her only holidays being the enforced leisure of transatlantic liners.

Then, in 1933, Hitler was elected Chancellor of Germany. Leider's violinist husband was Jewish: 'I was completely unprepared for this news, which caused me great distress. But artists are too easily inclined to ignore what might otherwise disturb their art, so, after the first excitement, I threw myself into my work even more intensely.' She paid dearly for her naïvete. Wagner became a standard-bearer of the Nazi ideology of German culture, and to sing his music under the new régime was seen, in America especially, as a political act. Hitler was a regular visitor to Bayreuth and a close friend of the English-born Winifred Wagner, who had inherited control from her late husband Siegfried. She won all sorts of exemptions from the tyranny which stifled everyone and everything else in Germany, and Hitler personally guaranteed the festival's financial security. In 1933 the Führer patronized a new Bayreuth *Ring* lavishly produced by Heinz Tietjen, who also ran her home opera house in Berlin and who imported his singers for the summer. Leider sang Brünnhilde. When she had first sung at Bayreuth in 1928, she found the approach old-fashioned, although she learnt much from Bayreuth-trained singers. It was here that she considered herself to have mastered the role of Kundry for the first time, and when Tietjen (the first person outside the Wagner family to have control of production) was appointed, he did away with many of the more antiquated conventions of staging. But by 1938 the festival had been turned into a glorified political rally, with swastika flags in the Festspielhaus and Hitler in formal residence at Wahnfried. Leider's husband was forced into exile in Switzerland, and she herself suffered a nervous collapse which effectively ended her operatic career.

Leider had few vocal problems in her later years, apart from the natural contraction of her topmost register. However, in her first season at the Met, during that fateful year of 1933, there was an electrifying incident of which Vincent Sheean gives an eloquent account. The occasion was a performance of *Die Walküre*:

> She was on her knees before Wotan (Friedrich Schorr), with her noble head humbly bent and her left hand at her throat . . . She had reached the point where she had to sing '*War es so*

*schmachlich?'* She sang the first two words and notes—that is, '*War es*'—after which a strange, very small sound came out of her throat and no note followed. That weird small sound is quite impossible to describe and if I had not been sitting so close I could have not heard it; I suppose most of the three thousand people there present did not. The click (if it was a click) seemed like the electrocution, the murder of the great voice . . . Leider kept her head down and I saw her shake it in a kind of fury . . . She had been singing the whole performance over a bad cold, so bad that she could not even speak. Now the voice itself, the very sense of her existence, refused its divine grace, and there she was, on her knees, with the ruin of a great career in plain view in front of her. Such a concentrated ordeal seldom befalls an artist. I felt, or imagined I felt, the struggle of her will to conquer her body. Then she threw back her really grand head and looked out beyond all the three thousand of us to some utter truth beyond us, opened her mouth with confidence, it seemed to me, and by some power (I could see her throat quivering) the voice was given again. From then on to the end of the act Leider sang with everything an artist has to give, although the sacrifice of her voice must have been tragic.

As Sheean goes on to consider, this sense of knife-edged excitement, tension, and awe are all fundamental to the experience of Wagner's music, and it was the induction of so much over-wrought emotion that led Nietzsche to pose his 'physiological objections' to it. An artist like Leider could bring her audiences to a pitch of silent hysteria, as Sheean also demonstrates: 'Isolde and Brünnhilde were hers, and there are no moderate ways of expressing how deeply she could move us in them . . . I have been so shaken by her Isolde, again and again, that I could no longer stand up, and had to go and sit on the floor of the house in that area at the back where the standees go. Some of those *Tristan* performances left me very uncertain of my own surroundings—so dazed that it was physically difficult to get out of the crowd and into the cold, wet street where reality slowly returned.' Wagner himself had understood the nature of the monster he had given birth to, writing to Mathilde Wesendonk during rehearsals that 'This *Tristan* is turning into something *dreadful* . . . only mediocre performances can save me. Completely good ones are bound to drive people crazy.'

Leider recovered her voice, although Sheean claims that she was 'never restored to full vocal power'. She herself does not even mention the incident in her memoirs. The Met re-engaged her in 1934, but after that she remained in Europe, for reasons that are not clear: she claimed that anti-German feelings were running high, while the Met archives suggest arguments over fees.

After the beginning of the war, Leider gave only recitals, and then retreated to her country estate near the Russian border. Her memoirs give a long and harrowing report of the last days of the hostilities, which she was clearly amazed to survive. There was a grotesque incident when the advancing Russian army passed through and a party requisitioned her house: 'They noticed a picture of me in my *Walküre* costume with helmet, shield and spear, whereupon the chauffeur, pointing at it, cried "Soldier!" and aimed his pistol at me. The officer immediately knocked it out of his hand.' Later the soldiers found a trunk full of her wigs and stage accoutrements and cavorted around dressed as Valkyries.

Leider's withdrawal opened the American door for another singer, about whom Leider sagely says nothing in her book and who was herself to suffer from the humiliations of war. Kirsten Flagstad (1895–1962) is the second Nordic phenomenon of opera. Like Jenny Lind, Flagstad transfigured her innate dullness. 'When I am not dealing with art I am the most commonplace person in the world. I am not a bit mysterious or unusual or complex. I am an absolutely average Norwegian,' she claimed in all sincerity. Whereas Lind was calculating and deeply self-aware, Flagstad always appeared faintly bewildered by her immense gift. Her voice poured forth like a torrential force of nature, something beyond her own reason or control. Before going on stage, she played Patience, as if innocent of what was about to befall her. 'I see her now,' wrote Vincent Sheean, 'in her dressing room at the Metropolitan . . . calm and majestic, smiling kindly, braiding her hair with a vocal score of the opera open on the table before her, an Isolde who had never suffered humiliation of spirit or the wish to die. She had been knitting and put the work down beside the *Tristan* score while she talked to us. After we left I imagine she resumed her knitting . . . No more tranquil approach to unbridled passion has come under my observation.' Her family background was strongly musical and she had undergone a sound and steady provincial training, but she had no burning motivation: there was no great dedication to singing or the theatre, and a few lessons in Dalcrozean *plastique** gave her all the ideas about acting she thought she needed.† 'I don't know anything, really, about my voice . . . why it behaves as it does I have no idea,' was another typical Flagstad disclaimer. All she wanted, she said, was a husband, a family, and a quiet, comfortable life.

In her operatic backwater of Oslo, she had sung everything from Tosca and Aida to musical comedy, and over twenty quiet years her voice had slowly increased in size and weight. In the early 1930s, without any sense of approaching her destiny, she began to sing some of the lighter Wagner roles—Elisabeth, Elsa, and Eva in *Meistersinger*. Even though she had been given a score of *Lohengrin* for her tenth birthday and had immediately learnt parts of Elsa's music, Wagner played little part in her life, and as late as 1930 she had almost fallen asleep with boredom at her first hearing of *Tristan*. But in 1932 she herself sang Isolde in Oslo with enough *éclat* to win a recommendation to Winifred Wagner at Bayreuth, where she sang in the 1933 and 1934 *Rings*. A talent scout from the Met had heard her as early as 1929 and had evinced interest, but it was only after Bayreuth that they followed it up. 'If I had known what this engagement would lead to, I really believe I would have refused it on the spot,' she later reflected. She was summoned to St Moritz, where she underwent a gruelling audition in a heavily curtained room that muffled the splendour of her voice. The Met had lost Leider and were anxious for a new soprano who could satisfy New York's insatiable Wagner-lust, but they do not seem to have had any high hopes of a raw and gauche Norwegian who had only just begun to sing in German. She was accepted diffidently and bundled off to Prague for some intensive coaching under George Szell. Her début was as Sieglinde in February 1935. It was an instant, overnight, copybook sensation: the soprano Geraldine Farrar, scheduled to give a radio talk in the interval of the performance, was moved to throw away her script and instead gushed about the astonishing newcomer. Four days later Flagstad sang Isolde; by the end of the month she had appeared as the *Walküre* and *Götterdämmerung* Brünnhilde, and in

---

* 'Rage: clenched fist and five steps downstage in a majestic manner; sexual passion: hands clasped on breast and head turned away' is how Sheean describes her stage manner.
† What do you need to sing Wagner? she was asked: 'A pair of comfortable shoes,' she replied.

April she was Kundry in *Parsifal*—all three operas being quite new to her.

Flagstad did not have Leider's intensity or Lehmann's intelligence. There were always plenty, Toscanini among them, who thought little of her interpretative power. What she had was the ability to sing Wagner with calm, literal accuracy. She was an absolutely faithful singer of music that had previously seemed to defeat that possibility. As the *New Yorker* put it, 'Madame Flagstad has the superlative gift of being able to do her job.' She was fortunate in having perfect pitch, but her musicianship went deeper than that: W. J. Henderson remarked at the time of her first New York appearance that 'There are no evasions of the demands of the music. She does not alter rhythms, introduce questionable tone-qualities or indulge in any of the other tricks which some singers use.' Vincent Sheean wrote that her voice was the greatest he had ever heard, 'the greatest in volume, range, security, beauty of tone, everything a voice can have, and all of one piece, never a break in it, all rolling out with no evidence of effort or strain even in the most difficult passages. The only defect to be found in her remarkable performances was that they did not express what Wagner wrote.' The qualification is, of course, somewhat crippling. It is not just the fact that German was not her native tongue—in her autobiography she describes the painstaking way she found out 'what it all meant', at least in terms of the dictionary—but the lack of an entire dimension of passion and urgency. Her singing is placid through music which bespeaks rage and obsession. We complain about the tonal imperfections of other Wagner singers and shake our heads at the thought of the Bayreuth 'bark', but Flagstad's straightforward perfection—for it is something near that—is not the answer either.

Until 1941, she maintained an effortless supremacy in the Wagnerian repertory. The gap between supply and demand was such that she was given little opportunity to try anything else, although Edward Johnson, the manager of the Met, begged her in vain to sing Norma. She was married to a lugubrious Norwegian lumber merchant and hotel-owner, Henry Johansen, whose wealth meant that she need only sing what, when, and where she wanted. Most of her professional year was spent in the major North American centres and it is no exaggeration to say that her box-office drawing-power saved the Met from bankruptcy in the final phase of the Depression. She loved Hollywood and movie magazines and the thought of herself as a celebrity: despite Garbo-like protestations of a desire to be left alone, anonymous, etc., she relished every last handclap of public adulation with a pleasure of which only the pure in heart are capable. And like Jenny Lind, she did achieve a general fame beyond the opera-going audience. Ogden Nash wrote comic verse celebrating the singer from Scandinavia, 'land of peace and sane behavia'; she sang on the Bing Crosby Show and in the movies. Again like Lind, her appeal came from a well-projected simplicity of manner which, after sophisticated prima donnas like Maria Jeritza or Lily Pons, made her seem wholesome and 'unspoilt by success'.

It was this very aspect of her public image which left her so cruelly exposed during the Second World War. She immediately suffered from the automatic association of Wagner with Hitler and from the revulsion from any aspect of German culture. By 1940 and the fall of Norway, she declared herself 'exhausted to the verge of hysteria' by five years of American fame. Everyone expected the unsullied Flagstad to do the right and noble thing—fight the Nazis—but she took the course of returning to Norway and her husband, a member of the extreme right-wing and later collaborationist Quisling party. She had 'no idea' about politics, she had 'no political views at all': she only wanted to be reunited with her husband as a private citizen, not as a national symbol. Norwegians in America tried to persuade her to stay, arguing that her return would be a propaganda victory for the occupying régime, and the ambassador himself stepped in. But Flagstad was adamant, even though her passage back to Norway would take her across Germany, where she was suspected of having secured a visa through friendly Nazi contacts. In fact, once back in Norway, she had rigorously refused any public engagements in occupied territory, singing only occasionally in neutral Sweden and Switzerland. 'Like millions of others,' she later explained, 'I had no choice but to sit it out. There was nothing I could do, nothing my background and temperament had prepared me to do but to wait.' After the war, however, she began to show quite exceptional courage and determination in salvaging her reputation.

Her husband had continued to operate his timber business through the war and had supplied the enemy, even though he had resigned from the Quisling party. After the war, he was arrested but died in a prison hospital before being committed to trial. All the family's assets were sequestrated, and Flagstad had no alternative but to resume her career. The beneficial side effect of her withdrawal was a wonderful Indian summer for her rested voice, which remained at its peak until she was in her late fifties. London gave her the benefit of the doubt and reaped the reward of tolerance. Flagstad's pre-war performances at Covent Garden had been very successful, despite the continuing presence of Leider, and a début marred by a bad cold and a wound caused by a powder-compact falling from a box on to her head while she was watching a performance of *Götterdämmerung*. After the war, Covent Garden reopened without much money and cleverly re-established its international reputation by engaging singers such as Flagstad whose wartime conduct was politically dubious and whom other houses were initially reluctant to engage. She relearnt her roles in English, and sang Wagner in four fondly remembered seasons.

In the USA things were very different. Her first return there was primarily a private visit to her daughter, married and living in Arizona, but the protests began almost immediately. The Met had refused to take her back, but although their reasons were not altogether political—Helen Traubel had since assumed Flagstad's roles, and the management could not simply dispose of her—this gave a sort of official confirmation to the public's suspicions of her integrity. Before the war she had had her little vanities, problems with unsympathetic conductors, and pique if her appearances were not sold out. She now faced a barrage of hostility unparalleled in opera history. Apart from a flood of unpleasant press allegations, friends and colleagues, including her regular tenor partner Lauritz Melchior, with whom she had quarrelled violently in 1938, publicly wanted nothing to do with her; recitals at Carnegie Hall were picketed; in Philadelphia, a businessman hired a claque of college boys at $15 each, who booed her from the first note and hissed 'Nazi' while she was singing. Stink bombs were thrown and when fisticuffs broke out, the police were called into the concert hall. But she persevered for, as Henry Pleasants put it, 'She could be small in small matters, not so much childlike as childish. But in big matters she was big.' And there were plenty who stood by her, notably the young conductor and pianist Edwin McArthur, whom she assiduously patronized.

By 1951 she had won her way back to the Met. Her singing for a Jewish relief charity undoubtedly mollified her opposition. The tumult of applause which greeted her as Isolde lasted right the way through the Steersman's song, at the end of which a lone voice shouted, 'Welcome back'—but Rudolf Bing, the new manager of the Met, also reported a letter from the Broadway impresario Billy Rose comparing the re-engagement of Flagstad to the hypothetical appointment of Ilse Koch (the extermination camp official who had made lampshades out of human skin) as wardrobe mistress. Flagstad herself was dry-eyed throughout. She accepted the invitation to return to the Met not because she wanted to sing, but because she wanted to complete her moral rehabilitation. Having won this battle, she faced another, albeit much lesser, scandal. A recording of *Tristan und Isolde* conducted by Wilhelm Furtwängler was made, with Flagstad giving a superb account of herself. For some years in the theatre she had missed out Isolde's top Cs—yet in the recording they sounded gleaming and forceful. It eventually leaked out that incidents of the note had not been contributed by Flagstad at all, but by Elisabeth Schwarzkopf, whose husband Walter Legge had produced the recording. Flagstad had shown her appreciation with the gift of a superb diamond necklace. There was a good deal of outrage at this fairly innocent trick, and Flagstad was accused of artistic dishonesty. The incident, trivial as it was, had a peculiarly demoralizing effect, and hastened her retirement.

In her last years in the opera house, Flagstad broadened her repertory to take in two classical roles—Gluck's Alceste, with which in 1952 she took her farewell to the Met, and Dido in Purcell's *Dido and Aeneas*, which she sang for nothing but love in the tiny Mermaid Theatre in the London back garden of her friend the actor-manager Sir Bernard Miles. She expressed regret that she had not sung more Mozart and Strauss—she gave the first performance of his *Four Last Songs* at a London Promenade concert of 1950, also under Furtwängler—but it was typical of her to have turned down the opportunity to sing Strauss's Elektra on the grounds that the text was 'coarse and indecent'. In the concert hall she could range wider, as long as she included the obligatory chunk of Wagner, and some of her loveliest records are of songs by Grieg and Sibelius.

Her years of semi-retirement do not seem to have been very happy. She settled in Norway where she coped with an undercurrent of unpopularity caused by her wartime conduct. She did, however, become the first director of a newly founded Norwegian opera company and continued to make a few records for Decca. Their producer John Culshaw persuaded her in 1958 to learn the mezzo-soprano part of Fricka in *Das Rheingold*, for what was to be the first

**1.** Jacopo Amigoni (1682–1752), Portrait Group, *c*.1752, oil on canvas. Farinelli sits in the centre; the woman to whom he hands the music has been thought to be Faustina. One of the most relaxed and attractive of the many pictures of Farinelli.

**3.** Mara as Gluck's Armida.

**2.** Mrs Billington in 1801, the year of her return from Italy.

**5.** Isabella Colbran in the 'cantata' *Il Sogno di Partenope*, which she sang at La Scala in 1817.

**4.** Angelica Catalani as Susanna in *Le Nozze di Figaro*. Water-colour sketch by Chalon, 1815.

**7.** The young Giulia Grisi, who sang with Pasta in the first performance of Bellini's *Norma* in 1831.

**6.** The great Giuditta Pasta.

8. Maria Malibran, in a drawing by Léon Noel which extraordinarily catches her vulnerability and charm. 9. *above right* Malibran's sister Pauline Viardot as Gluck's Orphée, an interpretation of melancholy passion extolled by Berlioz and Dickens.

10. Grisi at the height of her career as the first true dramatic soprano: the winsome beauty has become handsome and formidable.

11. Therese Tietjens, Grisi's successor in roles like Lucrezia Borgia and Norma, as well as a powerful singer of Verdi.

12. Henriette Sontag, first of the nightingales, engraved in a style popular in the 1820s and 1830s. 13. *above right* A photograph of Jenny Lind taken during her American tour.
14. *right* Adelina Patti, the child prodigy.
15. *below* A postcard of Craig-y-nos, Patti's Welsh castle.

**16.** Wilhelmine Schröder-Devrient, *c.*1830: her immense personal magnetism is barely hinted at in this engraving.

**17.** The invincible Lilli Lehmann, with dog.

**18.** Her rival Lillian Nordica, the first American Brünnhilde. **19.** *right* Frida Leider as Isolde, an interpretation still remembered with awe.

20. *left* Olive Fremstad, photographed by Mishkin as Isolde. 21. *above* Birgit Nilsson rehearsing for the famous 1962 Bayreuth *Tristan und Isolde* with Wieland Wagner.

22. Kirsten Flagstad attained a popularity that no other Wagnerian soprano has ever approached: here the press catch her with a bevy of Girl Scouts paying their respects.

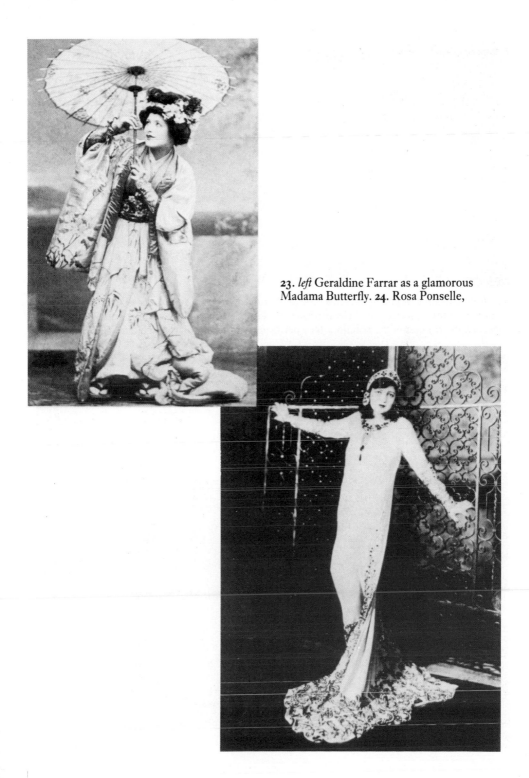

23. *left* Geraldine Farrar as a glamorous
Madama Butterfly. 24. Rosa Ponselle,

579664--WATCH YOUR CREDIT--INTERNATIONAL NEWSREEL PHO
SLUG (SCHUMAN HEINKE)

A BELOVED SINGER CELEBRATES HER 70TH BIRTHDAY
IN THE KITCHEN

LOS ANGELES....MME. ERNESTINE SCHUMANN-HEINK,
WORLD RENOWNED SINGER , IS HAPPY IN HER HOME
LIFE AND CELEBRATED HER 70TH BIRTHDAY ON JUNE 15TH
AT WORK IN HER KITCHEN . BUT SHE'LL CONTINUE TO
SING AS LONG AS SHE IS ABLE, AND WHILE PROUD OF
HER MUSICAL CAREER IS PROUDER STILL OF BEING,
ALL AT ONCE, A MOTHER, A GRANDMOTHER AND A GREAT
GRANDMOTHER. MME. SCHUMANN-HEINK HAS JUST WON
A JUDGEMENT AGAINST EDWIN CAREWE,FILM PRODUCER,
FOR $75,000 ALLEGING BREACH OF CONTRACT.
B-JUNE-16-31

**25.** *above* Ernestine Schumann-Heink, one of the first singers to exploit successfully the resources of the American publicity machine. **26.** Grace Moore impersonating Jenny Lind, receiving the tributes of the nobility after a performance of *Norma*, from the film *A Lady's Morals*.

27. A surprisingly pretty Nellie Melba in a title-role written for her, Saint-Saëns's Hélène: later photographs show her immovable and granite-faced.

28. Emmy Destinn, another great pre-war favourite at Covent Garden, seen here as a seductive Carmen, a role she sang during her Berlin years at the turn of the century.

29. *left* Eva Turner's first Turandot, Brescia, 1926. **30.** *above* Zinka Milanov rehearsing with a stage director for *Il Trovatore* at the Met. The reasons for her nickname '*la donna immobile*' are not hard to gauge.

31. *top left* The castrato caricatured: Velluti in 1825. Note the obvious symbolism of the double bass. 32. *above right* Catalani caricatured, quite unfairly, as a prima donna free with her favours. The occasion was the Cambridge Musical Festival of 1824. 33. *above* Patti caricatured in Paris in 1880 as a cat spewing forth money into an impresario's hat: the artist could equally have shown her swallowing the coins herself. 34. Madame Vera Galupe-Borszkh, the alias of Mr. Ira Siff, of the Gran Scena Opera Company.

35. Lotte Lehmann as Sieglinde in Act I of
*Die Walküre*. 36. *right* Maria Jeritza, one of
the great beauties among prima donnas,
possibly as Jenufa.

37. In 1963, Lehmann and Jeritza, brought together to discuss *Ariadne auf Naxos* with John
Gutman, buried the hatchet with a hysterical good humour that belied the violence of their
animosity during the Vienna years.

38. Emma Calvé in Massenet's *Hérodiade*.

39. Conchita Supervia.

40. *left* Mary Garden's scandalous Salome in Strauss' opera. 41. *above* Garden at her iciest, with the psychologist Professor Coué, whose methods briefly amused her.

**44**. Amelita Galli-Curci.

**42**. *above left* The enigmatic Claudia Muzio as Berthe in Meyerbeer's *Le Prophète*, photographed by Mishkin. **43**. *top right* Luisa Tetrazzini with her third husband. One of the more pitiful prima donna marriages, it ended in the law courts, with Tetrazzini suing for extortion. **45**. *above* Maria Callas as Norma, Catania, 1951. This rare photograph provides interesting evidence that Callas was not, as is often assumed, chronically fat throughout the early years of her career.

**46.** One of the finest of all musical intellects at work on her score during a recording session: Elisabeth Schwarzkopf in 1962.
**47.** *left* Janet Baker as Penelope in the famous Glyndebourne production of Monteverdi's *Il Ritorno d'Ulisse*.

49. Elisabeth Söderström as Janáček's Katya Kabanova, an unforgettable and deeply moving performance devoid of any false glamour or histrionics.

48. Two antipodean prima donnas: Kiri Te Kanawa and Joan Sutherland, during a recording of Gay's *The Beggar's Opera* in which they sang the rivals Polly Peachum and Lucy Lockit.

50. Shirley Verrett and Grace Bumbry happily acknowledge the reception of their Covent Garden concert in 1983.

**52.** Kathleen Battle in *Ariadne auf Naxos* (1985).

**51.** Jessye Norman in *Ariadne auf Naxos* (1985).

**53.** William Matteuzzi and Cecilia Bartoli in Rossini's *La Cenerentola*.

studio recording of the *Ring*, and the cool slow majesty of her voice is still evident there at the age of sixty-three. Then a long and lonely struggle against cancer began. Culshaw sent her records of Gilbert and Sullivan to convalesce with, hoping to the very end that he might get her for the *Walküre* Fricka: but she died painfully in 1962.

Flagstad was a popularizer, the most famous of all Wagner singers, in Britain and America at least, with a reputation beyond the ranks of opera-lovers. She was also very much the type of singer who carried her interpretation in her luggage, as it were; Flagstad's Isolde was the same in London as in New York and differences of production affected it minimally. This was not wanton sloppiness on Flagstad's part: she was simply following standard operatic practice. At this time, the idea of 'production' was generally slight in any case, consisting more of strategic marshalling and positioning of forces against the geography of the set than the realization of the director's ideological vision of the opera in question. No one changed this state of affairs more than Wagner's grandson Wieland who, in collaboration with his brother Wolfgang, reopened the Bayreuth Festival in 1951 after the post-war years of disgrace.

A new Germany had to look at its old heroes in a new light, and the Wagner stable had to be cleaned out. Wieland's singers not only had to act, they had to act in a style which fitted his approach. A Flagstad's small repertoire of attitudes and poses would have been no good to him. Cosima had aimed at once-and-for-all definition, but Wieland constantly explored possibilities: his later productions often contradicted the implications of his earlier ones. In 1951 Bayreuth had little money and Wieland made a virtue of necessity by sweeping away spears, helmets, forests, and the detritus of realistic presentation, replacing them with austere 'timeless' settings and sophisticated lighting—with the effect of emphasizing the universal mythic content of his grandfather's works, rather than their roots in Germanic folk-lore. None of Wieland's first prima donnas were singers of Flagstad's or Leider's stature, but both Astrid Varnay and Martha Mödl were remarkable examples of a new breed of 'singing actresses' prepared to commit themselves to long rehearsal periods and to work as closely with the producer as with the conductor. Neither of them, however, could boast what would commonly be described as a 'great voice'.

Perhaps it is unreasonable to expect any generation to nurture more than one true Wagnerian soprano, and an era that boasted

Birgit Nilsson can hardly feel cheated. The primal Wagnerian gifts of security, volume, and stamina were granted her, and if she lacked Mödl's or Varnay's impulsive power on stage, she became an impressive actress. But the most extraordinary thing about Nilsson was her continual development, her steady capacity to learn, even when her position was assured. 'I think I can say that each of my 208 performances of Isolde . . . has in some way differed from all the others,' she claimed. She was the opposite of complacent, and her granite features conceal what is evidently a complex personality. Schuyler Chapin, manager of the Met, described her as 'a very self-contained person, extremely sensitive and easily hurt'; the record producer John Culshaw found her 'not easy to get close to', outwardly jovial and sociable, but untrusting in herself and others. She managed herself and drove a hard deal; her fees were very high; no one got the better of her; and she was a supreme professional—'in all the years,' wrote Culshaw, 'she has never of her own volition wasted as much as a second of our time or money.'

A farmer's daughter from western Sweden, she was born in 1918—some books give 1922: either way, the power of her last performances is almost unbelievable. Her father hoped that as his only child she would take over the farm, and the night before her audition at the Stockholm Academy of Music made her milk ten cows. She won her place, but the first years were unhappy, with a teacher who did not understand her voice and a début at the Stockholm opera in 1946 which left her close to suicide. But eight solid years of consolidation followed in Stockholm, singing heavy roles like Aida, Tosca, and Donna Anna, which she continued to sing, even when firmly identified as a Wagnerian. She claimed that having to master her voice over a bad head cold put the seal on her technique. In the mid-Fifties she began on the major Wagnerian parts, first in Stockholm and then internationally: Munich, Vienna, San Francisco, Covent Garden, Bayreuth, and, from 1959, the Met. Canny, hard-working, independent, and persevering, a part of Nilsson has clearly never left the farm, but her essential seriousness has been overshadowed by her much-publicized knockabout wit. There were clashes with conductors, Knappertsbusch and Karajan ('Herbie', as she disrespectfully called him) especially; and a long-standing and good-humoured battle with Rudolf Bing, the manager of the Met, which led to various incidents, including her putting him down as a tax-deductible dependant on her Internal Revenue form—

it did her no good, and in 1975 she had to abandon America for a few years when a dispute with the IRS came to a head. During a performance of Puccini's *Turandot* the tenor Franco Corelli sulked in his dressing-room after being drowned by Nilsson at the end of 'In questa reggia'. Bing humoured him by suggesting that in the clinch that closed the final love duet he give her a small sharp bite on the neck. Corelli cheered up at once and followed Bing's notion. Bing shortly received a phone call from Nilsson: 'I cannot go on. I have rabies.' At Bing's farewell gala, she sang the closing scene from *Salome*, during which the severed head of John the Baptist, presented to her on a tray, was modelled on Bing's own. How did she manage to scale her voice down when appearing in a small theatre? a journalist asked her. 'Oh, I just use one vocal cord,' Nilsson replied.

Yet, for all the fun backstage, Nilsson's early performances were often criticized as 'cool', and 'the icy Birgit Nilsson' became a cliché of operatic criticism. There certainly is something chilly about the cutting force and occasional sharpness of her tone, especially compared to Flagstad's warmer and deeper sound. But Nilsson was an infinitely more intense singer than Flagstad, a singer born for extremes of emotion, for the peaks that leave the rest of us breathless. Her Brünnhilde, compared with Leider's or Helga Dernesch's, is relentlessly the Valkyrie: she fails to dramatize vocally the contrast between the unawoken goddess of *Die Walküre* and the woken mortal of *Siegfried*. Her Isolde, on the other hand, was an interpretation which simply grew and grew. She had sung Isolde 87 times when in 1962 Wieland Wagner asked her to re-create the role for a new production at Bayreuth. Wieland regarded her as something of a *pis aller*, for in 1960 Anja Silja, a lithe twenty-five-year-old beauty had arrived at Bayreuth to sing Senta. She had a modernity which fascinated Wieland as an angle for his productions, and she became his muse as well as his lover. Silja might have been a reincarnation of Schröder-Devrient: she too came from a theatrical and musical background and was a child prodigy, making her concert début at ten, and her operatic one at sixteen, as Rosina in *Il Barbiere di Siviglia*. Her singing was wild and wayward—sometimes enthralling, sometimes plain ugly and off-pitch. For Wagner's music she quite lacked those necessary gifts of stamina and security and she was never allowed much time for calm growth. Wieland wanted her for everything he did, at Bayreuth and elsewhere, and she did too much too soon. There was nothing statuesque or restrained about her acting style—as Fidelio, she would fling off her cap at the moment of revelation in the Dungeon Scene, letting long blonde hair tumble over her shoulders, making nonsense of the idea of 'disguise as a man', but creating a tremendous *frisson*; as Salome, she lay on her back, her head dangling over the edge of the stage. She was openly and convincingly erotic, with something strangely evasive behind her arresting stage manner. Against her Nilsson may at first have appeared conventional, inflexible, uninteresting, but Silja was not remotely ready at twenty-seven to sing Isolde at Bayreuth, and Nilsson it had to be. There was initial tension and disappointment on both sides, but she and Wieland went on to forge a production that lasted for eight summers and which witnesses would rank among the greatest operatic experiences of their lives. Nilsson later said of Wieland, 'I get down on my nose to him,' and he seems to have opened some floodgate in her art: the live recording made from performances in 1966 communicates much of her splendour in the role.

Perhaps her most shattering achievement was as Elektra in Strauss's gruesome opera, memorably recorded under Georg Solti. Here is awe-inspiring singing. In Elektra's monologue, one can hear the variety and subtlety of which Nilsson was capable, as well as a power that cuts the air like a sword ripped out of its sheath, the sound of will triumphant. There is yearning in her cries to her dead father, madness in the imperturbable steadiness of tone as she remembers his murder, and a winsome softness as she recalls her childhood. In the dialogue with Clytemnestra, she is light and frosty, simpering, mocking, and insinuating; in the greeting to Orestes there is a searing tenderness. Somehow she can bring all this to a climax of vengeful fury and ecstasy, the voice rolling through and over the orchestra tumult. Nor is this the fabrication of the recording studio. I came away from an actual performance of Nilsson's Elektra with a splitting headache and a shaken soul.

Since Nilsson, there has been nobody as decisively and consistently in command of the Wagnerian repertory. No one could pretend that we are in a golden age of Wagner singing. There have been some wonderfully warm and sensitive Brünnhildes, like Rita Hunter and Helga Dernesch, but they have been short-lived, and Dernesch, a potentially major singer much patronized by Herbert von Karajan, was forced to give up soprano roles altogether, the top of her voice having disintegrated. A Scot, Linda Esther Gray, is one of several enormously promising young Wagnerian talents who have recently vanished early; those who stay the course, like Gwyneth Jones and Hildegard Behrens, often do so at the expense of accuracy and control of intonation, relying instead on blasts of sound and vivid stage presence.

As I write in 1995, two very different sopranos tend the sacred flame: the slow-maturing Welshwoman Anne Evans, broad and firm of voice, unfailingly musical; and an enthralling American Deborah Polaski, still proving herself.

It must be difficult to be a Wagnerian prima donna. The jokes about heaving bosoms, spears, helmets, and 'Ho-jo-to-ho', with the Ride of the Valkyries crashing away in the orchestra, must get very boring. No other representative of the species has such a strong stereotype to contend with, as fixed, for instance, in Anna Russell's famous spoof version of the *Ring*. But Wagner himself dealt in female stereotypes, and to return in *Ring*-like fashion to our starting place, it could be argued that he did not present the prima donna with a set of dramatic possibilities substantially more complex than anything in Donizetti or Bellini. In some ways, less so. Most of Wagner's heroines are maidens of the sentimental tradition, with the single sublime mission to save men through the power or example of their love. In this, as in so many other respects, Wagner was thoroughly the Victorian, and it was left to Richard Strauss to provide German opera with broader images of womanliness.

# 5

# *Great Names of New York*

When Henry James returned to New York after a long absence in Europe, his mind saturated with the complex and hierarchical culture of the old world, he was intrigued by the paradoxical escalation of an *haut monde* within a democratic society. No royal court, no rights afforded by birth existed in the United States, but the Very Rich had to cultivate fields in which to display their ever-burgeoning wealth. Money was made to be conspicuous: the style with which this could be managed gave claim to aristocracy. Charity, art collecting, balls, all played their part, but nothing at the beginning of the twentieth century had quite the immediate cachet of a box at the opera. 'The opera function,' wrote James, was 'the only approach to the implication of the tiara known, so to speak, to the American law.' But who was there to curtsey to? he wondered.

James went on to talk of the 'general extravagant insistence' on the opera, and its role as 'the great vessel of social salvation . . . the whole social consciousness thus clambering into it, under stress, as the whole community crams into the other public receptacles, the desperate cars of the subways or the vast elevators of the tall buildings.' With the move to Lincoln Center in 1966, the Met has theoretically democratized itself (Peter Conrad talks of 'a reluctant metamorphosis from private club to public amenity'). Even so, opera in New York still feeds off this crush of hysterical competitiveness. Crisis, scandal, triumph, spectacle: New York loves its opera at the *n*th degree of excitement, and no applause is worth having if it is not a thirty-minute standing ovation.

New York audiences are both fiercely loyal and cruelly fickle, sentimental about overnight sensations and old favourites, débuts and farewells. Quiet respect and patient interest are not on their agenda. They want big voices, top notes and gut-busting intensity. They want stars, they want a climax. It all makes the city an intensely conservative operatic centre, but a uniquely exciting one as well.

Behind so much that is silly or trumped-up, behind the predominantly kitsch aesthetic of production, lies the force of the city's own irresistible vitality and a remarkable history.

There had been regular seasons of Italian opera in New York since 1854 and the establishment of the Academy of Music on 14th Street. Malibran, Alboni, Sontag, Grisi, Tietjens, and Patti had all sung opera in the city before the Met was even built. From its beginnings with Garcia's little troupe, Italian opera was a fashionable artistic import, an example of the aping of European style which beset the aspiring nineteenth-century American. The old 'Knickerbocker' families had filled the boxes of the Academy of Music for over a quarter of a century before they realized a revolution in high society was upon them.

The flood of money-making which followed the Civil War had bred a generation of *nouveaux riches* for whom there were no boxes available in the existing opera house. A cabal of these parvenu millionaires, led by J. P. Morgan and representatives of the Astor and Vanderbilt clans, decided that they, their wives, and their wives' jewels should shine forth in a brighter and better auditorium which they themselves would build. New money would be seen to outclass old money, and each shareholder in the scheme would have the right to his own box.

The opera house which opened on Broadway and 39th Street in October 1883 was modelled on Covent Garden and La Scala, with a passing nod at the splendours of Garnier's Opéra in Paris. This first Metropolitan Opera House proved peculiarly unsatisfactory in a number of ways: its yellow brick made it look like a brewery, its sight-lines were poor and its backstage facilities primitive, but the boxes (which made up a quarter of the total seating capacity) were properly prominent. The shareholders kept a form of control over artistic policy by leasing the opera house to an impresario who remained accountable to them. They wanted someone efficient who could negotiate with the stars and provide a standard repertory—Morgan himself was said to be partial to *Il Trovatore*—but beyond that they were not unduly bothered. There was, of course, the (perhaps not apocryphal) lady who tapped the conductor on the shoulder in the interval of a performance of *Meistersinger* and asked whether he would mind playing the third act before the second, as she and her friends always left early, and she had therefore never heard it—but such instances of musical passion were rare.

The Swedish prima donna Christine Nilsson sang Marguerite in the house's opening performance of Gounod's *Faust*. She received $1,000 for her efforts, more than ten times what the average orchestra member earned in a month, but the real success of the first season was the Polish soprano Marcella Sembrich. Between them, Nilsson and Sembrich accounted for two-fifths of the Met's total payroll and contributed substantially to the $¼-million loss sustained by the manager Henry Abbey.

This initial lack of success can be ascribed to two major impediments: one was the all-surpassing attraction of Adelina Patti, singing under Mapleson's management at the old Academy of Music; the other was the fact that, although the boxes were full, the upper regions remained empty. The Met's historian Martin Mayer has pointed out that the $2 required for the cheapest seat was about what an average workman would have earned in a day: the equivalent sum in 1995 might be $90, or about four times the actual current price of a cheap seat at the Met.

Apart from its autumn-winter orientation, the pattern for this first year was modelled on much the same lines as the spring-summer season at Covent Garden—the same repertory and many of the same singers were presented in a similar style. But then something bizarre occurred. Abbey withdrew and his place was taken by Leopold Damrosch, a German immigrant of high standing in the New York musical scene. Damrosch proposed a season of German opera (strictly, opera in German, for Verdi and Meyerbeer were performed but in German translation), with modestly priced and hard-working German singers who would provide a high standard of ensemble and rehearsal. For the boxholders this meant long evenings sitting in the dark in an atmosphere of unremitting earnestness, yet it worked. Artistic fervour became glamorous; seats for the public became much cheaper; the critics, most of them of German extraction anyway, applauded, as the romance of Wagnerism settled in Manhattan.

Damrosch died after one year of heroic labour, but his place was immediately taken by his twenty-three-year-old son Walter, who continued the assembly of a remarkable team. From Bayreuth came Anton Seidl, Wagner's erstwhile assistant and tireless international champion, as conductor; Amalie Materna, the first Bayreuth

Brünnhilde; Albert Niemann, the ageing but imposing *heldentenor*; Marianne Brandt, a powerful mezzo from Vienna; Max Alvary, a matinée idol Siegfried; and most significantly Lilli Lehmann, determined to conquer the heavy Wagnerian repertory, and the prima donna who would stand as Minerva to all American aspirants.

This regime lasted until 1891, buttressed by the support of New York's large German population. But finally the boxholders decided that they had had enough. The management was transferred back to Abbey and Maurice Grau, on the understanding that Italian opera in Italian with a healthy roll-call of stars would be produced.

A fire in 1892 gave further opportunities for reassessment. The opera house was reconstructed with improvements, including electric light. Only nineteen of the original shareholders remained, and Morgan and Vanderbilt closed their grip on the vacated boxes. Grau, a man of strong financial instinct, took the helm firmly, and under his steerage the Met committed itself to star singers at the expense of all else. The same old war-horses would be trotted out night after night, execrably decked up and accompanied by an orchestra not much better than that of the vaudeville pit. But those stars were refulgent: Melba, Calvé, Sembrich, the de Reszke brothers, Lassalle, Scotti, and Plançon among them. Grau made over $½-million for himself and plenty of singers topped Nilsson's $1,000 fee. In the boxes, society had settled into its routine—to deviate from which, as amusingly recorded in novels such as Edith Wharton's *The Age of Innocence*, was considered vulgar (it was certainly *not* done to listen to the entire opera). Two bejewelled and Worth-coutured ladies would sit in the front of the box, with four white-tie gentlemen behind them. On the fashionable Monday night, the leader of the pack, Mrs Astor, would appear promptly at 9 p.m., regardless of the performance, and receive guests in the next intermission. After she left, her imitators felt that they too could go—the real show was over.

For the prima donna's prestige these were golden years and circumstances, and it is in the last years of the nineteenth century that the female American singer finally established herself as a serious musical proposition. The standard of music teaching in America had been immensely improved by the influx of German and Italian immigrants, and the Met's tours across the States set many young provincial hearts palpitating with ambition. But as for Henry James's heroines, the education that mattered still began in Europe.

Americans like Sybil Sanderson and Emma Eames both started their careers in Paris after studying with Marchesi: Sanderson, a beautiful Californian with a small silvery voice, captivated Massenet, who wrote *Esclarmonde* and *Thaïs* for her; while Eames, described by Shaw as 'well educated, and with no nonsense about her', went on to become Melba's rival at Covent Garden and the Met—'Good day to you, Eames,' Melba would snap if their paths crossed, sweeping past without a backward glance. (According to Max de Shauensee, who discussed the matter with Eames's husband, Melba was completely indifferent to Eames and certainly had no vendetta against her. It was Eames who suffered the pangs of jealousy, referring to Melba only as 'MY ENEMY'.) The most famous Carmen of the era before Calvé, Minnie Hauk, was a native New Yorker who toured the States with Mapleson, but whose sole Met appearance was a failure. She ended her days living in Wagner's villa at Triebschen.

The finest émigré American prima donna, and one of the finest women of her time was Lillian Nordica, born Lillian Norton in Maine in 1857. Hers was good New England farming stock, and her grandfather had been a Revivalist preacher. In her family circle the stage was considered an improper destiny for a young woman, but Lillian Norton was never one to be discouraged, and accepted the drudgery of being a clerk and seamstress so as to pay for singing lessons. While studying in Boston, the great dramatic soprano Therese Tietjens heard her and gave real praise, but one feels that her Yankee grit was such that she would have got there entirely on a 'Teach Yourself Great Opera Singing' manual, had all else failed. 'A young person with a chin so expressive of determination and perseverance,' wrote another early American prima donna, Clara Louise Kellogg, 'could not be downed. She told me at that early period that she always kept her eyes fixed on some goal so high and difficult that it seemed impossible, and worked towards it steadily, unceasingly, putting aside everything that stood in the path which led to it.'

She won her way to the impossible goal without natural musicality. Rehearsal for her was a matter of endless repetition. 'There are plenty of singers with voice and talent equal to mine. But I have *worked*,' she claimed. She began professionally by singing in churches and concerts, and later joined Gilmore's American Band, singing ballads and arias on long whistle-stop tours. She reached London with the band in 1878, passing on to Paris and Milan where she continued her crash-course studies. Having changed her name to Giglio Nordica ('lily of the North'), she began in opera, singing the Patti repertory in Italy and Germany. In 1881 she had great success in St Petersburg and in 1882 went back to Paris to study Marguerite in *Faust* and Ophélie in *Hamlet* with their respective composers, Gounod and Thomas. She then made the first of three disastrous marriages to Frederick Gower, a speculator in telephones, who insisted that she retired from the stage. Gower was a bully and a shark: fortunately for Nordica he vanished over the English Channel in a balloon and was assumed dead.

Her career recommenced in America with a Mapleson tour and in 1887 she made her first appearance at Covent Garden in *La Traviata*. London high society fêted her fresh and vital personality, while the critics praised her sterling efforts—'courageous to the point of audacity', wrote Shaw—even more than her achievements. 'She was a most wonderful coloratura singer and had a perfectly placed voice . . . She could have gone on, I am sure, many years longer than she did, had not her tremendous ambition to sing in German opera overruled her judgment,' wrote the contralto Ernestine Schumann-Heink, one of her greatest friends from these years. But the fashion for Wagner caught her, as it caught every other prima donna of the age. At first she sang only Elsa in *Lohengrin*, which fitted well enough into her French-Italian repertory. Shaw was cutting on the subject, labelling her 'Elsa of Bond Street', because of her 'well-corseted waist' and 'bumptious, self-assertive' manner. For the first Bayreuth presentation of the opera in 1894 she studied the part in German with Cosima Wagner, who found her gratifyingly co-operative. Her success there was the watershed: she would work to become a dramatic soprano in the mould of Tietjens and Lehmann—and work she did.

In 1895 at the Met she sang Isolde to the Tristan of Jean de Reszke in a memorable performance which set new vocal standards for Wagner interpretation, as well as decisively showing that 'French-Italian' singers could keep their purity of style while singing in German. Nordica 'simply amazed those who thought they had measured the full limit of her powers'. Yet even now her star began to fall. After this triumph, she was eager to tackle Brünnhilde at the Met and felt a justifiable claim to the role—only to discover that her friend Melba was scheduled to sing the part in *Siegfried*, apparently at the personal request of Jean de Reszke. It was an inexplicable and inexcusable insult to a native singer, and Nordica was mortified. She tore up her contract with the Met, publicly accused de Reszke of plotting against her, and stormed off to sing elsewhere. Melba's subsequent *débâcle* has already been mentioned: whether de Reszke did recommend Melba to sing Brünnhilde is unclear, but it is possible that he was worried that Nordica would drown him in the final duet, Siegfried having been on stage for about two and a half hours before Brünnhilde is awoken.

Nordica may have been vindicated, but she was still miserable, and in the same year of 1896 she took her second husband, a hopeless gigolo and drawing-room tenor of charm and military good looks called Zoltan Döme. In her story about Nordica, 'The Diamond Mine', Willa Cather remarks that her heroine 'tried to give good fortune to an unfortunate man, *un misèrable*; that was her mistake. It cannot be done in this world. The lucky should marry the lucky.' Döme was a loser, who attempted to ride his way to success on Nordica's shoulders. He was also intolerably lazy and a womanizer. Nordica finally and sadly announced that she would sue him for divorce. Nordica made her escape, only to be informed later the same day that he had made a rather feeble effort to kill himself. She persevered in her resolve, however, and after the divorce, Döme took to the disconcerting habit of sending her notes before concerts, informing her that he would be sitting in a box with a gun, ready to shoot her while she was singing.

Nordica's relations with her colleagues were much more satisfactory. She and Melba had risen at Covent Garden together and felt mutual respect and affection which survived the Brünnhilde episode, and de Reszke soon became a friend and partner again. Her direct rival was Lilli Lehmann, who at first regarded her efforts to emulate her with contempt. At Bayreuth one summer Nordica had a mutual friend ask Lehmann whether she might pay a social call, as one prima donna to another. 'Tell her I am not taking any pupils this season!' Lehmann snapped back. Two years later at the Met they were singing in the same performance of *Don Giovanni*. Lehmann's dresser sent out a frantic request for a pair of black stockings— Lehmann had left hers at the hotel. Nordica could easily have taken the opportunity of returning the Bayreuth snub, but was not so petty-minded. The next day she received a touching note which serves as an object lesson in the ease with which the paranoiac sensitivities of a prima donna can be dispelled.

My dearest Mrs Nordica!
With heartfelt thanks I send back the stockings you lent me last
night; I washed them myself so you can be sure they are clean. I
already told your husband that I was glad to hear your voice is so
much better better [*sic*] now as two years ago, I hope you will be
pleased.

   With much love and thank [*sic*], yours sincerely and affec-
tionately,
Lilli Lehmann Kalisch

Lehmann became positively affable. One day she emerged from the
stage door with Nordica, who stepped into a waiting carriage.
Lehmann pulled up her skirt to reveal a pair of stout and sensible
boots. 'You ride,' she called out, 'I valk!'

   Nordica was particularly generous with the time she gave to young
singers, remembering kindnesses done to her in her youth by
Tietjens and others. When the New Zealander Frances Alda made a
début which the critics slammed, Nordica at once wrote to her:
'There was never a young singer who appeared at the Metropolitan
who wasn't severely criticized on her début. Melba, Sembrich,
Farrar, myself . . . all of us have gone through what you are going
through today. Have courage.'

   Nordica certainly lived by her own precepts. After ten years in the
major centres as a dramatic soprano, singing the heaviest of Wagner
and Italian roles, as well as making the odd return to her earlier
repertory, her voice was wearing thin. In 1907 she left the Met for
Hammerstein's new but short-lived Manhattan Opera, where she
was shabbily treated and virtually dismissed when attendances at her
performances did not reach the required level. Her records date from
this later period and fail to reveal a voice which must have still had
enormous trumpeting power and accuracy: the first recording
equipment was defeated by voices of such size. She herself was
bitterly disappointed by her failure in the studio, and instead
embarked on a useful project to record vocal exercises for students—
a very good idea, which foundered as sadly as did her scheme to
found a 'Bayreuth-on-the-Hudson', something along the lines of a
modern arts centre.

   In 1909 she sang Isolde for the last time and never again appeared
at the Met. In what was interpreted as sour grapes, she then attacked
the domination of the house by Italians and the casting of a non-

American singer (Destinn) for the première of Puccini's *La Fanciulla del West*. Her third marriage, to a banker who 'borrowed' nearly half a million dollars off her to buttress some failing operations, soon terminated. With the decline of her operatic status, she had embarked on some devastatingly exhausting tours. She travelled in her own railway carriage, 'The Brünnhilde', which had a music room, a salon, three bedrooms, a bathroom, kitchen, and servants' quarters, but such comforts were purely external. She had acute rheumatism at all times and a trail of other respiratory ailments. The baritone David Bispham toured with her, and relates her reaction to an attack of bronchitis: 'I have never seen any woman in such abject despair, walking up and down the little dining-room of the car like a caged tigress, every now and then touching a note on the upright piano which had been placed therein, and trying her voice . . . tears and misery had ravaged her comely face so that it was hardly recognizable.' But at 8 p.m. she would emerge in her concert toilet and sing her programme—very, very badly. 'During that entire week, this tragi-comedy would repeat itself every day. Her bronchitis never left her, and from my room I could hear this poor woman, as she entered the dining-room, touch the piano furtively and sing a few notes.' Once she faced Bispham with the truth: 'Do you think, now I am getting old, I should be doing this if I didn't have to?' Between 1910 and 1913 she suffered a series of nervous collapses.

She became an active campaigner within the suffragette movement, took to cycling, and spoke up for equal pay and a female President. 'If I thought I would help the cause of woman suffrage by going out and throwing a brick through a window or adopting any other militant tactics I would do it,' she asserted in an interview. Such feelings of solidarity with their sex are very rare among prima donnas, who have to regard other women as hostile to their always precariously held positions. Nordica, however, always sought friends. She was a lonely woman who had created a golden cage for herself, furnished with all the luxuries but without a key by which to let herself out: she could understand that other women's cages were not of their own making.

In 1913 at the age of fifty-six she embarked on a final concert tour which was to take her round the world. In Australia she had a complete physical and emotional collapse: then, *en route* for Java, her ship foundered on a reef off Thursday Island and the passengers were forced up on deck. Nordica caught pneumonia as a result of the exposure and died in hospital in Batavia. For her funeral, she wanted 'some great speaker' who could say 'she did her damnedest'. It would have been the appropriate epitaph, but there was more to commemorate. Thirty years later, reviewing the début of Kirsten Flagstad as Isolde, the veteran New York critic W. J. Henderson cast his mind back to Nordica and paid her a handsomer tribute.

> She sang Isolde so intelligently, so opulently in respect of gradation, subtlety of tint and significant treatment of text that she left the hearer convinced that she was the real Irish princess of the drama . . . the singing was . . . beautiful in tonal quality, sustained and exquisitely moulded in phrasing and nobility of style.

While American singers were passing into Europe to win their first necessary laurels, European singers could hardly wait to sail out in the opposite direction. Like the millions of immigrants of these years, they saw America as a passport to freedom and fortune—which indeed, for singers trapped in the provincial opera houses of Italy or the court theatres of Germany, it often was. But the market conditions in America were quite different from elsewhere, and the rapidly developing communications technology—wireless, movies, recording, amplification—all meant that it was possible for an opera singer to make a career outside the traditional arenas of opera house and concert hall.

Whether this worked to the detriment of art and technique is a moot point: it certainly involved singing a lot more ninth-rate music than the Lehmann-Melba-Nordica generation ever bothered with. We live at a time when the spheres of 'light' and 'serious' music are much more self-consciously separated than they were at the beginning of the century, and a properly trained singer of aspirations would certainly not have felt a loss of caste when tackling a 'popular' ballad—yet it is depressing to look back at the American years of, for instance, a contralto as rarely endowed as Ernestine Schumann-Heink and see how much time she spent in America with music that could get along without her quite nicely, while others hooted and bellowed their way through Verdi and Wagner.

'*Ich bin nichts als eine gewöhnliche deutsche Hausfrau*,' 'I am nothing but an ordinary German housewife,' was Schumann-Heink's favourite disclaimer, and it became her public image. She was not a glamorous soprano, flaunting her diamonds over Worth gowns, but a hard-working, cooking and sewing mother of seven. She had the common touch: her singing was aimed at the woman with her hands in the washtub and the soldier longing for home. It was an attractive persona, but one which obscured the real nature of her achievement.

Ernestine Schumann-Heink was born in 1861 as Ernestine Rössler, the daughter of a soldier of fortune, and had a rough peripatetic childhood. Her family had strong musical connections and Italian blood, and like Patti she communicates the feeling of having been born to sing, of someone for whom singing was as natural as breathing. In fact, she underwent a long and rigorous training, followed by a four-year apprenticeship in Dresden and a fifteen-year contract in Hamburg, where she clashed violently with her regular conductor, Gustav Mahler. She sang everything from Katisha in *The Mikado* to the Third Boy in *Die Zauberflöte* to Carmen and Amneris in *Aida*. At first she struggled through real poverty and hunger, bringing up the first four of her children on a meagre salary after her first husband had deserted her. Her breakthrough came in the 1890s when she made a name for herself as the finest interpreter of the contralto and mezzo Wagner roles, such as Brangäne in *Tristan*, Ortrud in *Lohengrin*, and Erda, Fricka, and Waltraute in the *Ring*. In 1896 she began her long association with Bayreuth, where she managed Cosima consummately and even won her affection. Once she complained to the 'Frau Meisterin' that the armour she had to wear as Waltraute was too heavy for her to sing in. Cosima was outraged at the thought, but Schumann-Heink managed to get her to try it on herself and admit the justice of the case—no small feat.

In the later 1890s she alternated between Bayreuth, Berlin, Hamburg and London, where she sang at Covent Garden and at a Windsor Castle Command Performance of *Lohengrin*, with a cast which also included Nordica, Bispham, and the de Reszkes, given to celebrate Queen Victoria's eightieth birthday. It was Nordica, a staunch friend and ally, who suggested America to her, and in 1898, heavily pregnant with what was to become George Washington Schumann-Heink, six other realized children, and her ailing second husband, she set sail.

For four successful seasons at the Met she repeated her Wagner roles and added to her repertory what was probably her favourite part, the distraught mother, Fidès, of Meyerbeer's *Le Prophète*. When Grau left the Met in 1903 his replacement as manager,

Heinrich Conried, did not meet with Schumann-Heink's approval, and it was from this time that her career took its distinctively American turn. Her Met appearances petered out, she broke her imperial contract in Berlin, and virtually stopped singing opera in Europe. In 1905 she became a naturalized American and set up home in the Villa Fidès in New Jersey with her third husband (the second, whom she deeply loved, having died), a lawyer who soon evanesced in a nasty lawsuit.

What made her take this course was her success in a musical comedy called *Love's Lottery*, which ran on Broadway and on tour in 1904–5. Schumann-Heink played a German washerwoman burdened with lines like 'Mine English, iss goot, ya?', and clearly relished the whole exercise. She then began on the round of concert tours and recording, and by the end of the decade she had a following outside urban musical circles comparable to that of Caruso, with whom she memorably recorded the duet from *Trovatore*, 'Ai nostri monti'. Everywhere she went, a bevy of local press would foregather and Schumann-Heink, making an embracing gesture, would boom forth some sentiment to the effect that here, at last, was her true home—with the result that she was said to be honorary citizen of half the cities in the USA.

Her last significant operatic appearance was as Clytemnestra in the first performance of Strauss's *Elektra* in 1909 in Dresden. 'It was frightful,' she later recalled. 'We were a lot of mad women. There is nothing beyond *Elektra* . . . We have come to a full stop.' Strauss commented bluntly that she was miscast. Back in America, the First World War gave new meaning to her role as a singer to the nation. The troops called her Mother Schumann, and eyes filled with tears as she sang 'Just Before the Battle, Mother', 'The Star-Spangled Banner', and 'When the Boys Come Home' at endless fund-raising functions. The irony was that sons of hers were fighting on both sides, and the boy in the German army was killed in combat.

After the war she became one of the first musical stars of wireless, and is still remembered today for her annual singing of 'Silent Night' on Christmas Eve. She even made guest appearances in a comic radio soap opera, *The Goldbergs*. In 1926 she returned to opera for the first time in ten years and to the Met in twenty to sing the Earth-Mother Erda in the *Ring*, a role she repeated again in 1932 at the age of seventy, and of which a recording exists. A couple of years earlier she had made a studio recording of Waltraute's narration to Brünnhilde, the moving description of the desolation of Valhalla, and although the music is cut and the voice is worn to a ravelling, it reveals singing of real beauty and deep understanding.

Unfortunately Wagner could not pay the bills. Schumann-Heink's investments were wiped out in the 1929 crash, leaving her with twenty-eight dependants. She had now passed into the realms of the old joke, and her tours became desperate efforts to keep her creaking bulk afloat. She returned to Katisha in *The Mikado*, and sank as far as singing in movie houses between the features, finishing up performing four times a day in vaudeville with an outfit known as 'Roxy and his Gang'. Finally, in 1935, after she had moved to Los Angeles, she made a film, *Here's to Romance* with Nino Martini: the next year she died of leukaemia.

She had given honest pleasure to millions—of that there can be no question—and half of her over fifty professional years had been spent in opera, but it is surely not snobbery to lament the dissipation of the other half. Schumann-Heink has been called the American Clara Butt, but her singing is more than lush, plummy *portamento* geared to the lachrymose and patriotic, as Butt's is too. It has none of the usual lugubrious limitations of a contralto voice: there is wafery delicacy, as well as superb coloratura and a staggering high register. Her Brindisi from Donizetti's *Lucrezia Borgia* is warmly playful in style, with a firm trill and some fabulously sustained top notes. Every memory of her Wagner praises its grandeur and conviction. How wonderful then if in her latter days she had recorded Brahms's Four Serious Songs or some Mahler rather than another version of 'Danny Boy'! America may not have torn her to pieces, but it distracted her from a mission far finer than national anthems and musical comedy.

In stark contrast to the jovially outgoing and familiar figure of Schumann-Heink stands that of Olive Fremstad (1871–1951), a woman who did not understand the meaning of the word distraction and of whom her biographer wrote, 'The one thing for which there was never any room in her life was mediocrity.' She was reclusive and enigmatic, perhaps something of a mystic. 'Through suffering,' she said gnomically, 'I have learned to seek the light to guide me through dark waters, and in that search, as humbly as a small child, I am seeking an understanding of life.'

Needless to say, it was Wagner that she mostly sang, and Fremstad conveniently embodied all the most Romantic notions of

Wagnerism. Lady novelists took her story (as far as it was ever known) and made extravagant fictions about it, the most famous being Willa Cather's turgid *The Song of the Lark*. Far more enjoyable is Gertrude Atherton's *Tower of Ivory* (1910), which tells of Margarethe Styr, formerly Margaret Hill, who arose from the depths of destitution and prostitution to become a prima donna. When the man she has dared to love deserts her for a pert American heiress, her panacea is a blazing performance as Isolde: 'What is mere human passion to art, what indeed, but its necessary but inferior partner?' she ponders. 'Nurse this, nurse this!' Atherton's novel is part of a 'spiritual' feminist literature which appeals for acknowledgement of the power of the outstanding woman's emotions and abilities in areas other than sexual love. The dross of womankind are venal in their desires, but some hold the sacred torch. Styr can give up passion and marriage, but she cannot surrender her art. Painful as the responsibility is, it is her appointed mission.

> There are many disappointments in my profession, and bitter, bitter contempts . . . If you love the good thing vitally, enough to give up for it all that one must give up, then you must hate the cheap thing just as hard. I tell you there is such a thing as creative hate! A contempt that drives you through fire, makes you risk everything, makes you a long sight better than you ever knew you could be.

Rather more polished and ironic, though no nearer conventional feminism, is Marcia Davenport's novel *Of Lena Geyer* (1936), which conflates elements of the careers of Melba, Nordica, Farrar, and Lotte Lehmann, as well as the author's mother Alma Gluck. But the core of the character of Geyer—a lonely, intense, unworldly dramatic soprano, sacrificing love and making do with lady companions, incapable of relating to ordinary life—is still Fremstad. Her true story is scarcely happier than Geyer's.

Olive Fremstad was born illegitimate, and was adopted by a Swedish father and Norwegian mother who emigrated to Minnesota. Her father was a surgeon turned evangelical missionary, and Olive's musical career began at prayer meetings, where she sang and played the harmonium. At the age of twelve she was giving piano lessons to adults, but in her teens she turned to singing. Cather's *Song of the Lark* makes much of the stifling small-town ignorance and philistinism which the heroine had to combat, but there must have been a certain amount of encouragement as well. She studied singing in New York for three years, sang regularly in St Patrick's Cathedral, and saved enough money to take a two-year course with Lilli Lehmann in Berlin. It was later said that she became involved with Lehmann's tenor husband, and certainly neither teacher nor pupil ever evinced much affection for each other in later years. Nevertheless, as Lehmann's pupil, she was given a hearing. She sang in the 1896 Bayreuth *Ring* and in Vienna as Brangäne and Adalgisa in *Norma*—all with Lehmann.

Although she sang predominantly mezzo roles in this first stage of her professional life, she claimed to possess what she referred to as a 'long voice', and from her return to New York in 1903 onwards she sang as a soprano. Critics sometimes doubted the wisdom of this, but the occasional weaknesses of her top register, like comparable flaws of Lotte Lehmann or Callas, somehow became an integral part of her vocal personality. On record her art comes across as an introverted one. In, for example, Tosca's 'Vissi d'arte', no one—not Muzio, Destinn, Callas, or Scotto—quite captures as Fremstad does the essential privacy of the plaint that Scarpia is not meant to hear; and in Eboli's 'O don fatale' from *Don Carlos* she begins not with the attention-grabbing chesty declamation of most Italian mezzos, but with a quiet bitterness and melancholy. All her Wagner excerpts have much to offer, although the discomfort and constraint of singing in a small studio is also evident.

Fremstad's success at the Met conveniently came at the time when Nordica was falling exhausted. Although she sang some of the standard repertory roles such as Tosca, Carmen, and Santuzza in *Cavalleria Rusticana*, it was for her Wagner that she was most valued. Not for her the statuesque proprieties of Lilli Lehmann: Fremstad's magnetism was not impersonal or monumental. 'The opera glass will never betray any of Mme Fremstad's secrets,' explained Willa Cather in the course of an interview.

The real machinery is all behind her eyebrows. When she sings Isolde, no one can say by what means she communicates the conception. A great tragic actress, her portrayal of a character is always austere, marked by a very parsimony of elaboration and gesture.

Henderson wrote further of her as 'no raging Isolde, but a woman smothering a devastating love which presently was loosed from its restraint and poured itself out in longing, sighing accents. There was little of the majesty traditionally associated with the role, but an abundance of . . . feminine lure.' There is a frustrating lack of more concrete documentation of Fremstad's theatrical style, but one remarkable piece of evidence has been revealed by Mary Watkins Cushing, who has deciphered the notes scrawled all over her score of *Tristan*. As with Pasta, everything in Fremstad's performances was calculated, rehearsed, and thought through: her interpretations did not change so much as intensify. ' "1-2-3 wide step—4-5-6 half-turn . . ." "Head up" is repeated over and over,' writes Cushing. 'The right or the left hand, even their fingers, have their special instructions, as well as the shoulders, the chest, the spine, the knees . . . perhaps most characteristic is her repeated reminder to herself "stand quite still".' Sometimes she is simply practical: at Brangäne's return from delivering the message to Tristan, she marks, 'Rush toward her, but *Caution* . . . don't arrive too soon because danger of bumping.' Elsewhere, she is more reflective, as at the opening of Act II, where she tells herself to gaze 'longingly into the forest where all her thoughts now are . . . *whole* body expecting the loved one . . . Here she *thinks* of torch,' then, 'just sing beautifully, gestures not necessary'; for the *Liebestod*, she is rather more blunt: 'take great breaths like a horse.'

About her other interpretations we can surmise less, although we know that her Brünnhilde was the first to emphasize the Valkyrie's girlishness. She personally commissioned Mahler's designer Alfred Roller to make her a costume which would allow her more freedom of movement than the traditional chain-mail cuirass, and then startled audiences by leaping about from rock to rock during the 'Ho-jo-to-ho' passage.

Fremstad's attention to the details of her performance and her fanatical dedication made her a difficult, even eccentric, colleague. When in 1907 she sang the sole performance of Strauss's *Salome* to be given at the Met until 1933 (J. P. Morgan's daughter was so shocked by its lasciviousness that she made her father use his influence to have it removed), she was noted to stagger while carrying the plate bearing John the Baptist's head. When questioned on this, she admitted that she had been to the morgue and spent some time rehearsing with the real thing—all 12lbs of it!

Those she worked with found her exacting. Mahler, himself uncompromising, admired her enormously and she sang her first ever Isolde when he made his début at the Met on 1 January 1908—also the first time New York had heard the opera played without cuts. Toscanini, however, deplored her refusal to rehearse the day before a performance. Finally, Gatti-Casazza, then manager of the Met, seems to have tired of her and let it be known that he would be engaging another singer to share her roles in the 1914–15 season. Fremstad immediately resigned. Her last performance, as Elsa in *Lohengrin*—Gatti refused her request for a *Tristan*—was greeted by one of the longest and most fervent ovations in the history of the house. 'May we all meet again in that far beyond where there is eternal peace and harmony,' she called over the footlights, bowing out at the height of her powers. She was only forty-three: at her age, Flagstad was only two years into her Wagnerian career. Gatti's action was a terrible tactical error: Fremstad had no successor, and the quality of Wagnerian sopranos at the Met did not recover for nearly twenty years. Gatti remembered her in his memoirs as 'a woman with a great sense of responsibility, thoroughly serious in her approach to her tasks, and sensitive to the point of being quixotic . . . rather nervous and difficult to keep happy'. That the Met could not accommodate such a temperament is a sad indictment of its priorities.

Fremstad sang on in Chicago for two years, and Gatti seemed to be on the verge of inviting her back for the 1917–18 season, had it not been for the cancellation of all German opera during the period in which America was at war. Her final public appearance was at a concert in New York early in 1920. Later the same year she wrote Gatti one of the most painful letters imaginable. Bowing to anti-German feelings caused by the war, a plan was announced for the Met to perform Wagner in English only. Fremstad played her last card:

There was a time during the War when it seemed almost impossible to convert Wagner into English without a tremendous artistic loss. However, I am now convinced that it is the only way at present of giving Wagner to English-speaking audiences. Therefore, I am learning the operas in English—*Tristan, Parsifal, Lohengrin,* and *Tannhäuser*—I am also adding *Forza del Destino* to my repertoire, making in all for the present, with Tosca and Santuzza, seven roles.

I expect to do better work than I have ever done before, and, naturally, in the event of your having a place for me, I should like to do that work at the Metropolitan, on the stage which has seen so many of my life's successes. Could you make this possible?

Gatti's reply is not on record, but it must have given him an awkward moment. However he phrased his refusal, its effect on Fremstad was decisive. She retreated completely, and for nearly thirty years lived on in New York State as a recluse.

Her personal life had scarcely existed outside the opera house. 'I spring into life when the curtain rises,' she said, 'and when it falls I might as well die. The world I exist in between performances is the strange one, alien, dark, confused.' Her eccentricities could be gruesome: on top of her grand piano at home sat a bottle containing half a pickled human head, sliced to reveal the physiognomy of the throat. No, she was not quite all there: even the most violent impingements of reality did not seem to affect her. When caught in the 1906 San Francisco earthquake, she insisted on returning to her hotel room to salvage some crimson roses. Hours later she was discovered calmly sitting in a small park on Van Ness Avenue distributing them to refugees. She was briefly married twice, once to a man who 'owned all the gold mines in Tierra del Fuego', but her strongest personal relationship appears to have been with Mary Watkins Cushing, a girl she employed as her living-in secretary and buffer from the world. Cushing's book about Fremstad, *The Rainbow Bridge*, reveals a woman who lived at an intolerable pitch of tension. In bed Cushing would have to sleep with a piece of string tied round her toe, which Fremstad pulled from the next room if she woke up in the night and felt the need for company. Even on walks she could not relax, but would improve the shining hour by measuring the number of lamp posts she could walk past without drawing breath. 'Friends are not for me . . . Think of me as a stage creature only,' says the heroine of *Tower of Ivory*—but Fremstad was even more estranged and isolated than the fictional characters she inspired.

This in itself gave Fremstad her glamour, albeit of a rarefied kind. The contemporary prima donna who had 'a hold on the baseball type of American' (as Willa Cather smartly put it) was Geraldine Farrar.

Hers was the comforting kind of sophistication achieved by a clean-cut healthy all-American female that anyone could see the point of. You couldn't have taken Fremstad home to meet the folks—she would have stared into the ether and refused offers of refreshment. But Farrar was recognizable to any reader of *Little Women* as a female of vivacity and candour. She took the trappings of stardom in her stride and enjoyed them extravagantly—her dress account at Henri Bendel was said to run up $80,000 a year. Farrar had, with all possible capital letters, personality. The exposure she experienced in her period of fame was the sort that film stars became accustomed to: indeed, she became a film star herself. Her fans knew all her movements, her measurements, what she had for breakfast, lunch, and tea. She was canvassed for her views on matters great and small, and her life was an endless source of public interest. When the cameras were there, Farrar never forgot to smile.

The driving force behind this success story was Farrar's mother, a woman who had married at seventeen and felt vicariously ambitious for her daughter, born in 1882 in Melrose, Massachusetts. Farrar's father was a store-keeper who pitched for a Philadelphia baseball team, and both parents had good voices. Geraldine was a determined child with a strong histrionic bent. She later remembered how once she went out and 'purchased a pair of lurid plaid stockings and told her family and friends that when she had these on she was not to be spoken to or taken any notice of whatsoever'. At the age of ten, she impersonated Jenny Lind in a school pageant and decided to cultivate the role further. Her mother pushed her hard, and for that she was always deeply grateful. When it came to writing her autobiography, *Such Sweet Compulsion*, she claimed to have communicated with her mother's dead spirit, and a third of the book is related by a voice from beyond the grave—a literary device which allowed Farrar to pay herself some astonishing compliments.

Farrar began to study seriously in Boston, where she was heard by Nordica who recommended her to make her way to Berlin, and by Melba who recommended Paris. At this her mother decided that only the best was going to be good enough for her Geraldine. With financial subsidy from a local lady of means—Farrar scrupulously repaid her a debt of $30,000—mother and daughter went to teachers in New York and Paris. In 1901 Farrar made a successful appearance in *Faust* at the Berlin Opera, and after a number of unacknowledged letters of self-introduction, Lilli Lehmann summoned the Farrars to an audition.

> On arrival my mother thanked Mme Lehmann for receiving us but added that her daughter had already written two or three times without receiving any answer. 'I know,' came the severe reply, 'but I could not read the handwriting. It is too big and illegible.'
>
> I said I always wrote that way, which brought no further comment. Then I sang for her. But I felt she was not greatly impressed, and so I said, 'Mme Lehmann, will you *please* take me? I am intelligent and I am very hard-working. But you will never know that unless you give me a chance.'

Lehmann took Farrar on and, against all the odds, the relationship proved a great success. They clashed constantly but not bitterly, for Lehmann admired the girl's pluck and Farrar wheedled out Lehmann's frustrated maternal instinct. There was, however, never any question of emulating Lehmann's own accomplishment, Farrar's voice being expressive but physically limited. 'Technical control to her meant everything,' she wrote of Lehmann, 'while emotional colour was my natural asset and delight.' In a letter to the music critic Henry T. Finck, she admitted, 'I do not long to, nor do I believe I can, climb frozen heights like the Great Lehmann.'

But Lehmann made Farrar into a real singer: when J. B. Steane notes the 'bracing vitality and precision' of her singing, he is praising the Lehmann aspect of her training. Farrar may not have been an interpreter of Fremstad's stature, but she was certainly not an impostor.

At the Berlin Opera she became enormously popular. She was regularly seen in the highest court circles, and the Crown Prince paid her such persistent amorous attentions that her father had to knock down a man who cast aspersions on her honour. All this was duly reported in the American press. One of her humblest German admirers was the young Frida Leider: Farrar's appeal was always as potent to girls as it was to men. To girls who had very little, she exuded the fantasy of having very much: wealth, talent, beauty, fame, admirers, independence. 'It was said,' Leider recalled, 'that when singing Marguerite she wore really and truly genuine jewelled buckles on her shoes. She seemed to me the most elegant and bewitching creature, and I used to colour all the sepia postcards which showed her in a long evening gown, a little diadem of pearls in her gently waved hair, with long white kid gloves, her head gracefully rested on one hand.'

Over five years Farrar built herself up in Europe, developing her repertory and making some appearances in Paris, Monte Carlo, and at Salzburg as Zerlina to Lehmann's Donna Anna. In 1906 she returned to New York to a public burning with curiosity. Her début at the Met in Gounod's *Roméo et Juliette* brought a certain inevitable critical resistance—Henderson reported that 'largeness, power, brilliancy, are what this young woman has sought instead of mellowness, liquidity, and perfect poise'—but her stardom was undeniable. For over fifteen years she dominated the French and late Italian repertory: with Caruso as her most frequent partner, her presence would guarantee a full house.

Her manner on stage had naturalistic immediacy that compensated for a lack of vocal *éclat*. 'I am an actress who happens to be appearing in opera,' she said. 'I sacrifice tonal beauty to dramatic fitness every time I think it is necessary for an effect and I shall continue to do it. I leave mere singing to the warblers. I am more interested in acting.' She played up to her audiences with an energy bordering on vulgarity. Caruso baulked at having his face slapped by Farrar's Carmen; as the music-hall singer Zazà in Leoncavallo's opera of that name, she created a scandal by 'raising her skirt to perfume the panties with an atomiser'; as the Goose Girl in Humperdinck's *Königskinder*, she would take her curtain call carrying one of the birds under her arm. Her most famous role, despite Puccini's initial disapproval, was that of Madama Butterfly, which she sang nearly a hundred times at the Met and of which she made recordings with Caruso and Scotti, whence her warm and intimate tones, combined with a firm line and intonation, are still pleasurable, even if she falls short of the dignity of Scotto or Los Angeles. Both Henderson and Schumann-Heink also single out her achievement as the pure-minded Elisabeth in *Tannhäuser*, but most of the rest of her time was spent conveying degrees of coquettishness.

The teenage girls who screamed and waved flags at the stage door on Farrar nights were christened the 'Gerryflappers', and their collective crush became something of a nuisance at the Met, which was fast losing its dignity. There were those who found the lady herself even worse than a nuisance. In an open letter she expressed her distrust of the newly appointed manager Giulio Gatti-Casazza, demanding that a second consul be appointed to govern with him; and like Melba she insisted on the key to her own dressing-room. With Toscanini, the great conductor of the Met during the years 1908–15, her relations proved catastrophic. After a first notorious skirmish—'I am the star,' asserted Farrar, in a quarrel over tempo; 'The only stars I know are in heaven,' retorted Toscanini—they became embroiled in a long and passionate love affair, kept a close secret from the press. Farrar finally demanded that Toscanini leave his wife and marry her: Toscanini, with his Italian conception of *la famiglia*, refused, and Farrar terminated the relationship. Toscanini's sudden and apparently unmotivated departure from the Met is now thought to be largely explained by his pain at the unavoidable encounters with his lost lover. Many years later Farrar invited him to dinner, at which caviare was served. Toscanini was furious, and whispered to his neighbour, 'I slept with that woman for seven years. Wouldn't you think she'd remember that I hate fish?'

From 1915 Farrar's life followed new directions. Her annual spring trips back to the Berlin Opera had been curtailed by the war, and instead she took to the movies once the Met season had ended. None of her fourteen pictures—which included a version of *Carmen, Joan the Woman* (about Joan of Arc) for Cecil B. de Mille, *The Woman God Forgot, The Hell Cat, Temptation,* and *Flame of the Desert*—were of any distinction, but it was in Hollywood that she met a handsome actor, Lou Tellegen, a former stage partner of Sarah Bernhardt, whom she swiftly married. Unmitigated disaster ensued. Tellegen was lazy and spendthrift, and his own career was inexorably collapsing. He drank heavily and involved himself with other women. Farrar was not used to being treated so lightly, and within a few years divorced him. When some years later he committed suicide, Farrar showed no mercy on his memory. 'He had the perceptions of a moron,' she wrote in her autobiography, 'and no morals whatsover.' As her mother's spirit put it, Geraldine was not made to be 'good material for tandem-going', and she never tried marriage again.

The strain of it all was beginning to tell. In 1918 Farrar developed a node on her vocal cords, and for six months was unable to sing, the silent procedures of the film studio being useful to her in her months of recovery. In fact, she does not seem to have regained her full powers, although she refused to diminish her work-load at the Met and continued to sing rumbustious *verismo* music which she had always found vocally exhausting. Vincent Sheean remembers Farrar's last years in the opera house:

> Her personality was more remarkable than her voice by the time I heard her. The voice had grown wiry thin in all its upper reaches and it never could have had much to offer in the lower part. By compensation there were wonderfully expressive tones still at her command in the middle voice [even though she] had pushed out her repertoire in all directions without regard for her special gifts.

Fortunately she could save face, in that she had always publicly, and probably sincerely, proclaimed her resolution to retire at the height of her powers. 'I have one very decided ambition,' she told an interviewer. 'I wish to develop my powers to the fullest extent and most complete beauty, and then—I wish to have the courage, when physical strength no longer responds to the creative demands, *to abdicate in favour of youth*!' Various factors conspired to make her fulfil her wish. Vocal problems, the stresses surrounding her divorce, and the advent of her fortieth birthday joined with the even more crucial advent of Maria Jeritza. The Met was captivated by this beauty from Vienna, with her new repertoire of startling theatrical tricks and a voice bigger than Farrar's had ever been. Without crossing swords with the newcomer, Farrar announced a short series of farewell performances. Just as he had refused Fremstad an Isolde, Gatti refused Farrar a last fling as Tosca, a role already assumed by Jeritza, and at a Saturday matinée in April 1922 she went out as Zazà, perfumed panties and all. 'I don't want any tears in this house,' she said in her traditional curtain speech. 'I am leaving this institution because I want to go.' The Gerryflappers then clad her in crown, sceptre, and robes, and she was borne aloft on to Broadway through an enormous cheering crowd.

Surprisingly, she did not make for Hollywood—in fact, her films had not proved particularly successful at the box office and Sam Goldwyn had terminated her contract. Instead she embarked on ten years of concert tours from which she made a good deal more money than she had made at the Met. On one such tour she sang a truncated version of *Carmen* 123 times in 125 days! There were constant whispers of a return to opera or a break into the legitimate theatre, but none of the schemes materialized. Promptly, at the age of fifty, she retired from performance altogether. She did make a return of sorts to the Met, but only as the interval commentator for the famous Saturday matinée radio broadcasts, and it was she who was on the air to announce the miraculous first appearance of Kirsten Flagstad in 1935.

In her quiet retirement in Ridgefield, Connecticut, she became a pillar of the community, involved with worthy causes such as the Girl Scouts and the women's voluntary service. Her fate was to become a spinster *grande dame* with unforgettably piercing blue eyes, respectfully visited by those with long and loyal memories, but there could well be a lot more to Farrar's story than has emerged in this sketch. At her death in 1967 she bequeathed her letters and papers to the Library of Congress, where they await an imaginative biographer.

Farrar was the first and most substantial of the American 'glamour' prima donnas, with a solid vocal talent to underpin her well-projected charms; but New York has also paid court to a series of lesser singers who could not have made their way without certain more venal and sensual endowments.

The most sheerly beautiful of them was indisputably Lina Cavalieri (1874–1944), who arrived at the Met in 1906, the same year as Farrar, but who failed to establish herself in a comparable repertory. Cavalieri let it be known that she was the barefoot daughter of a Roman washerwoman and a newspaper vendor, that she had slept in the gutters and sold oranges in the Piazza Novona, that she had begun by singing outside cafés. It may have been true, but supposition becomes verifiable fact in the mid 1890s when she became the mistress of Prince Alexander Bariatinski and then, from 1900, a prima donna. At the Met she sang with Caruso in the first house performance of Puccini's *Manon Lescaut* and Cilea's *Adriana Lecouvreur*, but her art was a fragile thing. By 1909 she was concentrating her activities on a Fifth Avenue *atelier* where she sold cosmetics made according to the recipes of Catherine de Medici, and in 1910 she married one of the Astor clan, from whom she was separated less than three months after. A brief film career (including appearances in *Eternal Temptress*, *The Shadow of her Past* and *Woman of Impulse*) was curtailed by the damage that studio lights did to her eyes. With the outbreak of war, she returned to Europe and lived off her jewels and divorce settlement. There were two more marriages, out of a total, she claimed, of 840 proposals.

Cavalieri had an insubstantial but pretty little voice which went well with her diaphanous beauty. As a singer she could not be taken very seriously, but as a late manifestation of the courtesan—a courtesan with a career and a press agent—she was magnificently successful. Perhaps the outstanding instance of a prima donna building her status on a combination of modest musicianship and mass public appeal is that of Grace Moore. Born in 1901 down in Slabtown, Tennessee, she made her way up through musical comedy and Broadway to make her début at the Met as Mimi in *La Bohème* in 1928. According to Vincent Sheean, she had a nice warm soprano, but no memory, imagination, or stamina, and 'she lived in terror twenty-five hours a day of her own shortcomings'. None the less, she lasted in opera until she was killed in an air crash over Copenhagen in 1947, singing a minuscule repertory and rehearsing with futile persistence.

Moore's ambitions did not lie in the direction of art. She wanted to be rich, famous, and admired, and she used her voice to attain the glittering end. 'She expected music to serve her,' wrote the recording producer Charles O'Connell, and had little interest in it beyond what was absolutely necessary or relevant. Her one estimable achievement was the title-role of *Louise*, which she had studied with the aged composer Charpentier.

It was the movies which gave her the exposure and publicity she craved, as well as keeping her afloat in the opera house. In a succession of musical romances, starting in 1930 with a 'biopic' of Jenny Lind and continuing through, among others, *One Night of Love*, *I'll Take Romance*, and *Love Me for Ever*, she became Hollywood's first true singing film star. As such, she was often regarded as the sinister portent of a new vulgarity. When the Covent Garden management attempted to hire Moore, Thomas Beecham and his partner Lady Cunard were roused to fury at the compromise of standards the engagement would represent. Miss Moore was much more concerned, according to a letter from her agent, that 'she should make her début night on the best and most fashionable one of the week; she also hopes that it will be possible to arrange a performance attended by the King and Queen'. In the event she was denied the royal presence, but she filled the house, as she always did, with a lot of people who had never been to the opera before—and who probably never came again. Between performances she fluttered her eyelashes at eligible scions of the aristocracy, indulging the outrageously naïve snobbery for which she was notorious. 'What she did to this world in the way of snooting,' commented Sheean, 'was good for us poor folks to witness.'

Farrar, Cavalieri, and Moore represent the prima donna as 'star personality'. All three specialized in the sentimental and sadistic operas of the turn of the century—Massenet, Puccini, *verismo*—which gave them maximum opportunity to fulfil sexual fantasy, and all three allowed their lives to be fed into an inexorably voracious publicity machine. A satire of the whole phenomenon is contained in Welles's and Mankiewicz's film *Citizen Kane*, in which Kane's second wife Susan has an opera house built for her meagre talent. She makes her disastrous début in an exotic French opera (faked by Bernard Herrmann) entitled *Salammbô* and is never heard again. According to Pauline Kael, Welles and Mankiewicz may also have had in mind both Randolph Hearst's one-time fiancée Sybil Sanderson, later the creator of Massenet's Thaïs, whose parents sent her to Paris so as to keep her from Hearst's clutches; and also Samuel Insull, who built the Chicago Lyric Opera inside a skyscraper block of offices before his empire collapsed spectacularly in the Depression.

But the most pathetic of the ephemeral prima donnas of this period was Marion Talley, a 'girl-next-door' prima donna whose fate was nothing but the odd appearance in a 'where are they now?' magazine feature. Her father was a telegraph operator in Kansas City, Missouri. As a boy his best friend had been Walter Chrysler, who went on to become the motor tycoon. In 1922, the chubby fifteen-year-old Marion had auditioned for the Met and was told to go away and study. She duly departed for Milan, financed by some benefit concerts held in Kansas City, and returned to the Met. Someone was foolish enough to engage her, and in 1926 amid a barrage of press coverage, this wretched eighteen-year-old made her début as Gilda in *Rigoletto*. Trainloads from the home town came to New York to cheer her on. A telegraph line was specially installed backstage for Talley's father to tap out a report on the performance back to Kansas City. The press also reunited him with Walter Chrysler: now, in the great melting-pot of American democracy, they could meet on equal ground.

The critics naturally deplored the whole incident, and as Talley went on to sing a variety of coloratura roles including Lucia, the Queen of the Night, and the title-role in Stravinsky's *The*

*Nightingale*, they did not spare comment on her 'hard, pinched manner', 'hollow' middle voice, and 'harsh and strident' top register. The public, however, continued to be entranced by the idea of the 'Little Red Riding Hood of the Met', whose 'only vice was candy'. Her face was plump and inexpressive, her temperament placid and priggish: more important, she had a voice quite unripe for serious singing. After a coast-to-coast concert tour from which she was claimed to have made $350,000, her tender instrument had virtually collapsed. Further appearances at the Met were disastrous, and by 1929 she was a dead letter.

Perhaps Talley was taken on because someone remembered an even greater risk that had been taken back in 1918 with a girl of twenty-one and which was now paying off triumphantly. We have now come to one of the giants—one of the very greatest names, in fact, in the history of Italian singing: Rosa Ponselle.

The commonly repeated story of how Ponselle, a poor Italian girl singing in lowly vaudeville, was spotted by Caruso and then shot to stardom after an untutored performance, is misleading. Rosa Ponzillo was born in Connecticut in 1897 into a typical first-generation Italian immigrant background: her father was a baker and small-town operator who never showed any pride or interest in his daughter's music unless money was being discussed. In fact, it was Rosa's elder sister Carmela who first went out into the metropolis, singing between reels in the nickelodeons, while Rosa was still being asked to keep her voice down and stop drowning everyone else in the school choir. 'I never had what I would call a "girl's voice"—the light, breathy-sounding, high-pitched voice we normally associate with young children. My singing voice was always big and round, and even as a teenager I could sing almost three octaves,' she wrote in her autobiography. She heard Tetrazzini, Calvé, and Melba in concert, and then quarrelled with the local priest at confirmation when he refused to allow her to take Melba as her saint's name. The singer who most influenced her, however, was Schumann-Heink, whose warmth and fluency would find their way into her own style.

Like her sister, Rosa Ponzillo began her career in the movie house, before graduating to the Café Malone in New Haven, where she accompanied herself on the piano and sang standard arias from opera and operetta. Her great hit was Victor Herbert's 'Kiss me again'. Carmela meanwhile had found her way into a Broadway musical and it was decided that a sisters act would go down very well in

vaudeville. Together Rosa and Carmela proved enormously successful with their duet rendition of the Trio from *Faust*, and were soon
'headliners' on the prestigious Keith circuit, touring the nation with
Harry Lauder, George Burns, Sophie Tucker, Jack Benny, and the
Marx Brothers.

There is thus no question of her being an untried unknown when
the Met approached her in 1918. Carmela had gone for lessons to
William Thorner, a fashionable voice teacher whose studio was
frequented by agents and impresarios, and Rosa again tagged on after
her. Both of them wanted to get out of vaudeville. Rosa had only
been to the opera twice, but Caruso and Farrar in *Butterfly* and
Muzio in *L'amore dei tre re* was no mean initiation. One day Caruso
himself appeared in the studio, and asked to sing some duets with
Rosa. He was sufficiently impressed to mention her name to Gatti-
Casazza, who was looking for a soprano for the Met première of
Verdi's *La Forza del Destino*. (It would be interesting to know why
the resident *spinto* soprano at the time, Claudia Muzio, did not take
the role.) Gatti auditioned both sisters, and even though she fainted
half-way through, it was Rosa who was eventually offered a contract
for the forthcoming season. It was a significant act, for as Gatti told
her, 'If you make good, I will open the door to American talent as
long as I am here. You will be the first American to appear at the
Metropolitan without having been to Europe first.'

Ponselle, as she was now to become, was then closeted away for
five months with Romano Romani, a *protégé* of Puccini and Mascagni
who was to remain her lifelong teacher, mentor, and close friend. All
went well until the day after the dress rehearsal, with Ponselle riding
high on the sudden realization of her miraculous natural capacities.
Then she read a newspaper review in which a respected Met singer
was adversely criticized, and for the first time contemplated the
possibility of her own failure. 'All I could think was, *just what have I
gotten myself into?*' she remembered. Overcome with the crippling
nerves that would dog the rest of her career, she was dragged to the
opera house by sister, mother, and Romani. When she finally
reached the wings, she looked pleadingly to Caruso for encouragement, only to find him in as bad a state as she was. No two singers on
record communicate a greater sense of spontaneous technical
mastery than Ponselle and Caruso; no two singers suffered more
agonies of uncertainty before a performance. And *Forza* is not easy
for anyone, even a Ponselle.

As an opera, *Forza* is supremely difficult . . . The one thing that stands out . . . is my constant thinking 'Top, top, top. Up, up, up,' to keep my voice light and sustain that extremely high pitch Verdi established for the tone of the opera . . . I always felt that the duet with the basso was the most difficult part of the opera. By the time I got to the Vergine degli Angeli at the end of the act I was in seventh heaven, for I knew that the worst was behind me. In that scene with Padre Guardiano, Leonora has to be a lyric, dramatic and near mezzo-soprano. She must express fear, fatigue, piety, desperation, remorse, relief, and a dozen other assorted emotions—all in phrases placed all over the scale and above and below it as well!

Having been pushed on to the stage, her success on that evening in November 1918 was decisive, although perhaps not the sensation that history has generally consecrated. Every critic was impressed, but urged caution and sustained study: 'She has an arduous road to travel before she can call herself a finished artist,' wrote Richard Aldrich. The next five or so years did indeed turn out to be arduous ones, and in the view of many she slipped back and failed to fulfil her initial promise. In retrospect, it was the necessary period of consolidation during which she worked steadily with Romani on developing a type of voice unparalleled among her contemporaries, neither lyric, dramatic, nor coloratura, but capable of embracing all three. Her repertory was highly unusual, and did not follow the pattern which we would expect from comparable post-war singers such as Leontyne Price: a lot of later Verdi, some Puccini, Strauss, and Donna Anna in *Don Giovanni*, with perhaps the odd Donizetti or Wagner role. Ponselle sang no Puccini, Strauss, or Wagner on stage, nor did she undertake Verdi's *Ballo* or *Otello*; even though she considered it 'the greatest opera ever written', she only sang *Aida* twice at the Met, so terrified was she of the exposed high C in the Nile Scene. All this may have been partly to avoid clashes of repertory with Jeritza, Rethberg, and Florence Easton, the three other leading lyric-dramatic sopranos of the 1920s and 1930s—and she was clearly very influenced by the tastes and advice of Romani. Nerves and caution were other factors, but whatever the reasons, the result was some interesting revivals and reassessments.

She worked slowly, always with Romani, and prepared new roles over a period of years rather than months. In 1925 she assumed the taxing title-roles in Ponchielli's *La Gioconda* and Spontini's *La Vestale*, an almost forgotten early Romantic opera. The natural fullness of Ponselle's voice—seamlessly even throughout its range, surprisingly flexible in coloratura—was matched to a deep musicality with a subtle sense of phrase and response to the composer's dynamic marking, as well as a real ability to communicate theatrically. Like Caruso's or Schumann-Heink's, Ponselle's tone *floats*—it never sounds pushed. It is like a liquid that does not freeze or congeal or evaporate. Victor Gollancz recalled it in Proustian fashion: 'I was given the other night a wine that tasted beautifully equable, yet was quite devoid of an exaggerated *velouté*. That was what Ponselle sounded like.' The cutting edge of a Nilsson is not there, nor is her coloratura as brilliant as a Sutherland's: Ponselle had a 'short top', and frequently transposed down to avoid high Cs and Ds. Otherwise, her singing is of a matchlessly satisfying completeness.

In 1927 she triumphantly put herself to the ultimate test of *Norma*, a work not heard at the Met since Lilli Lehmann sang it in 1891. There was also a superb Donna Anna in *Don Giovanni*, Selika in *L'Africaine*, and roles in some then little-known Verdi operas such as *Ernani* and *Luisa Miller*. In 1930 she sang, at Covent Garden, her first Violetta in *La Traviata*. The collapse of commercial recording in the Depression years means that the only faint echo of this interpretation which survives is an amateur pirate tape from 1935, on which the distortion is almost intolerable. Fortunately, the splendour of the singing remains blazingly evident. This Violetta is no nightingale exponent of *bel canto*. She begins a little loud and sharp—the effect, no doubt, of nerves—and in the first act one does not hear the sickness which Callas etched into her singing of the role, nor the fragility in Cotrubas'. This Violetta is a good-time girl, who knows how to enjoy life, and in a stunning 'Sempre libera' grabs excitedly at it. The second-act duet shows a wonderful range of emotion—anger and bitterness as well as grief and self-sacrifice—while the splendour of 'Amami, Alfredo' seems to overpower the pirate tape-machine altogether. Ponselle was not beyond the occasional extravagant vulgarity, as in the screeching noises she makes when Alfredo denounces her in the third scene, but how fully she braves the extremes of this great part, its ecstasy and despair as well as its purely technical challenges. What these records conclusively prove is that Ponselle was so much more than an obedient musician with a natural vocal gift: she was an enthralling performer, whose art also had a rare power and excitement.

Apart from three glorious seasons at Covent Garden, during which she did much to restore London's sorely tried faith in Italian opera—'I do not think I have ever heard anything to surpass or perhaps even to equal it,' wrote Francis Toye of her Violetta—and one visit to Florence in 1933 for *La Vestale*, she never sang opera outside the United States and indeed rarely left the Met company at all. The thought of new audiences and new opera houses paralysed her. Her enchanting letters to Covent Garden's managing director Eustace Blois are full of pleas, requests, apologies, and worries. Here among other things she tries a rather desperate means of avoiding those dreaded top notes:

> I hope you'll give us plenty of stage rehearsals for Traviata, as I won't have a chance to prepare it here. *You will won't you???* I do want to do it well you know . . . I do want to put it over big . . . I forgot to mention to the designer the colour of the *walls* in the bedroom scene, last act—if possible please have them a real mysterious lavender, more on the orchid shade. This color with my costuming of white is very impressive. Another great favor I ask of you is to get after the *orchestra pitch*. Have your German director keep pulling it down until you get it to 435 and *keep* them down. Get them to adjust their instruments before beginning your season.

Then in 1935 she sang Carmen, and everything suddenly went horribly wrong. Although the part lay very comfortably within her vocal range (Carmen is notoriously useful for sopranos worried about top notes), 'she played fast and loose with time and rhythm' and 'showed a cheerful disregard of laws of good singing for which she has won richly deserved eminence'—thus Olin Downes in the *New York Times*. Her acting was also considered an embarrassing miscalculation, the nadir being a vampish dance in the tavern scene which apparently had its origins in the Black Bottom and the Charleston rather than anything authentically Hispanic. She stuck by her interpretation and a minority claimed to be convinced by it, but there is no doubt that her confidence was badly shaken.* She

---

* Beverly Sills, Ponselle's pupil some twenty years later, found cartons

asked the Met management for a revival of Cilea's lyrical *Adriana Lecouvreur* and was refused, on the grounds that it was not a box-office attraction. She offered to sing it for nothing and was still refused. Outraged and exhausted, Ponselle announced her retirement. Her last performance at the Met was as Carmen in 1937. After the annual provincial tour and a few concerts, she never sang in public again. She was barely forty.

Some months earlier she had put paid to years of gossip and speculation by marrying Carle A. Jackson, the son of the mayor of Baltimore. For all her dedication, Ponselle had none of the asceticism of a Fremstad. She had had a string of romances and was known to enjoy herself uninhibitedly. Her great hobby was cycling, and Gatti-Casazza is said to have banned her from riding down Broadway to the Met from her apartment on Riverside Drive, lest she was involved in an accident. At a Met gala, she and Carmela once presented an acrobatic cyclist act left over from vaudeville days. In personality she was volatile and sensitive, quick to react to pressures or criticism. She argued with Jeritza, and once threw all her belongings out of their shared dressing-room; she argued fatally with her manager and long-serving secretary; and she argued with Carmela, who sang sporadically at the Met as a mezzo, without ever establishing herself as much more than Ponselle's sister.

Marriage to Jackson did not work well, despite the building of the famous Villa Pace (from the aria 'Pace, pace, mio dio' in *Forza*) near Baltimore, which is now the Ponselle Museum. The war took him away on active service, and Ponselle was also faced with the death of Romani, the conversion of Carmela to fanatical born-again Christianity, and a series of threats and demands from her mad brother Tony, who also had operatic aspirations. Shortly after Jackson's return, Ponselle, in a deep depression, took an overdose and spent a long convalescent period in hospital. Jackson then left her.

Music seems to have played relatively little part in her life during this dismal period, but after her divorce in 1950, some sense of purpose seems to have been re-ignited. She became artistic director of the small Baltimore Civic Opera and achieved some excellent results with limited resources; her guidance, formal and informal, of

upon cartons of this edition of the newspaper stored in her basement: evidently she had been so appalled by the review that she attempted to buy out the evidence.

singers such as Beverly Sills and Sherrill Milnes, was inspirational; and her opinion of every aspect of American operatic life was sought after and respected. Perhaps most important of all, she became less reluctant to sing, and in 1954 songs and arias from her concert *soirées* were recorded at the Villa Pace. After nearly eighteen years of retirement, the voice had retained its *grandezza*. At either end of her range the tone may be a little frayed and edgy, and the breaks in register are audible. Sometimes her style sounds archaic or unidiomatic, as in a swooping 'Liebestod' from *Tristan und Isolde* and a ludicrously stately rendition of 'Là ci darem la mano' from *Don Giovanni*, in which Zerlina '*vorrrrrrei*'s and '*non vorrrrrrei*'s like a Gioconda. But the 'Vergine degli Angeli' is loveliness itself, and the two arias from *Adriana Lecouvreur*, delicately shaped and sustained, reveal why she so coveted the role.

Ponselle died in 1981. She remains a beacon for every prima donna who aspires to the nineteenth-century Italian repertory, although it was not until the emergence of the black soprano that anything approaching her splendour was heard from an American singer. The necessary exception is the case of Helen Traubel (1899–1972), a strapping six-foot-tall soprano, flamboyantly costumed by Adrian of Hollywood, who assumed the Wagnerian niche at the Met during Flagstad's wartime absence. 'Nobody knows the Traubels I've seen,' lamented Rudolf Bing, punning on the spiritual: Traubel spelt trouble. Her voice was invaluable—huge, firm, and accurate, if unlovable. Like Flagstad herself, she had no difficulty in negotiating and enduring Wagner's challenges. The problem was her lack of commitment. 'I can admit that opera bored me,' she announced in her autobiography, and she sought a number of ways to alleviate the tedium, one of which was playing games with her regular partner, Lauritz Melchior, who by this late stage of his career could have sung Tristan or Siegfried in his sleep. In performance, they habitually competed to see who could get the other to 'crack up' first: Melchior would appear in the wings while Traubel was on stage, wearing a hula-hula skirt over his chain-mail and launch into a Highland Fling. In the next act Traubel would parry by pulling funny faces during a love duet.

'All culture has is hard seats' is another gem from Traubel's memoirs, and shortly after Flagstad's return and a front-page quarrel with Bing, she left the Met for the plush banquettes of the Chez Paree club in Chicago, making further cabaret appearances in

New York and Las Vegas. Here she sang what Bing quaintly referred to as 'programmes of folk music': opera—but not only soprano arias—'Vesti la giubba' and the Toreador's Song were aired as well, the St Louis (her hometown) Blues, musical comedy, and numbers from the hit parade. She then took to Rodgers and Hammerstein, where her impersonation of a brothel madam in *Pipe Dream* was a major factor in the show's collapse. She also made television appearances with Jimmy Durante and Jerry Lewis which usually involved some obvious guying of the conventions of opera. It was as though she wanted revenge: she even wrote a bad thriller entitled *The Metropolitan Opera Murders*.

The *reductio ad absurdum* of the prima donna aping herself and her art was the bizarre Florence Foster Jenkins. The unmistakable dreadfulness of her singing has remained a joke for forty years, although in fairness it ought to be remembered that when her infamous record was made in 1944 she was seventy-six, an age at which even Ponselle would have sounded distinctly unimpressive. It is conceivable that she may once have been able to sing competently, and it is more than conceivable that the whole thing was a hoax, perpetrated by someone who was well aware of the commercial potential in such a preposterous noise.

Little is known of Foster Jenkins's background, although her nobility is attested by her membership (as recorded in her obituary) of the Colonial Descendants of America, the National Association of Patriotic Women, and the American Huguenot Society. It has been said that she was the daughter of a rich attorney who cut her off when she announced that she wished to become a singer. It has also been said that she lived for thirty-eight years in a common law marriage with a ham Shakespearean actor, St Clair Byfield, while teaching the piano and—here we run into verifiable fact—running something called the Verdi Club, under whose auspices she would give her annual private recital at New York's Ritz-Carlton Hotel. Madame Jenkins preferred a light coloratura repertory, which she delivered in a variety of eccentric costumes. Winsome dances and *tableaux vivants* representing 'Grief', 'Dawn', and so on, were other features of the occasion. Her one public recital at the Carnegie Hall was an enormous success and is reported to have grossed $6,000. Unfortunately the artiste died from a heart attack only a month after giving it, mortified, so it is said, at the constant laughter which accompanied her singing and which she attributed to the claques of rival prima donnas.

Her torch is carried today by the even more bizarre and mysterious Madame Mari-Lyn, whose show on cable television in New York has become essential viewing for all connoisseurs of camp. Dressed in a peach polyester trouser suit and literally garlanded in sparkling paste diamonds, Madame Mari-Lyn gives earnest and execrable renditions of celebrated operatic highlights, complete with commentary, and accompanied by piano and violin. She appears to take herself very seriously indeed, claiming to be the protégé of the soprano Frances Alda (Gatti-Casazza's wife), but almost nothing about her career—not least the extraordinary number of awards with which she was showered in Czechoslavakia—is open to verification. Her astonishing records appeared on the Philips label, but nobody in the company knows anything about them. If she is a fraud, one would like to know her true story.

Such nonsense feeds into the camp tradition more self-consciously exploited by a series of artistes through Anna Russell to the drag queen Vera Galupe-Borszh of the burlesque Gran Scena Opera Company. Such acts can be witty and stylish; more often they are coarse and offensive, with a nasty undercurrent of contempt for women, especially fat ones. By now, one might have thought that the joke would have worn as thin as that of the mincing *ballerino*—but it hasn't. The camp prima donna has become one of the more tedious obsessions of gay culture.

Since eighteenth-century comic squibs such as Mozart's *Der Schauspieldirektor*, there has been a tradition of presenting prima donnas as avaricious monsters, unable to tolerate rivalry or criticism. By the 1920s the image had consolidated to that of a middle-aged lady, Junoesque in build, imperious in manner, but also ridiculously susceptible to flattery. Presumably this was conditioned by the appearance of figures such as Melba, Tetrazzini, and Schumann-Heink; it certainly bears no relation to Ponselle, Jeritza, or Garden. A perennially popular caricature in this vein is Madame Castafiore in Hergé's 'Tintin' series of cartoon adventure books, originally published in Belgium from the 1930s onwards.

What is most regrettable about this camp image of the prima donna is that it denies her any sincerity on stage or any reality off it. A romantic novel like Gertrude Atherton's *Tower of Ivory* may now seem over-heated to a ludicrous degree, but at least it suggests that a prima donna could be serious about her art, that real sacrifices are involved, that her motives might be something finer than vanity and greed. New York idolizes its prima donnas, turns them into icons and then debunks them: but does it ever give them a fair hearing?

## APPENDIX

Owing to the kindness of Mr Robert Tuggle of the Metropolitan Opera Archives, I was able to look at the house's paybooks for the years between 1898 and 1975. The following is a brief comparative table, culled from these fascinating documents, relating to the fees paid to prima donnas. All figures are for a single performance unless otherwise stated.

In 1898–9 Melba earned $1,650; Lehmann, $1,250 plus hotel expenses; Nordica, $1,000; and Sembrich $800. However, the highest earner was Jean de Reszke at 11,000 francs or $2,101. His brother Edouard took $668, while the other great bass of the time, Pol Plançon, sang for $220.

1899–1900: Schumann-Heink, $9,000 for 90 performances (later renegotiated at $16,000 for 80 performances, then $24,000 for 100); Eames, $1,000, payable in gold the morning after a performance; Sembrich, $1,000 plus two orchestra stalls (a fee that remained the same until 1906, when it became $1,200); Calvé, $1,719, with a dressing-room as near the stage as possible (in 1903 this rose to $1,920 for appearances outside New York).

1905–6: Melba was promised $2,000 but never appeared; in 1907 Oscar Hammerstein at the rival Manhattan Opera paid her $3,000; Nordica, $1,250; Eames, $1,500; Fremstad, $1,382 for ten performances a month. An average family's annual income in New York was estimated at *c*. $850.

1907–8: Caruso, $2,000; Farrar, $800; Fremstad, $750; Chaliapin, $1,344.

1908–9: Fremstad and Farrar level-pegged for one season at $1,000; Mahler earned slightly less at $5,050 a month for six performances, while Toscanini got only $4,800 for twelve performances a month.

1909–10: Destinn, $900; Farrar, $1,200 (making a total of forty appearances and singing at least twice a fortnight); while Fremstad stayed at $1,000 (also for forty appearances); Nordica kept to her

1905–6 fee of $1,250. Hammerstein at the Manhattan paid Tetrazzini $1,500 and Mary Garden $1,400.

1911–12: Destinn, $1,200; Farrar, $1,250; Fremstad, $1,000. Toscanini was still down at $7,000 a month, averaging twelve performances in that period. Seats at the Met were priced, as they had been for some years, at between one and five dollars.

1914–15: Caruso, $2,500; Destinn, $1,300; Melanie Kurt, Fremstad's replacement, $500.

1919–20: Muzio $625; Farrar, $1,500; Ponselle's second season—she had started at $150 for up to three performances a week—$100 with guaranteed fourteen days' rehearsal: the norm was seven.

1921–2: Jeritza's first season, $1,500; Farrar the same. Muzio, $800. Ponselle, $1,000 per week, singing 24 times in 15 weeks; Galli-Curci, $2,000; Chaliapin, $3,000.

1926–7: Galli-Curci on tour commanded $3,500, in New York, $2,250, with Jeritza a whisker ahead at $2,300; Schumann-Heink's return cost $500; Talley, $500 per week, three performances. The tenor Martinelli took $1,700, the baritone Ruffo $1,500; Gigli, $16,000 per month for approximately eight performances. In the mid-Twenties a motor car cost c. $1,000, a gramophone record $1, and a round-the-world cruise c. $2,000. A seat at the Met could cost up to $8.25 in 1929.

1930–1: the Depression had begun, but had not yet bitten into the upper end of the earnings scale. The charming and stalwart lyric soprano Lucrezia Bori, $1,400; Jeritza, $2,500; Ponselle (after her Covent Garden triumph), $1,700; Rethberg, $1,200.

1935–6: the Depression had hit. Flagstad and Lotte Lehmann, $750; Grace Moore, Ponselle, Bori, $1,000; Melchior, $1,000; Rethberg, $900; Martinelli, $800—less than half what he earned in 1926–7. Average earnings in 1929, $1,300; in 1935, $850.

1956–7: in the intervening twenty years, fees had not increased either in real or inflated terms. Tebaldi, Milanov, and Callas all earned the $1,000 top. By comparison in 1931 it took an average wage-earner 580 hours to earn enough to buy a refrigerator; in 1956, 168 hours.

According to Robert Turnbull's researches, published in the *Sunday Telegraph* on 15 March 1992, the top fee at La Scala now is about £14,000; at the Liceu in Barcelona £17,000; at the Met £6,500; at Covent Garden, £10,000. Mirella Freni, Jessye Norman and Kiri Te Kanawa are probably the only three prima donnas who can consistently command these fees (which can rise much higher in smaller opera houses anxious to buy the kudos of a star name).

# 6

## *The Verdian Soprano*

The prima donna's art is a primitive one. Very little about the production of the singing voice is fully understood, partly because until the recent developments in laser and micro-technology it was impossible to observe a 'throat' in action. (Mirror devices, like Garcia's laryngoscope, inhibit the musculature and cannot reflect the underside of the vocal cords.) Singing teachers all have their own ideas, their own metaphors and peculiar tricks for schooling what in physical essence remains nothing more than a form of expiration. Singers themselves rarely have much to say about their methods. Patti and Flagstad both claimed that they had no idea at all how they could sing as they did. The American bass Jerome Hines compiled a series of interviews on the subject with a number of eminent practitioners and concluded that 'most of the interviewees had difficulty at first in verbalizing their universe of vocal experience. This does not mean that they don't understand it, it means that they are accustomed to thinking about it in the non-verbal language of kinesthetic sensation. As a result they tend to describe their private world of vocalism by gesture, shaping the hands and fingers to represent laryngeal and pharyngeal configurations, or using arms and elbows to demonstrate use of the diaphragm.' In textbooks one often finds only what for a non-singer is sheer gobbledegook: here, for instance, is a much-mocked passage from Lilli Lehmann's *How to Sing*—'In order to make the vowel sound ā, the larynx is with energy brought in closer relation with the nose. By dilating the nostrils a preparation is made. The sensation is then as if the larynx were under the chin.' Try it and see . . .

Just as no two speaking voices can be precisely identical, so no two singing voices are either, and whatever one's preferences, there cannot be one universal and objective standard of perfection applied to them. An individual voice will change in range, timbre, and control over the years. Contraltos become sopranos, coloraturas become 'dramatics', Brünnhildes become Lucias, steady voices begin to wobble, others fray and sharpen. The standard categories of soprano, mezzo-soprano, tenor, baritone, and bass are not written in stone. Much depends on fashion and the demands of the composers of the day. Contraltos and *bassi profondi* have become rare; instead we have a glut of high-lying mezzos and bass-baritones. Vibrato is out of fashion, an efficient coloratura is in. Breath control is not what it was; the constant upward nudge in standard pitch doesn't help.

Every voice has its eccentric weaknesses and strengths. Birgit Nilsson could sing the Queen of the Night's aria with its top Fs and literally breath-taking runs, but only *after* she had warmed her voice up through a performance of *Götterdämmerung* or *Tristan*. Pasta and Malibran, like a number of 'sopranos', were stronger at the top and bottom of their ranges than in the middle; the impeccable Rosa Ponselle could not be relied upon to hit top C; while Jenny Lind's F# (just at the point where most singers have trouble in focusing the tone) was universally considered glorious. The singing voice is dogged by historians who bemoan declining standards and past golden ages, but it is much more realistic to think in terms of constant modifications, in which one strength compensates for another weakness. This may not be a great age for Wagner, but it certainly is for Mozart.

'I think too much is talked about technique,' claimed Joan Sutherland's husband Richard Bonynge in an interview. 'Singers should have a technique that's as simple as ABC. There is a great danger in analysing technique too much, putting its anatomical and physiological aspects under a microscope.' He's right, of course, and science will not take us much further. The physical mechanism of singing is based in the controlled expulsion of air through the vocal cords, two highly sensitive vibrating membranes stretched across the larynx. Resonators such as the larynx itself, the pharynx, palate, and sinus, pick up the sound created and amplify it: here the voice finds its unique timbre and character. The process begins with deep and gentle breathing into a relaxed system, then a smooth emission which leaves the singer with enough 'supporting' air in the lungs on which to 'float' the sound and finish a phrase comfortably. A good *legato* depends crucially on this. Nervous tension or any gustiness in breathing out soon produce the common faults of tremulous tone and aspirates ('haah' instead of 'aah'). Melba is a model here: her 'commencement' (otherwise known as 'attack' or *prise du son*) of a note was without breathiness or any sense of thrusting or grabbing at the sound—it simply arrives, whereas Lotte Lehmann's breathing and attack were noticeably imperfect.

A major area of controversy among singing teachers is the issue of the 'register'—breaks of tone in the voice at which some claim that the larynx decisively changes its shape and position. Chest, middle, and head registers are the terms that have been used in this connection since the thirteenth century, although the scientific evidence for their existence is exiguous and many say that the feeling of a decisive gear-change is illusory. Nevertheless many sopranos, for instance, have difficulty knowing quite what sound to make around E and F at the top of the stave. Teachers struggle to 'equalize' the registers so that the whole range of the voice sounds as seamless and homogeneous as Ponselle's or Leider's, an achievement which involves working hard on the passage-notes which link the so-called registers. The voice must also be 'placed'; that is, the air must be directed, at least mentally, towards the appropriate resonating cavities which will give the sound full and firm tone. Some singers centre it all at the back of the mouth, others concentrate on their sinuses: most agree that the tongue must not block or deflect the sound. Intonation, or the maintenance of correct pitch, is another problem, particularly in an age where *vibrato* is prevalent. It is impossible for a singer accurately to hear the sound she or he is making, and within any audience there will be surprisingly different reactions to a singer's intonation. Very few singers sing at a perfect regularity of pitch, and a small degree of sharpness or flatness is part of a voice's personality. However, a real problem with pitch—as suffered notably by sopranos under pressure, like Pasta or in our own day Gwyneth Jones—is excruciating.

There is so much that can get in the way. A sneeze can release a lot of phlegm and block paths of sound. A stomach upset can impair the breathing. Menstruation affects the abdominal muscles and can cause flatness. Ponselle could not sing near any artificial heat and would telephone the stage-door manager before entering the opera house to make sure it was suitably freezing. Perhaps the most common nightmare comes from the idea of nodes, tiny growths on the vocal cords which among other things are ruinous of a singer's ability to sing *diminuendo* and *piano*. They are probably caused by strain, can sometimes be cured by surgery or prolonged silence, and affect sopranos more than any other sort of voice. A celebrated victim was Lucrezia Bori, who for two years after an operation to remove a node did not raise her voice above a whisper. A more inevitable fate awaiting the vocal cords is sheer exhaustion. The right amount of exercise keeps them in trim, but there is a point beyond which they simply become flabby and unresponsive. For a top C they are estimated to vibrate at something like a thousand times per second, and that is a pitch that cannot be kept up indefinitely.

Beyond this, there isn't much which can be incontrovertibly said on the subject. Singers, especially the great ones, have their own ways of achieving their ends, a process in which (as Richard Bonynge implied) conscious intellect has little place. It's like riding a bicycle.

Somewhere at the heart of this debate is the music of Verdi. Few singers (least of all sopranos) would dispute that his operas provide the healthiest vocal diet, even though the style he requires is far from easy to negotiate or interpret; in particular two of his most famous creations, Violetta in *La Traviata* and Aida, contain radical difficulties. But in opera no one (except perhaps Mozart) has composed music which requires so little forcing or faking and which contains so much gratifyingly expressive and beautiful melody. His career and achievement stand as one of the marvels of musical history.

Giuseppe Verdi was born in 1813; his first surviving opera was produced in 1839, the last in 1893, and throughout his great span he showed an astonishing capacity for growth and self-renewal. As a citizen, he stood at the centre of his society, its aspirations and struggles, and a fervent liberal patriotism runs through his works up to *Otello* in 1887, by which time Italy was free of invaders and united as a nation. As a composer, he instinctively maintained the directness and simplicity of a rich popular musical tradition, and although he was intelligently sensitive to contemporary innovations, he kept his own counsel, immune to vogues, patiently developing his art at his own pace in a spirit of stubborn peasant tenacity.

Not that he was reactionary or complacent: in his own way, he was as dedicated to the reform of operatic abuse as any Wagnerian. From his first opera onwards he was fighting with hard-nosed managements, narrow-minded censors, and lazy prima donnas, all of whom treated his scores much as it suited them. Verdi was nobody's lackey, and as early as 1843 he refused to supply the soprano Sophia Loewe with the showpiece aria for the finale of *Ernani* which she considered her due. He also spent much of his life battling for a system of copyright protection which would prevent opera houses making random cuts, alterations, and substitutions, as well as ensuring the dignity and income of the composer.

The young Verdi, however, did not command the terms, and his survival entailed compromise with singers' capacities and audiences' tastes. Later he talked about his 'years in the galleys', churning out operas to order on harshly commercial terms and following helplessly many of the standard bad practices of the time. Nor was he invariably successful. For a long time his music was considered rumbustious, noisy, and ugly, especially in England, where connoisseur critics such as Chorley regarded even *Rigoletto* as symptomatic of the decline of Italian music into sheer vulgarity. Now, with the hindsight of *Otello* and *Falstaff*, it is easier to appreciate the virtues of works such as *Ernani*, but the modern reaction in favour of early Verdi has surely been excessive. It is refreshing to find the leading Verdi authority Julian Budden admitting that *Attila* is not a rough-diamond masterpiece, but 'blunt in style, daubed in thick garish colours; full of theatrical effects with no depth to them and containing more than its fair share of brash *cabalettas* . . . despite a genuine strength of construction much of it remains no less than *Alzira* on the level of commonplace vigour.'

It is in the music for the prima donna that these first operas most often show distinction. Two female stereotypes recur: there are the noble and pure-hearted ladies such as Amalia in *I Masnadieri* (written for Jenny Lind) and the eponymous Giovanna d'Arco (Joan of Arc), who are given music of Bellinian grace and the sort of wide-arched melody the Italians call *cantilena*; then there are the fiercer more energetic schemers like Abigaille in *Nabucco* or Lady Macbeth, whose roles demand powerful lower registers and some fiendish top notes. Both these types of heroine remain basic to Verdi's operas.

Like all major opera composers, Verdi's feelings about prima donnas were equivocal. In his youth he heard Malibran and the memory was never effaced. No contemporary prima donna offered him comparable inspiration, and he was scathing about the latter-day 'caricatures of Malibran who have only her oddities without any of her genius'. Bellini had worked closely with Pasta, but Verdi missed out on the strongest soprano of his day, Giulia Grisi, who had crossed the Alps and made for the fleshpots of Paris and London, never to return to Italy.* Of the various sopranos he did encounter, Giuseppina Strepponi (1815–97) was the most important to him, even if she was far from the best singer. She came from a well-connected musical family, and when Verdi was still a novice, she was an established prima donna in the dramatic repertory of Bellini and Donizetti. Her encouragement and patronage of the young composer was practical and genuine. In 1842 she created the role of Abigaille in Verdi's first real success, *Nabucco*: unfortunately, it proved the final nail in her professional coffin. She had sung too much over ten exhausting years and borne two illegitimate children as well as undergoing an abortion. The part of Abigaille was very taxing, and although she continued to sing it for a few years in the provinces, it must have finished her voice. At the age of thirty-one she retired from the stage and set up in Paris as a singing teacher. Verdi encountered her there by chance, and in 1849 they set up house together on the farm at Sant' Agata that remained Verdi's base for the next half century. Ten years and a lot of scandal later, they were married. Strepponi's correspondence reveals a splendid woman, warm-hearted, intelligent, and devoted to a man who with all his honesty and integrity could be moody and irascible.

Romantics like to believe that Verdi's experience of Strepponi's status as a 'fallen woman' seeking out happiness in rural retreat brought a new sympathy and emotional intimacy into his creation of the courtesan Violetta in *La Traviata* (1853). The idea is not altogether satisfactory. For one thing, although Violetta has passion, dignity, and independence of spirit, she is still primarily motivated by the ideal of noble self-sacrifice in the name of love which governs so many nineteenth-century operatic heroines. What does distinguish the role is the peculiar difficulty of singing it—a fact obscured by the opera's enormous popularity. Even sopranos as accomplished as Patti and Ponselle had to cheat by making cuts and transpositions, however easy it is to make an effect in the role. Most sopranos either garble the hectic coloratura of the first-act 'Sempre libera' or nervously speed up the wonderful 'Amami, Alfredo' passage, which needs to be sung with a Wagnerian breadth and depth. The orchestra is not overpowering, the opera is not long, the notes involved are not unduly high: it is just very difficult to sing it all as written.

Violetta's successor, the veiled court lady Leonora of *Il Trovatore*

* She did sing a few performances of *Il Trovatore* very late in her career.

(also 1853) is much more straightforward. This is a role that makes no dramatic demands whatsoever, and the stoutest soprano can walk through it all without a moment's embarrassment, so long as she can sing two gorgeous and stately arias in Verdi's most elevated style, each capped by the last of Verdi's old-fashioned *cabalettas*. These fast and brilliant passages tacked on to the end of each leading character's major arias usually had no purpose beyond showing off technique and stimulating wild applause: there was no other feature of conventional Italian opera that Verdi was so anxious to be rid of. In Violetta's Act I aria, he manages to make the *cabaletta* an expression of the character's nervous and self-deceiving love of worldly pleasures, but from the mid 1850s he managed to do without them altogether, developing a far more integrated aria structure.

Verdi's liberation from the *cabaletta* came at a time when he was moving decisively towards the model of French Grand Opera. He spent some years in Paris and wrote for the Opéra after the Meyerbeerian fashion. Sometimes he shows an awkwardness in reconciling the Italian and French traditions, but from *Les Vêpres Siciliennes* to the culmination of *Aida*, we can hear Verdi's steadily growing mastery of a more sophisticated and fluid technique. The orchestration becomes warmer and more varied, and the relentless energy of the early operas is replaced by more measured contrasts and colours. Situation and character are more expansively portrayed.

It is here that the *spinto* soprano makes her appearance. This term—properly *lirico spinto* or 'pushed lyric'—will be applied to several singers in the following pages (although Tietjens, Destinn, and Turner are better described as *soprani drammatici*) and it refers in particular to the type of soprano needed for the middle and late operas of Verdi. Gone are the agility and top E♭s exploited by Rossini and Donizetti: now a different conception of virtuosity prevails. In operas such as *Un Ballo in Maschera*, *Don Carlos*, *La Forza del Destino*, and above all *Aida*, the soprano needs rich, full tone over a wide range, with a perfect *piano* on high notes and strong projection in the lower reaches; breath control which can sustain and colour a long modulating *cantilena*; and the ability to make straightforward emotional dilemmas powerfully vivid. The feelings of Aida, for example, as she weighs '*amor*' against '*patria*' are generalized enough, and her psychology is not explored in any modern sense—but her music is exquisitely refined and full of the most taxingly delicate effects, ruthlessly contrasted with passages demanding something much more brazen and splendid in the middle of the voice. Thus after the infamous exposed ascent to a *diminuendo* top C in 'O patria mia' (the phrase which petrified Rosa Ponselle to the point where she would not sing the role), the soprano has to change *tessitura* within minutes and find a harsh, metallic edge for the confrontation with her angry father, before changing colour and range again for the love duet with Radamès. In the final entombment scene, at the end of a long evening, comes music involving wide and unfamiliar intervals, in a difficult key, which should be sung so as to convey a gradual ebbing of life and breath. Even Aida's first aria, 'Ritorna vincitor', depends entirely on the force of the switch between stern declamation and an exhausted prayer for pity. Technically then, Aida is a role of constant changes of gear, and it is rare to find a soprano who claims to sing it without trepidation. A successful Aida, like a successful Norma or Isolde, has nothing to fear elsewhere.

Far less problematic for the *spinto* is Desdemona in *Otello*, a role often used as a confidence-boosting trial run for Aida. Verdi wrote of Desdemona as 'the type of goodness, resignation, self-sacrifice. There are beings who are born for others, who are quite unaware of their own egos . . .' This characterization could equally be applied to the other *spinto* ladies, and one has to admit that there is a disembodied monotony about the presentation of these victimized and generally passive women which all the grandeur of their music cannot eradicate. For female wilfulness, energy, and anger we have to turn to the three dramatic mezzo-soprano roles that Verdi created in the Azucena of *Il Trovatore*, the Eboli of *Don Carlos*, and the Amneris of *Aida*. In these operas Verdi was in effect setting off the two female types of his early phase (maidenly Giovanna d'Arco and wicked Lady Macbeth) against each other, although the music assigned to them both is radically different in style. The soprano line arches, soars, and falls in comfortable harmonic relation to the orchestra, while the mezzo is more explosive and combative. The dramatic mezzo is another distinctly middle-late Verdi vocal type, a modification of the old Rossinian contralto (itself a replacement of the castrato) with the range pushed higher and the upwards strain used to great effect. The dramatic mezzo originates in Meyerbeer's Fidès in *Le Prophète*, of which Pauline Viardot was the great exemplar; the *spinto* soprano grew out of another phenomenon of French Grand Opera, the *falcon* voice.

Marie Cornélie Falcon (1812–97) belongs to a tragic band of prima donnas whose apparently powerful instruments have prematurely collapsed after a few years of overwork (Ljuba Welitsch provides a modern example of this). Falcon left her mark, however. After Malibran's marital problems caused her to withdraw from Paris, Falcon filled the gap, albeit in a French rather than Italian repertory. At twenty she made her début at the Opéra as Alice in *Robert le Diable*, and went on to create Rachel in Halévy's *La Juive* and Valentine in *Les Huguenots*. She had a withdrawn and intense personality, and a presence on stage which was later compared to that of the actress Rachel. Her voice was of a new and extraordinary character with, as one contemporary described it, 'an incomparable metal, a timbre like nothing that has ever been heard'. She did not have the easy coloratura or top register of an Italian-trained prima donna, but there was something dark, strong, and womanly in her voice, something that suggested both ardour and grief.* Falcon came to represent the romanticism of French Grand Opera, and her name is still used to indicate its range of soprano roles. Her name conjured up a mysterious but potent figure of immense dignity and restraint, and this was the image strongly received into Verdi's middle-period operas—*falcon* is, as it were, French for *spinto*.

Falcon herself met a swift nemesis. In 1838, not six years after her first success, her voice gave out in the middle of a performance. There was consternation in Paris. Such a thing was unheard of—but then so was such an exhausting weight of singing. Falcon went to Italy for a long holiday and some lessons. In 1840 she returned to the Opéra, where she was greeted by such rapturous applause that a combination of nerves and emotion caused her to faint. When she recovered, the audience heard a singer whose vocal extremities remained brilliant at the expense of a feeble hollowness in the all-important middle. Falcon retired immediately, and never sang in public again.

After Falcon, one might note the interestingly transitional voice of Grisi, a soprano deeply influenced by Pasta, who attempted without conspicuous success to enter the *falcon* repertory. It is an odd fact that few first-rate *spintos* have been Italian, and the muse that Verdi found for his later operas was Bohemian. She was Teresa Stolz (1834–1902), whose reputation was made in the eastern opera houses

---

* My own guess is that she sounded something like Jessye Norman.

of Odessa and Constantinople. In 1865 she came to La Scala, where she was to sing in *Un Ballo in Maschera*, *La Forza del Destino*, *Don Carlos*, the Requiem, and, most of all, *Aida*—as well as the *falcon* roles in *Robert le Diable* and *La Juive*. Her manner was commanding and impressive, and one may assume that she gave these rather nebulous characters theatrical definition. The American Blanche Roosevelt reports thus on her singing: 'The power she gave a high C is something amazing . . . the tone swells out bigger and fuller, always retaining that exquisite purity of intonation, and the air seems actually heavy with great passionate waves of melody.'

Her relations with Verdi are shrouded in mystery, despite exhaustive detective work published by Frank Walker and Mary Jane Phillips Matz, and it is impossible to tell whether or not she was his mistress. All we have are Strepponi's letters, full of jealousy and misery at the attentions Verdi paid to Stolz, who came to live at Sant' Agata for an uncomfortable length of time. Strepponi wrung her hands, but tried to maintain friendly relations with Stolz, who in turn appears to have been fond of Strepponi. The situation righted itself eventually, and it is perfectly possible that the affair only existed in Strepponi's head. It is also equally possible that she was being forced to accept an unsatisfactory *ménage à trois*.

There is no doubt, however, about the power of Stolz's vocal endowment, and in her day there was only one other soprano to match her in the *spinto* repertory: a singer whose voice united 'great volume with rare sweetness . . . sufficiently powerful to fill the largest house. It was soft as velvet, and even when it grew weaker there was no flaw to be detected in its mellowness, none of those qualities, which, miscalled "wiry" and "silvery", cover in reality ill-disguised attempts to enforce a pretence which no longer exists.' This is a description by the French critic Brémont of Therese Tietjens (or Titiens), who dominated the London opera scene much as Stolz dominated Milan: neither singer ever trespassed into the other's territory.

Tietjens was born in Hamburg of Hungarian extraction in 1831. Her background remains obscure, and her father has variously been recorded as of 'ancient and noble family' and as the keeper of a *bierkeller*. She sang in Central Europe until 1858, when the impresario Lumley wooed her from Vienna to Her Majesty's in London. It proved to be his last and most steadily profitable managerial coup. She arrived 'horribly nervous', and made her début as Valentine in *Les Huguenots*, before an audience led by Queen Victoria, who was to become one of her greatest admirers. The conductor Luigi Arditi recalled that 'ere she had sung half a dozen pages of music, significant looks passed amongst the audience, murmurs of approval grew into exclamations of pleasure'—and Tietjens went on to triumph. She became a naturalized Briton in 1868, living with her mother in St John's Wood. She was believed to have remained a spinster, but in 1896 *The Times* carried a report that a man claiming to be her husband had just died in Montevideo, the last refuge of the Victorian scoundrel.

A contemporary tribute by Sutherland Edwards shows how well her qualities suited the temper of the time: she was not just a fine singer, but a noble, earnest soul, more robust than Jenny Lind, and much more likeable.

Nor will it be by her artistic merits alone that Mdlle Tietjens will be remembered. The qualities that go towards the making up of a really great prima donna are many and varied. Besides a fine and powerful voice, a perfect style, and high dramatic ability, she must possess great physical strength and that particular kind of force, half physical, half moral, which is known by the name of 'nerve'. This species of courage enabled Mdlle Tietjens to do her duty, and more than her duty to the public at times when many a vocalist, of perhaps equal merit in a purely artistic point of view, would have given way.

Compared with Patti (the obviously implied 'vocalist' who 'would have given way'), her demands were modest and matronly. She was noted for taking an excessive amount of luggage on tour with her, but her fee—£800 for four performances—was never in the Patti league. She devoted her Sundays to charitable causes—'singing in a poor neighbourhood ... many persons actually stopped to kiss the ground where she had trodden'. Lumley's successor Mapleson admits that he was kept solvent by her steady appeal and utter reliability. Again unlike Patti, she was a staunch trouper and easy to deal with professionally; she was also extremely hard-working, and Arditi tells how after a performance they would repair to his home for supper, and at 1.30 a.m. start rehearsing again. Even in her mid-forties, when her supremacy was unassailable, she had the humility to seek lessons from Marchesi as part of an effort to rejuvenate the brilliance at the top of her voice.

Her repertory was extensive, although Lumley was of the opinion that the now old-fashioned 'florid music of the Italian school' suited her far less well than the more modern 'declamatory dramatic style'. But her range was remarkable, embracing Rossini's Semiramide and the mezzo role of Fidès in *Le Prophète*, as well as the first London Amelia in *Un Ballo in Maschera*, Leonora in *La Forza del Destino*, and Marguerite in *Faust*: she also valiantly championed works of neglected merit. *Aida*, of which she would have been superbly capable, did not appear in time to catch her, but on the strength of her performance as the evil Ortrud in *Lohengrin*, Wagner wrote to her in 1864, offering the part of Isolde in his forthcoming opera and even prepared to negotiate cuts in the score to win her over. Unlike some more easily seduced sopranos, Tietjens wisely refused.

Donizetti's Lucrezia Borgia was Tietjens's most famous assumption, as well as her last. Already suffering from the cancer from which she was to die, she gave her last performance at Her Majesty's Theatre in 1877. Mapleson reported on the event: 'As the evening progressed she felt she could hardly get through the opera. Her voice was in its fullest perfection, but her bodily ailments caused her acute agony.' In the final scene when Lucrezia sees that her son is dead, Tietjens uttered a terrible scream of agony: 'As it rang through the house the audience shuddered. Only the initiated knew how much reality there was in it.' At the end of the opera, Lucrezia collapses: when the curtain rose for applause, Tietjens continued to lie insensible on the floor. Having become extremely stout, it required four men to lift her. She died some months later: on the night before her death she received a personal message of sympathy and encouragement from Queen Victoria. Her funeral in Kensal Green cemetery caused something close to a riot, 'amid tokens of public grief such as no artist before her had ever been vouchsafed on English soil'.

By the 1890s that great iconoclast George Bernard Shaw was heartily sick of the Tietjens myth. She had become 'obsolescent':

Imagine being inured from one's cradle to the belief that the sublime in music meant Titiens singing the Inflammatus from Rossini's Stabat Mater; that the tragic in operatic singing, far overtopping anything that Mrs Siddons could ever have done, was Titjens as Lucrezia Borgia ... that Valentine in *Les Huguenots*, the Countess in *Le Nozze*, Pamina in *Die Zauberflöte*, all weighed eighteen stone, and could not be impersonated without a gross violation of operatic propriety by anyone an ounce lighter ... in spite of her imposing carriage, her big voice, her general intelligence, and, above all, a certain good-hearted grace which she never lost, even physically, the intelligence was not artistic intelligence; the voice, after the first few years, was a stale voice; there was not a ray of creative genius in her; and the absurdity of her age, her pleasant ugliness, and her huge size ...

Another critic of the period wrote that 'a certain number of operatic characters may be said to die with Mdlle Tietjens. For a time, at least, it will be very difficult to find a Norma or a Lucrezia Borgia.' In a sense, there was no need for another Norma or Lucrezia Borgia. There was a new Verdi and Wagner repertory for the dramatic soprano, and the only operas of the old Italian school whose popularity survived the turn of the century were *Il Barbiere di Siviglia* and *Lucia di Lammermoor*. The art of coloratura singing was no longer part of every prima donna's training—instead it would become the province of specialists such as Tetrazzini and Galli-Curci.

Tietjens's truest successor emerged twenty-five-odd years after her death, but for all the similarity we can assume between their respective vocal equipments, Emmy Destinn sang none of the 'old Italian' roles of Grisi, which Tietjens had kept alive and flaming. Destinn's voice is dark, heavy, and ardent, never brilliant or flexible. Desmond Shawe-Taylor described it as 'a voice full of meaning, a strongly emotional voice to which the sensitive listener cannot remain indifferent'. For the young Victor Gollancz, crouched up in the Covent Garden gallery night after night and growing to love opera through her singing, Destinn communicated 'a sort of spiritual urgency that can never be explained to anyone who hasn't heard her'. On record, her singing can now sound leaden and over-emphatic, even crude in its effects: she clearly had problems with her intonation and what should rise and fall smoothly (like the end of Aida's 'O patria mia') can sound clumsy and effortful. But the more one listens to her, the more what Gollancz referred to as 'spiritual urgency' does shine out. It was this intensity, as well as an underlying fullness of power in the voice, which made her such an outstanding interpreter of the *spinto* repertory and the first great Puccini prima donna.

Her art embodied the spiritual urgency in her life. She was a Romantic in the grand style, a woman of immoderate feelings, interests and appetites—a recent film has needlessly falsified what needs no exaggeration. She was born Ema Kittl in 1878 in Prague: her family owned mines and breweries. As a child, she showed marked literary leanings and throughout her life she produced poems, novels, and a drama, *Rahel*, which has been occasionally revived. She studied singing under Marie Loewe-Destinn, and took her name in gratitude. In 1898 she made her début in Berlin where she soon became prima donna. For such a weighty voice, she sang a mixed bunch of roles—Pamina in *Die Zauberflöte*; the lyric title-role in Charpentier's *Louise*; the *falcon* Valentine in *Les Huguenots*; and one of the heaviest of all Italian soprano parts, Ponchielli's La Gioconda. She also undertook Strauss's *Salome*, and was that composer's first choice for Ariadne in *Ariadne auf Naxos*. In 1901 she sang at Bayreuth, and in 1904 she arrived in London, which became her second home in the pre-war years. She took a house in Regent's Park and sang at Covent Garden for eleven consecutive summers. Over half a century later, in *Journey Towards Music*, Victor Gollancz reminisced about her art in seasons in which her tenor partners included Caruso, Slezak, and Martinelli.

> The apogee, I suppose, was the Nile scene in *Aida*, interpreted by Destinn, Caruso, and Dinh Gilly. No young opera-goer of today could possibly realise what it was all like; all the beauty and drama came to life for us in those incomparable voices, not as an occasional rarity, but in note after note and phrase after phrase . . . I adored Destinn: we used to say that her twiddly bit in the first act of *Tosca* was alone worth our whole half-crown 'and then some', and she accomplished the change of register in 'Vissi d'arte' with almost inconceivable mastery. But best of all were her soft high notes. They were like exquisitely rounded pearls, suddenly appearing, perfectly poised, out of nowhere: and were specially breath-taking when they opened a phrase, as with 'Un bel dì' in *Butterfly*.

Her voice had by now firmly settled in the *spinto* regions, and Aida, Tosca, and Butterfly became the centre of her repertory. One oddity that she sang was an ephemeral adaptation (in Italian) of Hardy's *Tess of the D'Urbervilles* by Baron Frédéric D'Erlanger, a banker whose money shored up the Covent Garden deficit. In 1908 she abandoned her contract in Berlin and made for New York, the Met having offered her a four-fold increase in salary. Here she was Minnie in the world première of Puccini's *La Fanciulla del West*, as well as singing more Verdi and Wagner.

With the outbreak of the First World War, Destinn's fortunes changed. She returned to Czechoslovakia, then a non-existent nation, its territories part of the Austro-Hungarian Empire. Destinn's nationalism was fierce, and the embattled Austrians interned her in her castle in Stráž, which some like to claim was used as a secret Resistance cell. The authorities refused to let her out, even to fulfil a contract at the Met, unless she agreed to sing for the Austrian Red Cross—which as a Czech patriot she refused to do. The castle, fortunately, was not dull. It contained a large aquarium and a choir of frogs, each of them named after a prima donna, who croaked at different pitches. There was a room full of relics of Napoleon and a huge library mostly consisting of books about 'alchemy, astronomy, black magic, necromancy, mantology, witch-craft, flagellation, somnambulism, spiritualism, and the occult'. There was even a ghost room containing a skeleton, fake tropical spiders dangling from the ceiling, and a coffin full of worms. A newspaper report listed Destinn's other hobbies as 'cats and collecting antiques' but there is no doubt that her ruling passion was sex. She lacked straightforward beauty, but occasionally there is a photograph which hints at the allure and sensuality that coloured her singing as well. Always desperate in search of the ideal, she made do with promiscuity, taking what she needed wherever she could: in her novel, *In the Shade of the Blue Rose*, the heroine finds that 'the desire for a man and his hot embrace were as necessary to her as a draught of liquid to one whose lips are dry and parched and to whom the vessel from which the drink came was of no importance'. Her lover in Berlin was the conductor Karl Muck; in New York, Caruso asked to marry her, and Puccini and Toscanini were besotted; but during the rehearsals for *La Fanciulla del West*, in which all these three were involved, she fell instead for the French Algerian baritone Dinh Gilly, who often sang opposite her as Aida's father. Together they lived in internment at Stráž, deeply but tormentedly in love. Eventually, Gilly could stand in no longer—Destinn took up, *à la*

Lady Chatterley, with a forester on the estate, and Gilly spent the remainder of the war in a camp. Later he railed to the accompanist Ivor Newton against the whole breed of prima donnas:

> They should all be burnt at the stake. I detest them all, I lived with one for five years. In the old days, if they hadn't lovers around them they used to drag the scene shifters into their dressing rooms before their mad scenes [probably a reference to a rumoured habit of Nellie Melba's].

Destinn's public eminence did not survive the war. In the years following the armistice she returned to Covent Garden and the Met, celebrating Czech independence by rechristening herself Ema Destinnová and refusing to utter a word in German, but her career soon lost momentum. Why this should have been is not clear—she was scarcely forty and the enforced years of silence left her voice, according to more than one critic, better than ever. But the collapse of her affair with Gilly must have left her demoralized and in New York, the novelty of Jeritza and Ponselle counted against her, especially as they poached on areas of her repertory. Even Victor Gollancz's enthusiasm waned.

Back in Czechoslovakia she married a young air force pilot, and became enormously fat and indolent. Food and drink were other passions of hers, and her expenditure proved considerably more lavish than her income. She sold her collection of jewels, took pupils, and occasionally sang in concerts, increasingly confining herself to Czech music. In 1930 at the age of fifty-one she died of a massive stroke. The beautiful city of Prague still commemorates its Destinnová with a museum in the Smirice Palace dedicated to her life.

Listening to Destinn on records is something that demands effort and imagination on the listener's part. One has to distinguish between what is plainly and permanently bad in her singing, what is the effect of recording, and what is simply the effect of a style now anachronistic. Destinn is often arresting, but in the Verdi *spinto* regions individuality of character does not count for as much as a pure legato. On this score Destinn is immediately outpointed not only by her 'successors' Rosa Ponselle and Claudia Muzio, but by several other *spinto* sopranos of the Twenties and Thirties: among them the elegant, well-schooled Elisabeth Rethberg, who sang both

German and Italian lyric-dramatic repertories in New York, and Meta Seinemeyer who was a spearhead in the revival of Verdi's lesser-known operas which took place in Germany in the 1920s and who died young of leukaemia. Another interesting figure of this epoch is that of Dame Eva Turner, born in 1892 in the bleak Lancashire cotton town of Oldham (which also fathered the composer William Walton, another musician who opted for the Italianate). For a nation with such a persistent and significant tradition of patronizing Italian opera, Britain has produced extra-ordinarily few internationally famous singers, at least until the 1960s. Between Mrs Billington and Turner, there were really only Adelaide Kemble (1814–79), daughter of the actor Charles Kemble and a pupil of Pasta's, who sang Norma throughout Italy and was greatly admired by Liszt but retired into marriage after only four years of success; and the contralto Mary Shaw (1814–76) who was in the first performance of Verdi's *Oberto* at La Scala in 1839, but who also prematurely retired after her husband fell seriously ill. Both these singers were stars of the 'opera in English' seasons at Covent Garden in 1841–2.

Eva Turner also began with 'opera in English'. After studying at the Royal Academy of Music, she sang between 1916 and 1924 with the valiant Carl Rosa Company who toured grand opera round the British provinces for over eighty years. Neither Turner's voice nor personality were made to languish in obscurity. 'I wasn't a Lancastrian for nothing,' she said. 'Even in the chorus I said to myself, "I must get to the front." ' By 1924, she was firmly at the front of the Carl Rosa and was heard by Ettore Panizza, Toscanini's assistant, during a London performance of *Madama Butterfly*. Panizza persuaded her to audition for Toscanini at La Scala—a tremendous step, even though the way had been paved for English-speakers by the success there of a pretty Irish soprano, Margaret Sheridan. At the audition Turner boldly sang Aida's first aria: Toscanini was impressed, and engaged her to sing two Wagner roles. She lived on in Italy until the outbreak of the Second World War, building herself a villa on the banks of Lake Lugano, and centring her career on the northern Italian opera houses, Turin in particular. What made her reputation was the short but crucifying title-role in Puccini's last opera *Turandot*, which only the most heroic of *spintos* dare to undertake. Ponselle, for instance, could not have coped with the burgeoning volume and pitch of the aria 'In questa reggia', but

Turner's voice was huge, and expanded magnificently to that unforgettable climax at which most singers have to pull back. ('The scoring that could drown Miss Turner has not yet been put on paper,' wrote Ernest Newman in 1928.) She sang Turandot in Chicago, South America, and elsewhere in Europe. Alfano, who completed the unfinished score after Puccini's death, thought her 'perfect' as the dead-hearted, fanatical, and ruthless ice-queen, and Turner's voice had the enthralling power to sustain the role in a way that perhaps only Birgit Nilsson has since matched. Elsewhere on her sadly few recordings she is a little too over-weening and unyielding to be as beguilingly melancholy as an ideal Aida or Leonora should be: but everything else bespeaks singing of towering accomplishment. Apart from her Italian roles, she was not surprisingly an accomplished Wagnerian, and in her long post-retirement teaching career taught Amy Shuard, Rita Hunter, and Gwyneth Jones, her three leading British successors in this area. She remained an awe-inspiring and honoured figure in London musical life until her death in 1990, serving the cause unswervingly. At ninety, she still stood erect as a guardsman, her speaking voice orotund and precise, her faculties thoroughly marshalled.

What is never said is that Turner should have gone even further. She should have recorded more, she should have sung at the Met and returned regularly to La Scala, working with the great conductors of the day. Even at Covent Garden, she was sometimes overlooked; on Coronation Night in 1937, an Italian singer was preferred as Aida, Turner being assigned the inferior task of leading chorus and audience in 'God Save the King'! The shortcomings of her career are emphasized by comparison with that of Zinka Milanov, a far less exceptional singer, albeit a very fine one.

In 1962, on the twenty-fifth anniversary of Milanov's début at the Met, 'the usually staid Monday night audience (Monday is "fashion night" at the Metropolitan) was beside itself . . . Radiant and deeply moved, Miss Milanov suffused the house with the glow of her emotions. She has one of those elemental temperaments whose very naivety is a great strength.' This last sentence, from a report in *Opera* magazine, politely hints at the truth—Milanov was very imperious and very determined. 'There was no false modesty about Zinka Milanov,' wrote George Jellinek. 'She was securely convinced of her own greatness.' Even in retirement she remained indomitable: when the comedian Lily Tomlin announced in the programme for her one-woman show on Broadway that her standby (understudy) was Zinka Milanov, the prima donna was humiliated by the joke to the point of suing for $2 million. Throughout her years at the Met, she kept a close eye on potential rivals. When Callas made her début there in 1956, she chose the part of Norma, in which Milanov had flopped two seasons earlier. As the second act was about to begin, Milanov made a slow pointed entry into the auditorium, gathering as much applause and attention for herself as possible. This remained a favourite habit of hers—I myself remember seeing her, long after she had retired, advance regally down the aisle before a performance of *Adriana Lecouvreur* with Montserrat Caballé. The applause was respectful and intimidated—we all knew at once that it was Milanov who had come to pass authoritative judgement, and that hers was the truly significant presence. At the Met's Centennial Gala, she was still there, sitting in a place of honour on the stage and surveying the proceedings with an icy and imperturbable stare.

She was born in Yugoslavia in 1906 and studied with Milka Ternina. In the early 1930s she took, like Turner, the best possible apprenticeship, singing regularly with the same company in a variety of roles. In 1937 she left her Zagreb nest, and again like Turner had her first international success under Toscanini, in the Verdi Requiem at the Salzburg Festival. From December of that year (in which Ponselle had retired) until the closure of the old house in 1966, with only one real break of three years after the war, she sang at the Met.

Milanov's early performances were marred by an uncertainty of pitch and a lack of general confidence, giving, as the Met historian, Irving Kolodin, put it, 'alternate sensations of pleasure and pain'—partly due, perhaps, to her difficulty with the Italian language. She continued to take lessons and worked hard with her accompanist brother, who clearly exerted considerable musical influence over her. By the 1950s everything had fallen into place. She married a Yugoslav general; she sang at La Scala and Covent Garden; she made LP recordings of her major roles with distinguished colleagues such as Jussi Björling and Leonard Warren; and, apart from the mistake with Norma, she stuck firmly to what she could do well—*Tosca, Trovatore, Aida, Un Ballo in Maschera, Andrea Chénier, La Gioconda*, and a very few others. She never bellowed or throttled her tone; her *pianissimo* was ravishing; she sang sparingly on her chest voice, so as to keep a pure soprano sound. She knew her limitations:

'A dog is a dog,' she told one interviewer portentously, 'and remains a dog even if he wishes he were a cat. The laws of nature cannot be changed. You are what you are.' She was cautious at all times and adamant about what she would not and could not sing: thus the Marschallin, Butterfly, and Turandot she had sung in Zagreb never passed her lips at the Met.

The result of this, confirmed by records, was a copybook art without much edge or flavour, apart from the wonderfully floated soft singing. One can start by finding Milanov relaxing but end up feeling a little bored. She can make a night-time reverie like 'D'amor sull' ali rosee' (from *Il Trovatore*) evanesce into the heavens, but any climactic open-throated cry—'Maledizione!', 'Suicidio!', 'Ritorna vincitor!'—finds her ladylike. The grand and sudden contrasts and modulations of mood upon which depends so much of Verdi's drama, and of *Aida* in particular, are not fulfilled.

Milanov epitomizes a certain idea of refinement and 'good taste' in Verdi singing, but it was Leontyne Price who broke the mould and brought back an uninhibited splendour. Price's voice has an unmistakably individual fragrance—husky, musky, smoky, misty (on a bad day, foggy!)—and a palpitating sexiness. It is not the voice of a good girl. When she sang Puccini or Strauss the sheer opulence became almost too much, like cream on top of a rich chocolate pudding. 'I think I've one of the most beautiful lyric soprano voices I've ever heard. I'm mad about my voice. It was gorgeous,' she told one interviewer after she retired from opera in 1985. 'I loved it so much that from time to time I would take out one of my best crystal glasses, sip a little champagne and toast it.'

The first thirty-five years of her life were dominated by her skin colour black. 'My career was simultaneous with the opening up of civil rights,' she complained. 'Whenever there was any copy about me, what I was as an artist, what I had as ability, got shoveled under because all the attention was on racial connotations.' She was born in 1927 in deep south Mississippi to parents who were active in the music of the local church. At the age of nine, Leontyne heard a recital given by the black American contralto Marian Anderson and decided that she wanted to sing for her living. The fact that a rich white family helped her with the money for lessons was later played up by the press, to the point where Price had to reassert the encouragement she had also had from her parents. She won a scholarship to the Juilliard School in New York, and studied with Florence Page Kimball, a pupil of Marcella Sembrich's.

In the early 1950s a serious black singer could only hope to follow Anderson into a career in concert and recital. A hundred years after the 'Black Malibran' and fifty after the 'Black Patti', Sissieretta Jones, the notion of a black prima donna had still not gained acceptance in the major opera houses. But Price heard Welitsch sing Salome and was entranced; it would be opera or bust. She spent her first years as a professional in Broadway productions of the next best thing—'all black' American operas, such as Virgil Thomson's *Four Saints in Three Acts*, and *Porgy and Bess*. In 1955, Bing opened the Met door to Marian Anderson, against considerable conservative opposition, and engaged her to sing the relatively small role of Ulrica in *Un Ballo in Maschera*.

A barrier was down and a precedent established: the event heralded a decade in which blacks would fight for a full role in the world's greatest democratic society. Price made her way steadily, although her token-black status meant that, as she put it, she had 'to walk on my tippy-toes'. She sang Tosca on American television and in *Dialogues des Carmelites* in San Francisco, but her real break-through was in Europe. In 1958 she sang Aida, the black soprano's inevitable *carte de visite*, in Vienna, the Verona Arena, and at Covent Garden. In 1960 she sang at Salzburg and La Scala. Karajan patronized her assiduously; her success was unremitting. Finally, in 1961, seven days after Kennedy's inauguration, at the dawn of a new America, Price made her début at the Met, in *Il Trovatore*. For all the immediate and lasting glory that she found there, it was never her happiest stage. One night she cracked in the middle of *La Fanciulla del West*—an opera for a Turner rather than a Price—and had to be replaced. In 1966, as America's undisputed prima donna *assoluta*, she was chosen for the première of Barber's *Antony and Cleopatra*, which was to open the new Met in Lincoln Center. The massive publicity culminated in anti-climax and Price herself was swamped by Zeffirelli's leadenly lavish production. In later years the Manhattan critics remarked on the blandness of her characterizations and decided that her singing was mannered. The rest of the opera-going public had little chance to test their verdict, since she was reluctant to travel far from her home in Greenwich Village in the latter years of her career.

Throughout the 1960s and 1970s, cut-Price imitations followed, as the black prima donna became fashionable rather than merely acceptable, and Mama Leontyne stood as a glamorous role model for a younger generation ready to take advantage of political and cultural enfranchisement. Several of them vanished swiftly—Felicia Weathers was one such nine-day wonder—but two of them, Shirley Verrett and Grace Bumbry hung on for dear life, spinning out their careers long past their impressive primes and playing with fire by changing from dramatic mezzo to *spinto* soprano and back again with no apparent concern for anything except naked ambition.

In the 1960s both of them had been magnificent. Bumbry, a pupil of Lotte Lehmann, became the first black singer at Bayreuth and her Eboli in *Don Carlo* was considered peerless; while no less an authority than Walter Legge soberly dubbed Verrett 'the best mezzo in the world'. For the two decades which followed, they kept their balances on a slippery slope, as finesse was sacrificed to sheer aggression. At a late stage, they joined forces to pull off a tremendous PR coup when in 1990 they inaugurated the new Opéra Bastille as Cassandre (Bumbry) and Didon (Verrett) in the first-ever Paris performance of Berlioz's *Les Troyens*. But their performances seemed harsh and coarse, making their effects through broad strokes, furious blasts and regal glares, rather than the wiser musicality for which both of them had initially been notable.

Jessye Norman (born 1945) carried the sacred flame far more surely. An astonishingly beautiful woman of voluptuous proportions and sensuality, she has a voice to match her physique—short of glitter at the top, but rich and broad and full, like some unstoppable force of nature: a waterfall, a tidal wave. 'Her whole body makes the sound,' as the American stage director Robert Wilson aptly put it. Her artistry was calculated to a degree which some found irritating— every nuance moulded, every gesture polished—and she never let rip with the thrilling abandon of which Price was capable. But every time she opened her mouth she commanded respect.

She has kept her career under strict control, mixing a limited number of appearances in opera (recently, she has concentrated exclusively on the Met) with a busier schedule of concerts and recitals. Wherever she goes, she calls the shots. The minute stipulations and specifications of the standard contract sent out on her behalf to anyone who hires her are never forgotten by those called upon to fulfil them—right down to the bottles of mineral water, the boxes of paper tissues and the minions forbidden to address her unless they have been previously spoken to.

Her repertory has been unusually idiosyncratic. Early in her career, when on contract in the 1970s to the Deutsche Oper, Berlin, she sang mainstream soprano roles like Aida, Countess Almaviva and Elisabeth in *Tannhäuser*. These were soon dropped and it is only on record that she has undertaken (to less than universal acclaim, it must be said) Carmen, Salome and Leonore in *Fidelio*. In the 1980s and 90s you were more likely to hear her in Gluck's *Alceste* or Schoenberg's *Erwartung*, off the beaten *spinto* track.

As she approached fifty, she was still havering tantalizingly over the role of Isolde—something which constitutes the furthest shore and the highest goal for the *spinto* (admittedly a category which Norman doesn't comfortably fit). She will doubtless spring some more arcane surprises on us, but in an age so scantily endowed with voices as splendid as hers one can't help regretting that she hasn't found the Verdi repertory more to her taste. To hear his mature music well sung is now the rarest of operatic treats; fifty, forty, thirty years ago, that was not the case. Verdi, like Shakespeare, can weather countless incompetent or mediocre performances, but nearly a century after his death, the dimensions of his genius which singers like Jessye Norman are capable of realizing seem to be falling beyond our reach.

# 7

# *Strauss and the Prima Donna in Vienna*

It would be possible to live in London or New York and remain quite unaware that the city contained a building called an opera house, but in Vienna one has no such option. The opera house dominates city life, both geographically and spiritually. It is as inextricably associated with Vienna as the Prater wheel, kitsch, and Sigmund Freud, presenting the Viennese with an unfailing source of controversy. As a symbol of the city, it is not an inert monument like the Eiffel Tower or the Golden Gate Bridge, but an institution whose personnel, character, and achievements are varying. Every performance puts someone's reputation at stake; every new production or appointment is a politically charged act (recent controversies have involved conductors Lorin Maazel and Claudio Abbado losing out to administrators, and the rise to power of Ion Holender, one of the toughest operators in the business). The opera provides Vienna with more than entertainment—it gives the city its honour, and after the bombing at the end of the Second World War, its survival in some form was regarded not as a luxury, the cream in the coffee, but as a precondition of decency.

Vienna's operatic tradition goes back to the seventeenth century and was long embroiled with the imperial court. Gluck, Mozart, and Beethoven all wrote for Vienna, and in 1821 Domenico Barbaia brought Rossini with him from Naples, when he took over the management of the Theater an der Wien and the Kärntnerthor. Colbran, Sontag, Schröder-Devrient, Lind, and Patti all had significant success there, but the modern era dates from 1869, when a new opera house was opened as the centre-piece of a massive urban redevelopment, along what is known as the Ringstrasse, embodiment of the pomp and pretension of the doomed Austro-Hungarian Empire. Six years later Paris was to open its own similarly grandiose opera house. Unlike the 'guest-star' oriented system of London, Vienna always maintained a permanent ensemble of artists, under long-term restrictive contracts as court servants. The prerogative of the prima donna did not obtain and perhaps more than any other opera house the history of Vienna is the history of its chief conductors rather than its leading singers. Musical standards were always abnormally high. Wagner found many of his singers for the first Bayreuth *Ring* here, and his operas were regularly and competently performed, sometimes under the composer's supervision and conducted by Hans Richter, at a time when most opera houses were still trembling at the strain of putting on even a mutilated version of *Lohengrin* or *Tannhäuser*.

The first unforgettable figure of the new Vienna Opera was Gustav Mahler, far more revered in his lifetime as a conductor than as a composer. He was chief conductor and artistic director there from 1897 to 1907, an appointment which caused immense controversy and which was violently resisted by Cosima Wagner on anti-Semitic grounds, despite his brilliant interpretations of her husband's works. Mahler enforced the Wagnerian etiquette of opera-going—dimming the house lights, refusing admission to latecomers and the claques. 'Tradition is slovenliness' was his militant principle as he ruthlessly revolutionized every aspect of opera performance, restoring passages normally cut and insisting on respect for the composer's written intentions. Melba, however, once bested him: in a guest appearance, she was permitted to give the entire Mad Scene from *Lucia di Lammermoor* as a tailpiece to *La Traviata*. Otherwise the prima donna was thoroughly subordinated to ferocious rehearsal and musical discipline. One of his most significant reforms was changing the position of the conductor's podium. Before Mahler, the conductor of Italian opera had stood up against the stage, as close to the singers as possible, the orchestra following him from behind: Mahler moved back to the modern position in front of the orchestra, where it could receive the full force of his electrifyingly volatile and expressive gesturing. In partnership with the designer Alfred Roller, Mahler also created restrained and beautiful stage-pictures, which in their use of simple colour schemes and subtle lighting effects heralded a new attitude to operatic spectacle.

His taste in singers was specific and his control over casting draconian. He had no great love of the sort of purely beautiful effortless tone represented by Melba, and put his energies into building up an ensemble of voices with power and expressive variety. It was unfortunate that his name was amorously linked with three of his prima donnas, since the coffee-houses and *salons* were all too eager for any evidence against him, and the casting-couch smear was as irresistible as it was unjustified. The only serious relationship he had was that with Anna von Mildenburg, a heroic Wagnerian soprano of great intelligence and melancholy mien. Mahler had fallen in love with her while conducting in Hamburg, where they were both contracted, and in 1897 she followed him to Vienna. To avoid scandal, the liaison was carried on in the utmost secrecy and discomfort, and soon broke under the strain, although she continued to sing for Mahler in Vienna throughout his tenure. Mahler's formidable wife Alma was later to write off Mildenburg's passion as 'wholly self-seeking', but if anything it seems to have been the opposite—a complete submission to Mahler's destiny, artistic principles, and temperament. Marie Gutheil-Schoder and Selma Kurz were also rumoured to have fallen under Mahler's baneful spell. Gutheil-Schoder's style was harsh, vivid, and forceful and she was initially dubbed 'the singer without a voice', but Mahler loyally nurtured her and she remained a feature of the Vienna Opera until 1926, a celebrated Carmen and the first Viennese Octavian in *Rosenkavalier*. Selma Kurz had a similarly long career in Vienna as a coloratura soprano with a staggering trill, still to be heard on record; Melba was said to be inflamed with jealousy by her acclaim at Covent Garden.

After Mahler left Vienna for New York and the Met, his heart condition fatally exacerbated by the intrigue and malice directed against him, there was a lull, followed by the First World War and the collapse of the Habsburgs. Austria emerged as a republic and Vienna's court opera became a state opera. The aftermath of war left the city impoverished and hungry, beset with inflation, strikes, and political unrest, but at least there was another conductor who could send waves of excitement through the opera house. In an unhappily ill-defined arrangement Richard Strauss (1864–1949) was appointed co-director with Franz Schalk in 1919. Strauss remained until 1924, when he too was prematurely pushed out.

In contrast to Mahler's high seriousness, Strauss leaned towards brilliance and charm. He was indulgent to singers and players, but knew how to achieve the best results. He was also, of course, an immensely self-assured and productive composer, who made a fortune fulfilling the middle-class musical taste of his time. Strauss remains fashionable as the opera composer of sophisticated romances and two out-and-out melodramas, all brilliantly orchestrated in an idiom which remains for most opera-goers an acceptable version of 'modern music', harmonically dissonant, sometimes bombastic but conveying recognizable moods and emotions in interesting situations. In *Elektra* one responds to the over-heated neurotic restlessness, the fantastic range of colour and dynamic, right down to the final crashing C major chords which close the work; in an opera like *Rosenkavalier* or *Arabella*, we all wait for the soaring ecstasy of the soprano passages, which swoop or droop over the passing of beauty, the smell of a rose, or the coming of Mr Right. Strauss's is music of pure—or impure—sensuality, sometimes physically assaulting, sometimes (as in the Four Last Songs or the *Rosenkavalier* Trio) spine-tinglingly lovely. Whether it is any more than this is a matter for personal taste or high musical debate.

Strauss was interested in women and their condition. Not since Mozart, one might go so far as to say, had a major opera composer treated such a variety of female psychologies. The Wagnerian mould was broken, and a Strauss heroine does not have to be branded angel, martyr, or virgin. She can let out her stays and uncover her cleavage without being thought a whore. Her sexual longings can be open and frank, her temper impulsive and melancholic rather than heroic and obsessive. Tricked or baffled by men, she can look in the mirror and keep a sense of proportion about life. She can even make jokes and snap at the servants.

Strauss's early career had been dominated by the composition of narrative orchestral tone-poems in which he played fancifully at the musical depiction of everything from a baby in the bath to mountain landscapes. The classicist Brahms devastated him by declaring that one of these pieces was 'too full of thematic irrelevancies', but Strauss continued to be a twentieth-century Baroque composer, in love with ornament, flourish, and gilded façades. In his operas the orchestra is always furiously busy making effects, and nowhere is this more overwhelming than in *Salome*, which Fauré described as a 'symphonic poem with added vocal parts'. Taken directly from Oscar Wilde's play, *Salome* was a sensation from its first performance in Dresden in 1905. Mahler then tried to get it for Vienna, but the censors forbade it as a distastefully lascivious treatment of a biblical subject; while in 1907, New York found its 'moral stench . . . abhorrent' and the Met did not perform it again until 1933. The shock value has now evaporated, but *Salome* still provides a marvellous opportunity for an imaginative prima donna capable of communicating the spoilt teenager in the character. Whatever one's view of Salome's moral awareness, she is always a virgin, and coy prurience is strongly drawn in her music. Great interpreters of the role like Ljuba Welitsch bring an ironic lightness and sweetness into their voices when singing it, and it is interesting that Strauss pestered Elisabeth Schumann, famous as the nice silly convent-educated Sophie of *Rosenkavalier*, to sing the role, even offering to reduce the orchestral counterblast to accommodate her.

Without the severed head, *Salome* could easily be turned into Viennese comedy—the story of a petulant rich girl who wants to kiss the high-minded but ineligible John the Baptist and flirts with her stepfather to get his permission. The decadent apparatus of the work now looks tawdry or ludicrous, but its successor, *Elektra* (1909), remains a genuinely terrifying study of the obsessive pathology of hatred, for which Strauss wrote his most dense, viscerally gripping and plain loud music. The libretto was adapted by Strauss's great collaborator, the Viennese poet and playwright Hugo von Hofmannsthal, from his own 1903 version of the Sophocles play. Its psychology, full of Oedipal situations, bad dreams, and sublimated sexual frustration, makes it a product appropriate to Freud's Vienna, and perhaps no other operatic part demands from the prima donna such a purely intellectual grasp of the implications of the text, such an amount of verbal inflection, or presents her with so many words to sing: this, as much as the length of the role and the volume required, sets it on its own. This Elektra is neither heroine nor victim, but a female Hamlet—unremittingly possessed by a mother's betrayal and a father's murder, driven by a suicidal tendency. Elektra is also a wit, and an interpreter who embraces her complex of moods should bring out the farcical aspects of the situation, her grovelling absurdity as well as her pathos. This is a brutally painful and exhausting opera for conductor, orchestra, the three women principals, and the audience. Strauss himself, easygoing by nature and bourgeois in his private life, was exhausted by composing it, and he never returned to any comparable subject-matter. Later he would write to Hofmannsthal of his ambition to be the Offenbach of the twentieth century—he had stripped off his Wagnerian armoury.

Strauss and Hofmannsthal's next opera was *Der Rosenkavalier* (1911), a roaring popular success everywhere from its first perform- ance in Dresden. More sentiment accrues to *Rosenkavalier* than to any other twentieth-century opera. It is 'loved' in the way that *Le Nozze di Figaro*, *Traviata*, or *La Bohème* are loved: the Marschallin's monologue, the Presentation of the Rose, the final Trio and Duet are listened to when all else seems lost. Every element and effect is carefully assembled to make up a pastiche of everyone's dream of the romance of old Vienna. There is a hint of Mozart in the period setting and the casting of lustful Count Octavian as a mezzo-soprano, a soupçon of Johann Strauss in the anachronistic waltzes, an Italian tenor to sing some mock-Verdi and even a little black page. The milieu is aristocratic but *louche*, and a married noblewoman is allowed her adultery without incurring any subsequent humiliation. The orchestra sweetens, spices, comments on, and imitates it all, from the startlingly graphic representation of sexual intercourse in the prelude to the final little twist in the coda. The core of its musical appeal, however, is surely the ravishing blending of three high-lying but differently coloured soprano voices, contrasted with the rough *buffo* bass of Baron Ochs—a beauty pursued by the beast principle, and one that Strauss returned to, partly to avoid having to deal with the tenor voice, which he disliked. The opera's emotional focus is the figure of the Marschallin, unhappily married, facing the end of her youth, involved with a younger man, well aware how it must all end, and facing that end, when it comes, with magnanimity and self- restraint. Towards the end of Act I she reflects on the inevitability of losing Octavian '*Heut oder Morgen*'; the passage of Time, '*ein sonderbar Ding*'; her daily round of church, lunch with an old uncle, a drive in the Prater—and a Lehmann, a Schwarzkopf, a Lott can engrave the poignance of it all on even the most cynical ear. The Marschallin is a symbol of the grace of aristocratic womanhood in an opera that depends a lot on nostalgia for the delights of the old order.

With *Rosenkavalier* Strauss reached a peak of fame and success. None of his later operas ever matched up to it in terms of public favour and he was to search in vain for the rest of his life for an equally happy formula. His next opera with Hofmannsthal, *Ariadne auf Naxos* (1912; second version, 1916), was considered too clever by half, although the pastiche is more economically contrived than its predecessor's, requiring only a small orchestra and ten singers. Originally, *Ariadne* was designed as a one-act opera to follow a spoken performance of Molière's *Le Bourgeois Gentilhomme*, but this proved impractical. After alterations it became an opera about putting on an opera, with another trio of high-voiced ladies in the leading roles. There is another breeches part for high mezzo-soprano in the Composer of the second version's Prologue, who lyrically defends the art of music against the philistines in some of Strauss's most pulsating and ardent pages; a grand prima donna part for the Ariadne, who has a grand monologue and a very grand aria and duet to negotiate; and finally the tiresome role of Zerbinetta, for a coloratura soprano who prances around giving the soubrette view on the proceedings. *Ariadne* was followed by *Die Frau ohne Schatten* (1919): its complex allegorical libretto delving into the mysteries of marriage and infertility inspired Strauss to a gorgeous score, but it was hardly designed for instant appeal in a society shattered by four years of war. It was the only Strauss opera to be given its première in Vienna, since Strauss ordinarily preferred to expose himself first in the smaller and kindlier opera house at Dresden. The first cast of *Die Frau* included Lotte Lehmann and Maria Jeritza, Vienna's two leading young soprano prima donnas, who were not on the best of terms. As such rivalries go, theirs was a sadly serious matter, fanned not by the press but by an artistic competitiveness centring on Strauss.

They entered the opera house by different doors on the nights on which they sang together, in *Die Frau*, *Ariadne*, *Carmen*, or *Die Walküre*; Lehmann refused to sing in a later opera of Strauss's, *Die Aegyptische Helena*, because Jeritza had cornered it before her, while Jeritza always claimed that Strauss had offered her either of the leading parts in *Die Frau*, and Lehmann had been handed her cast-off. Later, their territories separated: Lehmann never reached the Met until past her operatic prime, in the season after Jeritza had completed her thirteen-year sojourn there, and Jeritza never sang at Covent Garden after 1926, during Lehmann's legendary seasons. In her autobiography, Jeritza makes no mention of Lehmann whatsoever; Lehmann, in one of her many books, makes much of Jeritza, granting her genius but making a number of back-handed comments on her general deportment. She finally recalls how, many years into retirement, she and Jeritza were brought together for a radio interview, broadcast from the Met, in which they discussed the rehearsals for the second version of *Ariadne*. They 'exchanged remarks that in our youth would have been cause for blistering hostility or open battle . . . we were even served champagne, which I sipped with delight while Maria, in an astonishing display of abstemiousness, confined herself to ginger ale. Which, perhaps, was all to the good, for there is no way of telling what she would have said or done if the champagne had gone to her head.' The jibe ignores the fact that Jeritza was an avowed teetotaller.

Much of the feud went on unpublicized, but in 1925 Jeritza caused a real public scandal, when she clashed with the notoriously sensitive and excitable contralto Maria Olczewska during a performance of *Die Walküre* in Vienna. Jeritza stood in the wings with another singer, Hermine Kittel, waiting for her second Act II entry. Olczewska was on stage singing Fricka, deep in her debate with Wotan, sung by her fiancé who was widely suspected of dallying with Jeritza. In the circumstances, it was not surprising that Olczewska became thoroughly distracted by the sound of Jeritza's laughter and conversation. She hissed at her to stop, but Jeritza continued her merriment. Finally Olczewska marched towards the wings while Wotan was addressing her and spat at Jeritza. Unfortunately the force of the insult landed on the innocent Kittel, who was understandably outraged. Olczewska was immediately dismissed from the Vienna Opera, and according to Marcel Prawy a joke went round to the effect that the incident was symbolic of the new Austrian Republic—'The big powers quarrel and the small ones get it in the neck.'

Jeritza was certainly a big power, the only prima donna in the grandly authoritarian style of a Grisi or Melba which Vienna ever produced. She was born in the industrial city of Brno in 1887 and made a sensational début at the Vienna Opera in a forgotten opera, *Aphrodite*, in which she appeared in an unprecedented degree of nudity. She had a robust peasant beauty, with wonderful hair and a *retroussé* nose. Her voice was large, glowing, and somewhat ill-disciplined, and her acting style instinctive and energetic. Strauss and Hofmannsthal adored her. In rehearsal for *Ariadne* (she created the title-role in the second version), she was observed to be departing somewhat from the written score. 'Stop her?' replied Strauss to an anxious *répétiteur*. 'No, leave her alone, she knows what she's doing.*

---

* 'He makes phrases which go from here to Brook-e-Lyn. They make me choke,' Jeritza said of Strauss in the Met Radio interview, to Lehmann's evident delight!

Her unavailability for *Die Aegyptische Helena*'s première precipitated Hofmannsthal to blind panic, as the suggested substitute was without Jeritza's essential erotic aura.

She also stands with Mary Garden as the last 'star' prima donna to concentrate her repertory on modern operas. Apart from her Strauss, she was famous in Vienna and New York for the double role of Mariette-Marie in Korngold's *Die Tote Stadt* and Janáček's *Jenufa*, as well as taking part in a lot of ephemeral flops like *Siberia* and *Quo Vadis?* She complained about contemporary composers' preoccupation with the 'degenerate, neurotic, mad or imbecile', and it is interesting to read her opinion of an opera in which she sang by the *avant-garde* Schreker as being full of 'unvocal shrieking'—not the last time a prima donna was to express such a view of the operatic music of the twentieth century. On the whole, however, her memoirs—which rejoice in the title of *Sunlight and Song*—are unilluminating as to her musical experience, and by far the longest chapter is devoted to a fawning description of her relations with the imperial Habsburgs: 'The archdukes and archduchesses—with some of whom I stood on a footing of intimate personal friendship— were the most amiable, unaffected persons one might wish to meet.'

From 1921 she went every autumn and winter to the Met, where she replaced the retiring Geraldine Farrar as the star attraction: the Gerryflappers turned into Jerryflappers and women's magazines published her beauty tips—'How does Maria Jeritza keep the most beautiful elbows in the world? She soaks them daily in grapefruit juice', etc. Yet she continued hard vocal studies with the revered soprano Marcella Sembrich, as well as maintaining a fearsome keep-fit programme of Swedish gymnastics, swimming, and mountain-climbing.

Vincent Sheean gives his reasons for her popularity in New York: 'a fresh, strong voice, an eager awareness of the public, a sort of all-out unreserve . . . There was not a trace of subtlety in her voice or acting, but what she had to give was given so lavishly, so honestly and *de bon coeur* that no audience could resist her.' Her physical energy was inexhaustible. As Santuzza in *Cavalleria Rusticana*, Turiddu's push would send her rolling down a huge flight of steps, and when Alfred Piccaver revenged himself for some slight by refusing to administer the push, she simply rolled down anyway. As Carmen, writes W. J. Henderson, 'she was very busy. She made a vigorous attempt at a Spanish dance; she sprawled on tables and chairs, put her feet on men's laps, jumped on tables and off again and smoked cigarettes even while singing.' Her most sensational effect came as Tosca. When rehearsing in Vienna with the composer, who admired her enormously, she fell accidentally to the ground just before the aria 'Vissi d'arte', and discovering she had a nose-bleed, decided to stay there. Puccini approved the idea as a means of sustaining the dramatic impetus at a point where it is otherwise dissipated. Jeritza worked it up into a complicated piece of grovelling business, her hair falling over her face and her head sinking over her hands in a fit of sobbing. At first, wrote Lotte Lehmann severely, 'the effect was electrifyingly natural. Later on, however . . . that shock of hair always coming undone at precisely the same moment began to seem awkward and embarrassing because the artifice, the practised gesture with which she removed her hair-pins, became so obviously contrived.' Geraldine Farrar, herself a great Tosca, was bitchily terser: 'I obtained no view of any expressive pantomime on her pretty face, while I was surprised by the questionable flaunting of a well-cushioned and obvious posterior.'

Her records give little idea of her abilities: they are competent but uninspired to the point of sounding perfunctory. In view of her description of a typical recording session, she is not to be blamed:

> The records were made in a small room, a room so small that the members of the little orchestra of ten or fourteen men which accompanied me had to sit close together, knee to knee. With the orchestra so close to the singer the sound of the instruments is so overpowering that it drowns the voice and I could not hear myself sing . . . I found myself able to overcome this difficulty by holding my hands over my ears . . . Then there is the matter of adjusting your position as you stand and sing, so that you are at exactly the right distance from the receiver. For deep register tones one comes closer, for high register tones one moves further away.

Like Leider's, her art was one which was cruelly inhibited by this situation, and Jeritza does not seem to have been born with the caul of inhibition. Strauss was probably right not to stop her in her tracks: far better to lose or gain a quaver than cramp such flamboyant self-projection, even if there were times when the sloppiness of her singing verged on the disastrous.

In 1932 the Depression-stricken Met decided that they could no longer justify her exorbitant fees, and she was not re-engaged. With a new American husband, she settled in America, making regular return trips to Vienna. After the Second World War she made some embarrassing farewell appearances there, donating her fees to the rebuilding of the bombed opera house. By this time her voice was frayed, but although over sixty she still sang 'Vissi d'arte' lying on the floor and rolled down the steps in *Cavalleria Rusticana*; she braved Salome and her Seven Veils and rode bareback in *La Fanciulla del West*. The third of her four husbands (the first had been the grandson of Melba's singing-teacher Marchesi) was a rich American umbrella manufacturer. Umbrellas were then a rarity in Austria and with a prima donna's largesse Jeritza distributed a huge stock of them, flinging them from her hotel balcony to fans waiting below. In retirement outside New York, she bred horses imported from the Spanish Riding School in Vienna and was frequently conspicuous in the Met audience in dark glasses and large floppy hat. She died in her nineties in 1982.

For all the excitement associated with Jeritza, the memory of Lotte Lehmann (1888–1976) is a far warmer one. Her recordings are still extraordinarily vivid documents which communicate something of what everyone who witnessed her recalls as a radiant exultant intensity. There was no posing, no faking, no imposition of false effect in Lehmann's performances, and she must have left Jeritza looking stagey. In her autobiography, she spoke of an actor's 'faculty of forgetting himself entirely, of utterly losing himself in the part he has to play, of giving up his everyday self for the wonderful illusion of some strange destiny which, in the moment of living it, becomes his own, for weal or woe . . . The best teacher of all is life.'

Lotte Lehmann was no relation to her namesake Lilli: in style and personality, apart from a shared devotion to animals, they were as chalk and cheese. Prussian by birth, she was the antithesis of Prussian by nature. She had a difficult early passage, brought up in the family of a minor civil servant who disliked the theatre on moral grounds, and she was never to conquer technical inadequacies in her singing left by a variety of teachers in Berlin. She was expelled from the school run by Patti's former rival Etelka Gerster, where they signally failed to transform the grainy, earthy timbre of her voice into the nightingale mould, and went on to study with Mathilde Mallinger, the first Eva in *Die Meistersinger*, with whom she was happier. Yet she remained one of those singers with evident physical problems, miraculously exploited to expressive effect. Lehmann had a strange pinched attack on high notes and suffered from shortness of breath. She compensated for the latter 'by taking advantage of every comma in the text and by a skilful "catch-breath" which not only concealed breaks in phrases, but was even converted frequently into a characteristic Lehmann-effect—that of a sudden heightening of emotional tension.' If one has a heart of stone and can listen that objectively, this may be clearly heard on her famous recording of Act I of *Die Walküre*. She continued, like Jeritza, to be careless over small notated points, and above the stave glory came and went: her friend Elisabeth Schumann (as Sophie) often sang the Marschallin's top B for her at the climax of the *Rosenkavalier* Trio—but Strauss would not have minded.

She candidly admitted all this, and her autobiography also makes plain how difficult her first years as a professional were. Gauche, over-eager, and easily upset, she had only been to the opera twice in her life, when in 1909 she won a contract at Hamburg and took all the customary small roles. When *Rosenkavalier* was brought into the repertory, Lehmann was promised Sophie, but on the insistence of another member of the cast the part went to her superior of a few years, Elisabeth Schumann. Lehmann's feelings of bitterness were exacerbated by a personal rivalry with Schumann for the love of Hamburg's young lion of a conductor, Otto Klemperer. When Lehmann finally got the part of Sophie, in London in 1914, she went quite unnoticed. For all this, she won her way to the mecca of Vienna, where Strauss's operas were the favourite escapism of an opera public eating off ration cards.

Lehmann was at first thoroughly uncomfortable, surrounded by formidable competition, but her time came when Marie Gutheil-Schoder fell ill while rehearsing the newly composed role of the Composer in the second version of *Ariadne auf Naxos*. Strauss was so overwhelmed by the dedication of the understudy that Gutheil-Schoder was pushed aside and Lehmann given the première. She became famous overnight in a role that she adored: even when she had moved on to sing Ariadne, she would stand in the wings to inhale the Composer's generous but thwarted idealism. Her golden years in Vienna followed. If her fan club (and her fee) was smaller than Jeritza's, it was as vociferous, and the two prima donnas vied for everything, as the Mahler generation of singers declined into middle age. Lehmann's repertoire was broad, as the Viennese system of presenting about fifty operas every season necessitated. Apart from her Strauss—she became Vienna's regular Octavian in *Rosenkavalier*—and the lighter Wagnerian roles, she sang Verdi, Puccini, Mozart, French and Russian opera—all in German, as was customary. However, her excursions into contemporary opera were less extensive than Jeritza's, and she turned down an offer to create Marie in Berg's *Wozzeck*, the finest and most lastingly radical German opera of the 1920s.

These were also Strauss's golden years at the Vienna Opera. He was perhaps rather too full of his own works, which he loved conducting. He didn't rehearse over-much, his baton technique appeared slack, and he never worried about detail. 'All he wanted,' wrote Marcel Prawy 'was that his work should come to life, here and now, in the glamour of an evening at the theatre, and any deviation from the score that enhanced the brilliance of the occasion was not only tolerated but welcomed ... One could quote hundreds of observations of this kind at rehearsals of his own works, for instance: "If you can't hit that note, sing another. Whatever's easiest, it doesn't matter." ' But the casualness had inspired results, and everyone except the pedants and backstage bureaucrats were happy.

Strauss's next opera after *Die Frau ohne Schatten* was a domestic comedy, *Intermezzo* (1924), which represents a significant change in pace and style. The work is remarkable for its construction out of short 'cinematic' scenes and its light conversational vocal line, carefully imitating speech intonations and rhythms, which in an unaggressive way (for Strauss was no manifesto revolutionary) anticipates the more whole-hearted experiments of Berg's *Wozzeck* or Schoenberg's *Erwartung*, produced within the same few months. Strauss wanted to escape from the orchestral megalomania of his early works into music that was sharper, clearer, and closer to his beloved Mozart. Temporarily also rejecting the intricate fictions of Hofmannsthal, he based the plot firmly in a ridiculous incident in his own life and Lehmann, with some trepidation, accepted the delicate task of creating the central role of Christine, closely modelled, warts and all, on Strauss's bizarre wife: Jeritza had refused the dubious honour.

Pauline Strauss-de Ahna—the daughter of a general, she was ashamed of Strauss's bourgeois origins and insisted on asserting her family name—requires a little explanation. As a singer, she was probably not of the first rank, although she did take a leading role at

Bayreuth, and in their courting days Strauss conducted her as Isolde and in his own early opera *Guntram*. On their wedding in 1894 he composed for her four of his most rapturous *lieder* including the tear-jerking 'Morgen'. Up to the end of the First World War, husband and wife gave *lieder* recitals together, during which Pauline did not spare the histrionics. Sweeping on to the stage, she would unwind and toss aside an astonishingly long scarf; at the end of singing any song with a piano postlude, she would bow extravagantly to the audience, thus precipitating applause and drowning her wretched husband's efforts as accompanist. Everyone detested her, or at least kept as far away as possible, which fortunately suited Strauss's dislike of socializing. Mahler and Hofmannsthal could not bear even the briefest encounter, and Alma Mahler records her distaste for Pauline's vulgarity and material outlook. ' "Oh, men," ' Alma heard her say, ' "keep them on a tight rein, that's the only way"—and she went through the motions of holding the reins in one hand and the whip in the other.'

In fact, she did a lot more than hold the reins. She listened outside the study door to make sure Strauss was busy composing and bullied him mercilessly. She had no hesitation in humiliating him in public, and after the première of his second opera *Feuersnot*, loudly declared in front of the Mahlers that she held such music in contempt and refused to accompany its wretched composer home.

Lehmann spent a summer rehearsing at the Strauss home in Garmisch, where she observed that 'Pauline . . . derived an almost perverse pleasure from proving to her husband that no amount of fame could alter her personal opinion of him as essentially nothing but a peasant, a country yokel . . . she explained in great detail, how and why their marriage constituted a shocking *mésalliance* . . . nor was his music, as she readily explained to all who would listen, anywhere near comparable to that of Massenet.' Her other obsession was hygiene. All visitors to the house were immediately instructed to wipe their feet or take off their shoes, and even when Strauss was stricken at the news of Hofmannsthal's death, Pauline screamed at him about some mud on the carpet. She once paid a call to Lehmann's house: while waiting for her to appear, she inspected all the cupboards in the drawing-room and ordered the maids to make changes. She was entirely unintimidated, and remarks she made to high-ranking Nazi officials, mostly connected with the difficulties of collecting royalties during the war, caused Strauss considerable anxiety.

*Intermezzo* presents Pauline, as Christine, unflinchingly, but without viciousness. She was said to have enjoyed the opera. A character describes her as 'absolutely terrible', and she is shown as rude, hysterical, overbearing, and self-contradictory. Yet after the quarrels and farcical misunderstanding the real strength of the marriage is finally celebrated. Lehmann insisted that *Intermezzo* was 'a magnificent declaration of love', and played the part with as much charm as she could muster.

In the same year of 1924, Lehmann first took the Strauss role with which she will always be identified. Bruno Walter asked her to Covent Garden to sing the Marschallin in *Rosenkavalier*, and although she had never sung her before, she accepted for fear of losing a prestigious foreign engagement. She at once became a favourite in London, and returned in Wagner, Mozart, Verdi, and both Johann and Richard Strauss. With colleagues such as Elisabeth Schumann (now her dear friend), Frida Leider, Maria Olczewska, Friedrich Schorr, Richard Mayr, and Lauritz Melchior, German opera has probably never been better served or appreciated outside Germany or Vienna than it was during the pre-war seasons at Covent Garden, and one of its treasures was Lehmann's Marschallin. Her appearance in the part became a sort of annual summer fixture, a musical equivalent to Wimbledon or Ascot. Over the years she grew deeper and deeper into the character and its nuances of feeling; in later years, she was to write a long-pondered account of her interpretation. She was still singing the Marschallin at Covent Garden in 1938, the year of the Anschluss, when one evening she broke down. As the *News Chronicle* reported it:

> Throwing up her hands and exclaiming in German 'I can do no more,' Mme Lotte Lehmann suddenly staggered to the wings at Covent Garden last night and left the stage. The glittering audience was dumbfounded. The curtain was rung down—in the middle of Act I of *Rosenkavalier*. Herr Erich Kleiber, the conductor, carried on for a few bars, then the orchestra ceased playing. Thus was enacted one of the most amazing dramas in the history of opera.

A replacement, Hilde Konetzni, was luckily available and the performance continued: but what makes the incident interesting is the two different explanations on offer. Lehmann's own version is that the wonderful old team had disappeared, and the cast surrounding her was full of Berliners, some of them hard-line Nazis hostile to an unequivocal opponent of Hitler. She had just been informed of her husband's tuberculosis, and she was terrified as to what would become of his children, half-Jewish by his first marriage. The audience was told that Madame Lehmann was suffering from seasickness, but a doctor diagnosed hysterical paralysis of the vocal cords. Walter Legge, then Assistant Director at Covent Garden, remembers it rather differently. 'Next day, Lotte, in good spirits, gave a small lunch party. She said she needed a rest and explained privately . . . that a few minutes before the performance she had been told that relations of hers who were trying to smuggle valuables out of Austria had been held up at the customs, but now she knew they were safely through.'

Whatever the truth, Lehmann certainly suffered in the Nazi era. In Vienna, things had been going badly for her since the early Thirties. Her last new Strauss role, *Arabella* (1933), proved an altogether unhappy experience and she sang it very few times. This opera was the last of the collaborations with Hofmannsthal and for Strauss was something of a retreat from the innovations of *Intermezzo*. *Arabella* is a period comedy of a bright young girl's courtship and its attendant complications: the intrigues are fantastic, and Lehmann found some of it implausible. The vocal writing sounds mostly like a return to, if not a repeat of, Strauss's earlier romantic idiom, and the work has often been labelled as an inferior *Rosenkavalier*, without the same restlessly glittering orchestration. Lehmann was not selected for the Dresden première. Hofmannsthal for one, a hideous snob, found her too 'middle-class' in manner, and it may have been thought that she was a trifle old to impersonate an *ingénue*, but her most dangerous enemy was the conductor Clemens Krauss, who had led the Vienna Opera since 1929. He was determined to patronize a new crop of singers, and gave special attention to the Romanian soprano Viorica Ursuleac (1894–1985), whom he later married. The old guard felt slighted and pushed out before their time: an economic crisis also led to their salaries being cut substantially. Krauss was supported by Strauss, who thought Ursuleac the most 'faithful' of all of his sopranos—she sang an amazing total of 482 performances of his operas—and gave her the prestigious Dresden première of *Arabella*, specially written to exploit a top voice with more glittering lustre than Lehmann's. Lehmann was still given priority in Vienna (Ursuleac was singing in Berlin at the time), but on the morning of the first performance, she received news that her mother had died. Being Lehmann, she went on to save the evening, insisting only on avoiding the curtain calls. The piece had only a *succès d'estime*.

The silver lining to all this was the presence in the audience that night of Arturo Toscanini, who had never heard Lehmann before. She became one of the very few singers for whom he felt unqualified admiration. In 1935–7 she sang *Fidelio* under his baton at Salzburg: of her performance as Leonore, history records only superlatives. It was, wrote Walter Legge:

> . . . her most profoundly moving achievement . . . encompassing every facet of the character—its nobility and tenderness, pity and force, humanity, anxiety and courage, and, in the closing scene, 'nameless joy'. Scores of phrases, sung and spoken, echo down the corridors of memory after forty years as vividly as her acting of the part. That five cruel bars in the great aria have sometimes been more exactly vocalised by others is beside the point: Lehmann was Leonore.

Normally tyrannically demanding of singers, Toscanini made some rare concessions to accommodate Lehmann's vocal shortcomings. They eventually became lovers, but little is known about their apparently tempestuous relationship since they destroyed their correspondence.

By now the Nazis were tightening their hold on central Europe. People like Krauss and Ursuleac would spent the next years making skilful compromises to survive and even to prosper. Lehmann, however, had made an instant enemy of Goering by laughing at his wife's pet lioness and refusing to sing in Berlin as instructed, despite promises of high fees and captive critics: from 1934 she was banned from singing in Germany. Ursuleac later remembered it differently, claiming that Lehmann had been chronically jealous and a ruthless intriguer. Goering's offer had only been refused because she discovered that she would be sharing Sieglinde and Arabella with

Ursuleac. There could be a degree of truth in this, despite Ursuleac's self-righteousness.*

In 1938 Lehmann decided to emigrate to America, and she was to spend most of the rest of her life as a happy exile in the charming California resort of Santa Barbara. Europe was never to hear her in opera again. But her operatic career in America was not what it might have been. She first sang in Chicago in 1930, but by the time Jeritza had vacated her spot at the Met Lehmann was almost forty-six. Any success she had in her Wagner roles was soon overwhelmed by the miracle of Flagstad, and she also made a rare error of judgement in singing Tosca for an audience that had long been accustomed to the excesses of Jeritza.

The fact that the management offered Flagstad anything and everything first annoyed her: after the Norwegian had been given a revival of *Fidelio*, Lehmann refused the part ever again, probably nervous of those 'five cruel bars in the great aria' which got more difficult year by year, and the fact that comparisons would be made with Flagstad's effortlessness. As the Marschallin, however, she remained unassailable, and with a little help in ensemble from kind young Sophies, she continued to sing the part throughout the war as a melancholy and beautiful reminder of a culture now decisively shattered. In 1946, in San Francisco, she gave her last stage performance as the Marschallin.

Lehmann was far from finished. Since the early 1930s she had been giving regular *lieder* recitals of the type pioneered by Elena Gerhardt and Marcella Sembrich at the beginning of the century. Previously *lieder* had generally been given either at informal salon affairs, or as a group of items in a musical variety concert, at which the prima donna would sing only two or three times in the course of the evening, her appearances separated by a 'supporting prog-ramme'—this was the format favoured by Patti and Melba, for instance. Lehmann was one of the first to make popular the idea of singer and piano alone in a well-balanced programme of, say, Schubert, Schumann, Debussy, and Strauss. The mood was serious, and operatic gestures of the kind espoused by Pauline Strauss were

* In an article published in *Opera* in January 1986, two English sisters Ida and Louise Cook, opera fans whose devotion knew no bounds, claimed that both Krauss and Ursuleac helped them smuggle several Jews out of Germany in the pre-war Years.

eliminated: audiences were expected to listen hard and forget the spectacular gratifications of the opera house. *Lieder* has always been the province of the 'maturer'—but not necessarily older—singer, who likes to make a full range of effects without battling against orchestra, costume, stage lights, and upstaging colleagues. *Lieder* demands sensibility and intelligence rather than youthful power and virtuosity, and in properly intimate circumstances a recital can communicate a wonderfully vivid and varied impression of a singer's art. Lehmann's *lieder* embraced song cycles intended for male voice, like Schubert's *Winterreise* and Beethoven's *An die ferne Geliebte*, as well as French *mélodies*—at that time a genre hardly known. With her regular accompanist Bruno Walter she made recordings of which one can only say that so close is their intimacy that they seem to reach out and take the listener by the hand.

In 1951 Lehmann gave an unannounced farewell recital at New York's Town Hall. Vincent Sheean was there: she 'said that she had been before the public now for forty years and reminded us of the words of the Marschallin: "*Jedes Ding hat seine Zeit*", everything has its time. The howls of protest did not disturb her. She had Toscanini's orchids—he sent her orchids for each song recital, year after year, since she was "the greatest artist in the world"—and her mind was quite made up.' As a last encore, she sang Schubert's hymn of praise to music 'An die Musik': understandably overcome, she was unable to sing the last phrase.

The remaining twenty-five years of Lehmann's life were packed with activity. She painted furiously but not very well, and wrote somewhat better. Apart from her autobiography, published before the war, and a number of rather disappointing books on interpretation, she also wrote fiction—her novel, translated as *Eternal Flight*, is an action-packed saga of two sisters, one a ballerina, the other a prima donna called Aimée Françoise. An amusingly whimsical story featuring Richard Strauss in heaven, playing endless rounds of his beloved card game *skat* and worried as to whether Pauline has ended up in the other place, is almost worth reading.* In 1955 she returned to Vienna for the first time in seventeen years for the opening of the rebuilt opera house and received an overwhelming welcome. But she was not one to live off memories. Her public master classes in the late 1950s provided another unforgettable round of Lehmann evenings,

---

* It was published in *Opera*, February 1968.

her students including Grace Bumbry, Marilyn Horne, and Janet Baker (among her earlier pupils was Jeanette MacDonald, who briefly attempted to establish herself in opera). In 1962 she returned to *Rosenkavalier* at the Met, rehearsing a new cast that included Régine Crespin as the Marschallin.

Lehmann has often been cast as a noble soul who bravely resisted the corruptions of the 1930s. In fact, as she readily admitted, she did little against the Nazis beyond denying them her presence. In personality she was excitable, exacting, and sometimes quite cruel (Janet Baker bitterly recalls getting 'nothing at all' out of her master classes, 'except the resolve never to put anyone through the humiliations I suffered at her hands'). Yet it is hard to think slightingly of her. Her records alone tell of a passionate spirit. Vincent Sheean, who knew her art as well as anyone, does not feel that they do her any sort of justice, but for those of us who never heard her 'live', they serve as an arch and corner-stone: like Callas's records, they embody a power and intensity of expression against which all others are measured. Lehmann's voice was not large or tireless, and although she longed to sing Isolde ('I loved it with the stubborn tenacity of the unlucky in love,' she claimed), the advice of Melchior and others dissuaded her from it. Of her Wagner, we are lucky to have a recording of Act I and part of Act II of *Die Walküre* under her beloved Bruno Walter. On stage her Sieglinde had shocked Kirsten Flagstad into the immortal remark that 'She behaved as a woman should only do with her husband,' and one can indeed hear a keenly sexual note in Lehmann's singing here, as well as a terrible despair and an abandoned ecstasy: the gripping urgency with which she tells Siegmund the story of her wedding, followed by her recognition of the freedom now at hand, is equally enthralling. Someone who wants an instant idea of what the fuss is about could well listen to Elisabeth's aria 'Dich, teure halle' from *Tannhäuser*, where the joy of the music is realized in singing of almost reckless excitement. For the *Rosenkavalier*, follow a score or libretto, and mark the maternal kindness, the playfulness and wry humour, the held-back desire, the stillness of the resignation, the sudden assertiveness with which she invests music that can so easily sound aimless.

A third major Viennese soprano of the Strauss era was, appropriately enough, a direct descendant of Henriette Sontag: Elisabeth Schumann (1888–1952) inherited much of her sweetness and charm. Hers could never have been the heroic musical destiny of her friend Lotte Lehmann—as J. B. Steane puts it, Lehmann is at 'the centre of the spectrum . . . at the heart of human experience', while Schumann is confined to 'the qualities and colours of sunlight'.

Schumann's voice had little weight and under any pressure it could sound frail. There are those who argue that her technique was fundamentally weak, and Michael Scott (judging from records alone) claims that by the time she was forty, her voice held 'no more than a wisp of tone'. Today her Mozart sounds much too slow and squarely phrased, and nobody could think that her articulation of florid passages was crystalline. Occasionally, as Victor Gollancz wrote, 'she trembled on the edge of a Viennese archness'. Her repertory in opera was limited, and her stage career circumscribed: after her early days in Hamburg (where her passionate affair with the conductor Otto Klemperer caused enormous scandal), she was based in Vienna from 1919 to 1937, visiting Covent Garden between 1924 and 1931, with some appearances in Salzburg and Munich, and one brief visit to the Met in 1915.

Yet how can one quibble when confronted with singing as pretty as Schumann's? She may have played the soubrette—Mozart's Susanna or Zerlina, Adele in *Die Fledermaus*; Eva in *Meistersinger* was her biggest assignment—but it was always a soubrette with character, wit, and feeling. As Sophie in *Rosenkavalier* she is as fondly remembered as Lehmann is as the Marschallin, and her entranced singing of the phrase where Sophie breathes in the attar-soaked perfume of Octavian's silver rose is the indelible signature of her art.

Strauss loved the timbre of her voice, and it was he who brought her to Vienna for the first time. He tried to persuade her to sing Salome and offered to reduce the orchestration and make transpositions. Reluctantly she agreed, but then announced that the effect on her voice might be such that she could never sing Mozart again. Strauss backed off at once. Instead he accompanied her in *lieder*, where she effortlessly ranked among the greatest. Perhaps no other *lieder* singer seems to take such a radiantly simple pleasure in singing. Lehmann used to beg her to stay away from her recitals if she was singing Schubert, so awed was she by Schumann's mastery of that composer's genius. Their approaches were very different: to resume an inadequate metaphor, if Lehmann takes you by the hand and stares emphatically into your eyes, Schumann pulls you out of your chair and tells you a story or leads you off on a delightful walk—she is more companionable than communing.

For those not handicapped by race or moral outrage, the Vienna Opera remained a haven throughout the Second World War for both singers and audience. The Nazis largely left it alone, realizing the mollifying effect this would have on the city's bourgeoisie. For Strauss and many of the major conductors of the period like Furtwängler, Karl Böhm, or Clemens Krauss, it was all a matter of playing the game, keeping out of trouble, and maintaining a modicum of independence. Some valued Jewish artists or employees were won the right to continue working, but there was also a good deal of shabby time-serving. Strauss himself was a self-proclaimed 'non-political' man who, by reason of his international eminence, would have been useful to either side of the propaganda battle. He later excused his sidestepping on the grounds that he had to protect his Jewish daughter-in-law and his grandchildren, but he never lifted a finger to protect anyone whose survival was not in his own direct interest. Otherwise the war does not appear to have concerned him as more than a chronic inconvenience.

Strauss's last opera *Capriccio* was premièred in 1942. Clemens Krauss wrote the libretto in collaboration with Strauss and conducted, Ursuleac took the leading role of the Countess who must choose between her two suitors, a poet and a composer who are themselves collaborating on an opera. Set in eighteenth-century Paris, at the time of Gluck's operatic reforms, it is a clever conversation piece, with interludes of light relief, debating the claims of words and music to primacy in opera. The matter is still unresolved in the final monologue, in which the Countess, staring into a mirror, reflects on art, life, and love. With its obvious echoes of *Rosenkavalier*, its opportunities for wit and pastiche, as well as for another sweetly melancholic soprano *scena*, its long dying falls bathed in an orchestral 'mild blue light', *Capriccio* allowed Strauss to bask in his favourite element. It is a weirdly calm and sophisticated work to have come out of a time of such consuming crisis, and opinion is still split between those who find it a sure cure for insomnia and those who regard it as Strauss's most perfectly moulded and finished work. The Countess is certainly a grateful role for a prima donna who wants to indulge a bent for expressive and mellifluous *portamento*. As a character, she resembles the Marschallin in combining a mature aristocratic charm and a private vulnerability, but Hofmannsthal's conception is by far the more touching—the situation in *Capriccio* does not provide a very heart-rending dilemma.

One singer who has been able to extract the maximum of interest out of the role is Elisabeth Schwarzkopf, one of the dominating figures of the post-war era. Unlike Lehmann or Jeritza, she was never an improviser or one ready to skate over difficulties of detail. Following her recordings with a score, one is at once impressed by her scrupulous observation of the composer's markings—note-values, rests, dynamics, tempo. Nothing is shirked, everything is realized. Her regular accompanist Gerald Moore has written of her fanatic self-criticism, relentless rehearsal, and obsessive concern with accurate intonation. Her own scores were described by Edward Greenfield as 'covered with coloured pencillings, so close that she alone could read their meaning'. She was, one might say, a Prussian singer, the worthy heir to Lilli Lehmann's rigour and formidable inability to suffer fools gladly.

She was born near Poznań in 1915, the daughter of a classics master, and had two false starts as a singer in the Berlin of the late 1930s—first as a contralto, then as a soprano soubrette. From the beginning of the war she went for lessons to Maria Ivogün, a distinguished coloratura soprano of the Berlin Opera, and her husband Michael Raucheisen, a famous pianist and accompanist. These two seized on what André Tubeuf has called Schwarzkopf's 'demanding and proud nature, her intransigence, her capacity for monastic self-discipline'. Ivogün brought nobility into her voice, while Raucheisen introduced her to the *lieder* repertory: Schwarzkopf emerged as a singer with more than flexibility and high notes. In 1942 she won a contract at the Vienna Opera, but immediately suffered a year-long bout of tuberculosis, contracted in damp air-raid shelters. She sang with the German equivalent of ENSA throughout Nazi-occupied Europe, but could not get back to Vienna until 1945.

By 1946, she was singing leading roles in the Theater an der Wien, which was 'standing in' pending the reconstruction of the bombed-out opera house. The liberating Allied authorities tangled everything in administrative muddles: the degree of Schwarzkopf's involvement with the Nazis has never been satisfactorily explained and she herself has kept mum on the subject for fifty years. But according to Marcel Prawy, she was 'once banned by the British but cleared by the French, and later banned by the Russians and cleared by the Americans' in the chaotic course of denazification. At that time an English recording executive from His Master's Voice named Walter Legge was roaming central Europe in a ruthless effort to snap up musicians who had either begun their careers during the war years or who were now in limbo. Many of them had been Nazis, some of them active in the party and under official investigation, but Legge (who had Fascist sympathies himself) was only interested in their talent. He was brilliantly successful—Schwarzkopf, Karajan, Furtwängler, Hotter, Flagstad, Lipatti, and later Callas were all among his trophies—and he was subsequently criticized for indiscriminate opportunism.

Schwarzkopf herself was his most complete protégé, Trilby to his Svengali, it was said, and the closeness with which they combined their careers caused considerable resentment among other singers: Schwarzkopf was nicknamed Her Master's Voice, and Legge not only managed her engagements and produced her records, but later married her. He began by making her listen to records, so as to widen 'her imaginative concept of the possibilities of vocal sound'. Patti never heard the sound of her own singing until her career was over, but Schwarzkopf was able to learn from listening to herself over and over again, as well as using all the great singers of the past—Melba, Ponselle, Lotte Lehmann, Schumann, Leider—as her tutors, incorporating different aspects of their arts into her own highly wrought synthesis. Unlike so many prima donnas, she found the patient construction of a record uniquely satisfying, comparing it to the process of sculpture. Gerald Moore later wrote that Legge overestimated his formative influence on Schwarzkopf but the idea of using records thus was intelligent and original. It made Schwarzkopf into a uniquely self-conscious interpreter: it was perfectly natural to her that when asked on the BBC radio programme *Desert Island Discs* to select eight recordings to be shipwrecked with, she should choose only her own!

In 1947 she left Vienna and for five years based herself at Covent Garden, where she sang the standard lyric repertory—Mozart, some Verdi, Wagner, and Puccini—in near-impeccable English for a starting salary of £60 a week. Over the next fifteen-odd years, she was closely associated with the Salzburg Festival—Flagstad once said that the way Schwarzkopf opened the *Fidelio* quartet at Salzburg was the most beautiful thing she had ever heard. She was the very first singer at post-war Bayreuth, taking the small but honourable role of the First Rhinemaiden in *Das Rheingold*; in the same year of 1951, she created Anne Trulove in Stravinsky's *The Rake's Progress*. She also sang regularly under Herbert von Karajan, commuting with him between La Scala and Vienna in productions shared by both opera houses. All this went hand in hand with a careful balance of concerts and recitals, as well as a regular recording schedule. The only blot was the US: although she had operatic success in San Francisco, the Met refused to hire her, on the grounds of her Nazi affiliations, and for similar reasons, Schwarzkopf's records were banned from Israeli radio broadcasts. Until 1964, New York only heard her in *lieder* or oratorio.

By the late 1950s she had slimmed her operatic repertory down to six roles. Three of these were Alice Ford in *Falstaff*, the Marschallin in *Rosenkavalier* and the Countess in *Capriccio*. The remainder were Mozartian—Fiordiligi in *Così fan tutte*, Elvira in *Don Giovanni*, and the Countess in *Le Nozze di Figaro*. Her principle of fulfilling the score as closely as possible made for a style *vis-à-vis* the latter more subtly shaded but less forwardly emotional than had been the pre-war case. Influenced by the conductor Josef Krips, Schwarzkopf phrased cleanly, singing with a firm vibrato-free tone which became a standard on which the great Mozartians of the next generation have continued to model themselves.

About her Strauss one can feel some reservations. It has often been said that Schwarzkopf is a 'mannered' singer, but here 'over-literal' is the more accurate adjective. Compared with Lehmann's, her Marschallin is an impeccable aristocrat, much too proper to play around with teenagers. The text is picked and pecked at to the point at which hardly a single word runs free of special emphasis or colour. The sensuality and generosity of spirit that Lehmann's looser singing communicates is absent from Schwarzkopf's tight-lipped interpretation, which is finally meaningful but unmoving. Where she is quite irresistibly delightful is in comedy. Her sixth lasting stage role was Alice Ford in Verdi's *Falstaff*, which she sings on record with sharp wit and lightning playfulness and grace, while her series of Viennese operetta recordings, marketed by HMV as the 'Champagne Operettas', merit the accolade: Schwarzkopf has all that beverage's fizz and pop, dry, heady lightness, and strength of aftertaste. Her portrait of the outraged Prima Donna in a recording of *Ariadne auf Naxos* is a perfect vignette of her comic gift, sung with relish and broad humour. Many singers do a good Schwarzkopf parody, but Schwarzkopf herself does the best of them all.

All these qualities and more emerged in her *lieder* singing, especially in the subtle and complex songs of Hugo Wolf, for whose revived modern reputation she and Legge take a large amount of credit. Schwarzkopf continued giving recitals until the later 1970s, when she switched decisively to teaching, and as Dr Elisabeth Schwarzkopf has given public master classes for young professional singers which incidentally serve as a fascinating revelation of the powerful and dedicated mind which constructed her singing. She has always had a pedagogic streak (her father, remember, was a classics teacher). In Legge's memoirs he relates the wonderful story of an early pupil of Schwarzkopf's who demanded an impromptu lesson in the restaurant of Biffi Scala in Milan. This was none other than Maria Callas, who had been having trouble with her top register during a recording.

> Callas walked in as if unconcerned, pecked my wife's cheeks and without sitting down said, 'Show me how you sing top As and Bs and make a diminuendo on them. Walter says mine make him seasick.' When Schwarzkopf demurred, Callas, ignoring the astonished diners, sang with full voice the notes that were giving her trouble, while Schwarzkopf felt her diaphragm, lower jaw, throat and ribs. Waiters froze in their stride, while guests turned to watch and hear the fun. Within minutes Schwarzkopf was singing the same notes while Callas prodded her in the same places to find out how she kept those notes steady. After twenty minutes or so she said, 'I think I've got it. I'll call you in the morning when I've tried it out,' and sat down to supper.

Schwarzkopf was a good person to ask for advice: from *schmaltz* to Schubert, she was a singer who did everything right.

The same cannot be said for Ljuba Welitsch, whose name means, literally and appropriately, 'Love Great'. This Bulgarian soprano, born in 1913, was virtually a contemporary of Schwarzkopf's, and they started at the Vienna Opera at the same time. Welitsch's success was mercurial. She was compared to Jeritza, but her wildly extrovert behaviour is more reminiscent of Malibran, 'instinctual, impulsive, greedy and generous with no defences'. In 1944 she first sang her most famous role—Strauss's Salome, which she was to repeat almost six hundred times in the course of her short career: a New York critic described her performance as 'a crescendo of passion and neuroticism'. The elderly Strauss himself was the first to acknowledge that she had everything for the part—the sensuality, the innocence, a lithe and shapely figure, a shock of red hair, and a voice of spontaneous silvery freshness and power. It was too good to be true. Welitsch conquered London and New York, her Salome was sensational everywhere: she also sang Tosca, Aida, Musetta in *La Bohème*, Donna Anna in *Don Giovanni*, a heartfelt Tatyana in Tchaikovsky's *Eugene Onegin*, and her recordings of extracts from all these show just how exciting she must have been. The problem was her lack of caution and restraint. One night she sang with an inflamed larynx, and started the slow murder of her voice. By 1950, it had shrunk to the point of causing audiences familiar with her brief prime acute embarrassment. She was soon forced to retire from leading roles altogether, but Welitsch had far too much spirit to be crushed by her first demise. She had her beloved poodles and a traffic policeman for a husband, and now began a new career as a television and film actress, as well as making fruity cameo appearances in operetta.

Welitsch's extravagant personality made her an irresistible feast at a time when the national diet was otherwise limited by post-war austerities, but behind the flash of her stardom, a stronger and softer light was being cast by an exceptional generation of younger prima donnas who would lead the ensemble back into the reconstructed State Opera House in 1955. There was the lyric soprano regarded by Lotte Lehmann as her truest successor, Sena Jurinac, eloquent and dedicated in a large repertory, but best loved in Mozart; Leonie Rysanek, as admired in New York and Bayreuth as in Vienna, her powerful top register making her a superb exponent of the 'Jeritza' Strauss roles; Irmgard Seefried, another outstanding Mozartian and *lieder* singer; and Lisa della Casa, a beautiful Swiss woman, whose watery clarity of voice made her Arabella enormously popular. All except Rysanek were to some extent overshadowed internationally by Schwarzkopf and the dominance she achieved through her long recording career, but in Vienna their delicately differentiated virtues and personalities were savoured by an audience of connoisseurs.

From 1956, Vienna was rocked by another conducting genius,

whose tactics made him highly controversial. Herbert von Karajan took over from Karl Böhm, whose appointment to the new opera house was rescinded after a disastrous first season. Karajan insisted on Italian opera in Italian, a radical alteration in the old repertory system, and, like Mahler, control over production. Neither of these were universally popular measures. His Mahlerian inability to deputize or compromise caused even deeper frictions, and his departure in 1964 was spectacular, although he later returned as a guest conductor, as did the sacked Strauss. The results of Karajan's single-mindedness were predictably impressive, especially in the area of Italian opera, and he nurtured yet another school of prima donnas. Unlike Mahler, Karajan favoured voice with an instrumental beauty of sound, rather than those of vivid dramatic force and distinctive humanity. Two outstanding exemplars of his taste were Christa Ludwig, a bottomlessly rich-toned mezzo, who took some soprano roles and enjoyed remarkable professional longevity, and Gundula Janowitz, whose voice had the purity of a boy treble's.

So much to say about so many in so little space: where, asks the Viennese *aficionado*, is Rose Pauly? What about the Konetzni sisters? Maria Cebotari? One more name, however, cannot be omitted, for it conveniently embodies the best of modern singing style, as well as being representative of the Viennese tradition. Lucia Popp was born in 1939 in Czechoslovakia, motherland of a number of great Viennese singers including Jeritza. She first became famous on the strength of a miraculously well-articulated Queen of the Night in *Die Zauberflöte* at the State Opera in 1963, and over the next few years sang the part all over the opera world. At first she seemed cut out to be a successor to Elisabeth Schumann: with her pudgy, cheeky smile and charming demeanour, she inspired the same sort of undying affection in her audience. Then she found the measure of Sophie in *Rosenkavalier* and became a delightful Susanna and Despina, impeccably sung without the usual soubrette exaggeration or mincing. She also became, like Schumann, a lovely Eva in *Die Meistersinger* without further Wagnerian ambition.

Yet Popp's technique was inherently stronger than Schumann's—comparing their recordings of the same Mozart arias is a good way to illustrate the soundness of the best modern teaching. Popp's voice had a distinctive piquancy, which has been likened to the timbre of an oboe. It is not opulent or resonant, but it is very firmly under control, even throughout its range, accurate in intonation, and the breath is unobtrusively managed. Schumann could not have competed with Popp's command of coloratura, nor her linguistic versatility—she spoke Czech, German, Russian, English, and Italian.

Popp built on the security of her technical foundations by venturing slowly into a more ambitious Strauss repertory—the Four Last Songs, Arabella, Daphne, Christine in *Intermezzo*, the Countess in *Capriccio*, the Marschallin. At the time of her tragically early death from a brain tumour in 1993, she was proving herself the Schwarzkopf rather than the Schumann of her era.

Now she is gone—as loved and mourned as any singer since Kathleen Ferrier—there is much jostling for the creamy Strauss roles among a younger generation of prima donnas, Kiri Te Kanawa, Anna Tomowa-Sintow, Felicity Lott and Cheryl Studer eminent among them. They are all truly first-rate singers, gifted with the silver Straussian patina, and I think it is fair to say that their predominance means that the *echt* Viennese area of the repertory is currently better served and populated than any other. One may be unlikely today to hear a satisfactory Aida or Isolde; but there are still plenty of sopranos who can make Strauss's romantic dream of the female voice come true.

# 8

# *National Style,*
# *or the Lack of it*

Detecting national characteristics is a dangerous game. Singing presents a peculiar jumble of problems in this respect: perhaps one should simply stop here and acknowledge that every great voice is a freak of nature, without any root in race or culture, geography or heredity. The central nineteenth-century tradition of vocal schooling neatly endorses such a position. What was widely known as the 'Italian' style had its most famous teacher in Manuel Garcia II, a Spaniard who lived in Paris and then London, whose most distinguished pupil was a Swede, Jenny Lind; and Garcia's chief disciple was the German-born Mathilde Marchesi, whose model product was the technique of Nellie Melba, herself an Australian of Scots descent.

A singer is made more by how and for what she or he is trained than by climate or diet. Perhaps racial types of facial bone structure can make for certain effects of vocal resonance, but it is hard to take the idea of 'national endowments' further than that. If Slavonic sopranos are fierce and wobbly or English contraltos plummy and booming, that is because they have been taught particular means of tone formation, not because of some good or bad national fairy.

We have seen how a variety of Slavs, Anglo-Saxons and Black Americans have successfully interpreted the most demanding soprano roles in the Italian repertory; the French prima donna further confuses the picture.

French operatic tastes have always been insular, even chauvinistic. For all the lushly sensual melody we associate with Gounod and Massenet, the majority of French composers—and audiences—have been prepared to sacrifice beautiful tone to verbal clarity. The Italian style of vocal display has never much interested them: even the vogue for the castrati passed them by. The first great French opera composer, Rameau, kept close to the ideals of the early Florentines, writing pointed and austere declamation for his singers while his contemporary Handel followed the Italian Baroque form of the arias, with all its intricate artifice. As the eighteenth-century critic Charles de Brosses put it, 'Italian music can only trifle with syllables and lacks the expression which characterizes feeling.'

In the nineteenth century, grand opera made fashionable loud, impassioned voices like those of Cornélie Falcon, Josephine Fodor-Mainvielle, Laure Cinti-Damoreau and Henriette Méric-Lalande. Only in the 1860s did a more maidenly bourgeois style set in. Marie Miolan-Carvalho exemplified it, creating Marguerite in Gounod's *Faust* and title-roles in his *Roméo et Juliette* and *Mireille* (Micaela in *Carmen* and Massenet's Manon also occupy this territory). But for the greatest French soprano of the era such characters seemed feeble milksops, pallid and passive. Emma Calvé came from another France: the peasant south, where the emotional temperature ran higher. Her inspiration was not musical at all. 'The spark that set my art alight,' she wrote in one of her two volumes of memoirs, was the Italian actress Eleonora Duse, from whom Calvé learnt the intensity characteristic of the new naturalistic school of acting. 'I could never have thought it possible that anyone could have given so much of themselves,' she continued, 'she seemed to belong to a humanity more vibrant than our own. What accents! What communicative emotion! . . . no artist is more involving, more enveloping, and no artist possesses such an ability to induce emotion.'

Calvé followed Duse from theatre to theatre, saturating herself in every gesture and intonation and in particular modelling her operatic interpretation of the abandoned Sicilian peasant Santuzza in Mascagni's *Cavalleria Rusticana* on Duse's legitimate stage performance. Such emulation paid off, as Calvé's intensity of style was not only sensational in itself, but was also influential on a younger generation of 'singing actresses' including Garden, Farrar, and Jeritza—none of whom could match Calvé's classic schooling.

Calvé kept to her Provençal roots. She never forgot how, when she first returned to her native village following her professional debut and gave an impromptu outdoor concert, a peasant came up to her nodding his head sadly. 'Poor girl,' he said. 'How you scream! How it must hurt you! . . . Such a waste of strength! It's dreadful!' She was born in 1858, of farming stock but in early childhood her father moved on business from the Aveyron region to Spain. There, in unconscious preparation for her most popular role, she fell under an infant fascination for the gypsies and once invited herself to dinner at an encampment, much to her mother's horror.

Like Melba, to whom she is in so many ways comparable, Calvé hummed incessantly as a child, while the chants and canticles of her convent education further nurtured her voice. Moving to Paris, she went to a variety of voice teachers: she was unsure of herself and dissatisfied with her art. In 1882 she made her début in Brussels, then returned to Paris for lessons with Marchesi, who must have had a greater effect on her singing than Calvé ever gave credit for. Then followed three consolidating years at the Opéra-Comique, where the manager was Miolan-Carvalho's husband and where Victor Maurel, Verdi's first Iago and Falstaff, fervently urged her on. In 1887 she was hissed at her début at La Scala and returned to Paris for further study with a new teacher.

Only with the revelation of Duse did everything fall into place. Lying ill in bed with the image of her idol in her mind's eye, Calvé studied *Cavalleria Rusticana*, until, in the words of Marchesi's daughter Blanche, 'She felt she had overcome the natural shyness that stood like a barrier between her will and her execution.' The performance was to break many conventions of operatic decorum. Calvé's costume consisted of some clothes she had bought off an Italian peasant woman; her gestures were 'spontaneous and apparently unstudied'. But the result was an unqualified triumph, and by the 1890s Calvé was established as a prima donna of a defiantly modern and revolutionary kind, worlds away from the regal indolence of a Patti or Melba.

After Santuzza, Calvé began to work on the part with which she was to be most strongly identified, that of Bizet's Carmen. This masterpiece, first performed in 1875, with its simple plot, blazing orchestral colours, and miraculous succession of marvellous tunes, has shown a protean resilience to a broad variety of interpretations. Prior to Calvé, singers like the American Minnie Hauk had exploited a picture-postcard image of the Spanish gypsy; later, Farrar and Jeritza would present her as a sort of silent-movie vamp, at the opposite pole from the chaste and fatalistic conception of the part held by Lilli Lehmann and Fremstad. Latterly we have had Carmen as 'free woman' and feminist, valuing independence above security. Yet no view of the character has had quite the extraordinary shock value that Calvé's had. Shaw, deeply shaken by the naked display of animality, described it vividly:

> There is no suggestion of any fine quality about her, not a spark of honesty, courage, or even the sort of honour supposed to prevail among thieves. All this is conveyed by Calvé with a positively frightful power of divesting her beauty and grace of the nobility . . . which seems inseparable from them in other parts . . . To see Calvé's Carmen changing from a live creature into a reeling, staggering, flopping, disorganized thing, and finally tumble down a mere heap of carrion, is to get much the same sensation as might be given by the reality of a brutal murder . . . It was the desecration of a great talent. I felt furious with Calvé.

Calvé herself actually disliked the part. 'Carmen has only two redeeming qualities. She is truthful and she is brave,' she wrote. The problem may have been boredom: she claimed to have sung in the opera over three thousand times. The clamour to see this remarkable histrionic display was universal. Queen Victoria commanded a performance at Windsor Castle, rewarded her with the gift of a dog, and commissioned a marble bust of the singer which still stands there today. At the Met her début in the role was acclaimed by an audience including Ellen Terry, Henry Irving, and Tommaso Salvini. Such was the infallible effect of Calvé as Carmen on the box office that managements were loath to let her do anything else, and over the years up to 1904 when she sang the part repeatedly in most of the great opera houses, the interpretation became overloaded with exaggerated and excessive business: one of her regular Don Josés, Jean de Reszke, particularly objected to the way in which Calvé would suddenly park herself in his lap while he was trying to sing. 'Calvé's Carmen went to artistic pieces,' recalled W. J. Henderson. 'The prima donna could not stand her enormous success. She became extravagant, whimsical, erratic, irresponsible. She did anything that occurred to her to accomplish a passing situation.' Whether she was similarly cavalier with the music is disputable. Shaw claimed that she carried 'her abandonment to the point of being incapable of paying the smallest attention to the score', but other critics have contradicted this. Her own considered view of the matter was that, 'Unfortunately for me, no one dared utter a word of criticism: and in consequence, I was carried away by my passion for realism. It became an obsession, and occasionally I overstepped the mark.'

At one point she considered quitting opera altogether to become an actress—anything to get away from the Carmen for which she was paid ever more irresistible fees! Her repertory was never large. Massenet wrote for her the title-roles in what was intended as the French answer to *Cavalleria Rusticana*, *La Navarraise* (in which Shaw wrote of her as 'a living volcano, wild with anxiety . . . mad with joy, ecstatic with love, desperate with disappointment') and *Sapho*, a strange piece with a contemporary setting about an artist's model; otherwise she was largely restricted in her years of fame to alternating her Carmen with Santuzza, Marguerite in *Faust*, and Ophélie in Thomas's *Hamlet*.

In 1904 she announced her retirement from opera, although impresarios who opened their coffers wide enough dragged another few Habaneras out of her. She continued to sing in recital, where, apart from the inevitable *Carmen* numbers, she made a speciality of Provençal folk songs. On a recording of one of these, 'Ma Lisette', she finishes with a top D of unearthly purity and steadiness, quite unlike an ordinary soprano rendition of that note. It is widely supposed that this is evidence of what she called her 'fourth voice', a method of voice production she learnt from an aged castrato in the Sistine Chapel choir and which apparently involved keeping the mouth virtually closed, as if humming. It took her three years to perfect and she never succeeded in communicating the technique to any of her pupils.

Calvé's voice was an altogether unusual instrument, with a genuine and unforced extension in the lower regions beyond the scope of the other Marchesi-trained sopranos. Accompanists, however, would be driven mad by her persistent but inconsistent demands for transpositions. In the morning she would feel comfortable singing high; come the concert, everything had to come down. In the recording studio, she was even more eccentric. Before her first session, she refused to enter the door of the Gramophone Company's back-street London studio. 'Never in my life will I enter such a place,' she exclaimed from her carriage to her accompanist Landon Ronald. 'It is a tavern—not a manufactory. I shall be robbed there. You have brought me to a thieves' den.' Only when her fee of one hundred guineas was brought forth in golden cash did she relent. Once in front of the horn, there were further problems. According to

Roland Gelatt, 'She had the disconcerting habit of commenting on her performance in the midst of a recording—even uttering shrieks of joy or groans of disgust, depending on whether she had turned a particular phrase to her liking—and in the "Séguedille" from *Carmen* she insisted on dancing in front of the recording horn just as she was wont to do on stage.' None the less what we hear from Calvé's recordings is a voice of real loveliness, with a warmth that Melba's quite lacked.

She kept a simple love of the physical act of singing. Into her vocal dotage, she continued to give recitals, travelling as far as Honolulu (where she was gratifyingly greeted by 'a little fleet of balloons floating over the city, to each one of which was attached a large picture of myself'), and during the First World War toured North America raising money for the French wounded. In one concert hall she noticed a party of innocent Germans, doubtless anxious to transcend the limitations of nationalism. Calvé, however, could not restrain herself and half-way through her rendering of the *Marseillaise* spat in the direction of the enemy contingent. Such was her instinctive sense of theatre.

'Instinctive' is the key word in any discussion of Calvé. She was not interested in the conventional social success so highly valued by Melba. She lived the life of a manic depressive, and her memoirs alternate between the joys of music, painting, literature, travel, and references to long periods full of 'overwhelming catastrophes' and illnesses 'of which I still cannot speak'. She was married definitely once and possibly twice, although the memoirs contain absolutely no reference whatsoever to either the definite Signor Gaspari or the possible M. Boellman. She was a highly susceptible woman, and at one time fell deeply under the influence of a guru, Swami Vivi Kananda, who passed on to her the secrets of yogi breath control. All varieties of mysticism fascinated her, especially those of the East, and a friend recalls her singing her mantra: 'She became very calm, very serious too, and, closing her eyes, began in a voice deep, rich, full, and powerful: "*Om, om, Hari Om, tata sat*".'

Her other source of peace of mind was the castle she bought at Cabrières in her native Aveyron, no elegant country house, but a rough stone fortress perched on top of a crag. She continued restless, however, keeping up studios in Paris and Nice where she took pupils in order to relieve her growing financial embarrassment—and she continued to sing into her seventies. Colette encountered her in 1934 in a restaurant in Nice. She looked frail, and Colette wanted to order her a cab. 'What for?' Calvé asked. 'I have good legs. At home every morning, I climb, I climb. When I have enough, high up there, I sing, I sing for my mountain . . . For my mountain and also for some little shepherd boy. For a girl who beats out the washing . . . For a ploughman who stops his team and listens to me.' She died in 1942, shortly after losing the remains of her money in the aftermath of the German invasion.

The next great prima donna of French opera, Mary Garden (1874–1967), was not French at all, and in fact both spoke and sang the language with unmistakable American intonation. In a sense, she represents no style or school or even nation: if her art was French, her birthplace was Aberdeen, her passport always British, and her upbringing largely American. As a singer and a personality, she defeats all categories and comparisons: 'Mary Garden, as difficult of classification as a French verb,' wrote one journalist; 'a condor, an eagle, a peacock, a nightingale, a panther, a society dame, a gallery of moving pictures, a siren,' waxed another. It was almost as though she had already transcended the mortal condition. Whereas Calvé's life, as revealed in her memoirs, bespeaks a recognizable human being with ordinary enthusiasms, appetites, and failings, Mary Garden's is a glacial and flawless catalogue of achievement. 'I began my career at $50 a month and ended it with $3,500 a night. I call that a lot of fun.' Otherwise she enjoyed neither food, nor sex, nor curtain calls. She was the complete egoist, ruthlessly self-aware and self-centred, utterly cold-eyed and imperturbable. 'I believed in myself,' she proclaimed, 'and I never permitted anything or anybody to destroy that belief . . . I wanted liberty and I went my own way.'

Garden's parents had taken her to America when she was six, and the family had settled in Chicago, the city with which the name of Mary Garden remains indelibly associated. Liberty began in earnest when a wealthy family paid for her to continue her musical studies in Paris, where she walked out on teacher after teacher—including Marchesi, whose insistence on the virtue of pure virgin tone she found antipathetic—before her sponsors received a not-proven report of her lax moral behaviour and cut off their subsidy. Fortunately Garden was then taken up by Sybil Sanderson, a beautiful American soprano for whom Massenet had written *Thaïs*. In 1900 Sanderson introduced her to Albert Carré, director of the Opéra-Comique, who, like everyone else, was impressed by the girl's breezy self-assurance. She was told to learn the title-role of Charpentier's wildly successful new opera *Louise* and bide her time. In April of that year, on a day on which she recalled 'feeling particularly depressed over the death of a dog that had been run over by an omnibus', the original Louise fell ill in the middle of the performance and within minutes Garden had calmly stepped in and taken over without any stage or orchestral rehearsal: 'I have never been nervous in my life and I have no patience with people who are,' she asserted. Her feat brought her immediate fame, which she handled consummately. Over the next few years she consolidated her reputation and repertory at the Opéra-Comique, incurring the jealousy of Carré's soprano wife as she blithely carried on the *jeune fille Americaine* tradition established by Sanderson and her predecessors in Paris such as Marie van Zandt and Minnie Hauk.

In 1902 she was chosen by Debussy to create the part of Mélisande in his *Pelléas et Mélisande*. 'You have come to me from the mists of the north to create my music,' he told her. On the surface it was an unlikely piece of casting, for Garden was already notorious for her brisk, restless wit. Mélisande is a creature from nowhere, lonely, child-like, unawoken. Yet Garden was herself not quite of this world, at least in terms of feelings—'I never really loved anybody. I had a fondness for men, yes, but very little passion and *no need*,' she admitted—and perhaps she brought something of her own unfeelingness into her interpretation. 'She hardly moved her hands and arms for long stretches of the action: her head was usually bowed in submission, but when it moved it had something to contribute to the composition . . . The voice had the pallor of the tomb at times; it was difficult to understand how such misty rose-gray and blue-gray notes could spin from a human throat.' Thus Vincent Sheean: a fellow prima donna, Frances Alda, whose compliments were few and far between, also emphasized this ethereality. 'She was so still. Just that one little phrase, "Il fait froid ici", as it came from her lips, and you shivered under the chill winds that blow between the worlds of the real and the unreal. Contrasted with it, [Lucrezia] Bori's rendering of the line sounded like a schoolgirl who steps out of bed without her slippers.'

Debussy fell in love with Mary Garden, promising to write her a *Romeo and Juliet* opera if she accepted him—but she laughed him off and told him how charming his wife was; the conductor of the first *Pelléas*, André Messager, was also brushed away. To Mélisande alone did Garden remain loyal, and the impact of her performance was an important element in what initial success the opera had. It is not an easy work, and the first audiences were bemused and sometimes bored by its delicacy and understatement, as well as its brief explosions and searing climaxes. The vocal line, made up of brief, thwarted interchanges and little recognizable melody, is not immediately gratifying. There is no ballet, no spectacle, no *scandale* in the plot. A certain sort of person will always find the whole thing a sure cure for insomnia. Yet to others it represents a peak of opera's expressive potential. Imagine Wagner writing an opera to a libretto by Henry James, full of the mysteries of innocence and guilt and bottomless unexpressed tragedies, a dream rather than an apocalypse, with music that conceals more than it reveals and suggests more than it states—and there you have something of *Pelléas*'s quality. Mary Garden understood it all intuitively and Debussy recorded that she needed almost no direction during the long and painstaking rehearsal period. 'All of my creations went into me and out,' she later said. 'They were inside of me, and I threw them out to the public. I never really worked over them, not in the usual sense—I just knew them . . . I just had it in me, all of it . . . I was Mélisande . . . That was all there was to it.'

In 1907, Garden left the Opéra-Comique and Paris. She returned to New York and Oscar Hammerstein's new Manhattan Opera House. To avoid too much direct competition with the Met, Hammerstein sought out not only new stars but a new repertory, and Mary Garden in French opera became a corner-stone of his success. Louise and Mélisande were two of her earliest roles here, but she became equally celebrated in the operas of Massenet, making her Manhattan début as his Thaïs, the Egyptian courtesan turned nun. Eyebrows were raised at once and gentlemen dropped their monocles, for there was nothing healthy about either Garden or Massenet: for good clean frilly-knicker fun Geraldine Farrar was New York's prima donna, but Garden excelled in conveying the more sophisticated and exotic varieties of eroticism. Massenet himself, according to Garden, was 'the yes-man par excellence' who wrote 'endless letters dripping with the most sickening kind of sentiment, everything underlined not once, but two, three and four times': his later operas are composed on equivalent musical principles. Garden gave even his attempt at pious simplicity, *Le Jongleur de Notre-Dame*, a sexual *frisson* by taking the tenor title-role and dressing herself in a short jerkin and tights. Strauss offered her the travesty role of Octavian in *Rosenkavalier*, but she refused on the grounds that it would have bored her to make love to a woman on stage. His Salome was more in her line: she sang it in French, as she did all new operatic roles, and performed the Dance of the Seven Veils herself, swathed in layers of diaphanous tulle. In Chicago, the police banned it as an affront to public morality: the police report on the first performance read thus: 'It was disgusting. The whole show lacked high class. Miss Garden wallowed around like a cat in a bed of catnip. There was no art in her dance that I could see. If there was it must have been black art. I wouldn't call it immoral; it was not high class enough to be called immoral. To be sure Miss Garden can sing. She is the whole show . . . As for the music, it was simply one crash after another . . .'

But Mary Garden was to go a lot further than biblical virgins caressing severed heads. As Massenet's Cléopâtre, 'the queen, disguised as a boy, visits an Egyptian brothel and makes love to another boy'. 'Mary was very startling,' was the critic Carl van Vechten's thunderstruck comment! When Février's Monna Vanna appears before her captor clad only in a fur mantle, she is asked whether she is naked underneath: '*Oui*,' replied Garden, and made everyone believe it. Most meretricious of all was her involvement in D'Erlanger's *Aphrodite*, which included the crucifixion of a negro slave, overt lesbianism, and a multiracial orgy. It was hardly surprising that the evangelical Billy Sunday preached against Mary Garden's lascivious incitements, or that a teenage girl denied entry to Garden's dressing-room killed herself rather than suffer the pangs of unrequited infatuation for her prima donna.

Sadly, Garden's records communicate nothing of this fatal allure. In general, her singing makes a pleasant, correct, and unmemorable impression. There was always a faction that claimed she could not sing at all, and it is certainly true that in a 'heavy' role like Salome she was not beyond cheating by omission or abbreviation. At the same time, a recording of Violetta's first-act *scena* from *La Traviata* shows that there was some substance to her technique. Others noted her extraordinary ability to colour her voice to suit the character she had undertaken. Garden was in no doubt of the facts. Apart from a glass of milk with ten drops of iodine after a performance, her voice required no attention, let alone improvement. 'I did what I liked with my voice; I was always its master and never its slave. It obeyed me, and not I it . . . I never had to rest because it was tired—never, never, never. At all times, my voice was absolutely at my command.' Yet she could also be realistic about it. 'I know full well that I have not a great voice, and I do not make any claim to such heights. I am not a Melba or a Calvé and do not expect to be compared with such singers,' she told a reporter.

'My art, on the other hand, is one quite separate from that of other operatic singers, and the success I have won and hope to win is not the success of vocal cords; it is by an art quite different from that of other opera singers that I have found my way, and I want to be judged not alone by my singing or my acting or my stage appearance, but by these combined into one art that is entirely different from all the rest. That is the way I wish the critics to regard me, and that is all I ask of them.'

After the closure of the Manhattan Opera in 1910, Garden struck out west with many of Hammerstein's personnel and established a company on similar lines in Chicago. Here, over the next twenty years, Garden became as infamous as any gangster. Every year she would appear in a novel French (or at least Frenchified) opera, each of them flimsier than the last, as well as a few more conventional vehicles like *Tosca* or *Carmen*, and her established roles. She seems to have had very little musical discrimination: what attracted her was the chance to present some striking new variation on the old romantic dilemmas. To the *cognoscenti*, she was simply the greatest actress in America, with an imagination and originality which radiated through her bizarre repertory. She may not have been profound, but off stage as well as on, she astounded.

The Garden year began on her return to Chicago from a summer vacation in Europe, when she gave a press conference in her hotel suite, just before the opera season opened. She effortlessly publicized herself as the acme of sophistication and provided a feast of good copy. One year she was engaged to a Turkish pasha ('he smokes cigarettes constantly and he blows the smoke in such fascinating rings'); the next she announced categorically that she did not wear corsets but thought monocles or white spats very becoming. Then Coué, the apostle of auto-suggestion, had cured her of bronchial pneumonia; or she had met Mussolini whom she deemed 'the incarnation of Napoleon'. 'What is your weight?' she was asked.

'Ah! I am slender. I am chic. I am light and tripping on the feet. I have taken it off. I have lost it. It will never return again. Never more will I weigh an ounce more than I do right this moment,' came the reply.

'Yes. I know, but the figure—'

'I am speaking of the figure—my figure. Is it not superb?'

'I meant the weight . . .'

'It is one hundred and twenty-four pounds—spell it out.'

As the embodiment of modern womanhood her views on men and the question of sex took centre place. 'It is fine that women do no longer love as they did,' she said. 'It will be even finer if they can win absolute freedom. Formerly we were under the man's heel. Now just his little toe is on us. Yet how conscious we are of that little toe.' In Chicago her opinions and presence were ubiquitous: when a man who tried to assassinate her was asked why he had wanted to do it, he replied only, 'She talks too much.'

In 1921 pressure from the male little toe was finally lifted. Garden won herself greater worldly power than any prima donna had previously had when for one season she was made director or (as she insisted) directa of the Chicago Opera. Some magnificent artistic coups, including the première of Prokofiev's delightful *L'Amour de trois oranges*, were achieved at the expense of an administrative fiasco. 'I went as often as I could,' wrote Sheean, 'and reveled in the originality of the arrangements. An opera might be given once only—two performances was rather a long run—and a singer might make a debut which was simultaneously a farewell. These singularities are most often the prerogatives of failure . . . [but] Garden conducted her whole season through a tootling of success like the triumphal scene in *Aida*.' A large number of singers were engaged at vast salaries and then given nothing to sing while the directa went on two or three times a week, though, to be fair, she received no fee for her services beyond what she earned as a performer. No attention whatsoever was paid to proper budgeting and the final deficit was ruinous. Garden was quite happy with the result, announcing, 'If it cost a million dollars, I'm sure it was worth it.'

Garden last sang in Chicago in 1931 and in Paris in 1934. She made a fortune—fees in Chicago were even higher than the Met, in which she never appeared. Through the summer she augmented her income playing the casino at Monte Carlo where, being Mary Garden, she consistently won. She also made two silent films, including one of *Thaïs*, for which she was reported to have been paid $125,000. Olive Fremstad visited her on the set and was appalled.

'My God, Mary, you must be quite mad,' Mary Watkins Cushing heard her whisper. 'Why do you let yourself in for anything like this?' Miss Garden answered by tracing with one stiff finger in the icy air the cabalistic sign of the dollar. ' "Only that and nothing else," she declared, adding, "But even so it's not worth it, so DON'T." '

In semi-retirement (she continued to give lectures until her eighty-first year), she remained amazing and astounding. At the outbreak of the Second World War, she returned to Aberdeen, played bridge, and set up a military convalescent home with her sister. 'Gosh! How great it is to be British,' she wrote to an American correspondent. 'Charming she wasn't' remembered Beverly Sills, briefly her pupil. 'In fact Mary Garden often struck me as the meanest woman I had ever met.' But one wonders whether she was quite human at all—like the Mélisande she so eerily embodied. Even in the ranks of prima donnas Mary Garden stands out beyond the rule.

Her example was a dangerous one to follow—not that anyone dared. A more solid path for the French prima donna has been that of the heavy dramatic soprano. Calvé taught the Paris-born Gina Cigna, a famous Norma and Aida of the 1930s, while the half-Russian Félia Litvinne, a pupil of Pauline Viardot's, had a mastery of Wagnerian declamation. In her turn Litvinne taught Germaine Lubin (1890–1979), a gleaming heroic soprano who has been unfairly overshadowed by her contemporaries Flagstad and Leider. Her reputation was also affected by her sad 'collaboration' with the Nazis. In 1939 she sang in both Berlin and Bayreuth, where Hitler told her in his charming way that, 'In all my life I have never seen or heard an Isolde such as you.'

After the invasion of France she became a puppet in the direction of the Paris Opéra and sang as 'guest-artist' with visiting German companies. As so often, this appears to have been far more a matter of naïvete and time-serving than an active espousal of Nazi ideology, yet she was inevitably treated as a traitor after the Liberation, imprisoned, hounded, and broken: her son killed himself under the stress. 'Like Amfortas,' she told Lanfranco Rasponi at the end of her life, 'my wounds are destined to remain open . . . except for having eaten the flesh of children, there is nothing I was not accused of.' Whatever moral judgement one makes on her (and the evidence is by no means all on her side), the voice survives on record with a steely ringing confidence—fiercer than Flagstad's, less emotional than

Leider's—which has the exhilarating effect on a listener that we associate with Birgit Nilsson.

Lubin continued the direct line of succession when she coached Régine Crespin, the outstanding post-war French prima donna, in her assumption of the Wagner roles. Their encounters must have been interesting, for Crespin's highly idiosyncratic voice and style could never have developed the underlying physical stability of Lubin's. Lubin's is a lighthouse of a voice, shining out unmistakably, whereas Crespin is a siren, alluring and elusive, who like Shakespeare's Cleopatra 'makes hungry where most she satisfies'. It is hardly surprising that her career was so wayward, or that in a disarmingly frank autobiography she has revealed a life to complement it. Born in Marseilles in 1927, she was about to train as a pharmacist and only took up singing seriously when she failed her *baccalauréate*. From beginning to end she had a difficult relationship with the audiences and managements of the Paris Opéra, the house which should have garlanded her; and her most satisfying work was done in the French provinces, where she not only upheld all aspects of the French classical repertory (including Gluck's *Iphigénie en Tauride*, Berlioz's *Les Troyens*, and Fauré's *Pénélope*), but also sang Sieglinde, Tosca, and Desdemona. Internationally she kept the good name of French singing alive in an otherwise moribund period. She was a much-admired Kundry in *Parsifal* at Bayreuth and a knowing Marschallin at Glyndebourne, Covent Garden, and the Met, where she was coached by Lotte Lehmann. Later in the 1960s she was persuaded by Karajan to sing Brünnhilde in his *Ring* at Salzburg, but after nine performances she wisely renounced the role.

By the early 1970s she had reached a crisis point. At the Opéra she was mercilessly booed by what she claimed to be an organized anti-Crespin cabal. Her control over her voice was failing, as was her marriage to a man whose sexual appetite exhausted and terrified her. A wretched love affair, divorce, and psychoanalysis were followed by a radical retraining of her voice under a German teacher. Crespin forgot about her inimitably airy top notes and focused herself on lower-lying roles, including a stern Carmen. Then she suffered another unhappy involvement with the conductor Henry Lewis, Marilyn Horne's ex-husband, and a bout of cancer, but again recovered from both. The last years of her career, in which she memorably sang several cameo roles including the Prioress in

Poulenc's *Les Dialogues des Carmélites* and the Countess in *The Queen of Spades*, were probably her happiest.

Crespin's singing is probably the nearest we can come to a definition of French style, although some would think in terms of something more sweetly girlish and a multitude of others of Edith Piaf, another singer whose power lay in rich forthright enunciation. Few prima donnas have used words so clearly and expressively as Crespin, for whom, as her champion André Tubeuf puts it, 'good singing is first of all good speaking'. Her art is perhaps best characterized as being one of superbly inflected declamation, on the models of Racine and Rameau, in which mere smoothness of line and roundness of tone are subordinated to the communication of emotion and meaning.

Yet it would, I think, be impossible to identify a French voice blind and it would certainly not be easy to make out any significant similarities between the singing of Calvé, Garden, Lubin, and Crespin. A much stronger archetype is presented by the Spanish prima donna. Here we can isolate definite characteristics: vibrant tone, and an unerring sense for the subtleties of rhythm, for instance. Robert Rushmore further believes that a Spanish singer can be detected by 'a sound like the tiniest of hiccups' in the attack on certain notes in the middle and lower parts of their ranges. Even *Carmen* can recover some of her ethnic roots with a Spanish interpreter. A French Carmen like Régine Crespin will turn her mind to Racine and compare the cigarette girl to the great heroines of Antiquity, but a Spaniard knows what a gypsy is and what a *habanera* really sounds like. With no one is this more striking than Conchita Supervia, the mezzo-soprano whose voice breathes an unschooled peasant directness and charm which no other prima donna presents on record. Supervia was no drawing-room nightingale: her coloratura is not the disembodied carolling of one of Marchesi's pupils, but a dynamic emission of energy; her prominent vibrato (some say exaggerated by records) is not the result of tremulous over-refinement, but a sensual and robust buzz. The smell of fertile sunburnt earth pervades her singing.

Her origins are mysterious, and even her birth date is disputed, 1891, 1896, and 1899 having been variously suggested. It is now widely thought that she was born in Barcelona in 1895, although this makes her first recorded appearances in Buenos Aires in 1910 and Rome in 1911 (as Octavian in *Rosenkavalier*) almost incredible. Her musical training is equally mysterious. Her only known teacher was one Alfredo Martino, and it is conceivable that such a firm and healthy voice never needed much moulding. Most of her singing years were spent in Spain, Argentina, and Italy, where in 1918 she bore a son to a lawyer who begged her to marry him and give up singing. But for Supervia singing must have been as necessary as breathing and she refused him, strongly influenced by her dominating mother. In the 1920s, inspired by the conductor Vittorio Gui, she first sang in the operas of Rossini, the composer to whose spirit she was perhaps best suited. At that time he was only remembered as the composer of *Il Barbiere di Siviglia*, but Gui and Supervia reminded Europe of *La Cenerentola* and *L'Italiana in Algeri* as well, leaving matchless recordings of some of their major scenes and arias. For Supervia at her most inimitably vivacious, listen to the quarrel duet 'Ai capricci della sorte' from *L'Italiana*, for the spice of her wit and wickedness. Should you at the same time be contemplating suicide, allow Supervia to sing you out of it with Cenerentola's rondo 'Non più mesta'. Its embracing kindliness and sheer cheerfulness, as well as its irresistible rhythmic impetus, could make anyone feel that life was worth living.

Such was her success in these Rossini roles that, along with Carmen, she henceforth sang little else in the opera house. In 1931, in an attempt to give her son George legitimacy and a proper home, she married an English timber-merchant, Ben Rubenstein, and moved to London. The arrangement did not turn out well for either Supervia or her son, but the English public was delighted with its catch. She became an enormous favourite in the concert hall, where she did much to popularize the Spanish folk- and art-song. Her regular accompanist in these years was Ivor Newton, who described her as 'intensely alert and possessed of an apparently inexhaustible vitality. Her gaiety, good temper, sympathy and charm cloaked a keen intelligence and adamantine will-power . . . She needed only to say "I would like so-and-so" and whomever she addressed immediately said "Of course".' But there were times when the wheels of gallantry did not turn so smoothly, and nothing illustrates Newton's characterization of the singer better than the story of her only Covent Garden appearance in 1934–5.

She was engaged to sing Carmen and Cenerentola, but found the roles difficult to perform at the same time, since their vocal requirements are so different; nor did she wish to sing Carmen *before*

Cenerentola. When the fulfilment of these conditions proved impossible without a cut in the number of performances originally signed for, Supervia withdrew in a fury and threatened to sue for breach of contract. She went off to make a film of Beverley Nichols's novel *Evensong*, based loosely on the supposed rivalry between Melba and the young Toti dal Monte on their 1924 Australian tour. Eventually a compromise was reached: only *Cenerentola* would be performed, but Supervia's wishes would be met in the subsequent season. Sir Thomas Beecham, Covent Garden's musical director, had been thoroughly sceptical of the worth of Rossini's score and irritated by the instance of prima donna's privilege, but his resistance soon melted. When the ponies which draw Cenerentola's coach were unavailable during rehearsal, Supervia invited Beecham and the administrator Geoffrey Toye, who were sitting in the auditorium, to stand in. They gamely accepted and hopped around the stage dragging the coach behind them, while the triumphant prima donna whipped them on. The performance proved a wild success, and Supervia was so pleased with it all that she asked Ivor Newton to find her a graven image of Rossini somewhere in London: he came up with the frieze round the Albert Memorial, and together they went and laid a wreath of flowers at the master's feet—a snapshot exists of the little tribute.

Supervia then wrote to Toye suggesting the supporting casts that she would like for her forthcoming appearances: all her hints were taken. Opera historians have deplored this as unpardonable arrogance, but one must remember that it was Supervia who persuaded the management to take the risk on Rossini in the first place and that no one would have known more about who could sing his music than she did. And *L'Italiana in Algeri* emerged in London as happily as had *Cenerentola*, special delight being occasioned when Supervia made her entry carrying a small Pomeranian dog—a detail perfectly in accord with the character in question. Her Carmen followed, magnificently costumed by Lanvin: this divided opinion, some critics finding her too ingratiating. Yet the recordings communicate a creature of fierce determination, amoral yet not unfeeling, with an appeal that is anything but sugary—'predatory' is the word aptly used by J. B. Steane.

Supervia died suddenly in childbirth in 1936, having been warned by her doctor that pregnancy would be dangerous. Ironically for a singer whose art is so full of ordinary human happiness, she died sadly, miserable within her husband's tight-knit family circle and her son's hatred of his new situation. She was buried in the Jewish cemetery in Golders Green, having converted to Judaism to please her husband; her money and property were fiercely contested in an atmosphere of much resentment and recrimination. Fortunately these tragic complications could not affect the priceless legacy of her singing.

If she is irreplaceable, the line of Spanish prima donnas has continued and flourished. Victoria de los Angeles—another native of Barcelona, born in 1923—has had something of the same ability to inspire love in her listeners, although her charm is a much more shy and modest thing than Supervia's wonderful swagger. Los Angeles is the most restful of singers and whatever she sings has a natural intimacy and grace. 'For sheer quality of sound, Victoria's [voice] affects me more than any other,' admitted her accompanist Gerald Moore. Her Madama Butterfly is miraculously pathetic and dignified without ever sinking into the morass of sentiment implied by libretto and score, just as her Carmen (which she very rarely sang on stage) avoids any sort of snarling or strutting.

Despite an important operatic career in the mainstream—she was particularly popular in the 1950s at the Met, where her virtues and repertory recalled memories of another great Spanish soprano of the inter-war years, Lucrezia Bori—it has been in the intimacy of the song recital that her most essential qualities were fulfilled. Here her infallible gift has been the realization of the heart of the song, of its emotional point: Schwarzkopf could get more colour and subtlety into a song's *meaning*, but she is rarely as simply moving as Los Angeles. Truly, she has been a singer with a Midas touch, turning gold in the tender and melancholy reaches of Spanish song as well as in the less florid areas of Purcell, Handel, and Monteverdi. Nobody has better communicated the desperate, breathless happiness of Schubert's 'Mein' or more sharply tossed off the humour in Brahms's 'Vergebliches Ständchen'. To everything, she grants an artless beauty, and if Supervia is the singer to save one from suicide, it is Los Angeles who could sing one to a peaceful and painless grave.

Finally we come to the problematic case of Montserrat Caballé, without doubt one of the greatest singers since the war and a prima donna as people like to think of them.

Caballé's voice has all the vibrancy and her musicality the supple rhythmic sense that we associate with the Spanish. Her singing is on the grandest scale, filling vaults of sound with exquisite filigree detail. She could pull out a phrase to heavenly lengths, moving effortlessly from dreamy *pianissimo* to a thrillingly metallic top C. In the later 1960s and early 1970s after the eclipse of Renata Tebaldi and Leontyne Price, she was regarded as queen of the Italian repertory, a peerless stylist with a facile coloratura and astonishing versatility. She was also the fat lady prima donna, the elephant who had swallowed a nightingale, and so good when she was good that you'd forgive her anything—greed, laziness, megalomania. Like Patti, Caballé always had charm.

She had a long apprenticeship before her talent coincided with her luck. Born in Barcelona in 1933, her parents were very poor and badly hit by the Civil War: at sixteen, she was working in a handkerchief factory in order to pay for an operation on her father. For seven years her musical ambitions (which had begun with training for the ballet) were sponsored by the wealthy Bertrand family, on the sole condition that she never neglected Barcelona's opera house, the Liceo—which she never did, to the point of using it for many years as the base for her power and influence. In 1956 she joined the Basle Opera. Over the next few years she sang anything from Salome (her favourite role) to Mimi and took a long time getting anywhere. It was not until 20 April 1965, almost ten years since her operatic début, that she broke through the invisible barrier, when she stepped at short notice into a concert performance of Donizetti's *Lucrezia Borgia* at Carnegie Hall in New York, and provoked a sensation. The great years followed, during which she was particularly in demand for the more dramatic Donizetti, Rossini, and early Verdi roles, which had long been awaiting such a voice.

Then in the early 1970s began a bewildering series of illnesses and indispositions, affecting both her and her family. Scarcely a month seemed to pass without some contretemps: either she was walking off-stage mid trio (as she did during *Un Ballo in Maschera* at Covent Garden) or she was collapsing in her dressing-room as the curtain was about to rise. She suffered from salmonella poisoning, car accidents, kidney stones, cancer, heart problems, phlebitis and a brain tumour; she simply couldn't take the pace. With her erratic health came erratic singing. Much of the time it sounded as though she knew *what* she ought to be doing, but couldn't stop herself from doing otherwise. In particular her singing at Covent Garden, where she first appeared in 1972, was consistently disappointing, and

London only heard her at her best in concert, where she was probably happiest anyway, especially if she found a chance to engage the audience in some long (and usually incomprehensible) ramble about her accompanist, her hotel, her wardrobe or her health. She was capable of ravishing and memorable performances and even on an off-night could produce *belles minutes* of a splendour that none of her contemporaries could match. Yet she became an impossibly dodgy proposition for anyone trying to run an opera house, not least because her miraculous sight-reading abilities meant that she was a great one for learning her roles at the last minute, much to the aggravation of those she worked with. Sterner critics tutted at her tendency to collapse into hysterical fits of giggling at moments of high operatic drama and the dubious activities of her brother and manager Carlos Caballé, as well as at a bizarrely catholic repertory which could embrace a money-spinning stunt with rock star Freddie Mercury (in the hit single 'Barcelona', to which she contributed a hair-raising descant), Isolde and Sieglinde, Norma and Turandot, and such oddities as Salieri's *Axur*, Pacini's *Saffo*, Rossini's *Adelaida di Borgogna* and Respighi's *La Fiamma*. 'Quixotic' is probably the most charitable and ethnically appropriate way of summing her up.

# 9

# *The Callas Revolution*

Once the struggle for national unification in Italy was won, Italian opera abandoned the heroic romanticism which Verdi's music had so gloriously embodied. Inevitably, the new political stability left the public less engaged by the issues of war and peace, rulers and subjects, power and the powerful. Instead it turned inward to dilemmas more personal and subjective, psychologically intense rather than socially extensive: something of this is evident even in the different orientations of Verdi's *Aida* (1871) and *Otello* (1887). '*Verismo*' is the term used to describe this trend, but like '*bel canto*' or 'Wagnerism', it has become a label of operatic history so indiscriminately applied as to be misleading.

The origins of *verismo* are in fact French. The naturalistic novels of Zola which depict industrial and working-class life were the sensational modernism of their day, influential throughout the Italian *avant-garde*. The French playwright Sardou's meaty melodramas like *Fedora* and *La Tosca*, both written for Sarah Bernhardt, also had obvious operatic potential—*La Tosca*, of course, contains a prima donna as its central character—and Italian composers were deeply impressed by the heart-on-the-sleeve idiom of Massenet's early operas, which trade on emotional situations far more accessible to the average opera-goer than Wagner's complex mythologies. The moment at which all these elements decisively came together was the production in 1890 of a one-act opera called *Cavalleria Rusticana*, by the twenty-six-year-old Pietro Mascagni. This was, as it were, the musical version of a tough little play made very popular through Duse's performance as the betrayed Sicilian peasant Santuzza. Mascagni set the piece to boldly crude music and not only created a *furore* but set a new course for Italian opera. The concentration made possible by the single-act form was much imitated, as in the original version of Leoncavallo's *I Pagliacci* and Massenet's 'answer' to *Cavalleria Rusticana*, *La Navarraise*. Physical violence in a low-life setting, sometimes contemporary, involving characters who have compromised themselves sexually, became a standard format, and the fustian clichés of conventional operatic Italian—from '*padre, pietà*' to '*crudel fato*'—gave way to librettos closer to recognizably demotic speech.

All sorts of operas have been categorized as *verismo*, even if they really do not fit the above characterization. Ponchielli's *La Gioconda* appeared some fourteen years before *Cavalleria Rusticana* and is based, like *Rigoletto*, on a drama by Victor Hugo; Cilea's *Adriana Lecouvreur* is set in seventeenth-century Paris and deals with a noble-hearted actress of the Comédie-Française; Giordano's *Andrea Chénier* is a high-flown tale of the French Revolution—yet all are commonly thought of as '*verismo*'. The greatest Italian composer of the period, Giacomo Puccini (1858–1924), only wrote one opera, the one-act *Il Tabarro*, which can properly be called *verismo*, although his operas are generally lumped under that label.

What more intelligibly unites all these works are certain musical characteristics: not very salubrious ones, it has to be said. Under the twice-removed example of Wagner, the harmony is glutinously chromatic; the orchestration tends to the thick and lurid; and crashingly obvious '*leitmotivs*' blaze out repeatedly at crucial moments of looming doom and ultimate destruction. The vocal line depends heavily on overt rises and falls in pitch and dynamic indicative of emotional torture. To maximize the expressive potential, singers of the time resorted to a number of vocal tricks which had no place in the Italian training given by a Garcia or Marchesi: Michael Scott lists them as 'the sob and catch in the breath, the glottal attack, the aspirate and those sudden shifts from a *mezza voce* ... to a *forte* in which the words are uttered with explosive force'. *Verismo* also brought about a considerably more energetic and uninhibited style of acting, which in turn all too often descended into fits of hysteria, throat-clutching, extended death-throes, and other clichés in the vocabulary of melodrama.

For the prima donna, *verismo* caused a crisis comparable to that presented by Wagner. The agility required by Donizetti or Meyerbeer was of no use to someone singing Santuzza, nor could the Verdian *spinto* who had mastered legato and purity of intonation

267

always muster the dark colouring and throbbing heart-ache necessary for a Butterfly or Tosca. The result was a specialization in
particular areas of the repertory that had not previously been so
clearly demarcated. Before the turn of the century, a fluent
coloratura with a facility in runs, trills, and other ornaments, had
been part of the equipment of every prima donna, from Lilli
Lehmann and Nordica to Melba and Calvé; now it became the
province of a few singers revered as freak vocal acrobats.

Luisa Tetrazzini, for instance, with the biggest voice and most
striking personality among this new breed of show-off coloraturas,
did not infallibly impress. When she made her New York début in *La
Traviata* to wild public acclaim, the respected critic W. J. Henderson
pointed out that however accurate and powerful her runs and high
notes, there were some fundamental inadequacies underneath.
Tetrazzini's was as indisputably a badly schooled and unbalanced
voice as it was a phenomenally brilliant one. Her lower medium notes
'were all sung with a pinched glottis and with a color so pallid and a
tremolo so pronounced that they were often not a bad imitation of
the wailing of a cross infant . . . her *cantabile* was uneven in tone
quality, the breaks between her medium and her upper notes coming
out most unpleasantly', while her ascending scales were 'sung in a
manner which would not be tolerated by any reputable teacher in a
pupil of a year's standing'. When asked for her opinion of the new
prima donna, Melba replied with customary sharpness, 'Get her to
sing me a slow scale,' justifiably confident of the firmness of her own
grounds in such basic technical matters.

Tetrazzini herself candidly admitted in her autobiography that
'My actual training was probably the shortest of any prima donna
that the world has produced.' Born in Florence in 1871, she had the
initial advantage of coming from a musical family, in which her elder
sister Eva, later married to the chief conductor of the Manhattan and
Chicago Operas, Cleofonte Campanini, was also to become an
operatic soprano of some repute. Luisa spent a few unfruitful
months in a music conservatory before making her début in Florence
in 1890. She then embarked on the provincial Italian opera circuit,
where she was much in demand for her accomplishments in the 'old'
pre-*verismo* repertory. It was in Florence some years later that E. M.
Forster heard her as Lucia di Lammermoor. The comedy attached to
her performance found its way into *Where Angels Fear to Tread* and

provides a vivid picture of the theatrical conditions under which she performed.

> The climax was reached in the mad scene. Lucia, clad in white, as befitted her malady, suddenly gathered up her streaming hair and bowed her acknowledgements to the audience. Then from the back of the stage—she feigned not to see it—there advanced a kind of bamboo clothes-horse, stuck all over with bouquets . . . With a scream of amazement and joy she embraced the animal, pulled out one or two practicable blossoms, pressed them to her lips, and flung them into her admirers. They flung them back with loud melodious cries, and a little boy in one of the stage-boxes snatched up his sister's carnations and offered them. '*Che carino!*' exclaimed the singer. She darted at the little boy and kissed him. Now the noise became tremendous. 'Silence! Silence!' shouted many old gentlemen behind. 'Let the divine creature continue!'

From 1892, Tetrazzini also toured in Central and South America, which had recently developed a vigorous operatic life, relying strongly on imported Italian singers. Tetrazzini is an example of a prima donna famous for years on the 'Latin' circuit, while remaining completely unknown in the 'Anglo-Saxon' centres of London and New York. It was not until 1907, when she was engaged for the quiet autumn season at Covent Garden, that she made the breakthrough. The manager Harry Higgins was not enthusiastic at first and even tried to renege on the contract, but Tetrazzini was determined to sing where her idol Patti had sung. She arrived in London in November to find the city enshrouded in one of the legendary 'pea-soupers', which was hardly propitious. No one expected anything of her at all. The opera house was half empty—few ventured out to brave the fog which had even invaded the auditorium and rendered the stage half invisible. But when Tetrazzini started singing her first-act aria, Higgins was stunned. In the interval he rushed to telephone Fleet Street to send down some reporters to witness what was obviously going to be a sensation. Tetrazzini's status duly changed overnight, and *le tout Londres* came out to hear her. The greatest accolade came from no less a personage than Patti herself, who wrote an enthusiastic and generous letter.

My dear Madame Tetrazzini, *Bravo! Bravo!* and again *Bravo!* I cannot tell you how much pleasure it gave me to hear you last night and what a joy it was to me to hear your beautiful Italian phrasing . . . I shall take the first opportunity of going to hear you again. I heartily rejoice in your well-deserved triumph. Yours sincerely, Adelina Patti-Cederström.

Critics soon became rather more sceptical: 'Madame Tetrazzini's most striking characteristic as Violetta,' wrote one in 1908, 'is the unfailing good temper with which she puts up with the trying circumstances of that lady's career. Then comes the voice, that astonishing voice which is like some incredibly perfected mechanical toy. Her acting—but enough. Madame Tetrazzini knows that it is sufficient to be just herself.' That 'perfected mechanical toy' was enough to keep audiences happy, however, and for five subsequent seasons she dominated Covent Garden alongside Melba and Destinn. On one mind-boggling night, the Coronation Gala of 1911, the three of them appeared together: Destinn sang in the triumph scene from *Aida*, Melba the second act of *Roméo et Juliette*, and Tetrazzini the last act of *Il Barbiere di Siviglia*. The evening was capped with dancing from Karsavina and Nijinsky. Unfortunately the scent from the 100,000-odd roses decorating the auditorium was so overpowering that many of the audience (who had paid up to £1,000 for a box and £100 for a seat) fainted. Perhaps the whole occasion was a dismal anti-climax . . .

Tetrazzini repeated her London operatic success in New York and Chicago. At her Manhattan début Mary Garden was observed to applaud so loud that she split her gloves, and though the critics echoed their London colleagues' reservations, audiences remained frantic with approval. After the outbreak of the First World War, she abandoned the stage for the less taxing and more lucrative sphere of concert tours. These continued much, much too long, but Tetrazzini loved singing and loved her publics. She was not, like Patti, someone who immediately cancelled if she felt slightly off-colour. If people wanted to hear her sing, then she must sing. Part of her appeal was her simple but abundant warmth of manner: at the beginning of concerts, she would pass round the platform waving, shaking available hands and kissing available children. The ritual became increasingly painful, however, and by the early 1930s, when she was in her sixties, she only endured the agonies and indignities of touring because she was desperate for money. The record producer Fred

Gaisberg remembers a provincial matinée concert in 1933. The hall was virtually empty and the stage could only be reached from the dressing-rooms via a narrow spiral staircase, up and down which the wretched Tetrazzini, covered in costume jewellery, extremely stout and in poor health, had to be firmly pushed. Gaisberg saw her kiss her rosary, tears trickling silently down her cheek.

Her life had ended in a mess, largely due to her invincible gullibility and extravagance. 'I am of a very buoyant nature and am a born optimist,' she claimed, and it was just as well that she was. She lost fantastic sums of money, throwing it away on schemes run by any plausible swindler. Her third husband, for instance, twenty years her junior, turned out to be a charlatan and she was forced to sue him for extortion. Previously she had bought an entire mountain on the unjustified assumption that it was 'made of gold'. Her paranoid superstition made her even more vulnerable, as well as exasperating. Despite her terror of travelling and a readiness to see imminent disaster signified by anything from hunchbacks to paper-knives, she was equally game to try anything. Once, in San Francisco in 1919, she went up in a bi-plane for charity with the stunt pilot Ormer Locklear:

> Sailing over the bank of eucalyptus trees at the far side of the field, Locklear nearly lost control of the plane when Tetrazzini let loose an impromptu high C. Glancing round in terror, he was reassured by Madame's jolly cherubic face that the golden note had been thrown out on the breeze only as an expression of delight. He circled the field a couple of times and gave Tetrazzini an extra thrill by buzzing the grandstand twice before landing. 'Ah, it is so exquisite,' she told Locklear while getting out of her flying togs. 'So much more exciting than hitting high C when singing, and almost as momentous to me.'

She died in 1940 on *terra firma*, in some poverty and was buried in Milan at the expense of the Italian state.

Her 'successor' in the public's affections was Amelita Galli-Curci (1882–1963), a coloratura soprano of much less power and firmness, but an unfailing simple charm, gentler in manner than Tetrazzini and possessed with what one imagines to be something of Patti's gift for making her art sound spontaneous. Galli-Curci is an easy singer to like: she sounds such an innocent little thing. Uncle Matthew in Nancy Mitford's novel *The Pursuit of Love* could not get enough of her and woke the rest of his household up at five o'clock every morning with her dulcet tones emanating from records invariably played at the wrong speed.

The fact that Galli-Curci's singing could penetrate the murky depths of upper-class English philistinism is tribute indeed, but then few prima donnas have lent themselves so well to clever marketing. The voice was soft-grained enough to record both clearly and warmly, and she was assiduously exploited by the recording companies. She had married into the Italian nobility. Her long, languid face and olive colouring were the stuff of every chocolate-box Renaissance painting. An aura of romance was not hard to fabricate round her life and circumstances, once she had reached an initial point from which she could be exposed to the public.

That point was Chicago in 1916: before this her career had followed a standard pattern. Born in Milan into a musical home, she had begun as a pianist, but was encouraged by Mascagni to develop her voice. For ten-odd years she sang the 'old' repertory on the 'Latin' circuit, without making much of a stir. Her luck changed after the sinking of the *Lusitania*, when she was stranded in South America, with the Atlantic unsafe for the return passage to Europe. The obvious alternative was to go north, especially as with European sources effectively cut off, opera houses in America would be seeking out fresh blood. Gatti-Casazza at the Met turned her down because she sang flat, while in Chicago, the conductor Campanini (Tetrazzini's brother-in-law) unenthusiastically offered her two trial performances. Only at the dress rehearsal of *Rigoletto* did he realize her potential. She was immediately booked for the rest of the season at twice the fee for which she had originally signed, and after that the star-making machine took over. The début was sensational; every imaginable sort of offer followed. Her manager Charles Wagner mapped out the tactics:

We had at least one condition greatly in our favour. The public just about to plunge into a frightening and horrible war was in the mood for a new thrill that would give them pleasure and take their minds from this tragic prospect . . . Dressing her in old-fashioned gowns added considerably to her early popularity. The Mona Lisa story was well-timed*—appearing just when the famous master-piece had been stolen and was on all the front-pages. Then when a dear old lady in Columbus, Ohio, who had heard Jenny Lind, told me how much Galli-Curci reminded her of the Swedish Nightingale, I was inspired to give out the story of that celebrated singer of the past century. Papers were delighted to print it and the public gobbled it up.

None of this would have worked had the lady herself not delivered the basic commodity. Henderson, a critic notoriously hard to satisfy, was at first convinced that she did, calling hers 'a well-equalized voice, with a fine welding of registers ... lending itself readily to gradations of power, which its owner employs with the most delicate musical skill and admirable taste'.

A great majority of her records confirm this—the voice is physically a better balanced instrument than Tetrazzini's, and of a colour perfectly appropriate to the either sparkling or melancholic heroines in which she specialized—Amina, Norina in *Don Pasquale*, Lucia, Rosina, Dinorah, etc. On the other hand, Galli-Curci never communicates any particular shade of meaning or any sense of drama, nor can she match Tetrazzini's sheer knockout razzamatazz. She trips happily through the florid arias and wistfully spins out the ballads: more than this one must not ask.

After 1916 Galli-Curci's opera career was surprisingly circum-scribed. She very rarely sang on stage outside the Chicago or Met companies, and instead spent an extraordinary amount of time in the recording studio, where she was more of a perfectionist than most of her contemporaries. When her charms as a 'live' performer began to fade—and fade they very speedily did—her records continued to sustain her reputation. The problems began in the mid 1920s, when she discovered that, as her ludicrous biographer puts it, 'the path of art is never entirely one of roses. Wasps in human form attack the flowers.' Critics of her performances had first become bored with her obvious limitations and then fastened on to her painful tendency to sing off the note. One of her most decisive humiliations was her first London concert in 1924, given to an Albert Hall packed with an audience keenly anticipating the Galli-Curci of the records. One of

* Charles Wagner liked to claim that Galli-Curci had a strong facial resemblance to the subject of Leonardo's painting.

those most disappointed was Nancy Mitford's Uncle Matthew, whose 'disillusionment . . . was so great that the records remained ever after silent, and were replaced by the deepest bass voices that money could buy . . . These were, on the whole, welcomed by the family, as rather less piercing at early dawn.'

In 1929 she announced that she was giving up opera altogether, because of its 'essential absurdities' and henceforth would concentrate on world concert tours. By this time the flatness in her singing had become persistent and her control was generally in decline. Finally, a throat specialist risked operating on a goitre which had grown as big as a tennis ball. It was duly removed, and in 1936, presumably no longer inhibited by absurdity, she braved a return to Chicago and opera, in the undemanding role of Mimi in *La Bohème*. The trouble, however, must have lain deeper than her throat, because this too proved a complete failure and she was forced to move into teaching and thence into an idyllically happy Californian retirement, as memorably commemorated by her biographer C. F. Lemassena, whose pretentious book, in which each chapter is named after a phase in an inexorable spiritual cycle, as though its subject was some sort of female Buddha, does disservice to a prima donna whose art was not a pretentious thing:

> Evening were devoted to music, art, books, and conversation appertaining to some suggested mental trend, which, no matter whither it led, the hostess . . . could meet and carry on with erudite assurance, for she was a reader and a thinker, a scholar and a sage . . . Nothing gave her more delight than to scramble with a flock of gladsome children . . . they would inspect the cows and chicks and wind up in the dairy to sip sweet cream from earthen jugs, then lick their coated fingers clean mid laughter and enraptured merriment . . . No stray dog or cat or bird applied in vain at her open door for succour . . .

All the elevation of Galli-Curci's fragile accomplishment was substantially the work not of the press so much as the technology of recording and broadcasting, and the fact that by the 1920s gramophones and wirelesses were no longer luxury items. Girls of that time, the Mitfords included, grew up with the processed voice of Galli-Curci, and if they wanted to sing, they wanted to sing like her. It would not be an exaggeration to say that Galli-Curci formed a new style of prima donna. In the opera house, her most distinguished successors were probably Toti dal Monte and Lily Pons, her most ill-fated imitator Marion Talley;* but her influence spread deep into the new entertainment media, and it was in the even more modest talents of such singing movie stars as Deanna Durbin and Jeanette MacDonald that the style and tone of voice lived on. Coloratura did not, as is often said, die out, only to be revived by Maria Callas: its fate was not temporary death, but temporary emasculation. It became decorative, dainty, and harmless, associated with a bodiless femininity as sexually inert as the Hays Censorship Code could wish. Had the cinema and wireless public been listening to Ponselle as Norma or Donna Anna, the received image might have been different.

Opposite this new brand of 'old-fashioned' prima donna was what for convenience we shall call the '*verismo*' prima donna, specializing in the post-*Cavalleria Rusticana* repertory of the modern Italian school. The single greatest influence on the formation of this type was the actress Eleonora Duse, whose performances in the new dramas of social realism had a power and emotional range which shattered theatrical convention and stereotype. We have already seen how deeply Emma Calvé was affected by Duse, but the first true *verismo* prima donna was Gemma Bellincioni (1864–1950), the first Santuzza in *Cavalleria Rusticana* and a Violetta whose originality and force were much admired by the elderly Verdi. Puccini's favoured sopranos—Cesira Ferrani (the first Manon Lescaut and Mimi), Rosini Storchio (the first Butterfly), and Hariclea Darclée (the first Tosca)—are other historically significant names, but probably the best and certainly the most celebrated of the *versimo* prima donnas was the enigmatic Claudia Muzio. Charles Jahant remembers her acting as a mannered display of *grand guignol*, yet as a singer she expresses a purer form of tragedy. Like so many others of her generation, she over-cultivated the brown and purple colouring of her voice, and her technique shows many real shortcomings when compared to that of a Melba or Calvé: but Muzio always *sang*, and never resorted to the sobbing, rasping gasping which so many of her lesser contemporaries used to excess, at the expense of the smooth and steady emission of even tone. In Lanfranco Rasponi's book of interviews with prima donnas of the early years of this century, it is

* See p. 181–2.

certainly Muzio who wins the most extravagant tributes. Mafalda Favero went backstage after a performance and spontaneously dropped to her knees in front of her; on Eva Turner she made 'the most unforgettable impression of all'. Others spoke of 'the divine Muzio', 'Muzio, my idol', 'a case apart, you cannot classify her', or 'the only word to describe Muzio is sublime'. The ability she had to move her audiences seems to have been unique, and it is Muzio on whom the 'Duse of Song' accolade has most fairly stuck.

Her life seems to have been almost entirely unhappy—a fact which her voice, 'made of tears and sighs and restrained inner fire', as the tenor Giacomo Lauri-Volpi described it, does not allow one to forget. She was born illegitimate in 1889 as Claudina Versati, although her parents later married. Her mother was a chorus singer, her father a stage director at the Met and Covent Garden. An education at convents in Tottenham and Hammersmith bequeathed her the beautiful unaccented English audible on some of her song recordings, and Eva Turner remembered having a very English tea with her in Chicago years later at which she was plied with questions about those areas of London.

In 1906 she went back to Italy to study voice and made her début as Gilda in *Rigoletto* in Messina in 1910. After some success in Turin and La Scala, she returned to Covent Garden in 1914, singing among other roles Tosca and Mimi, opposite Caruso. Then in 1916 she was engaged by the Met to replace the indisposed Bori and the incarcerated Destinn. She stayed there until 1922 and created the role of the bargee's wife Giorgetta in Puccini's *Il Tabarro*, as well as introducing Tatyana in *Eugene Onegin* and Maddalena in *Andrea Chénier* to the house. Like Farrar, she was pushed out of New York by the arrival of the all-vanquishing Jeritza, and her career was thereafter concentrated in Chicago, Buenos Aires, and Rome. Her repertory was mostly later Verdi, Puccini, and *verismo* roles, but in South America she also sang the Marschallin in *Rosenkavalier*, Elsa in *Lohengrin*, and even Norma. In 1932 she opened the War Memorial Opera House in San Francisco as Tosca; in 1934 she created the title-role in Refice's briefly sensational 'mystical' opera *Cecilia* and returned to the Met. In 1936 she died in a hotel in Rome.

This is an impressive catalogue. There were no crises, vocal or otherwise, no lapses of taste or disastrous errors of judgement, no publicity stunts. The critics were almost invariably favourable, the public appreciative: Muzio's problems began outside the opera house. She was known to be acutely self-conscious about her height (five foot nine or ten inches), despite a face of great beauty and a dress sense and deportment to match. Perhaps her apparently pathological shyness was exacerbated by her illegitimacy; perhaps it was just the hauteur which prima donnas commonly use as a self-protective wall. Whatever its cause, Muzio was hardly bubbling with fun. The jokiness and camaraderie around Caruso infuriated her: 'She came to the theatre, rehearsed, sang and left, exchanging barely a few sentences with fellow-singers, who remember her as a soprano "who never said anything", "who acted as if we were all devils".' Frida Leider shared a dressing-room with her in Chicago:

Her Italian maid used to spend entire mornings arranging her costumes. When Claudia appeared for rehearsal, her maid would help her to change, for she had a kind of rehearsal uniform which consisted of a heavy black silk dress, a black jacket trimmed with ermine, and a little hat to match. Always the *grande dame*, she would stride majestically across the stage to the prompter's box, clasp her gloved hands, and simply mark her way through her entire role without moving an inch.

She shared her heyday in Chicago with Mary Garden, but more of a contrast cannot be imagined. Garden was a hard-boiled exotic who courted and flirted with publicity; no one could make anything of Muzio. In his memoir of the city in the 1920s Arthur Meeker claims that 'people who knew her painted a gruesome picture of rooms from which all daylight was excluded, full of jabbering relatives and cooking spaghetti, in the midst of which Claudia, wearing a gorgeous *robe de chambre*, with her hair down her back, lay prone and weeping over the machinations of her rivals, sentimental or professional.'

The key to it all seems to lie in her relationship with her mother. After her adored father had died, wrote Mary Jane Matz, 'her strange silent mother became her exclusive companion ... fanatically religious, suspicious, possessive, she kept Muzio apart from those of her father's cronies whom the singer had known. The two women gradually became virtual recluses.' On tour in South America, Muzio and her mother 'sat in the corner of the hotel dining-room farthest from the rest of the company "never speaking, never even nodding to the rest of us".' She lived 'almost as the older woman's slave', without any other friend or confidante. Throughout all this, she was deceiving her mother with a series of lovers, and here the story becomes depressingly familiar. One of them, according to Leider, was an impresario who absconded with a lot of her money; then in 1929, after her mother's death, she married a man seventeen years younger than herself, with the predictable result. The cause of her death at the age of forty-seven has been variously reported as suicide, nephritis, cancer, tuberculosis, Bright's disease, or a heart condition.

Shortly before, she had embarked on her last recordings, an event also surrounded with various pathetic tales. Out of the sessions came a record of 'Addio del passato' from the last act of *Traviata* which immediately became a classic. Like all classics, it has suffered some knocks from latter-day critics, but it stands up to them. Everything about it illustrates the best of the *verismo* style. Muzio sang the role frequently (including in a modern-dress production in Rome in 1928), but the overwhelming impression the record gives is of emotional immediacy. There is a superb command of *parlando* effects: this Violetta reads the letter from Germont like a sick woman who has been turning the words over in her mind obsessively for days. Her cry of 'E tardi!' ('It is too late') is heavy with fate. In the aria itself Muzio exploits the use of short breaths—not sobs, so much as an effortful intake of air—until the memory of 'l'amor di Alfredo' brings out a full passionate grief for what has been lost. A constant seesaw between *crescendo* and *diminuendo*, within both single notes and full phrases, further intensifies the feverishness. At the end the little spasms of breath return inexorably, culminating in a perfectly pitched scream of agony, cut sharply off into silence. The singing is graphically descriptive of Violetta's mental and physical state (whether Muzio herself was also dying of consumption is another question) in a manner that a Violetta of the older school, like Melba, would have thought horribly vulgar.

An earlier series of recordings made in 1917–18 shows Muzio's voice fresher in tone and freer in movement, the melancholy less pervasive than in the 1934–5 series. Some of her attempts at Verdi's most heroic arias may lack the last degree of power and expansiveness; her coloratura is sketchy; but in the music of Boito, Catalani, Puccini, Giordano, and their fellows, she is unforgettable and unsurpassed. All the temptations to mawkishness and morbidity offered by their music are cast out by her burning light of conviction. The pathos in Muzio's art remains quiet and withdrawn, where others fling their self-respect to the gallery. Her sense of a phrase's gravity is unfailing, and she shares with the greatest singers the gift of surprising the listener by turning a single word or note into something unexpectedly telling. A final little surprise—Garbo smiles and Muzio laughs!—is her pert and cheerful rendition of a ditty by Delibes, 'Good morning, Sue', which also exemplifies the purity of her English.

Only by bearing in mind this major division between the 'Galli-Curci coloratura' and the 'Muzio *verismo*' sopranos can we properly appreciate the revolution in the years after the Second World War which went under the banner of Maria Callas (1923–77). So much journalistic copy has been expended on this singer (of prima donnas only Malibran provoked such a degree of prurient international interest) that for many people, the idea of the prima donna still begins and ends with Callas. This is absurd. Callas was indeed a revolutionary, but not a revolutionary without a tradition to inherit or a band of comrades. And like many of the most successful revolutionaries, she was in many ways a restorer rather than an iconoclast.

The first important fact about Callas is that her principal teacher was Elvira de Hidalgo, a light coloratura of the Galli-Curci type who had been popular on the 'Latin' circuit between about 1910 and 1925. Callas's natural vocal colour, as a Hellenophile friend of mine pointed out, can be heard on any Greek island when the peasant women start shouting at each other. Peremptory, black, strident but *vibrato*-less, it is a sound of tragic absolutes, quite different from the dark tints of Italian *morbidezza*, let alone the white warblings of a Galli-Curci. Normally a voice of Callas's type would have been groomed for Tosca, Gioconda, and a round of *verismo* heroines, but de Hidalgo seems to have been concerned with brightening and colouring her timbre and with passing on the discipline of old-fashioned flexibility. She thus left her pupil in the odd position of having a great dramatic voice trained to sing little-girl roles like de Hidalgo's own favourites, Rosina, Lucia, and Gilda. Callas did go on to sing those roles, but she gave them a radically new complexion; and beyond them she brought back more grandly scaled figures such as Donizetti's Anna Bolena and Cherubini's Medea.

In the immediate post-war period, however, when her career began in Italy, Callas sang in the accepted heavy dramatic repertory, parts such as Turandot, Gioconda, and Isolde, none of which exploited the facility de Hidalgo had given her. It was only when she met the great Italian conductor, Tullio Serafin, that her voice met its destiny. At the end of 1948 she sang her first Normas under his direction, and a few weeks later he inspired her to the unprece- dented, almost lunatic feat of singing Brünnhilde in *Die Walküre* and Elvira in Bellini's *I Puritani* within days of each other. Serafin had a profound understanding of the great Italian tradition represented by the art of Pasta, Malibran, and Grisi, and the music Bellini and Donizetti had provided for them. It was above all he who led what became known as the '*bel canto* revival', meaning revival of the *dramatic* potential of coloratura singing, as opposed to its evergreen 'nightingale' aspect. This revival started long before Callas.

After Mussolini came to power in 1922, he instituted a far- reaching programme aimed at the regeneration of national culture. One of its more important platforms was an assertion of the glories of Italian music, too long overshadowed by Wagnerism and Teutonic morbidity. At first the state encouraged the staging of new Italian operas (notably Mascagni's *Nerone*), most of which proved embar- rassing flops. As a second-string therefore, the Ministry of Culture sponsored attempts to re-establish the worth of the forgotten Italian operas of the early nineteenth century. In the 1920s and 1930s many dramatic sopranos in Italy sang *Norma*, and some of the obscurer Donizetti and Rossini operas were also heard again after fifty or more years. In 1935, for instance, the centenary of Bellini's death, Gina Cigna sang his *La Straniera* at La Scala; in 1933 Vittorio Gui had conducted *I Puritani* and Donizetti's *Lucrezia Borgia* at Florence's Maggio Musicale. Supervia was singing superbly brazen Rossini coloratura from the mid 1920s all over Europe; there was also Ponselle, with whom Serafin had worked closely on *Norma* and Spontini's *La Vestale*. The war checked the impetus of the revival, but even without Callas it would surely have continued to gain ground in the 1950s. Yet Callas did provide a magic ingredient missing in the equipment of the fiery but technically ill-prepared sopranos of the previous generation—a true coloratura—and it was Serafin who appreciated the possibilities this presented. He taught her authority of phrasing and attack, the value of a pause, and the way to shape a recitative. In her own words, he 'showed me that there was a reason for everything, that even *fioriture* and trills . . . have a reason [*sic*] in the composer's mind, that they are the expression of the *stato*

*d'animo* of the character . . . He taught me exactly the depth of music
. . . I really drank all I could from that man.'

Sadly, Serafin was on bad terms with the La Scala management
and thus never conducted Callas in the opera house which offered
her the highest standards of production and musical preparation,
when her art was at its peak. Their partnership was however
substantially preserved on record, thanks to the good sense of EMI's
producer Walter Legge, one of Callas's most cogent critics and
admirers.

Callas's La Scala years have become the core of her legend, but her
triumphs there were not easily won and the stories of her skirmishes
are well known. Every performance was a battle with hostile factions
in the audience and backstage intrigue, doubtless exacerbated by the
tough business negotiations of her husband and manager Giovanni-
Battista Meneghini, and her own explosive temperament. Nevertheless, she was surrounded there by colleagues whose artistic ideals
were as high as hers and whom Callas could trust. She was not a
prima donna who simply wanted to be attractively framed or
delicately coddled. She wanted to work, and the capacity to work was
intrinsic to her genius. 'I do not believe with Descartes: "I think,
therefore I am," ' she said. 'With me, it is: "I work, therefore I am." '
La Scala gave her the tools—the innovative repertory, the extensive
rehearsals, conductors like Karajan, Bernstein, Giulini, producers
like Visconti and Wallmann, baritones of the calibre of Gobbi,
mezzos such as Stignani and Simionato, one of her closest friends,
and the best of the Italian tenors.

One of Callas's major problems at La Scala was Renata Tebaldi
(born 1922). Whatever their private feelings for each other and
whatever the justice in their feud, there is no doubt that as singers
Callas and Tebaldi were chalk and cheese to the public, and that the
fierce admirer of one was likely to be antipathetic to the other. Callas
was in the vanguard of a revolution, while Tebaldi stood tranquilly
for what had now become the 'classical' *verismo* style, her voice as
soft-grained and plangent as Muzio's, with whom she was frequently
compared. Their repertories did not overlap to any great extent and
Tebaldi had no pretensions to coloratura, although it is interesting to
note that early in her career she too sang in revivals of rare Spontini,
Rossini, and Handel operas. Callas never sang Puccini with the
ravishing intimacy and fluidity that Tebaldi could give to such arias
as 'Signore, ascolta' from *Turandot* or 'Senza mamma' from *Suor*

*Angelica*, and Tebaldi had little of Callas's fire and imagination in their mutual Verdi roles. It was mostly a matter of taste, and which singer one heard first; to anyone accustomed to Tebaldi's smoothness and steadiness, Callas would have sounded shockingly self-assertive, and Tebaldi was established at La Scala before Callas 'arrived' in 1950, replacing Tebaldi in *Aida* after she had fallen ill.

Professionally, a *modus vivendi* was reached. Tebaldi recorded for Decca, Callas for EMI–Angel; Tebaldi left La Scala in 1954 and sang at the Met for almost twenty years. Callas sang only a handful of performances at the Met, but stayed on at La Scala and sang regularly at Covent Garden, well out of Tebaldi's way. But as with the Faustina and Cuzzoni incident over two hundred years earlier, the press exploited the whole business *ad nauseam*, casting the two roles in starkest black and white. Tebaldi smiled sweetly ('She has dimples of iron,' remarked Rudolf Bing) and was presented as a homely body who consulted Cardinal Spellman on the advisability of taking the veil after her mother died in 1957; Callas snarled at the cameras and was reported in *Time* as having told her mother to 'jump out of the window' if she could not earn enough to support herself.

Tebaldi herself had other problems apart from Callas. She was always a stiff actress, physically inhibited by a childhood bout of polio. In 1963 she had a fiasco at the Met as Adriana Lecouvreur and retired for a year to retrain her voice, without ever quite recovering its earlier purity. Nothing, however, about her decline was anything but graceful, whereas Callas's failure—if that is the right word—was spectacular and controversial, her every vocal utterance mercilessly scrutinized.

None of the offered explanations for this are completely satisfactory, since great voices are not rational quantities. The weight-loss idea, for example, is absurd: muscular control, not bulk, is the key to healthy vocal production. Some of the causes for the failure are inherent in the fact that Callas had been schooled to push her voice beyond its natural limitations. John Ardoin, who knows Callas's art as well as anyone, writes in his book *The Callas Legacy* that 'There is no doubt that [she] demanded more from her voice than it could comfortably deliver. Yet a parallel conclusion is equally clear: had she put herself in less peril, had she taken fewer chances or remained within safer limits, she would never have been Callas.' He also notes from the recorded evidence that as early as 1950, she could be squally on top notes, heavy in style, uneven, over-forceful, and unable to sustain a *pianissimo*, but that as late as 1964 she could still be 'impressively secure'. Much of her difficulty stemmed from her psychology: what Walter Legge referred to as her 'superhuman inferiority complex' and her obsessive quest for self-improvement which must have started in her sad childhood efforts to win her mother's love. Something of this, as well as the cruel pace at which she was being worked,* is revealed by a letter she wrote from London to a close friend in New York early in 1957:

Dear Leo, It's been such a long time since I heard from you—Don't you love me any more? Some other soprano has taken your interest?

Last time I passed from New York—I didn't have time to see you and couldn't trace you even by telephone.

Everything since Chicago [where she had given a concert a few weeks earlier] has gone perfectly well—it's as though since the allergy I had in New York has cured me of something [*sic*] and I'm singing as I never did. Thank God!

My Norma here the other day [at Covent Garden] would have been the pride of all my admirers first of all you dear Leo! I'm so happy! They all say I've never done a performance like that before—tomorrow is my second and last. After that I'm recording the 'Barber' until the 14th and then on to the Scala for the 'Sonnambula' on the 23rd of February—on the 12th of April we have the 'Anna Bolena', just God [her début in the role], and then 'Iphigenie en Tauride', then Vienna with 'Traviata' on the 4th of July. On the 24th June opening of the Radio season with Lucia broadcast. And then around the first of July, Cologne, Germany, always with the Scala—Then some recordings of Turandot and Manon of Puccini, some rest and then Edinburgo with 'Sonnambula' [the series of performances from which she made one of her most notorious walk-outs]—San Francisco with Macbeth-Lucia [her failure to appear here led to her being sued], Scala opening with 'Moses' of Rossini and then 'Pirata' of Bellini and then finally New York—if I'm still alive by then. So dear Leo, please write all your news; and don't forget your favourite singer so quickly.

* How many of the performances listed here actually materialized may be checked in John Ardoin and Gerald Fitzgerald's authoritative *Callas* (1974).

Write about the 'Traviata' at the Met [which she was scheduled to sing in 1958]—also about the costume . . .

Perhaps the first decisive catrastrophe was the infamous *Norma* performed before the Italian President and other dignitaries in Rome in January 1958, when Callas abandoned the performance after a disastrous first act during which she had been heckled for her efforts to sing over bronchitis and tracheitis. The adverse publicity Callas received over this affair was savage enough to finish her career in Italy, since no opera house could afford the astronomically high insurance premium put on the possibility of her cancellation, quite apart from the bad feeling created. Later that year Bing dismissed her from the Met, after disagreements over repertory. Then in 1959 she left Meneghini, a dull husband who valued her artistic well-being,* for Onassis, an exciting lover whose interest in her singing extended only as far as the glamour and status she had incurred. She was now in a position to fulfil what Zeffirelli described as her 'stupid ambition of becoming a great lady of café society', and by 1960 she was in semi-retirement: a very few stage appearances and occasional recordings or concerts made up her professional life for the next four years. Onassis did nothing to sustain her. 'Hold your tongue, you are nothing but a night-club singer,' he once shouted at her in the hearing of her agent Sandor Gorlinsky. 'I just hoped that she would grab the nearest bottle and strike him over the head,' he recalled. 'But she just got up and left the room. She was completely under his thumb.' Callas did not take criticism, even of the abusive sort, lightly. 'My biggest mistake,' she said, 'was trying to intellectualize my voice . . . the press was writing so frequently that I had lost my voice, I got to the point of believing it myself . . . I got complexes for the first time and lost my audacity.' With the encouragement of the record producer Michel Glotz, she managed a triumphant return to the stage in 1964–5 for *Tosca* at Covent Garden, her tone harder and her control diminished, but her unique authority and intelligence still blazing. Yet she was again unable to sustain the pressure she put

---

* Walter Legge took the view that 'her breach with Meneghini coincided with the decline of her artistic achievements—or caused it. Her life with him had been built on community of interests, mutual respect, spartan domestic economy, rigorous self-discipline and hard work.'

on herself, and the impetus fell away. She wanted Onassis, and she couldn't have him.

In an interview given to *Life* in October 1964, she brightly proclaimed, 'Now at last I am a happy normal woman of my age, even though I have to say that life for me really began at forty.' The truth was that she was about to plummet into a period of barren misery, without marriage to Onassis or a resuscitated career. At the end of the 1960s, she began a protracted search for something to fill the hiatus. Apart from a ceaseless flood of rumours and abortive announcements, there was a film of *Medea*, directed by Pasolini, vastly underrated by the critics but obviously not the beginning of a solution; a misguided attempt to become an opera producer: and negotiations over the possibility of becoming Artistic Director at the Met. From the historian's point of view, the most interesting of all these enterprises was the series of master classes that she gave at the Juilliard School in 1971–2, from which a set of tapes was made. Her manner as a teacher emerges as scrupulous, polite, and patient, and she showed an almost comic concern for the health of her students, but the actual teaching had none of the engagement, energy, and precision that Schwarzkopf, for example, infallibly provides at similar functions. The points Callas made were very largely general interpretative ones, often with reference to Serafin, and assertions of basic principles: 'feel what you're singing', 'lean on the words', '*legato, legato, legato!*' were continual insistences. As she must have realized, the subtleties of her art were not easily communicated: the television interviews she gave to Lord Harewood reveal her as positively banal when she attempts to articulate her art.

Throughout the master classes, she was herself back at rehearsal with a *répétiteur* and John Ardoin is surely justified in thinking that the master classes 'were simultaneously serving a greater and somewhat ulterior purpose—the rebuilding of Callas's confidence before an audience'. Buttressed by the ageing tenor Giuseppe di Stefano, she made her return to public singing in a world concert tour. To those who had heard her in her prime, this proved a terrible disappointment, but to a new generation—of which I was one—it was something. In November 1973, she returned to her 'caro public di London', as she addressed us, and the city which had given her the most steady and sympathetic support. The hope that the disembodied voice which had haunted my discovery of Italian opera on records would be made flesh before me was not realized, but what I heard was more than the rattling of bones. There was still a lot of volume—she had no difficulty in projecting through the difficult acoustics of the Festival Hall; the unmistakable grainy tone of the middle of the voice, more resonant with emotion than anything I have ever heard in music, was still alive; and above all, there was that ability to arch a phrase in such a way that its absolute rightness of expressive shape, as clear and pure as the line of a suspension bridge, was revealed.* It was not, unfortunately, possible to ignore the shaky intonation, colourless *mezza voce*, and painfully raw top notes that ravaged her singing, but there was yet another dimension to Callas which seized one's attention. She involved her whole body in the dramatic import of the music and instinctively acted out its meaning. I felt this most in the duet from *Cavalleria Rusticana* as a desperate Santuzza, fighting back against the boorish Turiddu, clenching her fists on his chest, turning from him with scorn, watching him with hawk-eyed jealousy, emerged from Callas's elegantly coutured façade.

When the tour finished Callas's morale was no higher. 'Anything to survive, my dear. At my stage of the game, anything to survive,' she had told John Ardoin in 1968, and that was still the position in 1974. Everyone tried to help: Zeffirelli, for instance, suggested *L'Incoronazione di Poppea* (and how magnificently Callas would have sung Monteverdi), while Covent Garden offered her a *Cavalleria Rusticana* with Domingo. When this latter plan fell through in 1976, she asked Covent Garden to send her a *répétiteur*, as she wanted to work towards a concert there. Jeffrey Tate was duly sent to her Paris apartment and found her even more nervous than he was. In rehearsal she proved pathetically inhibited, constantly muttering remarks like 'I don't think I can do this . . . Is this possible? . . . I am frightened.' Then she secretly hired the Théâtre des Champs-Elysées to try herself out in a larger arena. A journalist sneaked in to the empty auditorium and went away to write a knocking article about La Divina's exiguous vocal resources. Callas was not only furious, but mortified. A few months after the petering-out of the

---

* As the conductor Nicola Rescigno eloquently put it, 'it is a great mystery how a girl from the Bronx born into an unmusical family and growing up in circumstances without any connection with opera, could have been blessed with the ability to sing the perfect recit[ative].' Also noteworthy is the fact that Greek was her first language, English her second, Italian—the language of her art—only third.

entire scheme, she died at the age of fifty-three in circumstances of some ambiguity. Meneghini for one suspected that she killed herself, and Jeffrey Tate's verdict is even bleaker: 'I think eventually she died of neglect. She just neglected herself as a person. She abandoned her life.'

As a victim of the images and prejudices that hedge a prima donna, Callas recalls none of her predecessors so much as Mrs Tofts, with whom this history began. Callas's life had an even harsher nemesis than that of the demented Mrs Tofts who retreated to her Venetian garden, and none of the popular treatments of the story detract from the waste and pain involved in either her professional collapse or her emotional difficulties. But it is important not to romanticize Callas. She was a martyr rather than a saint, and was fuelled by an overweening morality—'I am Victorian,' she told an interviewer—of 'self-excruciation' (Peter Conrad's word). Every failure was taken hard; she alone was responsible for her shortcomings. All this made her cold, withdrawn, and quintessentially self-centred. One searches her biography in vain for any instances of spontaneous generosity or kindness. Instead one finds the persistent insecurity of the unloved child, the anxiety to find people she could depend upon, and a proud automatic mistrust of anyone not completely dedicated to her. 'We are all vulnerable,' she told *Life* in 1964. 'I am extremely so and have naturally tried not to show it for my own self-preservation. My shyness and insecurity have often made me seem arrogant—it's a form of self-protection for timid people.' Other prima donnas would not have defended themselves thus. A Melba or a Mary Garden were blessed with a canny Scots self-awareness and never lost sight of their own value, but Callas, as Montague Halbrecht put it, 'carried within her a sense of her unworthiness, almost ugliness'.

None of this made Callas lovable. Walter Legge judged her on occasion as 'vengeful, vindictive, and malicious', and when provoked the younger Callas was not afraid of physical violence. Meneghini tells the story of her reaction in 1951 to the administrator of the opera house in Rio when he told her that she had given a 'lousy' performance and was being replaced. 'On his desk was a large bronze inkstand and paper holder. It weighed over twenty pounds. Maria picked it up and, holding it in the air, said, "Repeat what you just said, if you have the nerve, and I'll smash your skull".' When the administrator threatened to have her arrested, she threw herself at him 'striking him in the stomach with her knee. It could have been a fatal blow. Maria at that time weighed more than two hundred pounds, was twenty-eight years old, and had the power of a young bull.' Her victim keeled over, and Meneghini rushed Callas back to their hotel: 'Maria, however, was now very calm. She walked about the room humming, totally pleased with what she had done. "Don't you think you overdid it?" I asked. "I only regret not having broken his head," she said with a smile.'

At the end of her life, an unremitting fatalism set in. She became at best a terrible egomaniac: 'an evening with Maria was an evening talking about Maria,' complains Zeffirelli in his autobiography. 'How good she looked; how nice her hair, her dress; how she really must make a comeback etc., etc., etc. Frankly, it was frequently very boring.' 'Her view of the world was totally depressing,' said Jeffrey Tate. 'I had the terrible feeling that here was a woman who had gone beyond the edge of possibility.' The worst had indeed happened. Life did turn against her and she bore an immense burden of defeat. If one thinks back to the retirement of her great sister-in-art, Pasta, contentedly pottering about with her turkeys wearing an old coat, the cruelty of Callas's lot becomes all the more poignant.

Throughout her singing, as throughout her life, the tone of tragedy sounds deeper and truer than any other. To wistful lyricism (her *Sonnambula* is too earnest) or tearful melancholy (for which we listen to Muzio), let alone comedy, she was less well suited. To misquote Dorothy Parker, she ran the whole gamut of the emotions from A to about S: inevitably, there were moods and shades that eluded her.* J. B. Steane, yet again, best expresses in what lay Callas's extraordinary stamp: 'She will seize the moment, say, of noble or tragic decision, summoning all the dramatic force of what has gone before, evoking our knowledge of what the consequences are to be, and focusing precisely upon the moment on which all depends.' Anger, grief, contempt, passion, madness, despair, and isolation were her points of emotional reference.

Next one must emphasize the musicality which she developed

---

* A letter I received from a Swiss correspondent who witnessed her through her prime, contains the following interesting judgement: 'She was not the great Leonora, or Amelia, or Elisabetta . . . She did much better in early Verdi—up to *Trovatore* and *Traviata*—but even there, in spite of her outstanding merits as an interpreter, something was missing: the easy flowing soaring line of Ponselle's voice or the marvellously expressive sound produced by Muzio.'

under Serafin's tutelage and which remained even when a rich, firm tone had deserted her. She always found the proportion, scale, and depth of phrase required for any musical episode, be it recitative, arioso, or pure melody, and her sense of a climax was infallible. The way she sustains and colours the span of Norma's 'Casta Diva' *scena* is an egregious instance of this. The same gift for timing clearly applied to her acting as well. Connoisseurs will tell you that the film made of Act II of *Tosca* shows but the shadow of its impact—yet how much remains! This Tosca is not just an outraged prima donna, but a tough and direct woman trapped in a situation that makes her panic. There is no strutting or false dignity, rather a last-ditch effort to keep control. She gulps down the wine for quick Dutch courage, and then stands mesmerized by the sight of the knife, putting the glass down slowly as the thought of murder passes inexorably into her mind. Only at the last second does the animal release itself, the tension held in her hand clasped over the top of the glass. At the end of the scene she weeps with nervous exhaustion as she lurches round the chamber, grabbing at her stole, repelled at touching a dead body, unable to believe what she has just done, desperate not to leave incriminating evidence. The complexity of movement and the telling use of details and props, all matched to the musical cues, proves how extensive the thought behind this explosion was, how carefully Callas and her collaborators Gobbi and Zeffirelli had worked out the pace and shape it should follow. Yet Zeffirelli emphasizes her naïvete in rehearsal. She needed 'a simplified notion' to cling to: 'curiously she was always childish when asking about a role: she would talk in a babyish way—"Am I good or bad here?" "Why do I say that?" . . . then suddenly she would see it, would grasp the point and would begin to discuss it with intense sophistication . . . What Maria required of her directors was a vast input of ideas.'

Ironically, this naïve genius has ended up a profound influence on a whole generation of dramatic sopranos who have sought to imitate that very feeling for pace and shape, that intensity and command of the stage which the *Tosca* film allows us to glimpse. Just as Pasta was followed by the aptly-named Teresa Parodi,* so Callas has been

---

* Of whom Chorley wrote: She 'presented a singular imitation of Madame Pasta's voice out of tune . . . all the more singular because she was obviously no mocking-bird, bent to mimic the song of somebody else, but a sincere and careful artist'.

followed by Souliotis, Bumbry, Sass, Aliberti, Baltsa and a host of others, all at times exciting prima donnas, but all in varying degrees liable to lapse into what have become the 'Callas clichés' of scornful glances, rasping chest-notes, etc. Others have built on her example more creatively and at this point it is important to repeat that Callas is not, as it were, the first and last note in the '*bel canto* revival'. In the period preceding her emergence, Ponselle and Supervia, to name but two, had sung what by any standards were superlative accounts of parts of the early nineteenth-century Italian repertory; and in the 1960s the remarkable work of Callas, Serafin, and her colleagues in revaluing the operas of Donizetti and Bellini in particular would be carried even further by singers whose techniques were in some respects superior to Callas's.

The name which comes most immediately to mind in this respect is that of the Australian Joan Sutherland (born 1926). Her ample and inexhaustibly brilliant top voice recalls that of Tetrazzini, although Sutherland had the fuller middle range and sounder musicianship. Comparisons apart, Sutherland made her own distinctive mark on operatic history, and whatever her shortcomings as an interpreter, she had a long and distinguished career, steadily 'at the top' for thirty years, as long a reign as that of Patti or her compatriot Melba.

The history of Sutherland's voice and its development is an interesting and exemplary one, illustrating the importance of physiological good fortune and the effect of a powerful teacher. Sutherland was blessed with a broad face, strong jaw, powerful vocal cords, and strapping physique—all of which gave her the muscular foundation for resonance, flexibility, breath control and sheer endurance. From childhood, she also suffered from a variety of potentially crippling ailments: sinus trouble, bad teeth, abscessed ears, back pain, and poor circulation have all been enemies against which she fought long tactical battles in the war to perfect her technique.

Sutherland's apprenticeship began with her mother, from whom she learnt by imitation. Muriel Sutherland had studied with a Marchesi pupil, and by all accounts had a superb mezzo-soprano voice 'as powerful as Stignani's', which she never used professionally, choosing instead the roles of wife and mother (how many great voices must have been hidden thus!). Joan grew up in Sydney as a mezzo and shorthand typist, chronically self-conscious about her height and ungainly deportment but aware that she had a gift. Others were aware of it too, and a doctor had wisely refused to remove her troublesome tonsils in case her vocal cords were damaged in the process. At the age of nineteen she won two years' free singing lessons with teachers who pushed her voice into its soprano range, leading Sutherland to decide that she would become a Wagnerian singer along the lines of Kirsten Flagstad. She duly cultivated a bright, steely edge to the voice and won enough competitions on the strength of it to finance the trip to London, as inevitable for an Australian singer as Paris had been for an American fifty years earlier.

Before her departure in 1951, she had been giving song recitals around the New South Wales music clubs, accompanied by Richard Bonynge, a teenage piano prodigy who was also about to set off for London and who was to become the decisive influence over her life and singing. Like Legge with Schwarzkopf or Serafin with Callas, Bonynge had a great master-plan for her voice which he was gradually and tenaciously to put into practice. His childhood love of Chopin had brought him to Bellini, and from there he had developed an antiquarian's passion for the obscurer reaches of that period of Italian opera. He also became fascinated by the possibility of reviving contemporary styles, especially the custom of ornamentation, which Callas and Serafin had only very chastely adopted.

In London, Sutherland studied with Clive Carey, a pupil of Jean de Reszke who 'fattened up', as she graphically puts it, the top of her voice. Bonynge came along to the lessons, accompanying her, making suggestions, and throwing out criticism; at home, he worked on the flexibility of her voice, putting her through endless scales, runs, and trills, and by cheating her into starting her exercises at a higher pitch than she believed she was singing at, further developed the all-important top notes. He also married her.

When she first joined the Covent Garden resident company in 1952, everyone except Bonynge thought of her as a potential *spinto* soprano – an Aida or a Tosca, perhaps even a Wagnerian. Over the next few years she had a fair degree of success in the mainline repertory, but it soon became clear from her execution of the coloratura passages written for Gilda in *Rigoletto* or Jenifer in Tippett's *The Midsummer Marriage* that another and rarer sort of voice was secretly coming to maturity. In 1957 she showed the full extent of her accomplishment in concert performances of forgotten Handel, Scarlatti, and Donizetti operas, and the Covent Garden management decided to mount a new production of *Lucia di Lammermoor* for her in 1959, to be produced by the young Zeffirelli and conducted by the great Serafin himself. Callas came to the dress rehearsal and sat next to Schwarzkopf, whispering conspiratorially. 'That is not good,' she was heard to say of Sutherland's singing. 'It is *too* good.' She herself was about to bow out of the operatic arena for a life in Onassis's *haut monde*; her voice, although still passionately admired, was increasingly criticized for curdled top notes and thin tone. And here was a hefty and amiable Australian girl whose voice was in the pink of health, singing a role on which Callas had lavished all her unique tragic fervour, in a style which, in important ways, flew against everything Callas had restored to Donizetti's music. Sutherland and Bonynge appreciated Callas but they also appreciated Galli-Curci, and it was the latter model they followed in moulding a sweet, open, and girlish quality into the voice. Callas would also have heard naïvely perfect coloratura, replete with ornaments and used essentially as a vehicle of virtuosity rather than of emotion and meaning. Later Callas pointed the finger at Bonynge, accusing him of 'setting my work back a hundred years'.

It would have been futile for Sutherland to have emulated Callas. She had the sense to realize that she simply *was* a different sort of coloratura singer, and that she must present herself on her own terms. The public certainly accepted them ecstatically enough, and from her first Covent Garden Lucia, Sutherland sustained a supreme position in the wake of Callas's withdrawal. Strangely, Serafin thought that she ought to go on to sing the declamatory and mostly low-lying role of Verdi's Lady Macbeth, but apart from a glorious Donna Anna in a Giulini recording of *Don Giovanni* later in 1959, she preferred a softer-edged and more lyrical repertory.

From 1962 Bonynge began to conduct at his wife's performances, and the knives were drawn. The Sutherland-Bonynge 'circus' or 'package deal' was found to be a deplorable instance of prima donna's privilege, doubly so as Bonynge's conducting was considered noisy and amateurish (it has continued unpopular in some quarters, but singers invariably find him extraordinarily considerate of their needs). Sutherland herself came in for her share of criticism, as the bright, crisp, and open sound of her early recordings gave way to a drifting, mooning way with anything that was not perforce fast and glittering. Among the ranks of the *bien pensant*, she could soon do nothing right. 'Spot the consonant,' became a favourite opera buff's game every time a new Sutherland record came out, for her diction had been reduced to a series of vowels connected by the broadest and most generalized of *portamenti*. Victor Gollancz stormed out of a Sutherland evening at Covent Garden muttering the much-quoted remark, 'God, she's as dull as Melba,' while her Norma was compared to Callas's and found wanting in energy and temperament.

Sutherland had an immense support system, however, in the form of her husband (who by the mid 1960s was conducting virtually all her performances), a long-term recording contract, excellent management, and a band of regular colleagues. Her returns to Australia, first in Melba-style touring companies, later as prima donna of the new Australian Opera, were triumphant; in Italy the gallery dubbed her 'La Stupenda', a label which delighted the press; and in the US rumours that her fees were at least as high as any other singer's was in itself a potent recommendation. What is more important, Sutherland proved herself a real trouper, reliable, hard-working, and always ready to deliver the coloratura goods that her audiences were paying for. She is widely thought of as a sunny and extrovert Aussie, Antipodean to Callas in every way, but she kept a streak of the gawky outsized schoolgirl who didn't know quite where to put herself. 'Sometimes I wonder whether I can possibly be the person all the fuss is about,' she told the journalist Peter Conrad, but this self-deprecation never stopped her playing her part convincingly. Occasionally her habitual good temper has snapped, but as in the incident in Genoa when an understudy was mercilessly booed and she walked out on the performance, the generosity of feeling has been all on her side.

In the 1970s her reputation among the critics began to swing up again, partly because of a marked improvement in her diction and partly because, although younger sopranos of her range might be more expressive and imaginative musicians, she remained indisputably the supreme technician. There were some surprises too, such as a fabulous recording of *Turandot*, in which the *spinto* metal in her voice came to the fore again, and some Bonygne-inspired discoveries from nooks and crannies of the operatic archives. One may not want to hear Massenet's *Esclarmonde* or Bononcini's *Griselda* more than once, but without Sutherland and Bonynge one might never have heard them at all.

Sutherland could at times be a fussily correct singer, lacking in daring and vision; but, given the right music, she could also be a tremendously beautiful one and beside her almost every other coloratura comes to sound tinny, feathery or skidding. Few would, I think, claim that she could match the command of phrase, word, and inflection shown by Callas in Donizetti and Bellini or Janet Baker in Handel and Mozart. Yet, like Melba, her singing can still mesmerize, and for sheer brilliance it has only been rivalled by the mezzo-soprano who miraculously complemented her, Marilyn Horne.

Born in 1934, Horne represents some sort of ultimate triumph of technique, and the unique completeness of her vocal equipment opened up further paths for 'the *bel canto* revival'. After a bewildering start to her career, dubbing the voice of Dorothy Dandridge for the film of *Carmen Jones*, working with Stravinsky and Robert Craft, and a three years' stint as a lyric soprano in the German provinces, Horne encountered Sutherland at the latter's New York début in 1961. Their subsequent partnership has passed into history. Throughout the 1960s they sang together regularly, in *Norma* and *Semiramide* in particular, and became close friends, whiling away the dead hours of rehearsals, intervals, and recording sessions in elaborate needle-point projects. With the help of Bonynge and her own husband, the conductor Henry Lewis, Horne brought back much of the music in which 'Rossini' mezzos such as Pisaroni and Alboni had excelled, decorating it in authentic style and singing with a confidence and precision that no one could remember equalled. In the early 1970s she changed direction somewhat, breaking away from her image as 'Sutherland's mezzo' and embarking on a more mainstream repertory. She had success as Carmen, but was generally considered miscast in Verdi; plans to appear as the *Götterdämmerung* Brünnhilde never materialized. In her late forties, she turned decisively back to the Rossini and Baroque music for which she has ever since been most celebrated.

Horne has frequently and quite seriously been called 'the world's greatest voice' or 'the greatest singer in the world'; she has even been compared to the most legendary of the castrati. At certain levels, her claims cannot be easily dismissed. Her technique *is* staggering: listening to her one might well think—this is the human limit of such things. The power of the chest register, the fluency of the runs, the control of dynamics, are all immaculate. Talking to Jerome Hines, she revealed her belief that singing was 'ninety per cent' the economical emission of breath and 'ninety-five per cent brains'. She advocated 'military-type posture' and for coloratura a tightening of the buttock muscles, remarking that she frequently finished a performance with stiff legs.

More revealing to the uninitiated public is Robert Jacobson's feeling that in personality Horne resembled 'the High School overachiever who always has her hand up first'. 'Overachievement' is a particularly apposite word, for Horne's singing sometimes recalls the proverbial hammer brought in to crack a nut. In everything she sings there is an assertive dignity and intelligence, but a lot of Rossini, for example, also demands a lightness and individuality of touch that she largely lacks. One wishes in something like *L'Italiana in Algeri* that she would expend less energy on singing with the determination of an imperturbable steamroller, and more on the delicacy, wit, and playful *rubato* which make Supervia so enchanting.

With Horne, the '*bel canto* revival' reached its peak and inevitably lost some of its impetus. There was not so much vitally important work to be done—the better of the operas were recorded and to some extent re-established and the prima donnas had shown spectacularly how they ought to be sung. In the last twenty-five years, there has been a rise in the *general* standard of coloratura singing unimaginable forty years ago and sopranos currently in control of the repertory like Edita Gruberova and June Anderson no longer hit the headlines in quite the same way as their predecessors did.

One other American singer calls for mention, not only on the grounds of her own merits but also because she represents the full circle of the revolution. Unlike the big-voiced Callas and Sutherland, Sills had the small, soubrettish voice, all pip and ping, of pre-war coloratura sopranos like Toti dal Monte, Miliza Korjus and Lily Pons. By dint of good old American determination she pushed into dramatic soprano territory.

Sills, born Belle Silverman in Brooklyn in 1929, suffered—or enjoyed—the full indignity of being a child star, making her début at the age of three on a radio commercial. Her mother, not surprisingly, was a Galli-Curci fan, the proud owner of eleven of her records, which like Uncle Matthew she played compulsively. 'She would play them even before she made coffee in the morning, and they would echo throughout the house all day long,' Sills remembered. 'Before I was seven I had memorized all twenty-two arias on the recordings and could sing them in phonetic Italian.' With this training, Sills became a regular feature on a number of radio shows of the 1930s, including *Uncle Bob's Rainbow House, Our Girl Sunday*, and *Major Bowes' Amateur Hour* (on which Callas in her girlhood had also appeared, probably under the name of Nina Foresti).

What saved Sills from an ordinary fate was being sent for lessons to Galli-Curci's erstwhile coach, Estelle Liebling, last of Marchesi's pupils, with whom she was to remain for thirty-four years. In Liebling's studio she encountered many of the great operatic names of the time, not least that of Maria Jeritza, who patronized her extravagantly. More significantly, Liebling managed to curb the Sills precocity with a regime of scales and arpeggios without crushing her ebullience. 'Singing was always so easy for me, so natural,' she later told an interviewer. 'Iron lungs, that's me, and I was never really taught to sing, just helped by discipline.' By the age of twenty, she claims to have known fifteen roles by heart, some of them, like Salome, learnt for love alone. After a gruelling initiation in touring opera—she once sang sixty-three consecutive Micaelas in *Carmen*—and a spell with Ponselle's company in Baltimore, she joined the New York City Opera in 1955. For the next ten years she was the useful house soprano, and it was not until 1966 that she won wider recognition, when City Opera eclipsed the new Met's opening production of Samuel Barber's *Antony and Cleopatra* with a revival, appropriately enough, of Handel's *Giulio Cesare*, in which she sang a sensational Cleopatra.

She stayed loyal to City Opera, but moved on to even more ambitious undertakings, notably the queens in Donizetti's 'Tudor' operas, *Roberto Devereux*, *Anna Bolena*, and *Maria Stuarda*, to the demands of which her light, bright timbre was patently unsuited. But Sills gave them her all, and more—'*Devereux* shortened my career by three or four years,' she admitted—making a compelling impression by virtue of her vivid acting and eloquent musicianship. In vocally less taxing roles such as Lucia or Massenet's Manon she was even more satisfying.

Sills sang relatively little outside North America, mainly due to the needs of her two children, one deaf, the other mentally retarded, but the most difficult engagement to clinch was one only a hundred yards from home, at the Met. Rudolf Bing was well known for his dislike of purely American-grown singers, and was infuriated that the possibility of scheduling the 'Tudor' trilogy with Montserrat Caballé had been taken from him. He made Sills a couple of paltry offers, and created a little running scandal. Sills herself was not over-concerned: 'In an odd way, Mr Bing made my career by keeping me out of the Met for so long. Nothing infuriates the American public quite as much as the notion of a haughty, foreign-born aristocrat being mean to one of its native-born girls.' Unfortunately, when in 1975 she finally 'crossed the Plaza', the dwindling of her voice was sadly exposed by the size of the house. She wisely retired from the stage in 1979, and became directa of City Opera, with distinctly mixed results.

Not since the days of Geraldine Farrar had a 'serious' prima donna projected so brilliantly as a personality. Farrar was from shopkeeping New England stock, whereas Sills was wisecracking Brooklyn Jewish, but they were both all-American girls with the right touch for the times. Sills's capacity to sustain exposure on the television and in the popular press made her the very first 'superstar'—otherwise the American translation of *diva*. She had infectious energy and enthusiasm, a broad and ready smile, a private tragedy in her children, and even a nauseating nickname, Bubbles. She performed consummately on innumerable chat shows including her own, and brought opera to millions, theoretically at least, by prancing about with puppets, muppets, and Carol Burnett. She was never high-falutin' about her considerable art and she never pulled the prima donna wool over her public's eyes. She was, as she put it, 'a communicator', and a natural theatre-bird. 'I found singing such a joyous experience that I couldn't wait to get on the stage . . . I was always the first person in the theater all the time. If it was an eight o'clock curtain, I was here at five-thirty, and it wasn't that I needed to vocalize, because I was all warmed up. I couldn't wait for it to begin.'

The traditions of Italian singing have not been altogether wrested from native Italians. Among its more impressive representatives has been Renata Scotto (born 1933), a cherub-cheeked soprano who first came to notice when she replaced Callas in *La Sonnambula*, after her default from the Edinburgh Festival in 1957. As a teenager she had communicated at a *séance* with the spirit of Malibran who had urged her to carry on her good work. Scotto certainly went on to show something of her predecessor's tremendous dedication, and of all the Italian singers of the post-Callas era she is possibly the most intelligent and original. Her repertory has been enormous, embracing virtually all the most challenging roles in the nineteenth-century and *verismo* repertories. Some dramatic coloratura roles like Norma have plainly over-taxed her, but she was a worthy heir to Muzio and Tebaldi in Puccini, with a genuine *morbidezza* in her voice as well as a stern and adult emotional temper that has made her Violetta, Desdemona, and Manon Lescaut unusually moving. Her most famous part was Madama Butterfly, from whom, in her own phrase, she sheared the *bambolaggiamento*, the Japanese-doll kitsch which many lesser singers fall back on as a means to pathos.

Scotto has had a long and sometimes controversial contract with the Met: perhaps that house has been too large for a voice that is inclined to force itself, and a stage manner liable to over-emphatic projection. Her contemporary Mirella Freni (born 1935) has been more cautious and moved her range slowly up from delightful interpretations of Susanna in *Figaro* and Marguerite in *Faust* to selected Verdi and Puccini, settling in her fifties on Tchaikovsky and *verismo*. One critic awkwardly but accurately characterized her as 'a Sauvignon singing roles which should be red Burgundy', but having been scalded by a catastrophically premature first bash at *Traviata* in 1964, on Callas's sacred patch of La Scala, she henceforth behaved with a caution and a calculation which earned her the soubriquet of La Prudentissima. On the strength of a head which wasn't easily turned and an immaculate musicality she sustained a top-flight, top-fee, top-billing career of consistent excellence. Luciano Pavarotti was her childhood friend in Modena; they sang together on occasion, providing an object lesson in lucidity of diction and sureness of intonation to a younger, sloppier generation too often eaten up (and eaten away) by the vain desire to cut a Callas-like dash at the expense of the composer's more precisely notated intentions.

# The Prima Donna
# Today

Opera buffs are not happy people, and at least nine-tenths of what they see and hear in the opera house fills them with amused contempt. Dare to praise any young singer in a particular role, the response will be either the unanswerable, 'Thirty years ago she would not have been tolerated,' or 'Have I never played you my 1922 recording of X singing it, you sad, sad person?' A lot of such gambits are part of a conspiracy to intimidate candid outsiders, but they are also the result of a millennial tendency to feel that civilization is generally in decline: we feel nostalgia for what we have never experienced and assume that good can only give way to worse. I do not mean to imply that singing is now as good or even better than it has been, or that Mme X of 1922 might not be enthralling—only that people have been talking about the collapse of standards in operatic singing since the beginning of the eighteenth century without acknowledging a constant process of *change*. Thus the pedagogue Tosi in 1723 lamented that only Faustina and Cuzzoni 'keep up the tottering profession from immediately falling into ruin'; in 1834 Mount Edgcumbe was unmoved by Pasta and Malibran and admitted, 'I never expect to hear again what I have done, or any new music, or new singers, that will make me amends for those which are gone'; in 1906 Henderson, worried by Wagnerism, reported that 'It is plain to every careful observer that the race of beautiful singers is diminishing with every year, and that in its place there is growing up a generation of harsh, unrefined, tuneless shouters'; while in 1982 Lanfranco Rasponi produced a book called *The Last Prima Donnas*, in which he interviewed the last 'members of an extinct race'. All along, local standards of taste and style are assumed to be historical absolutes, and the great living body of laws, traditions, and controversies connected with good singing is reduced to the pedantry of Beckmesser's slate.

In the post-war period a new set of complaints has accumulated without any real acknowledgement of loss and gain, of a complexity of factors. If singers 'over-part' themselves and find it hard to cope with large opera house orchestras, do we therefore have to return to Verdi and Wagner played with reduced scoring? Do we tolerate the random cuts and transpositions which composers of the nineteenth century fought so hard to eliminate? If aeroplane travel is so bad for singers, was lurching across the Atlantic in a steamer any more comfortable? And how did Catalani, Pasta, or Malibran feel after a month-long coach tour of one-night engagements, driving along bumpy and dangerous roads in wind and rain? If some singers are now 'over-exposed', does anyone remember that many nineteenth-century prima donnas regularly performed four or five times a week? If producers today often make unreasonable demands and impose trivial concepts, do we therefore reject altogether the fertilization that a theatrical mind like Peter Stein can bring to the musical egg, and listen instead to 'concerts in costume?' Is the producer's or conductor's prerogative any more or less desirable than that of the prima donna? None of these questions have simple answers.

Over the last ten years or so, the prima donna has come to seem a less problematic figure than she once was: we are accustomed now to dominant vocal females at all levels of society, from that of Head of State downwards; a prima donna is less egregious in the ranks of her sex than she was even thirty years ago. Two tenors, Luciano Pavarotti and Placido Domingo, occupy the focus of public attention once held by Callas and Tebaldi: in terms of fame and record sales they far outscore their highest-ranking sisters Mirella Freni, Jessye Norman and Kiri Te Kanawa. Only rarely does a prima donna hit the headlines, with the force that Malibran or Patti, Garden or Jeritza did. Perhaps this is not such a terrible loss; we can concentrate on the quality of singing instead. But just occasionally, a flare-up of old conflicts suggests that for women who sing opera the agenda is still a tricky one.

As when a black coloratura lyric soprano called Kathleen Battle (born 1948) was fired from the Met in February 1994. Her story is a sad one. Unlike Leontyne Price and Jessye Norman, both of middle-class origin, Battle came from a poor family—her father was a steel-worker in Ohio—and she had to fight her way through several social and financial hoops and barriers in order to make it as far as music school, let alone a career. Someone remembered as a smiling hometown girl then seems to have hardened her heart. She made her Met debut in 1977, the protégée of the house's omnipotent artistic director James Levine, and within a few years she had become one of its biggest stars; unfortunately, she had become one of its most cantankerous too. She peremptorily took over fellow-soprano Carol Vaness's dressing-room because it was situated marginally closer to the stage than hers; she began issuing instructions to other singers in rehearsal; she was disgustingly rude to chorus, stage-crew and dressers ('I survived the Battle' read a t-shirt which appeared backstage in San Francisco after she had passed through) and she developed a strange paranoia about people looking at her—specifically, people who 'stared at her mouth'. One who inadvertently did so was the mezzo-soprano Rosalind Elias, who became the object of Battle's furious hostility during rehearsals for a comic scene in Donizetti's *La Fille du Régiment*. The Met decided at that point to fire her—she had been warned repeatedly, and for all her promises of good behaviour had proved a recidivist. Since then, Battle—a radiant Sophie and Zerbinetta, a bright and lovely star—has not appeared in any opera house. It would be interesting to hear her side of the story, but with legal action pending, she has to date (July 1995) said nothing.

The episode constitutes yet another round of hostilities in the old war of singer and impresario, and it illustrates one of several ways in which the world of opera remains as tough as it ever was for the prima donna. Bully or be bullied; assert yourself or be crushed. 'I wish the house would al joyne to humble her and not receav her again,' said Lady Wentworth of Mrs Tofts in 1708; very much the same was said to Battle when she 'huft' in 1994.

From other angles, the prima donna's profile continues to alter perceptibly. She is, for one thing, richer than ever she was, not so much through the fees she commands in opera houses (which are relatively less than they were in 1830 or 1910) so much as through sound and video recording royalties. She is also able to rely on various artificial aids to clarity of projection unavailable to previous generations. In the opera house, sound today is often electrically 'lifted' in acoustically flat areas, while the advent of surtitles means that impeccable lucidity of diction has fallen to a somewhat lower priority in the catalogue of singers' virtues. Recording equipment becomes ever more flattering and its digital alchemy can redress unsympathetic balance between voice and orchestra with computer-ized ease and finesse. Antibiotics are swiftly effective against ear, nose and throat infections; laser technology allows nodes to be nicked off damaged vocal cords in seconds.

Yet in this air-conditioned, freeze-dried ecology, singers are still withering and perishing. We cannot produce the voices we need to fire the big guns for Verdi and Wagner, and the crop of talent in the lowest ranges is desperately short too—a phenomenon often blamed on the marked rise in standard orchestral pitch since the beginning of the century. The plummy sound of a contralto or a true bass has become ludicrous with unfamiliarity, and we now like the lower voices to have an upward gravitational pull, a slim and athletic character which eschews the once-prized 'flab' of *vibrato*. We have nurtured wonderful young bass-baritones and two generations of versatile mezzo-sopranos, from the older, grainier, fruitier Agnes Baltsa, Brigitte Fassbaender and Tatiana Troyanos to the younger almost-sopranos Ann Murray, Anne-Sofie von Otter and Susan Graham. We have been rich in silvery Mozart and Strauss specialists—Lucia Popp, Anna Tomowa-Sintow, Margaret Price, Cheryl Studer, Felicity Lott—and gentler lyric voices like those of Ileana Cotrubas and Frederica von Stade. The Americans churn out brightly confident sopranos (Carol Vaness, June Anderson, Dawn Upshaw); the Russians seem to come one size bigger, with grand old-school stand-and-deliverers (Galina Gorchakova, Nina Rautio, Olga Borodina); the British one size smaller, with new-school elegant performers (Marie McLaughlin, Joan Rodgers, Alison Hagley). But the generally perceived problem is one articulated in an interview by the Viennese soprano Leonie Rysanek. 'There are wonderful voices today,' she sighed, 'and they seem to be able to sing anything . . . What we miss are great personalities. I want someone who grabs at me the moment they step on stage.'

Rysanek has a point. Although we boast an embarrassment of fine 'singing actresses' of striking intelligence—one thinks of Julia Varady, Joan Carden, Maria Ewing, Catherine Malfitano, Josephine Barstow, Sheri Greenwald, Waltrud Meier, Sally Burgess—there is almost nobody who leaps out with an electrifyingly distinctive stage persona; the prima donna today is too disciplined, too attentive to conductor and producer for that sort of individuality to emerge.

Perhaps one might make an exception for Anja Silja; or for Teresa

Stratas (b. 1938), the Greek-Canadian soprano whose almost ridiculous spiritual fervour recalls the lofty Fremstad. Her neurasthenic temperament has made her notorious for her last-second cancellations and her voice in latter years has been worn to a ravelling. But how startling and dangerous she was on stage (and on film, as Salome and Violetta in Zeffirelli's otherwise kitsch version of *La Traviata*), how she flung herself into the abyss and survived!

Her art drew heavily on her tubercular childhood in a Toronto slum (she used to heave a floursack into her dressing-room to remind herself of what she was brought up sleeping on) and she remained deeply fixated on death and the dying, nursing both her father and her patron Rudolf Bing through the ghastly final stages of Alzheimer's Disease, as well as taking time out to work with Mother Teresa in Calcutta and in a Romanian orphanage.

She had many lovers, including the condutor Zubin Mehta and the poet Tony Harrison (who wrote lyrically of their relationship), but continued to live alone near the Met, in a vast and spooky apartment described by visitors as a mixture of Baroque library and nun's cell. There she brooded and dreamed. 'My voice is an extension of my soul. I have many voices inside my body,' she whispered. It sounds pretentious, but those who witnessed her Lulu, her Nedda in *Pagliacci*, her Marenka in *The Bartered Bride*, or her many assumptions of tortured Puccini heroines, could hardly doubt the truth of it.

Commanding more steady respect in the mainstream of the best traditions of the modern operatic scene are singers like Elisabeth Söderström and Dame Janet Baker. Not for them the shenanigans of stardom: they were servants of music and essentially prima donnas who sought to collaborate and co-operate in the extraordinarily complex process of mounting coherent 'music theatre'.

Elisabeth Söderström, a Swede born in 1927, is a soprano who miraculously avoided vocal compromises while still communicating the extremes of emotion demanded by the twentieth-century 'expressionist' operas. Her consistency and dedication throughout a very long career (she made her début in 1947, and retired only in 1992) was matched to a constant desire to challenge herself. Few prima donnas since the war have been so flexible, so responsive, so ready to work in ensembles and smaller companies taking long rehearsal periods—hence her long association with Glyndebourne.

Söderström's repertory was unique, although she was a very

careful singer who never 'over-parted' herself and who made a point of appearing regularly in smaller opera houses in which nuance can be more lucidly projected. She sang Monteverdi, Mozart, and a lot of Russian music, as well as Berg, Henze, and Britten; Boulez conducted her in a memorable series of performances at Covent Garden as Debussy's Mélisande and in Stockholm she created an erotic role in Ligeti's gloriously wicked *Le Grand Macabre*. One of her closest associations was with the Strauss *grande dame* roles, in which she won the blessing of no less than Schwarzkopf, who rehearsed her as the Marschallin and forthrightly expressed her admiration. Söderström did not have Schwarzkopf's mystique or aristocratic reserve: instead, everything she did had an evident sincerity and warmth. As Peter Hall noted while rehearsing her in *Fidelio* this could teeter on 'a radiant sentimentality' which Strauss gives the prima donna plenty of opportunity to indulge. The operas of Janáček have a harsher emotional cut, and here, on stage and records, Söderström achieved very moving results. No opera composer has shown a more overwhelming sense of the pain in ordinary human life, and for the prima donna Janáček offers release from the stereotype of the pure-hearted maiden who lives only to sacrifice herself for love and a violent contrast to the sophisticated dilemmas of the Strauss heroines, cushioned by lush orchestration and substantial incomes. Janáček's women have the stature of the heroines of nineteenth-century fiction—the betrayal of Jenufa, the frustration and vulnerability of Katya Kabanová, the desperate *ennui* of Elena Makropoulos, are the stuff of George Eliot and Tolstoy laid out naked in music. Underneath and beyond these distorted and deformed lives runs Janáček's tremendous affirmatory vision of the splendour of nature, of pity, hope, and continuity. Söderström's singing rose to this suppressed joy as well as the scalding anguish, without any evasion of the score's requirements. Janáček is tough on the vocal cords and the pace and concision of his music allow no respite. Many sopranos resort to *verismo* mannerisms—sobbing, shouting, *parlando*—to pile on the agonies and avoid the stress, but Söderström's musical honesty reaped rich rewards.

Honesty has been a corner-stone of the English mezzo-soprano Dame Janet Baker, although honesty alone cannot account for the full earnestness of her dedication to her art. At the beginning of her career, she remembers calling 'silently on the name of Jesus to help me. I was in this situation only because I honestly believed he had given me work to do as a singer.' Few prima donnas in this book can match Baker's religious depth of belief in herself as the bearer of a sacred flame, and anyone who doubted her commitment was given short shrift. A music critic of *The Times* once suggested casually that at a certain performance Dame Janet had perhaps not given her all: shortly afterwards a stinging retort appeared on the newspaper's letters page. 'He has absolutely no right to suggest that I in some way shortchanged the public by singing "as if marking her part, rehearsal-fashion". All my working life I have given my heart and soul to my audiences: last Thursday was no exception. To suggest I deliberately gave less than the best is to question my integrity . . . my intention to serve the public to the utmost cannot be questioned.' This diamond-hard conviction about herself brooked no obstacle. 'I approached my job as a matter of life-and-death,' she once told me. 'I couldn't take it lightly.'

She was born in Yorkshire in 1933 into a family in which music was not particularly important. But the flame ignited early: taken as a child to hear the D'Oyly Carte in Gilbert and Sullivan, she recalled that she 'thought it was all very well, but it wasn't really music'. In her teens she benefited from the North Country traditions of choral singing; when she was twenty she came to London, working as a bank clerk while taking singing lessons. Most of her early operatic appearances were in Baroque pieces, and it could be said that, working with conductor-scholars like Charles Mackerras and Raymond Leppard, she realized their dramatic potential much as Callas and Serafin did Donizetti's and Bellini's. Gluck's *Orfeo*, Purcell's *Dido*, and the operas of Handel have been central to Baker's art throughout her career, and to all of them she brought a revolutionary energy and depth of expression which made the previous generation of interpreters sound both stolid and light-weight. A steady loss of inhibition and what Lord Harewood described as her 'rather English want not to wear your heart on your sleeve' led her to the performance which more than any other brought her sensational fame, that of Dido in Berlioz's *Les Troyens*, which she first sang in 1969 with Scottish Opera. She became a superb tragic actress, commanding a perfectly judged economy of movement and gesture and an extraordinary capacity to project pride, anger, and isolation. In all this, as in the splendour of her declamation and recitative, her ability to colour words and tone, it is Callas to whom one compares her.

In 1970 at Glyndebourne she sang Diana in an unforgettable revival of the seventeenth-century Venetian composer Cavalli's *La Calisto* (in which she incidentally brought off a brilliantly witty impersonation of Jove-dressed-up-as-Diana) and two years later Penelope in Monteverdi's *Il Ritorno d'Ulisse*. This latter interpretation will be remembered for its stillness and rapt introspection when Penelope cried 'Non voglio amar' or 'Torna, deh, torna, Ulisse', the grief spilled out in the voice, but the body held back—just as in the final duet, where Penelope is reunited with her husband, it took her an eternity before she dared touch Ulisse and believe in his physical presence, so long denied her. Outside Glyndebourne, she gave Covent Garden a Vitellia in Mozart's *La Clemenza di Tito* where the stress of an almost soprano tessitura became integral to the expression of the character's full vicious self-centredness; and a chilling portrait of the small-minded and suburban Kate in Britten's *Owen Wingrave*, in which she credibly allowed a chink of vulnerability to show through the girl's monstrous complacence.

One more assumption should be singled out, that of Donizetti's Mary Stuart (as the English National Opera had it), which gave full rein to her impeccable technique and intensity of temperament, as well as transfiguring what can seem third-rate music. The mounting fury of her encounter with Elizabeth, and the last burst of fanatical self-justification, her body shaking with defiance as she ripped stunningly through the *cabaletta*: this must have been the art of Pasta and Malibran too. I remember, in fact, fatuously asking her at the stage door one night what she had thought when one critic had written that the first Mary, Malibran herself, could not have been better. 'How does he know?' was her typically blunt and proper answer.

In 1982, after a mountain of publicity which even Patti's or Melba's farewells cannot have equalled, she closed the door on opera. Her timing was just, for there were moments at which exhaustion was evident, and her irritation with *The Times* critic shows how impossible she found it to give less than everything. At her last performance—a staged Prom in the Royal Albert Hall, where she took the title-role in Glyndebourne's production of Gluck's *Orfeo*—she left the stage with a striking image. Acknowledging the final applause, she held up above her head the lyre she had been using as Orfeo, as if to direct the audience's tribute back to the spirit of music itself. It was a gesture that signified the depths of her idealism and her somehow Victorian conception of the nobility of the singer's calling, with its exalted mission to communicate the essence of music—but it amused a certain section of the public. Her diary of her last year as an opera singer was published to patronizing sneers at her reflections on art and life; and a glossy magazine nicknamed her 'Dame Granite'. Peter Hall, who knew her well and produced that last *Orfeo*, saw it from another angle in his diary: 'My goodness, she seems to be together, that woman. She knows what she wants, and she knows the sacrifices she has to make in order to get it. She also treats her talent not as a meal ticket, but as a serious responsibility that's got to be used to the full. She's a very remarkable person.'

A very remarkable singer too, if in her case the two can be separated. Matthew Arnold once wrote of Aeschylus that his plays conveyed 'the most agitating matter under the conditions of severest form'—a statement that seems to suggest some of Janet Baker's fundamental qualities. She takes the most intense and essential human emotions to the very limit that physically perfect singing allows: one never, for instance, finds her obscuring her diction, fudging a high note, or breaking *legato* to make a cheap effect. Hers is lean, purposeful singing without frills, fakery, or rhetoric; impassioned, evangelistic, but not wantonly sensual. It is the singing of a born and bred Yorkshire Protestant, as much an expression of that landscape and culture as *Wuthering Heights*. Other mezzo-sopranos have had more volume and ample caressing warmth in their voices, and in that respect her Mahler or Brahms is not as satisfying as, say, that of Kathleen Ferrier to whom she was so frequently and inevitably compared. Ferrier was a mother-earth contralto whose art had great simplicity of feeling, while Baker is a dramatic mezzo of the post-Callas dispensation, *our* singer, as Pasta was Stendhal's and Chorley's.

Much more accessible to a broad public is Kiri Te Kanawa (born 1944), a prima donna of irregular but exotic beauty with a gorgeous and healthy lyric soprano. Glamorous, dressy, jokey, a keen golfer, with two adopted children and a nice husband, she has provided plenty of innocent copy for newspapers in search of a good-sport prima donna along the lines of Geraldine Farrar, acting up to the part without taking it too seriously. Kiri is marketable. She is televisable, if there is such a word. She is advertisable too (as Rolex watches and Sainsbury's supermarkets confirm), and all because she sang at the wedding of the Prince and Princess of Wales in 1981.

Her life has an attractive story-line. She comes of Maori ancestry and her first singing teacher in New Zealand was a nun, Sister Mary Leo. Like Sutherland, she collected a lot of prizes in Australia and came to London on the proceeds, joining the now defunct London Opera Centre. The first shock, appropriately enough, was a master class with Richard Bonynge, at which he told her that she was not a mezzo, as she had previously thought, but a soprano. For some time, she was utterly disoriented. 'At twenty, I was *dreadful*,' she claimed, 'always late, untidy, just totally useless.' She was not happy at the Centre, and word got around that she was not completely serious in her approach. At a number of Covent Garden auditions she was rejected on her personal reputation rather than her vocal merits, which were glaringly obvious to anyone who heard her. Fortunately she found Vera Rosza, a formidable Hungarian émigré, who took the girl and her singing in hand. Madame Rosza continues to be centrally important in Te Kanawa's career, and she is said to remain in mortal terror of her judgements. By 1971 she was ready to be cast in her first major role at Covent Garden, the Countess in *Le Nozze di Figaro*, since when she has been that opera house's nearest thing to a resident prima donna. Her popularity is also particularly high in Paris— which likes its prima donnas to have style, if not chic—and in New York, where in 1964 she first stood in at short notice as Desdemona in *Otello*, replacing a stricken Teresa Stratas. Schuyler Chapin, acting General Manager of the Met, remembers the self-assurance of his hot new property. 'She knew exactly what she would do and what she would not do, the repertoire she wanted to sing over the next several seasons, the directors she wished to work with, the conductors she would tolerate, the costumes she would wear and the attitude of the theater she wanted when working in it. She said all these things while sitting seductively on the couch, her knees tucked up, her long hair touching her shoulders, her deep-set brown eyes staring out of a *café-au-lait* face.' In other words, Te Kanawa had learnt how to cope, bargain, charm, and get her way. Peter Hall records an incident in Salzburg in 1979 when 'Kiri made a number of forays to the hotel's jewellery shop which seems to stay open all night. She kept reappearing every few minutes with a ring worth £1,000 or a necklace worth £50,000. She tried them on, paraded them for a giggle. Perhaps that's how a *diva* should behave.'

Te Kanawa the singer is easily sneered at. Vanilla-flavoured, they say. She is not notably individual in her musicianship and although she is a great dotter of Is and crosser of Ts, she does not apply any great imagination to the text. In her Strauss repertory—the Marschallin, Arabella and the Countess in *Capriccio*—she sails closer to Lisa della Casa's silvery shimmer than Schwarzkopf's insistent subtlety; in Italian opera she is a little too cool and in control to move an audience in the way of a Freni or Scotto. She is slow to learn and not over-keen to challenge herself. Her end-of-term report would probably contain the word 'underachiever' and she made no bones about sharing Patti's view that one should always sing on one's interest rather than one's capital. But the sheer consistent loveliness of the sound she makes, the sureness of her schooling and her shrewd sense of what she can and can't do: don't these give an audience satisfaction and deserve a respect which the press has been reluctant to give her?

Te Kanawa's self-control and self-preservation are rare virtues in opera today (or perhaps any day). For all the injunctions of teachers and sages, young singers face enormous pressures from greedy agents and desperate opera houses to sing louder, higher and more often than they should. Audiences want their prima donnas hot rather than cool and they want them sounding as golden and glowing as they do on the lying compact disc. It makes for trouble.

There is always talent coming up to warm the heart of even the most jaded opera queen—how can one follow opera in 1995 and not be impressed by the promise of Cecilia Bartoli, Elena Prokina, and Amanda Roocroft?—but equally it is impossible not to worry about the loss of the old system of apprenticeship whereby novices were weeded out early by a solid stint on contract to one provincial house, during which stamina and experience could be built up without all the extra pressures of travelling. Bartoli, for instance, fabulous talent that she has already proved herself on record and in recital, was launched on the international scene far too early and has since proved a disappointment in the major opera houses: she should be singing in a small and stable house like Glyndebourne, but the management reportedly refused to break their normal ceiling and pay the fee which her agent demanded. Instead she appears in the vast caverns of Salzburg and Houston where the smallness of her voice disappoints audiences who expect to hear the full glory—'at once bright, warm, smooth, sparkling and ductile' as Max Loppert put it in *Opera* magazine—of the recordings.

The other longer-term crisis facing the prima donna is the

reluctance of contemporary composers to write big roles for specific singers. It is not true to say that this century has seen opera definitely on the wane: as we approach its end, there is a substantial repertory of works written since the end of the First World War—Berg's *Wozzeck* and *Lulu*, several Strauss pieces, Stravinsky's *The Rake's Progress*, the entire oeuvre of Britten, as well as pieces by Poulenc, Tippett, Ligeti, Berio, Birtwistle and Adams—which show strong signs of standing the ultimate test of time. But apart from some rather crazy acrobatics demanded by Berio, Stockhausen and such, living composers don't seem to write with any great passion or imagination for the voice and rarely seem to find a great singer an inspiration. Think of what Mozart wrote for Cavalieri, Bellini for Pasta, Wagner for Schröder-Devrient, Strauss for Jeritza, and one may ponder the gravity of this loss.

So the prima donna, to put it bluntly is no longer the big deal she once was. She has become simply another form of professional and can no longer rank as the awesome and menacing exception to the rule that she was in the days of Lilli Lehmann and Melba; we have prima donnas in politics, medicine, academic life, business, sport, prison, outer space—the stage is only one of many arenas in which women can now dominate. Women in opera are no longer out there on their own, a revolutionary example to their sex. Is this a liberation or a tragedy, a beginning or an end?

# ACKNOWLEDGMENTS

Among the many people who have helped me write this book, two (non-singing, as far as I know) prima donnas must take particular credit: Jill Black, my editor, whose patience and persistence have astonished and inspired me, and Caroline Dawnay, who has been a complete and dedicated ally throughout. My heartfelt thanks to them both, and to Will Sulkin and Jörg Hensgen at Pimlico for allowing me the luxury of a second edition. Among relations and friends, I must especially thank my mother and sister, Kay and Anna Christiansen, for their encouragement and support; Cassandra Jardine, who is no opera fan, but has nobly put up with it all; Robert Turnbull, who has kept a close musical ear on the proceedings and proved a marvellous sounding-board—his own book, forthcoming as I write, on the opera business, promises to be revelatory, and I am privileged to have read and profited from his research; and Gill Morgan, who did more for me than she knows. I have also benefited from the labours and favours of Francesca Franchi of the Royal Opera House Archive; Anthony Gasson, who generously allowed me to reproduce pictures from his unique collection; Bill and Virginia Nicholson; Patrick Bade; Robert Rattray; David Scrase; Joan Sutherland and Richard Bonynge; James Supervia: Robert Tuggle of the Metropolitan Opera Archive; and Alan Williams of Viking Penguin Inc., whose enthusiasm at a decisive moment fired me on; also in New York, Juliet Annan and Charles Jahant, who gave me some useful leads, and Victoria Pryor. Of the many libraries I have used, I must single out the London Library, and the British Sound Archive. I would also like to acknowledge assistance I have received in the British Library; Westminster City Libraries; Bibliothèque de l'Opéra, Paris; Library of the Performing Arts, Lincoln Center and the Pierpont Morgan Library, New York; the Museum of La Scala, Milan; and the archive of the Victorian Arts Centre, Melbourne.

Since I first published this book in 1984, I have received many letters from all over the world, some complimentary, some critical, but all gratefully received. Among my most constructive correspondents (whose thoughts have been incorporated into this new edition) are Carolyn Beckingham, Giovanni Carema, Antonio Cavalleri, E. J. Cooper, D. H. Clampton, Ivan Marinov and William J. McCarthy. My thanks to them all, and to *Harpers and Queen*, the *Observer*, the *Spectator* and *Opera*, in all of which I have written about prima donnas over the last decade.

Thanks are due to the following for permission to quote copyright material:

John Calder Ltd: Frida Leider, *Playing my Part* (tr. Osborne) and Stendhal, *Life of Rossini* (tr. Coe).

Duckworth: J. B. Steane, *The Grand Tradition*.

Faber and Faber: Elisabeth Schwarzkopf, ed., *On and Off the Record*.

Victor Gollancz Ltd: Jerome Hines, *Great Singers on Great Singing* and Vincent Sheean, *First and Last Love*.

Hamish Hamilton: *Peter Hall's Diaries* (ed. Goodwin).

Simon and Schuster Inc: Mary Garden and Louis Biancolli, *Mary Garden's Story*.

The Putnam Publishing Group: Schuyler Chapin, *Musical Chairs*.

The Society of Authors on behalf of the Shaw Estate: Bernard Shaw, *Shaw's Music*, Vols 1–3.

Thanks are also due to the following holders of copyright photographic material: The National Gallery of Victoria, Melbourne, plate 1; the Royal College of Music, plates 2 and 11; The Royal Opera House Archives, plates 6, 10, 14, 19, 24, 27, 29, 38; Bibliothèque Nationale, Paris, plates 8 and 33; Roger Viollet, Paris, plate 9; the Performing Arts Center, New York Public Library, plates 13, 18, 23, 25, 28, 30, 40; *Opera News*, Metropolitan Opera Guild, New York, plates 17, 22, 37, 42; Culver Pictures, New York, plate 20; Bayreuth Festspielhaus, plate 21; Austrian National Library, plate 35; G. Macdomnic, plate 46; Clive Barda, plates 48 and 50; Julian Sheppard, plate 49; The Trustees of the British Museum, plate 31; Glyndbourne Festival Opera, plate 47; the Gasson Collection, plates 3, 4, 5, 7, 12, 15, 16, 26, 32, 36, 39, 41, 43,

44, 45; Faith Wilson Arts Publicity (photo by Hashimoto), plate 34; Decca (photo by Vivienne Purdom), plate 53; Zoë Dominic, plates 51, 52.

# SELECT BIBLIOGRAPHY

For authoritative information on all matters operatic and full bibliographies, see the *New Grove Dictionary of Opera*, ed. Sadie (1992), 4 vols. *The Oxford Dictionary of Opera*, ed. Warrack and West (1992) is generally reliable, although more modest in scope. Alfred Lowenberg's *Annals of Opera* (2nd edn., 1955) is invaluable for the amount of information it provides about dates and places of operatic performance. D. J. Grout's *A Short History of Opera* (3rd edn., 1988), 2 vols., remains the best of its kind. For individual prima donna discographies, see *Le Grandi Voci*, ed. Celletti (1964); for opera plots, both *Kobbe's Complete Opera Book*, ed. Harewood (10th edn., 1987) and *The Viking Opera Guide*, ed. Holden (1993) are first-rate. A feminist critique of opera has been essayed in Catherine Clément *Opera, or the Undoing of Women*, tr. Wing (1989); and Susan McClary, *Feminine Endings* (1991). Neither of these can be confidently recommended.


*Chapter One*
On the period and its singers generally, see Charles Burney, *A General History of Music* (repr. 1935), 2 vols.; George Hogarth, *Memoirs of the Opera* (repr. 1969); Richard Mount Edgcumbe, *Reminiscences* (repr. 1973); Henry Pleasants, *The Great Singers* (2nd edn., 1981), esp. chs. 1–7; John Rosselli, *Singers of Italian Opera* (1992) and H. Sutherland Edwards, *The Prima Donna* (repr. 1978), 2 vols.; Eric Walter White, *A History of English Opera* (1983). For scholarly accounts of opera's beginnings see Robert Donnington's *The Rise of Opera* (1981) and S. T. Worsthorne, *Venetian Opera in the Seventeenth Century* (1954); for Handel's operas, Winton Dean, *Handel and Opera Seria* (1970) and *Essays on Opera* (1990); also Jonathan Keates, *Handel: The Man and his Music* (1985); and for a

translation from Marcello's *Teatro alla Moda*, see Oliver Strunk, *Source Readings in Music History* (1950).

**Mrs Tofts:** Mollie Sands, 'Mrs Tofts', *Theatre Notebook* (Spring 1966).

**Faustina and Cuzzoni:** Keates, op. cit.; Pier Tosi, *Observations on the Florid Song*, tr. Galliard (repr. 1926).

**The Castrati:** Angus Heriot, *The Castrati in Opera* (2nd edn., 1974); Vernon Lee, *Studies of Italy in the Eighteenth Century*, (1880); Rosselli, op. cit.; Dennis Arundell, *The Critic at the Opera* (1957), Part II, also gives a fascinating account of popular taste in opera in eighteenth-century London.

**Banti:** Lorenzo da Ponte, *Memoirs*, tr. Abbott (1929).

**Mara:** Alan Yorke-Long, *Music at Court* (1954)—excellent essays on an interesting subject.

**Mrs Billington:** Michael Kelly's entertaining *Reminiscences* (repr. 1975).

On Mozart's operas, see Volkmar Braunbehrens, *Mozart in Vienna*, tr. Bell (1989); Alfred Einstein, *Mozart* (1946); Andrew Steptoe, *The Mozart–da Ponte Operas* (1988); Wolfgang Hildesheimer, *Mozart* (1984); H. C. Robbins Landon, *1791: Mozart's Last Year* (1988) and the highly provocative Brigid Brophy, *Mozart the Dramatist* (1964). *The Letters of Mozart and his Family*, tr. Anderson (1938), 3 vols., are also well worth reading, and contain passages pertaining to Mara and Cavalieri.

*Chapter Two*

The finest book of the period is undoubtedly Stendhal's *Life of Rossini*, tr. Coe (1956), which contains witty and idiosyncratic thoughts about every aspect of early nineteenth-century opera, including his views of Colbran and Pasta. See also his *Memoirs of an Egoist*, tr. Ellis (1975); and *Rome, Naples, Florence*, tr. Coe (1959). For more soberly factual reading, Herbert Weinstock, *Rossini* (1968) and *Bellini* (1972); William Ashbrook, *Donizetti and his Operas* (1982); and the outstanding Julian Budden, *The Operas of Verdi*, vol. 1 (1973). Two more speculative books on nineteenth-century opera are Carolyn Abbate, *Unsung Voices* (1991) and Peter Conrad, *Romantic Opera and Literary Form* (1977). Henry Chorley's *Thirty Years' Musical Recollections* (repr. 1926) is a classic, and J. E. Cox's

*Musical Recollections* (1872) 2 vols., usefully supplements it. See also Luigi Arditi, *My Reminiscences* (repr. 1976); Ellen C. Clayton, *Queens of Song* (repr. 1972), 2 vols.; John Ebers, *Seven Years of the King's Theatre* (repr. 1969); Benjamin Lumley, *Reminiscences of the Opera* (repr. 1976); J. H. Mapleson, *The Mapleson Memoirs* (repr. 1966); Harold Rosenthal, *Two Centuries of Opera at Covent Garden* (1958). Also Hogarth, Mount Edgcumbe, Pleasants, Sutherland, Edwards, Rosselli op. cit.

**Pasta**: M. Ferranti-Giulini, *Giuditta Pasta e suoi tempi* (1935); *Opera News*, 13 February 1982; John Rosselli, *The Opera Industry in Italy from Cimarosa to Verdi* (1984) has much interesting material on the business and financial side of opera during Pasta's career.

**Malibran**: Howard Bushnell, *Maria Malibran* (1979) is a model piece of scholarship with an excellent bibliography.

**Viardot**: April FitzLyon, *The Price of Genius* (1964); Hector Berlioz, *Memoirs*, tr. Cairns (1968); George Sand, *Correspondence* (1964). For French Grand Opera, see the book of that name by W. Crosten (1948), a pioneering study, also J. Fulcher, *The Nation's Image: French Grand Opera* (1987).

**Grisi**: G. Pearse and F. Hird, *The Romance of a Great Singer* (repr. 1977) and Elizabeth Forbes, *Mario and Grisi* (1985).

*Chapter Three*

General pictures of various phases of the Victorian opera scene are provided by Arditi, Chorley, Cox, Lumley, Mapleson, Rosenthal, Rosselli, *Singers*, op. cit. Also Hermann Klein, *Thirty Years of Musical Life in London* (1903) and for the last years of the century, the incomparable G. B. Shaw, *Shaw's Music* (1981), 3 vols., and Clara Leiser, *Jean de Reszke* (repr. 1970). See Michael J. Baker, *The Rise of the Victorian Actor* (1978) and Tracy C. Davis, *Actresses as Working Women* (1991) for analysis of the status of the theatre in the nineteenth century. On Victorian taste, Zuzanna Shonfeld *The Precariously Privileged* (1987); my own 'George Eliot, *Armgart* and the Victorian Prima Donna,' *About the House*, Spring 1986 and 'A Victorian Lady Wagnerite', *Opera*, April–May 1987. On recording, Roland Gelatt, *The Fabulous Phonograph* (1955) and Joseph Horowitz, *Understanding Toscanini* (1987).

**Sontag**: Chorley's remains the best essay on Sontag in English; otherwise the German E. Pirchan, *Henrietta Sontag* (1946) and Bushnell, op. cit.

**Lind**: Joan Bulman, *Jenny Lind* (1956), particularly strong on her early years. For the Bunn Affair, see Lumley, op. cit.; and for the American tour Phineas T. Barnum, *Struggles and Triumphs* (repr. 1981), usefully complemented by the meticulous P. Ware and T. Lockard, *P. T. Barnum presents Jenny Lind* (1980) and Horowitz, op. cit. The letter quoted on p. 97–8 is housed in the Pierpont Morgan Library, New York.

**Patti**: John Frederick Cone, *Adelina Patti, Queen of Hearts* (Aldershot, 1994). The contemporary Hermann Klein, *The Reign of Patti* (repr. 1977) is obviously biased; equally Clara Louise Kellogg, *Memoirs of an American Prima Donna* (repr. 1978) and Mapleson op. cit. have axes to grind, entertaining as they are. For an interesting assessment of Patti in the 1860s, see Eduard Hanslick, 'Adelina Patti' in *Vienna's Golden Years of Music*, tr. Pleasants (1950). The letter quoted on p. 107 is housed in the Library of the Performing Arts, Lincoln Center, New York.

**Melba**: John Hetherington, *Melba* (1965) is an adequate modern biography, as is Therese Radic, *Melba: The Voice of Australia* (1986); and William R. Moran, *Nellie Melba* (1985) usefully collates the documents of her career; her autobiography *Melodies and Memories* (1964); makes painful reading. I have also consulted the archive of the Victorian Arts Centre, Melbourne. Sir Thomas Beecham makes some illuminating comments in *A Mingled Chime* (repr. 1976); also John F. Cone, *Oscar Hammerstein's Manhattan Opera Company* (1964); Blanche Marchesi, *A Singer's Pilgrimage* (repr. 1977); Mathilde Marchesi, *Marchesi and Music* (repr. 1978); Ivor Newton, *At the Piano* (1974).

On **Eames**, see *The Opera Quarterly*, Winter 1992.

*Chapter Four*
Ernest Newman's *The Life of Richard Wagner* (repr. 1976), 4 vols. is one of the great biographies of the century and also contains what amounts to a history of nineteenth-century German opera. Frederic Spotts, *Bayreuth: A History of the Wagner Festival* (1994) is excellent in every respect; Robert Hartford has collected reactions to and

comments on the first festivals in *Bayreuth: The Early Years* (1980). For Wagner in his own words, see *My Life*, tr. Gray and Whittall (1983); *Wagner on Music and Drama*, ed. Goldman and Sprinchorn and tr. Ellis (1970); and *Cosima Wagner's Diaries*, tr. Skelton (1978–80), 2 vols. See also Hanslick and Shaw op. cit., Newman, *Wagner Nights* (repr. 1977); and Barry Millington and Stewart Spencer, *Wagner in Performance* (1992) and *The Wagner Compendium*, ed. Millington (1992).

On the singing of Wagner on record see J. B. Steane, *The Grand Tradition* (1972) and Michael Scott, *The Record of Singing* (1977–9), 2 vols.

For a picture of nineteenth-century attitudes to Wagner production, see my 'Victorian Lady Wagnerite', op. cit.; for modern attitudes see Spotts, op. cit, also Geoffrey Skelton, *Wieland Wagner* (1971) which also contains an interesting account of Anja Silja's early years; and Penelope Turing, *New Bayreuth* (1971). Pierre Boulez, Patrice Chéreau, *et al*, *Histoire d'un 'Ring'* (1980) follows a notorious production from first to last.

**Schröder-Devrient**: see Newman's *Life of Wagner* and Chorley op. cit.

**Lilli Lehmann**: *My Path through Life* (repr. 1977) and *How to Sing* (repr. 1949); also Hanslick op. cit., *Opera News*, 20 February 1965; and Geraldine Farrar, *Such Sweet Compulsion* (repr. 1970).

**Leider**: *Playing my Part*, tr. Osborne (1966) and Vincent Sheean, *First and Last Love* (1957). Leider was interviewed a few years before her death in *Opera News*, 28 January 1967. Also *Opera*, August 1988.

**Flagstad**: Louis Biancolli, *The Flagstad Manuscript* (1953); Edwin MacArthur, *Flagstad: A Personal Memoir* (1965) and Howard Vogt, *Flagstad: Singer of the Century* (1987). For her post-war return to the USA, see Rudolf Bing, *5,000 Nights at the Opera* (1972) and for her last years, John Culshaw, *Ring Resounding* (1967). Also Newton, op. cit.

**Nilsson**: *My Memoirs in Pictures* (1981), which is delightfully unpretentious; interesting essays in Winthrop Sargeant, *Divas* (1973) and Peter Conrad, *A Song of Love and Death* (1987); and the interviews in *Opera News*, 15 February 1975 and 9 February 1980.

*Chapter Five*
The Met has been rich in historians: one can safely recommend Quaintance Eaton, *The Miracle of the Met* (1968) for its wit and narrative flair; Irving Kolodin, *The Metropolitan Opera* (4th edn., 1966) for its comprehensiveness; and Martin Mayer, *The Met* (1983) for both its lavish illustration and lighty-worn scholarship. *Annals of the Metropolitan Opera*, ed. Fitzgerald (1990), 2 vols. is the Met's encyclopedia. On opera in New York in this period *c.*1880–1950, see variously Cone, *Hammerstein*, op. cit, W. J. Henderson, *The Art of Singing* (repr. 1978); O. Thompson, *The American Singer* (repr. 1969); Frances Alda's acid *Men, Women and Tenors* (repr. 1970) and Giulio Gatti-Casazza's disappointingly bland *Memories of the Opera* (repr. 1980). For the Met of the 1950s and 1960s, see Rudolf Bing, *5,000 Nights at the Opera* (London, 1972). For the Met today, see Part III, Chapter 2 of Peter Conrad, *Song*, op. cit.; Frederic Dannen, 'Twilight of the Gods', *New Yorker*, 3 October 1994; Patrick J. Smith, *A Year at the Met* (1983).

**Nordica**: Ira Glackens, *Yankee Diva* (1963) is outstanding. See also Thompson, Henderson, Shaw, op. cit. and Mary Lawton, *Schumann-Heink: Last of the Titans* (repr. 1977).
**Schumann-Heink**: Lawton op. cit. is couched in the women's magazine idiom of the day, but is still revealing. See also *Opera* November 1967 and *Opera News*, 4 December 1965 and 24 January 1977.
**Fremstad**: Much about Fremstad remains a mystery but Mary W. Cushing, *The Rainbow Bridge* (repr. 1977) tells much, with humour and compassion, about her years of fame. See also Carl Van Vechten, *Interpreters* (repr. 1977) and Cushing's analysis of Fremstad's scores in *Opera News*, 14 March 1956. Letter quoted on p. 172–3 from the Metropolitan Opera Archives.
**Farrar**: *Such Sweet Compulsion*, op. cit.; Thompson, Vechten, op. cit. Harvey Sachs, *Toscanini* (1978) gives brief glimpses of the relations between singer and conductor. Many articles in *Opera News*: see esp. 12 January 1953, 25 February 1957, 29 January 1966, and 15 April 1967.
**Cavalieri**: Scott, op. cit., vol. 1.
**Moore**: Charles O'Connell, *The Other Side of the Record* (repr. 1970); her autobiography, *You're Only Human Once* (1947) is not edifying.

**Ponselle**: her posthumous autobiography, written with James. A. Drake, *Ponselle: A Singer's Life* (1983) tells much about operatic life in the inter-war period and contains Ponselle's frank views on the state of singing today. See also Walter Legge's essay in *On and Off the Record*, ed. Schwarzkopf (1982); John Ardoin's 'A Note on Ponselle's *Norma*', *Opera*, March 1976—a discussion of her musical practices, in particular her habits of transposition; and *Opera News*, 12 March 1977. Ida and Louise Cook, *We Followed our Stars* (1950) provides bizarre evidence of the prima donna fan mentality, as focused on Ponselle and others. For a negative appraisal of her art, see Scott, op. cit., vol. 2. Letter quoted on p. 186 from Archives of the Royal Opera House, Covent Garden.

**Traubel**: her autobiography is *St Louis Woman* (repr. 1977). See also O'Connell, Bing, op. cit. and *Opera News*, September 1972.

**Foster Jenkins**: *Opera News*, 16 March 1963.

I owe my knowledge of Madame **Mari-Lyn** to Robert Turnbull.

For opera singers on film, see John Ardoin, 'Operatic Shadows', *The Opera Quarterly*, Summer 1988 and *Opera News*, 19 December 1964;. Beverly Sills, *Beverly* (1988). For camp, Ethan Mordden's *Demented: The World of the Opera Diva* (1984) and Wayne Koestenbaum's amusing and often perceptive *The Queen's Throat: Opera, Homosexuality and the Mystery of Desire* (1993); the few issues of the magazine *Opera Fanatic*, published in New York, provide a certain sort of amusement. On fees, see Michael Scott's exposé in *Opera*, July 1977 and Robert Turnbull, 'Kings and Queens of the High Fees', *Sunday Telegraph*, 15 March 1992.

*Chapter Six*
On vocal technique, see Robert Rushmore's witty and readable *The Singing Voice* (1971), with its excellent bibliography. Also Rodolfo Celletti, *A History of Bel Canto*, tr. Fuller (1991); Scott, vol. I, op. cit.; Jerome Hines, *Great Singers on Great Singing* (1983), which includes interviews with Crespin, Horne, Milanov, Nilsson, Ponselle, Sills, Sutherland and Verrett and Helena Matheopoulos, *Diva* (1991) which similarly covers Caballé, Freni, Gruberova, Ludwig, Popp, Price, Studer, Sutherland, Tomowa-Sintov *et al*. On Verdi, see Julian Budden, *The Operas of Verdi*, 3 vols. (1973–81); David Kimbell, *Verdi in the Age of Italian Romanticism* (1981) and the authoritative biography by Mary Jane Phillips Matz, *Verdi* (1993), all of

which contain valuable material on **Strepponi** and **Stolz**. Gabriele Baldini's *The Story of Giuseppe Verdi*, tr. Parker (1980), although unfinished, is radical in its views and enthralling.

**Falcon**: Charles Bouvet, *Cornélie Falcon* (1927).

**Tietjens**: Arditi, Klein, *Thirty Years*, op. cit, and *Great Women Singers* (1931); Lumley, Shaw, and Sutherland Edwards, op. cit.

**Destinn**: Victor Gollancz, *Journey into Music* (1964), a delightful account of half a century of opera-going in England and Europe; A. Rektorys and J. Dennis in *Record Collector*, July 1971; *Opera*, September 1955.

**Turner**: Lanfranco Rasponi, *The Last Prima Donnas* (1983); J. B. Richards in *Record Collector*, February–March 1957; *Opera*, March 1987 and August 1990.

**Milanov**: Rasponi, op. cit.; *Opera News*, 1 May 1968 and April 1977; *Opera*, August 1989; *The Opera Quarterly*, Spring 1990.

**Price**: Matheopoulos, Sargeant, op. cit.; *Opera News*, 12 February 1972 and 6 March 1976; interview with Alan Blyth in *The Gramophone*, August 1971; Hugh Lee Lyon, *Leontyne Price: Highlights of a Prima Donna* (1973).

**Norman**: The profile by Charles Michener, *Vanity Fair*, February 1989; My own 'Stormin' Norman', *Harpers and Queen*, June 1993. On the black prima donna, see Roslyn M. Story, *And So I Sing: African-American Divas* (New York, 1990).

*Chapter Seven*

A generously illustrated and richly gossipy history is provided by Marcel Prawy, *The Vienna Opera* (1970). For Mahler and the Vienna Opera, see *Gustav Mahler in Vienna*, ed. Wiesmann, tr. Shelley (1976); and for a sane and modest critical biography of Strauss, see Michael Kennedy, *Richard Strauss* (1976). Detailed analyses of the operas are contained in William Mann's *Richard Strauss: a Critical Study of the Operas* (1966). Strauss's correspondence with Hofmannsthal, published as *The Correspondence between Richard Strauss and Hugo von Hofmannsthal*, tr. Hammelmann and Osers (1980), gives great insight into their compositional methods; Lotte Lehmann's *Singing with Richard Strauss* (1964) deals with both the facts of the collaboration and her own views of the roles she sang. See also

Bruno Walter's autobiography, *Theme and Variations*, tr. Galston (repr. 1981).

**Jeritza**: *Sunlight and Song* (repr. 1977); Prawy and Strauss/ Hofmannsthal op. cit.; *Opera News*, 18 March 1957 and 18 February 1961. I myself profited enormously from Nigel Douglas's radio programme on Jeritza, first broadcast by the BBC in March 1984.

**Lotte Lehmann**: see her autobiography *Wings of Song*—in USA, *Midway in my Song*—(1938); Prawy, Sheean, op. cit.; Walter Legge's essay in *On and Off the Record*, op. cit.; Marcia Davenport, *Too Strong for Fantasy* (1968); and *Opera News*, 22 December 1962. Two recent, gentle biographies, both entitled *Lotte Lehmann* are by Beaumont Glass and Alan Jefferson (both 1988). Also *Opera 66*, ed. Osborne (1966) and *The Opera Quarterly*, Summer 1991.

On music in the Third Reich, see Richard Grunberger, *A Social History of the Third Reich* (1974) and Henry Bair's articles on opera in Berlin 1933–39, *Opera*, January–February 1984.

**Ursuleac**: see the fascinating interview she gave Lanfranco Rasponi, op, cit., also *Opera*, January 1986.

**Schumann**: see the articles in *Opera*, August, September, November 1973 and January 1974 and in *Record Collector* 1952; also Peter Heyworth, *Otto Klemperer*, vol. 1 (1983).

**Schwarzkopf**: see *On and Off the Record*, op. cit. and her frank interviews with Edward Greenfield in *The Gramophone* October–November 1976. André Tubeuf's *Le chant retrouvé* (1979) devoted to modern prima donnas (also including essays on Jurinac and Rysanek) cannot be recommended too highly. See also Gerald Moore on accompanying Schwarzkopf in *Am I too Loud?* (1962) and his assessment of Legge in *Furthermoore* (1983). *L'Avant Scène: Opéra* devoted a special issue to Schwarzkopf in Autumn 1983.

Steane op. cit. treats the recordings of Lehmann, Schumann, and Schwarzkopf with particular sensitivity and wisdom.

**Popp**: *Opera*, February 1982 and January 1994.


*Chapter Eight*
On 'national style' in singing, see Rushmore op. cit. Steane and

Scott, vols. 1 and 2, op. cit. also have interesting ideas on the subject. For French opera in this period, see Martin Cooper, *French Music from the Death of Berlioz* (repr. 1969).

**Calvé**: in *Emma Calvé* (1983) Georges Girard has edited and filled in the gaps in Calvé's autobiographical volumes, the first of which was tr. Gilder as *My Life* (repr. 1977). See also Shaw, Henderson, op. cit.

**Garden**: see Mary Garden and Louis Biancolli, *Mary Garden's Story* (1952); R. L. Davis, *Opera in Chicago* (1966); also Sheean, Sills, Vechten, op. cit.; *Opera*, October 1984. A modern full-length biography is badly needed.

**Lubin**: N. Casanova, *Isolde 39* (1974). Her interview with Rasponi, op. cit. is poignant and revealing.

**Crespin**: see her autobiography, *La vie et l'amour d'une femme* (1982); Tubeuf, op. cit.; *Opera News*, 13 December 1975 and 13 January 1979.

**Supervia**: Newton, op. cit. gives an affectionate account, elaborated in *Recorded Sound*, 52 (1973)—although his facts are not reliable. See also H. M. Barnes and V. Girard, in *Record Collector*, March 1951 and Desmond Shawe-Taylor in *Opera*, January 1960; for the story of her Covent Garden appearances, Rosenthal, op. cit.

**Los Angeles**: Peter Roberts, *Victoria de los Angeles* (1982); Moore, *Am I too Loud?* op. cit.

**Caballé**: Matheopoulos, Tubeuf, op. cit., *Opera News*, 9 March 1974; Robert Pullen and Stephen Taylor, *Caballé: Casta Diva* (1994).

*Chapter Nine*

William Weaver, *The Golden Century of Italian Opera* (1980) is excellent as far as it goes. See also Julian Budden's article, 'Puccini, Massenet, and *verismo*', *Opera*, May 1983. Budden's book on the operas of Puccini is keenly awaited. See also Mayer op. cit. and Frances Donaldson, *The Royal Opera House in the Twentieth Century* (London 1988). Harvey Sachs' *Music in Fascist Italy* (1988) illuminates the inter-war years; Rosselli, *Singers* op. cit. provides vivid, specific sociology and history.

**Tetrazzini**: her autobiography *My Life of Song* (repr. 1977). Also

Cone, *Hammerstein*, Henderson, Newton, op. cit. Charles Neilson Gattey's *Luisa Tetrazzini: A Florentine Nightingale* (1995) is a full biography and appreciations.

**Galli-Curci**: C. F. Lemassena, *Galli-Curci's Life of Song* (repr. 1978); Rasponi, op. cit.; *Opera News*, 22 February 1964.

**Muzio**: Charles Jahant's article is in the *Saturday Review of Literature*, 30 November 1957. See also *Opera News*, 16 April 1960; *Opera*, June 1986; and *The Opera Quarterly*, Winter 1993–4.

**Callas**: the leader in this vast and ever-expanding field is still John Ardoin and Gerald Fitzgerald, *Callas* (1974), supplemented by Ardoin's review of Callas's singing on record, *The Callas Legacy* (1977), Jürgen Kesting's intelligent *Maria Callas*, tr. Hunt (1992) and Franco Zeffirelli's autobiography *Zeffirelli* (1986). Arianna Stassinopoulos's *Maria* (1981) is romanticized and hardly creates a profound picture of the artist, but is none the less full of interest and contains a useful bibliography. John Ardoin's article in *The Opera Quarterly*, Summer 1985, clarifies Callas's earliest professional years in Greece and Italy; G. B. Meneghini's *My Wife, Maria Callas* (1982), though much criticized, is probably the most accurate account we have of Callas in the 1950s. See also Legge, op. cit.; *Opera*, September–October 1970 and my own article, *Opera*, June 1987; Montague Halbrecht, *The Quiet Showman* (1975); and Jeffrey Tate, interviewed by Patrick O'Connor in *Harpers and Queen*, December 1983. Letter quoted on pp. 283–4 is housed in the Library of the Performing Arts, Lincoln Center, New York. Lord Harewood's two-part television interview, *The Callas Conversations*, was shown on BBC2 again in 1993.

**Tebaldi**: Kenn Harris, *Renata Tebaldi* (1975) is almost absurdly adulatory. See *Opera News*, 30 January 1965 and Rasponi, op. cit.

**Sutherland**: Brian Adams, *La Stupenda* (1981); Quaintance Eaton, *Sutherland and Bonynge* (1987) and Norma Major, *Joan Sutherland* (2nd edn., 1994); Sargeant, Tubeuf, and Zeffirelli, op. cit.; *Opera News*, 4 December 1982 and the interview with Richard Bonynge, *Opera News*, 22 January 1994; *Opera*, November 1990 and the essay in Peter Conrad, *Feasting with Panthers* (1994).

**Horne**: her autobiography, with Jane Scovell, *My Life* (1983) is well worth reading; see also *Opera*, December 1967; *Opera News*, 10 March 1973 and 14 February–14 March 1981; *The Opera Quarterly*, Summer 1993.

**Sills**: her autobiography, *Beverly* (1988); Sargeant, op. cit.; *Opera News*, 19 April 1975, 14 February 1976, and October 1980.
**Scotto**: *Opera News*, 17 December 1977; Matheopoulos op. cit.
**Freni**: Matheopoulos, op. cit.; *Opera*, May 1994.


*Chapter Ten*
On the decline of the modern prima donna, compare Rasponi with the more balanced views of Steane, op. cit., and in *Voices: Singers and Critics* (1992), John Stratton 'Operatic Singing Style', *Recorded Sound*, XXII, 3 (1966), and for another view of the matter, Koestenbaum op. cit. On twentieth-century opera, see H. H. Stückenschmidt, *Twentieth-century Music* (1969) and *The New Oxford History of Music x, 1890–1960* (1974) as well as John Tyrrell, *Janáček's Operas* (1992) and Humphrey Carpenter, *Benjamin Britten* (1993) and Michael Kennedy *Britten* (2nd edn., 1993).


**Baker**: *Full Circle* (1982), the diary of her last year of opera; Alan Blyth, *Janet Baker* (1973); Moore, *Farewell Recital*, op. cit.; *Opera News*, July 1977 and my own interview in *Opera*, September 1993.
**Te Kanawa**: David Fingleton, *Kiri* (1982); *Opera News*, 26 February 1983 and October 1994.
**Stratas**: Zeffirelli, op. cit.; *Opera News*, 9 December 1989 and *Opera*, October 1994. Also Harry Rasky, *Stratas: An Affectionate Tribute* (New York, 1988).
**Battle**: Dannen, 'Twilight', op. cit.
**Lott**: *Opera*, October 1989; my own 'A Cheltenham Lady's Dalliance', *Observer*, 8 July 1990.
**Studer**: Matheopoulos, op. cit.; *Opera*, June 1994.
**Bartoli**: my own article, 'Can't Stop the Music', *Harpers and Queen*, February 1992 and *Opera News*, August 1993.

# Concise Index of Names